EXPLORER
THE LOST ISLANDS

SEVEN GRAPHIC STORIES
EDITED BY KAZU KIBUISHI

AMULET BOOKS

NEW YORK

THANKS TO MY COEDITOR,
SHEILA KEENAN
—K.K.

Publisher's Note
This is a work of fiction. Names, characters, places, and incidents are
either the product of the author's imagination or are used fictitiously, and
any resemblances to actual person, living or dead, business establishments,
events, or locales is entirely coincidental.

Library of Congress Control Number: 2013935794

Paperback ISBN 978-1-4197-0883-1
Hardcover ISBN 978-1-4197-0881-7

Cover art © 2013 Kazu Kibuishi
Compilation © 2013 Bolt City Productions
Book design by Chad W. Beckerman

Text and illustrations © 2013 by the individual artists as follows:
"Rabbit Island," pages 4–19, © 2013 Jake Parker
"The Mask Dance," pages 20–37, © 2013 Chrystin Garland
"Carapace," pages 38–55, © 2013 Jason Caffoe
"Desert Island Playlist," pages 56–73, text © 2013 Dave Roman;
illustrations © 2013 Raina Telgemeier
"Loah," pages 74–91, © 2013 Michel Gagné
"Radio Adrift," pages 92–109, text © 2013 Steven Shanahan;
illustrations © 2013 Katie Shanahan
"The Fishermen," pages 110–127, © 2013 Kazu Kibuishi

Printed and bound in China
10 9 8 7 6 5 4 3 2

Amulet Books are available at special discounts when purchased in quantity
for premiums and promotions as well as fundraising or educational use. For
details, contact specialmarkets@abramsbooks.com, or the address below.

ABRAMS
THE ART OF BOOKS SINCE 1949
115 West 18th Street
New York, NY 10011
www.abramsbooks.com

CONTENTS

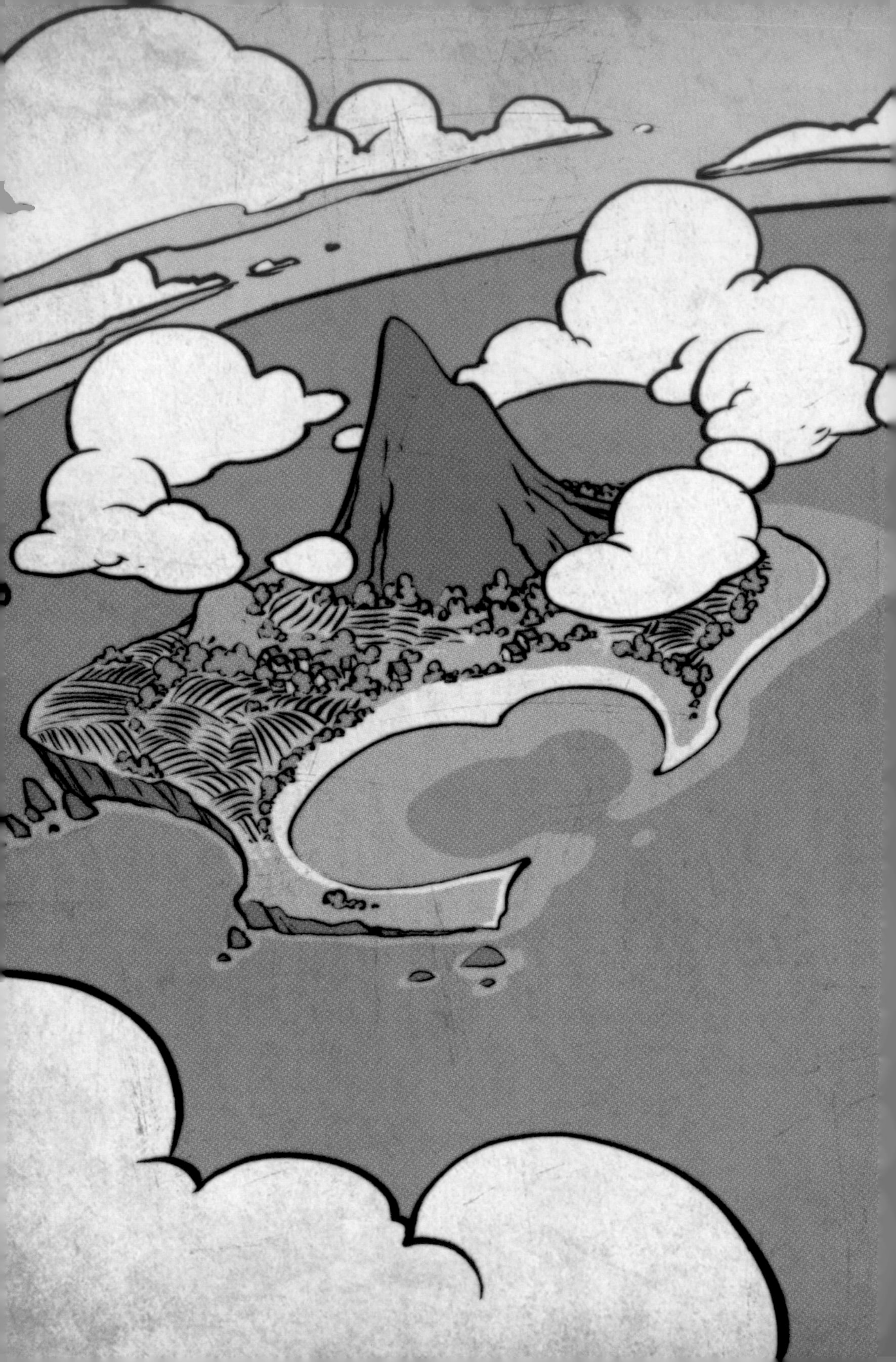

RABBIT ISLAND

BY JAKE PARKER

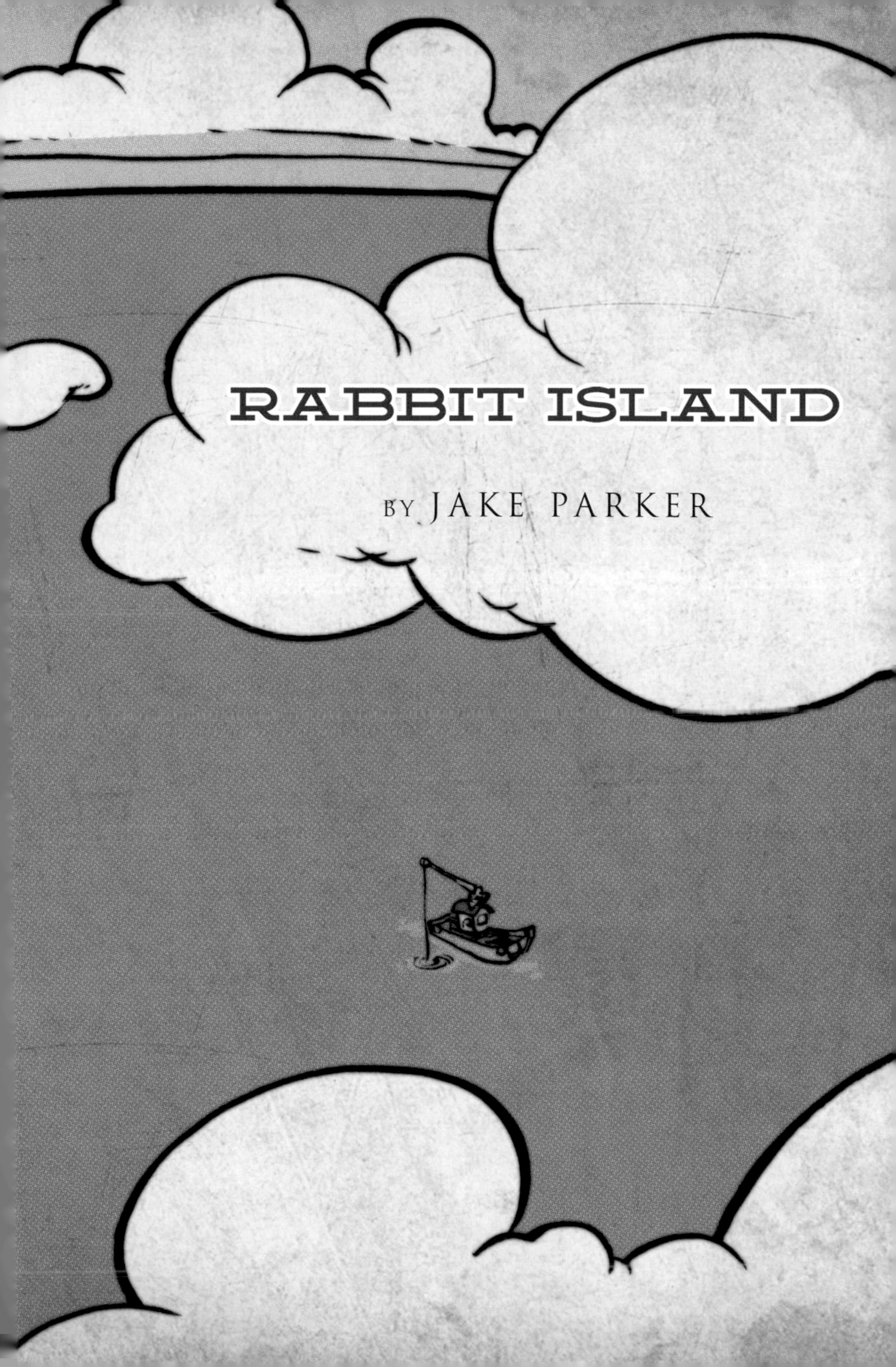

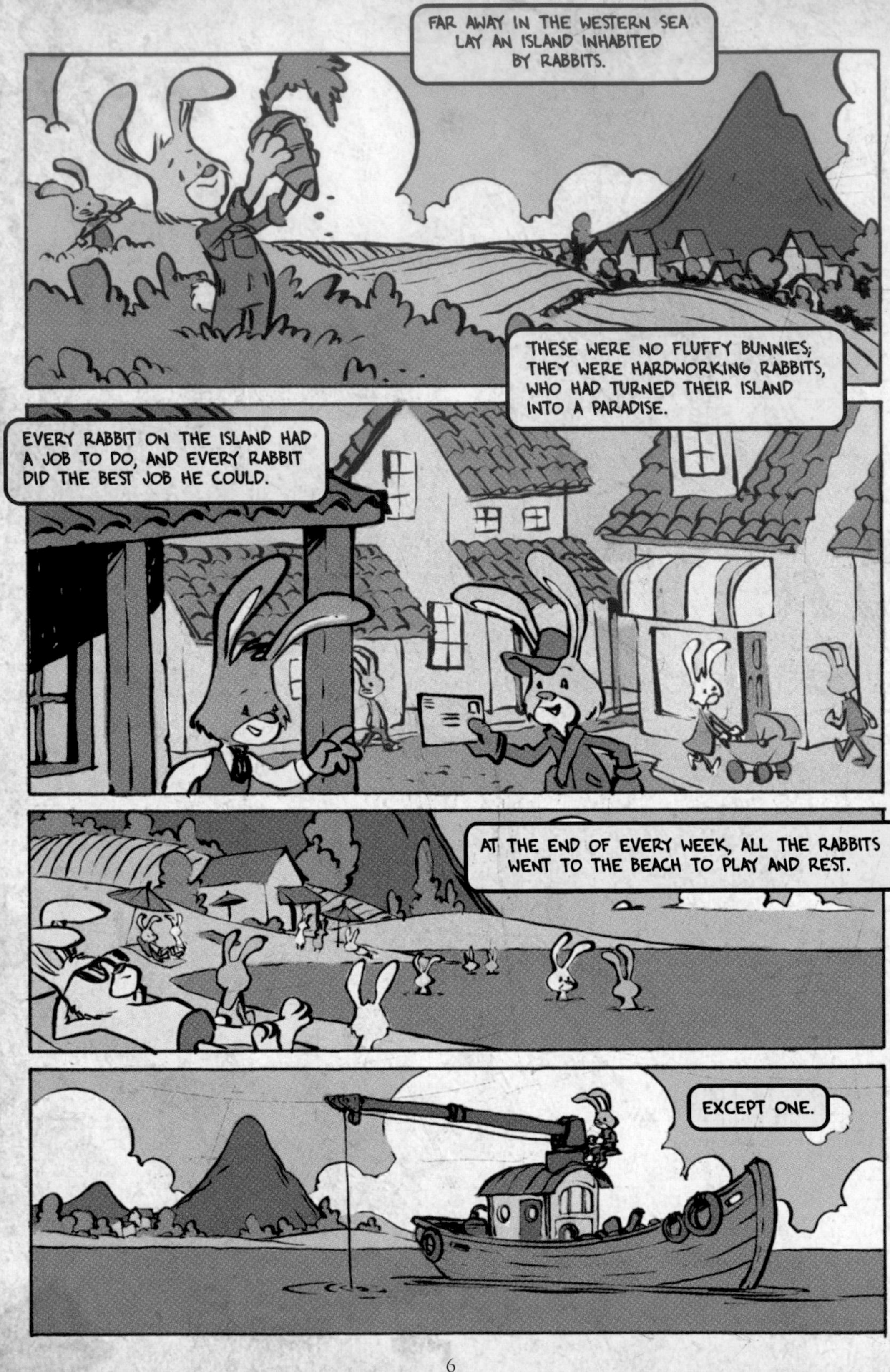
FAR AWAY IN THE WESTERN SEA LAY AN ISLAND INHABITED BY RABBITS.
THESE WERE NO FLUFFY BUNNIES; THEY WERE HARDWORKING RABBITS, WHO HAD TURNED THEIR ISLAND INTO A PARADISE.
EVERY RABBIT ON THE ISLAND HAD A JOB TO DO, AND EVERY RABBIT DID THE BEST JOB HE COULD.
AT THE END OF EVERY WEEK, ALL THE RABBITS WENT TO THE BEACH TO PLAY AND REST.
EXCEPT ONE.

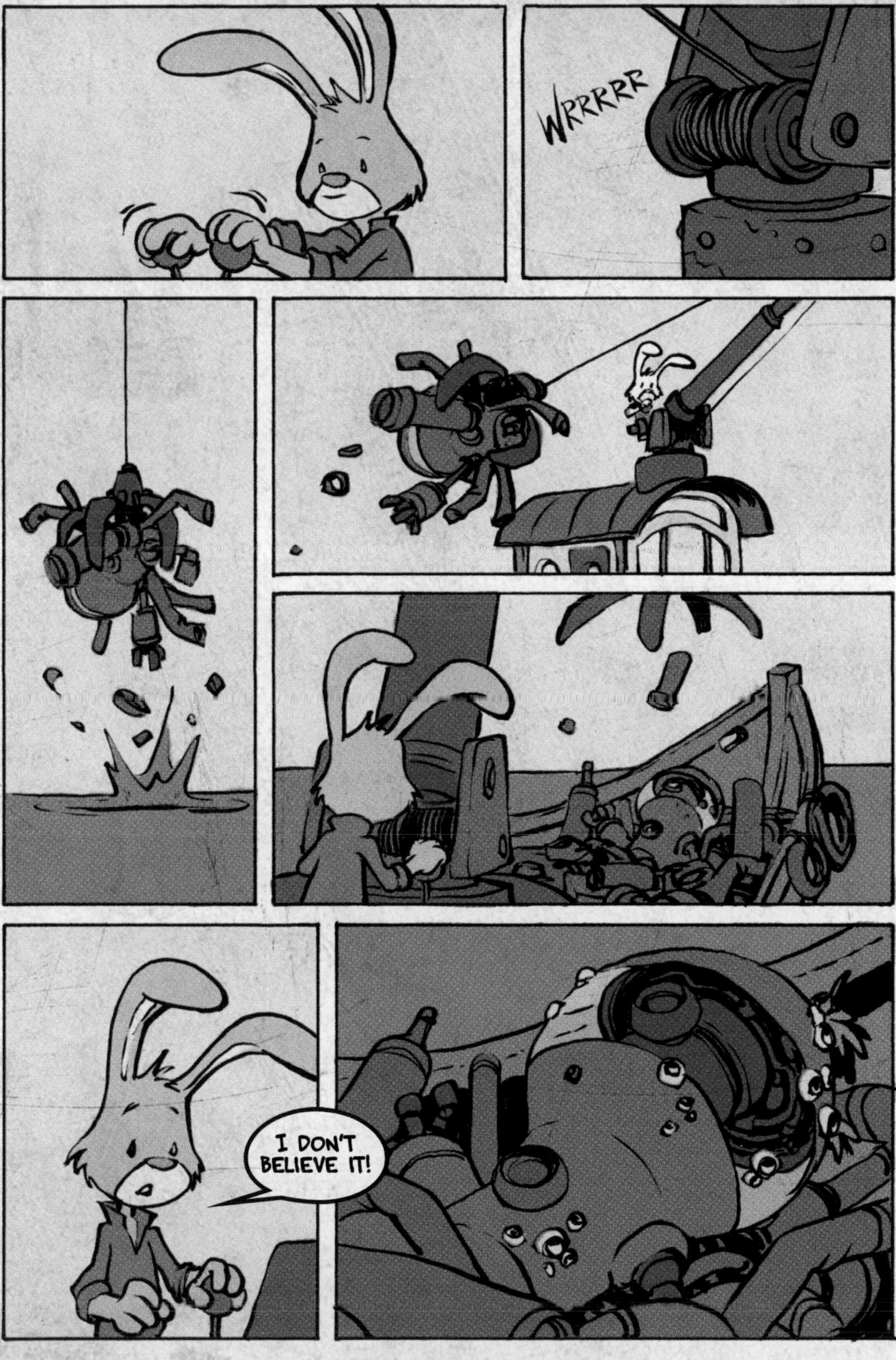
WRRRRR
I DON'T BELIEVE IT!

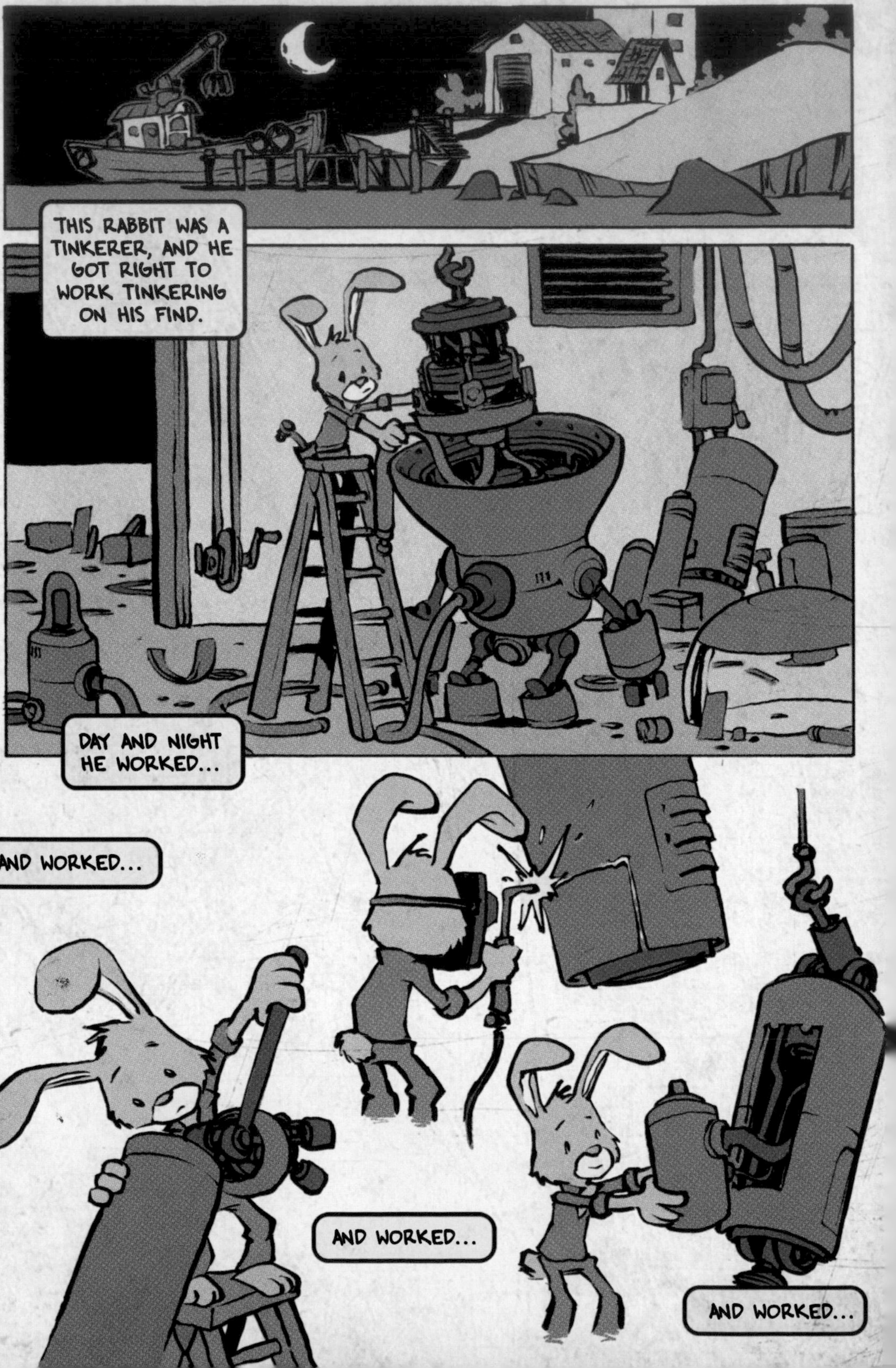

THIS RABBIT WAS A TINKERER, AND HE GOT RIGHT TO WORK TINKERING ON HIS FIND.
DAY AND NIGHT HE WORKED...
AND WORKED...
AND WORKED...
AND WORKED...

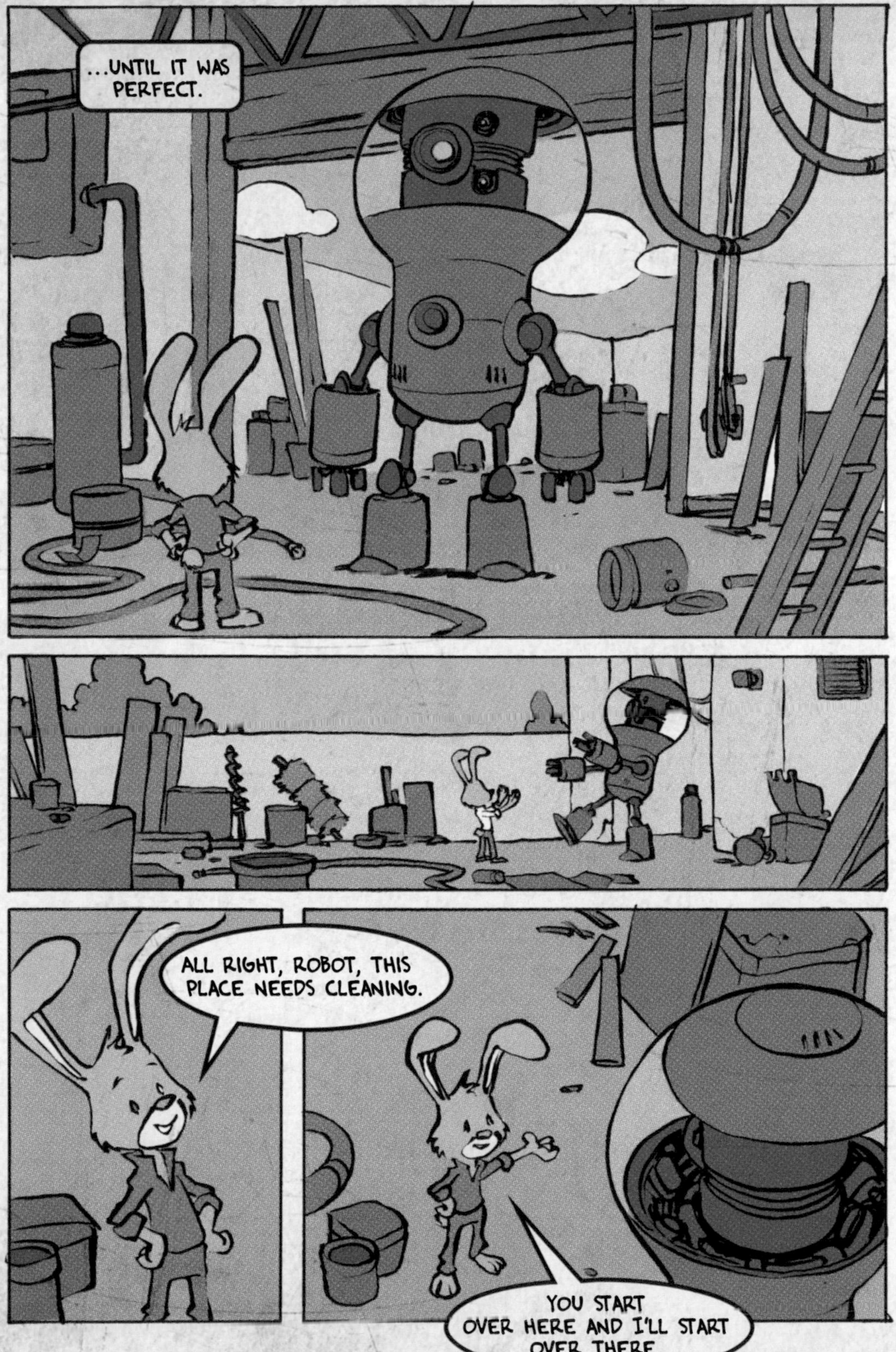
...UNTIL IT WAS PERFECT.
ALL RIGHT, ROBOT, THIS PLACE NEEDS CLEANING.
YOU START OVER HERE AND I'LL START OVER THERE.

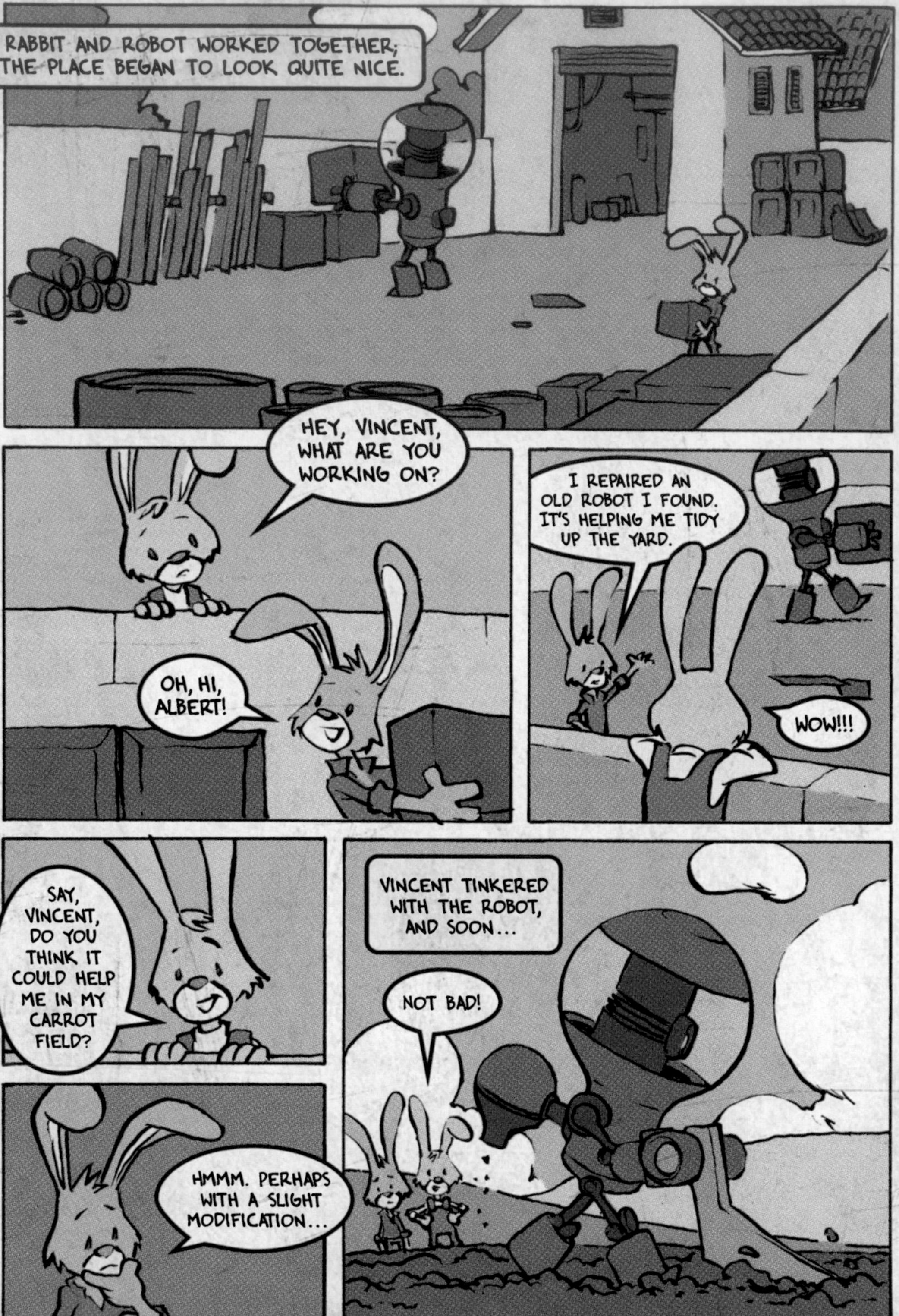
RABBIT AND ROBOT WORKED TOGETHER;
THE PLACE BEGAN TO LOOK QUITE NICE.
HEY, VINCENT, WHAT ARE YOU WORKING ON?
OH, HI, ALBERT!
I REPAIRED AN OLD ROBOT I FOUND. IT'S HELPING ME TIDY UP THE YARD.
WOW!!!
SAY, VINCENT, DO YOU THINK IT COULD HELP ME IN MY CARROT FIELD?
HMMM. PERHAPS WITH A SLIGHT MODIFICATION...
VINCENT TINKERED WITH THE ROBOT, AND SOON...
NOT BAD!

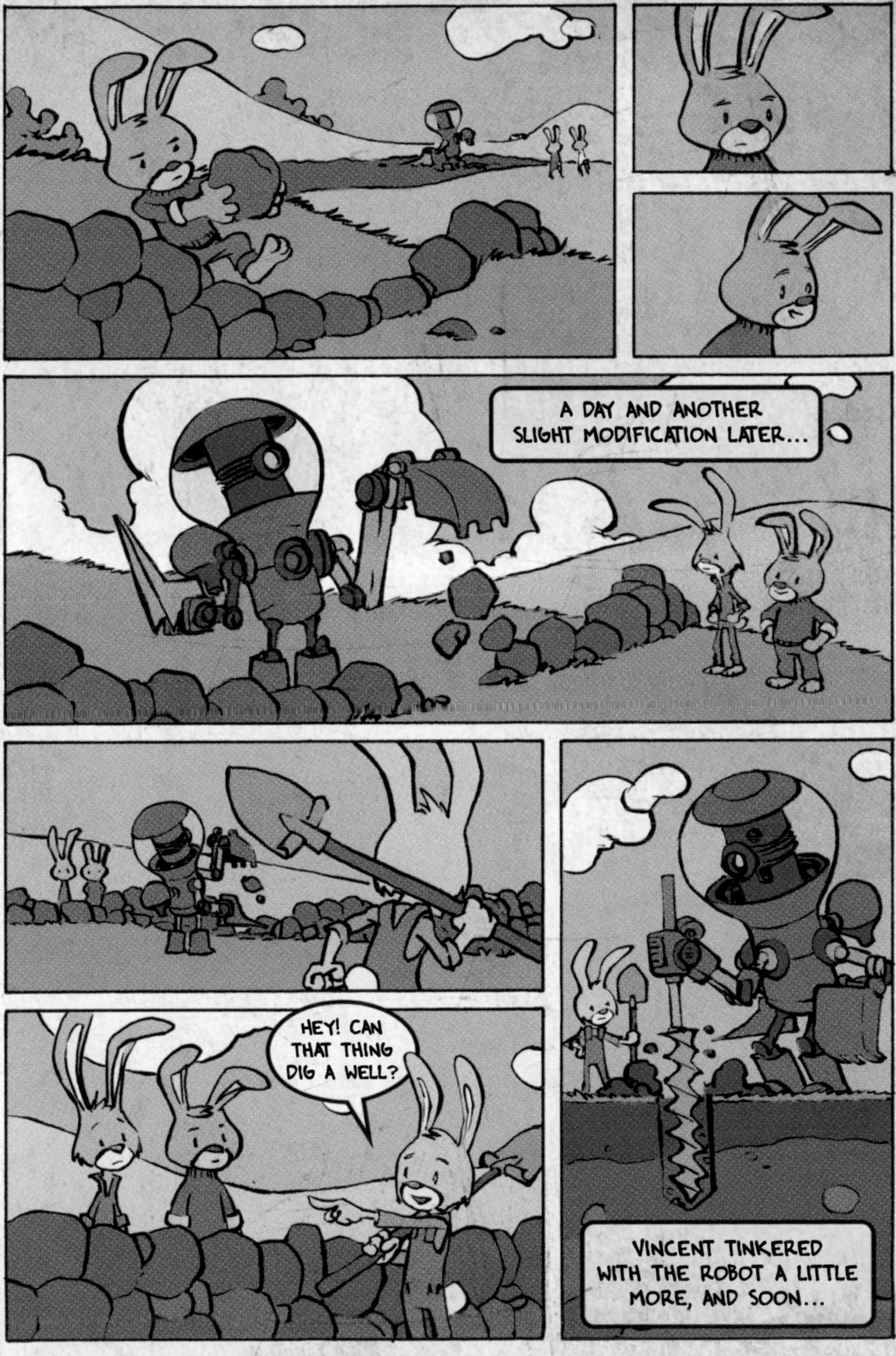
A DAY AND ANOTHER SLIGHT MODIFICATION LATER...
HEY! CAN THAT THING DIG A WELL?
VINCENT TINKERED WITH THE ROBOT A LITTLE MORE, AND SOON...

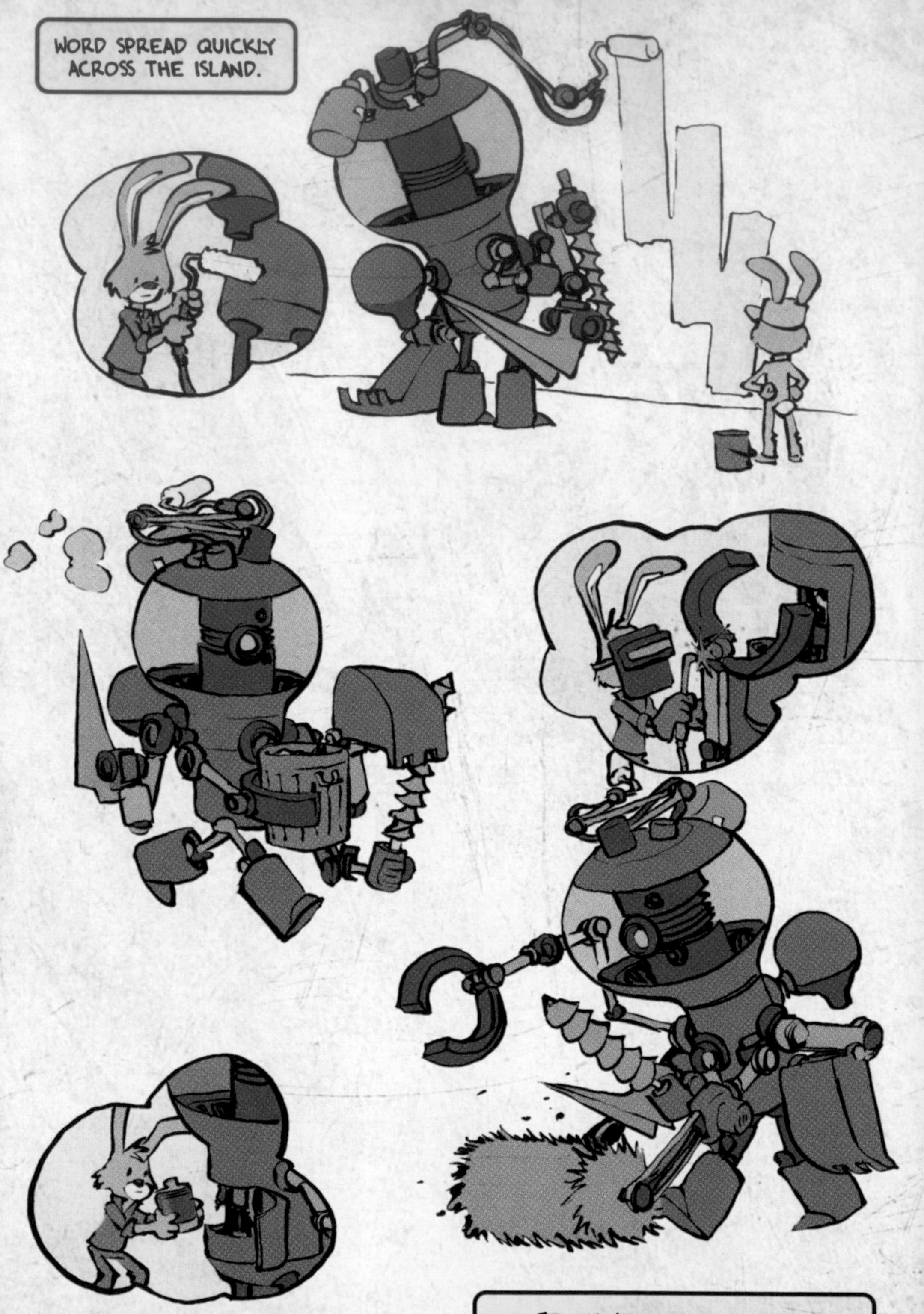
WORD SPREAD QUICKLY ACROSS THE ISLAND.
IT WASN'T LONG BEFORE THE ROBOT WAS HELPING OUT EVERYONE.

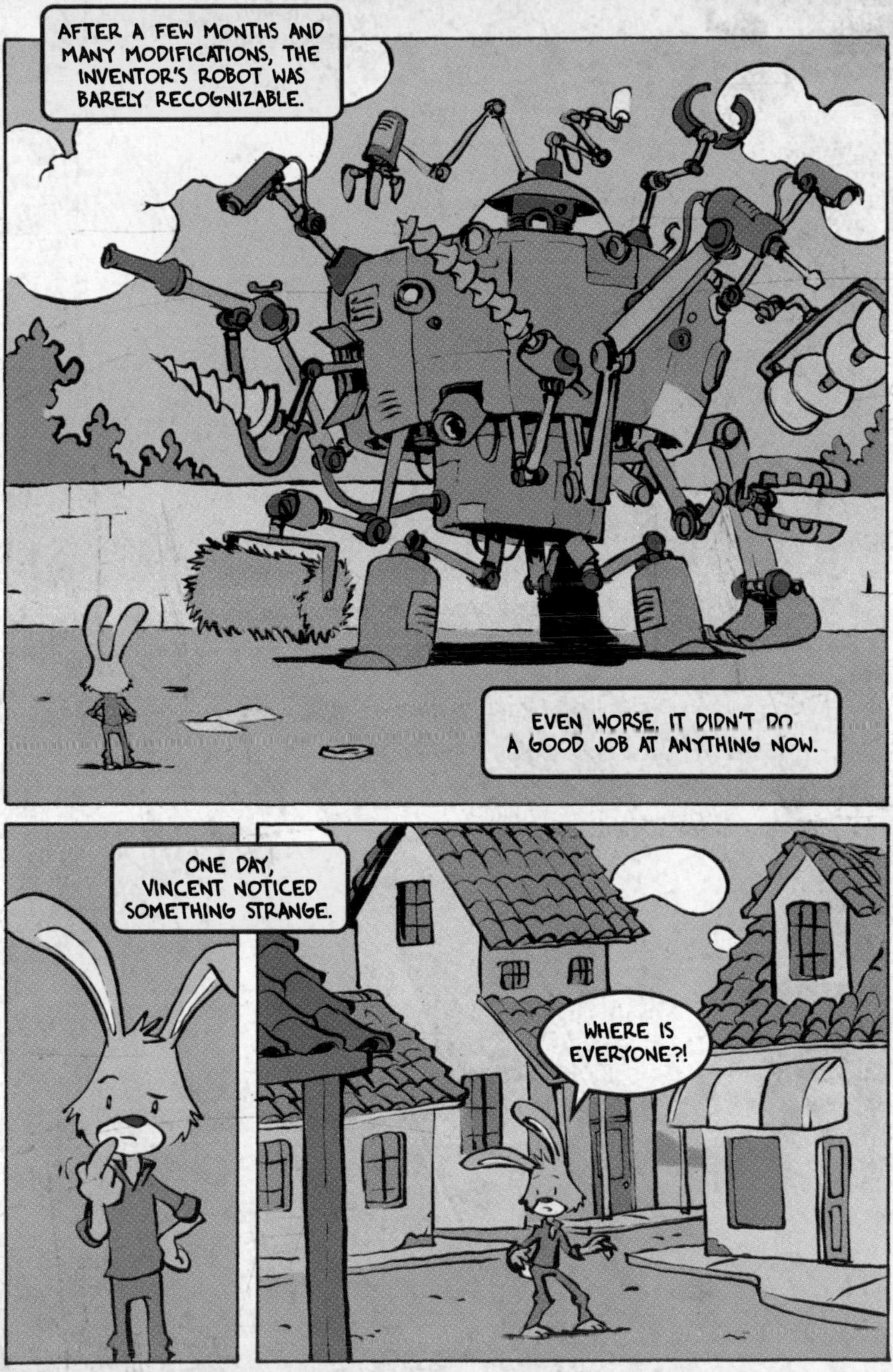
AFTER A FEW MONTHS AND MANY MODIFICATIONS, THE INVENTOR'S ROBOT WAS BARELY RECOGNIZABLE.
EVEN WORSE, IT DIDN'T DO A GOOD JOB AT ANYTHING NOW.
ONE DAY, VINCENT NOTICED SOMETHING STRANGE.
WHERE IS EVERYONE?!

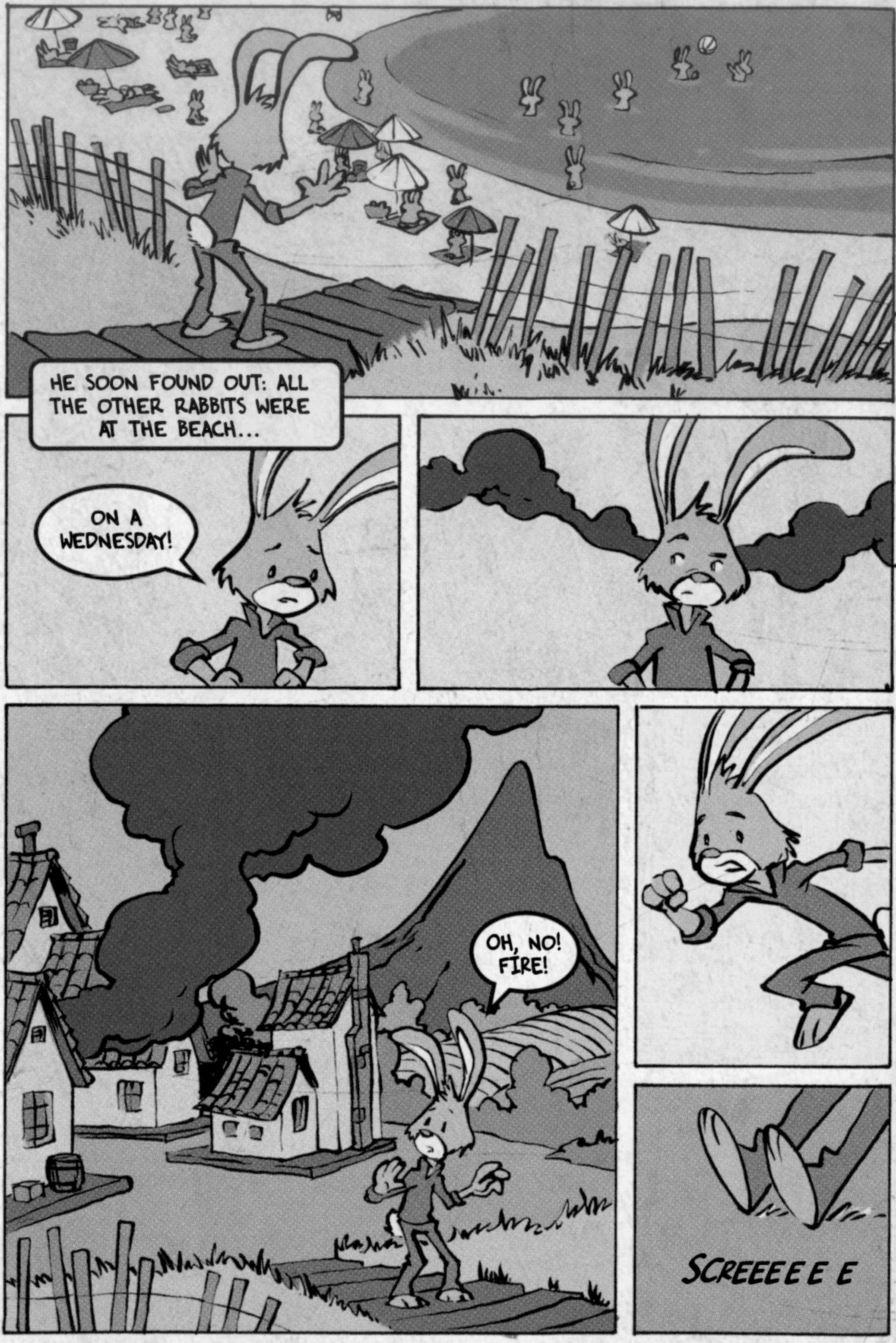
HE SOON FOUND OUT: ALL THE OTHER RABBITS WERE AT THE BEACH...
ON A WEDNESDAY!
OH, NO! FIRE!
SCREEEEE E E

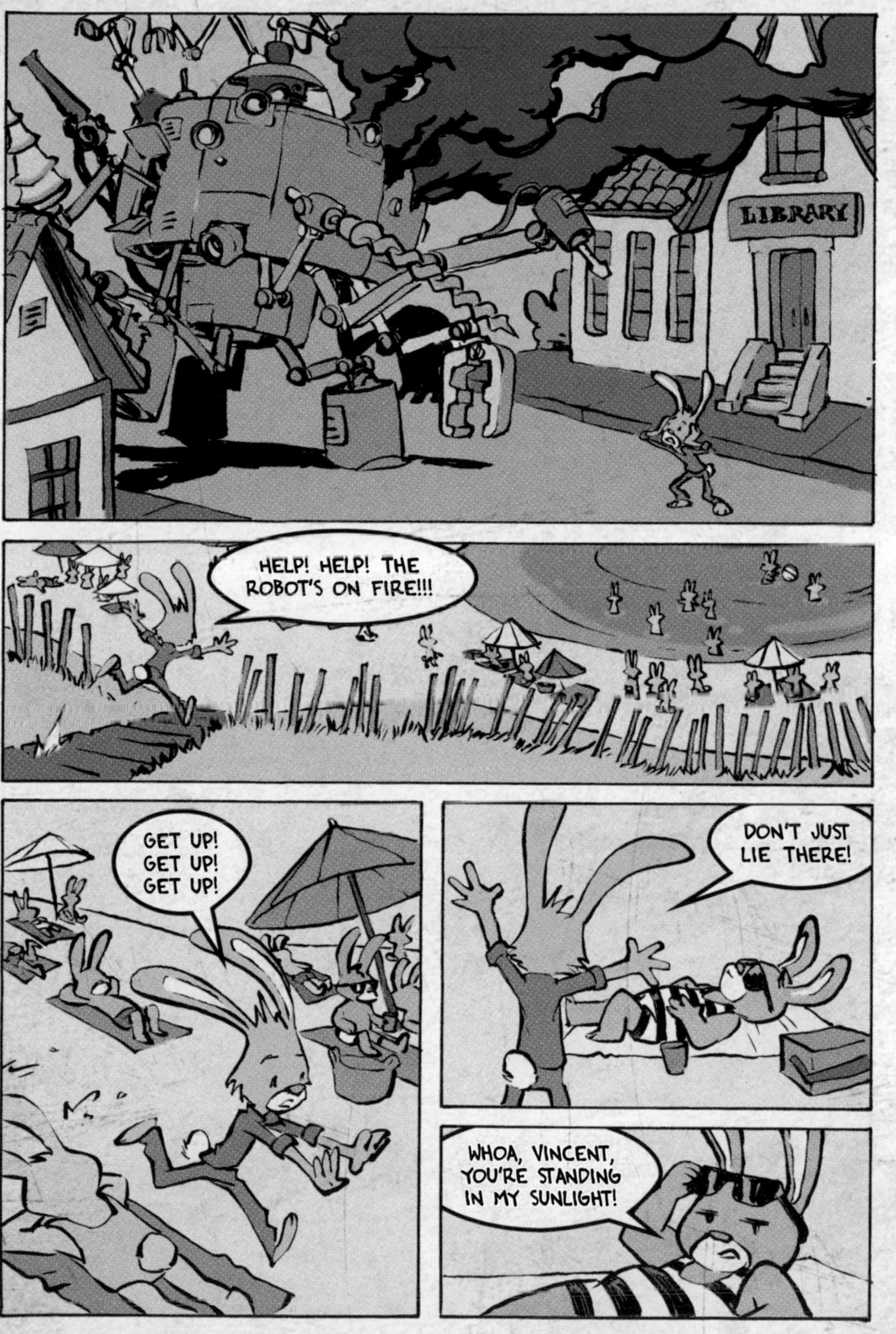
LIBRARY
HELP! HELP! THE ROBOT'S ON FIRE!!!
GET UP! GET UP! GET UP!
DON'T JUST LIE THERE!
WHOA, VINCENT, YOU'RE STANDING IN MY SUNLIGHT!

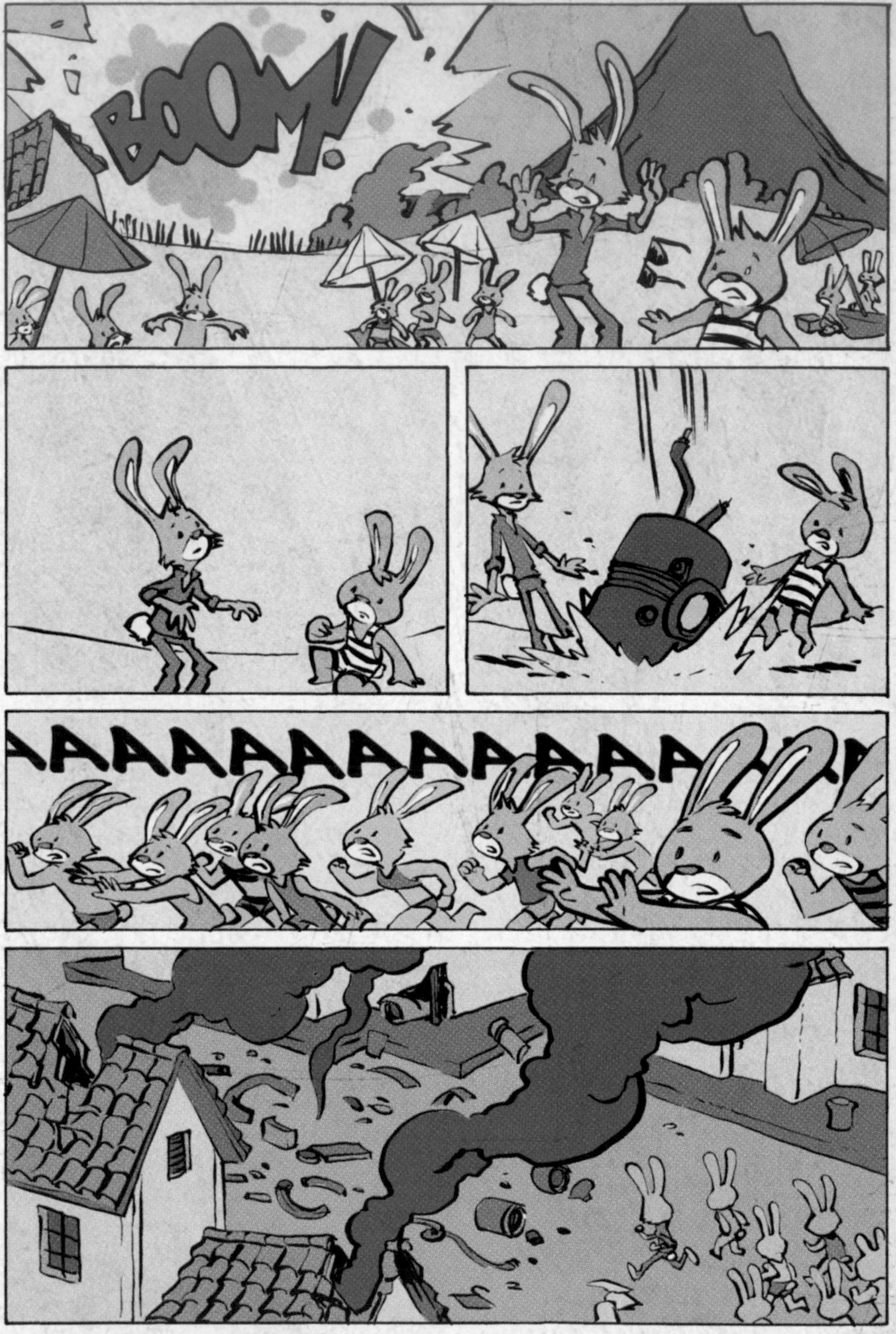
BOOM!
AAAAAAAAAAAAA

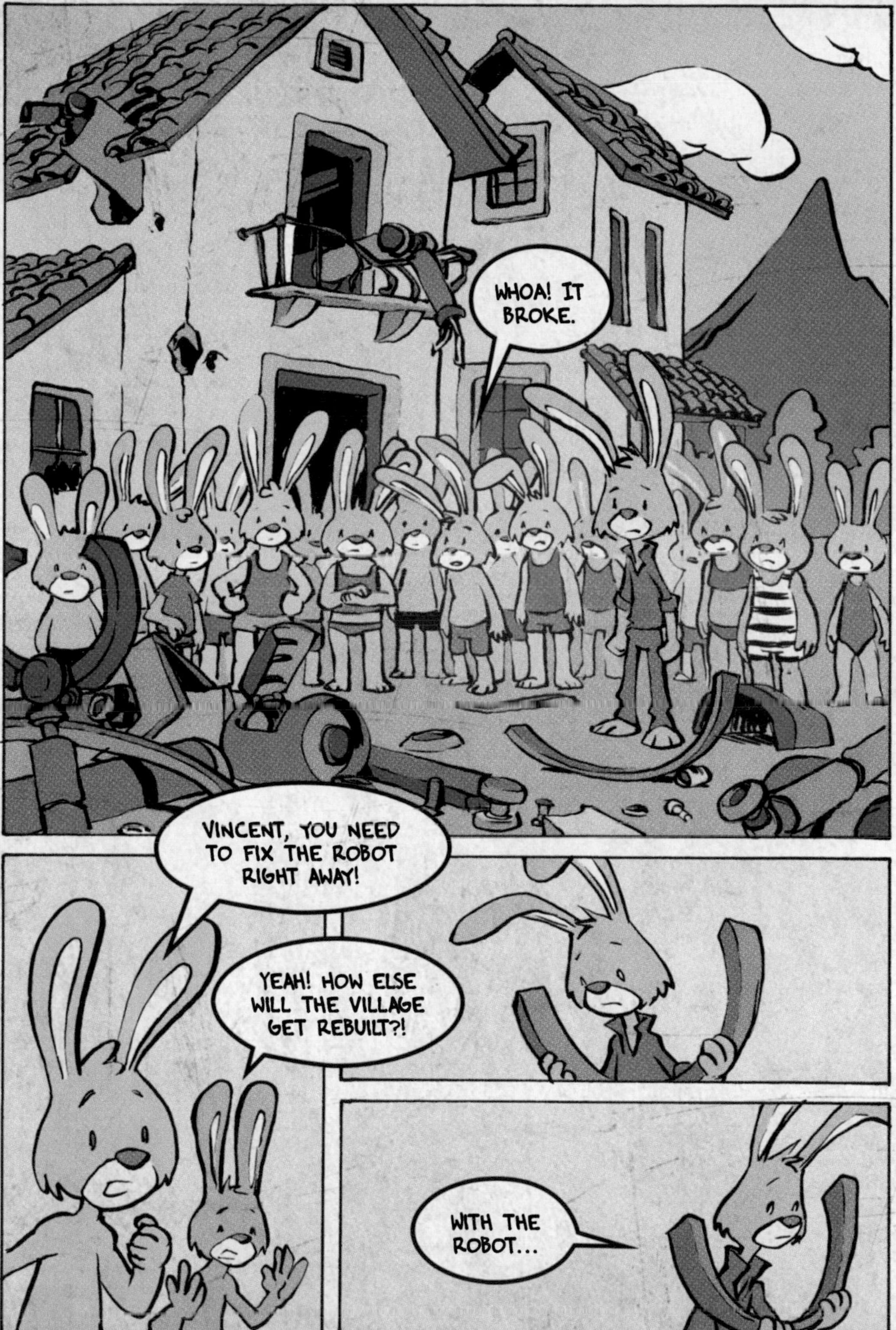
WHOA! IT BROKE.
VINCENT, YOU NEED TO FIX THE ROBOT RIGHT AWAY!
YEAH! HOW ELSE WILL THE VILLAGE GET REBUILT?!
WITH THE ROBOT...

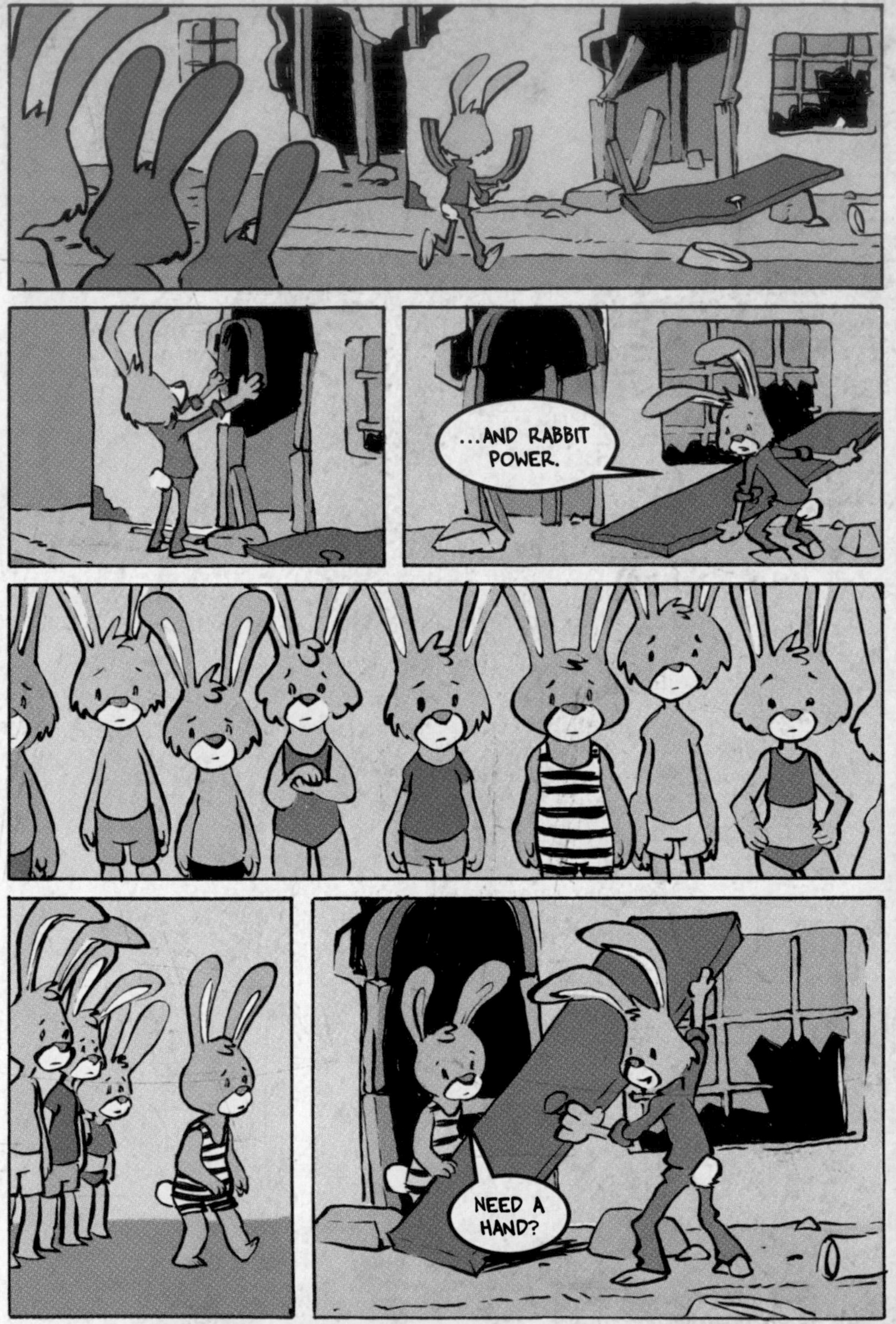
...AND RABBIT POWER.
NEED A HAND?

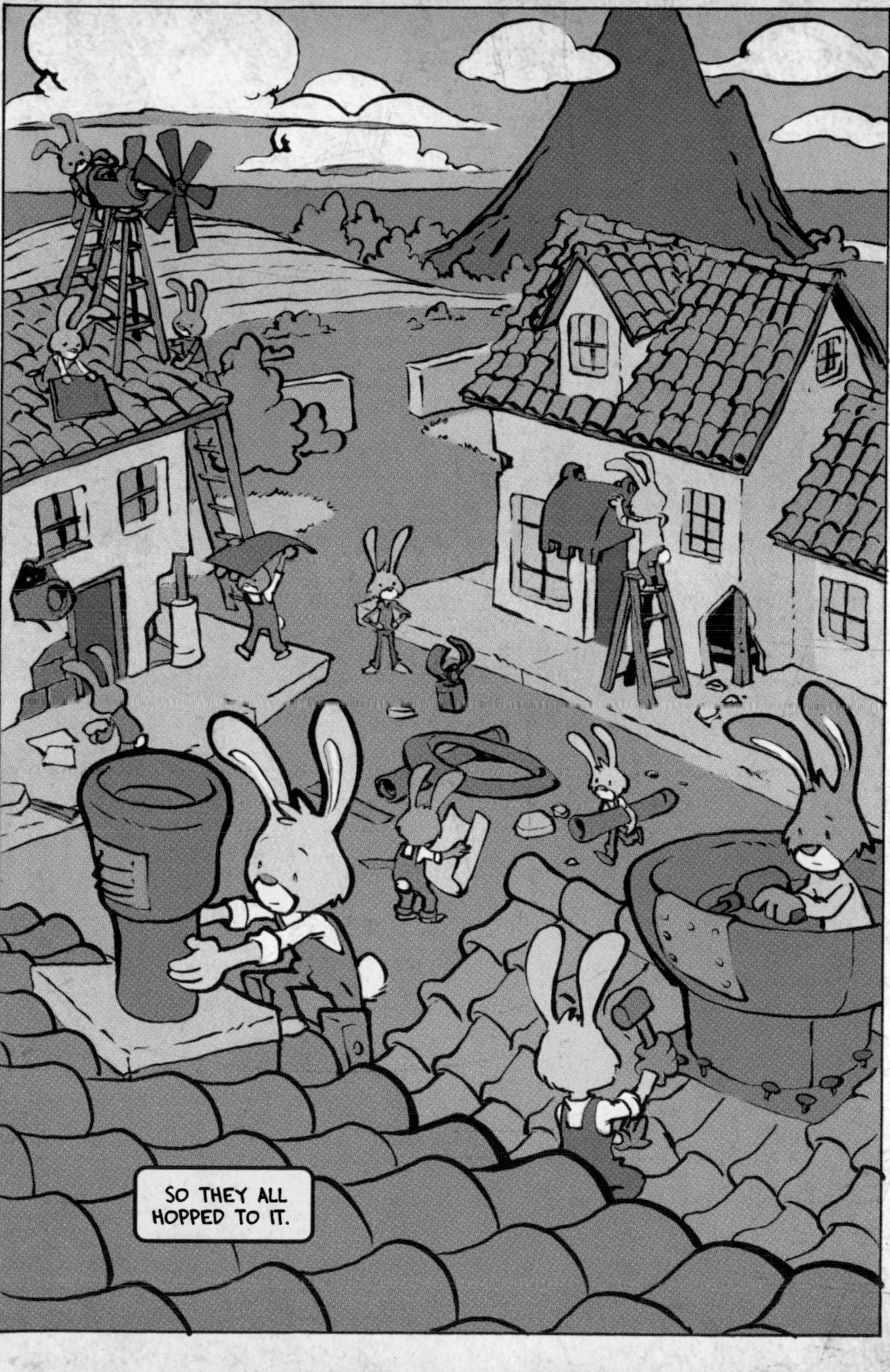
SO THEY ALL
HOPPED TO IT.

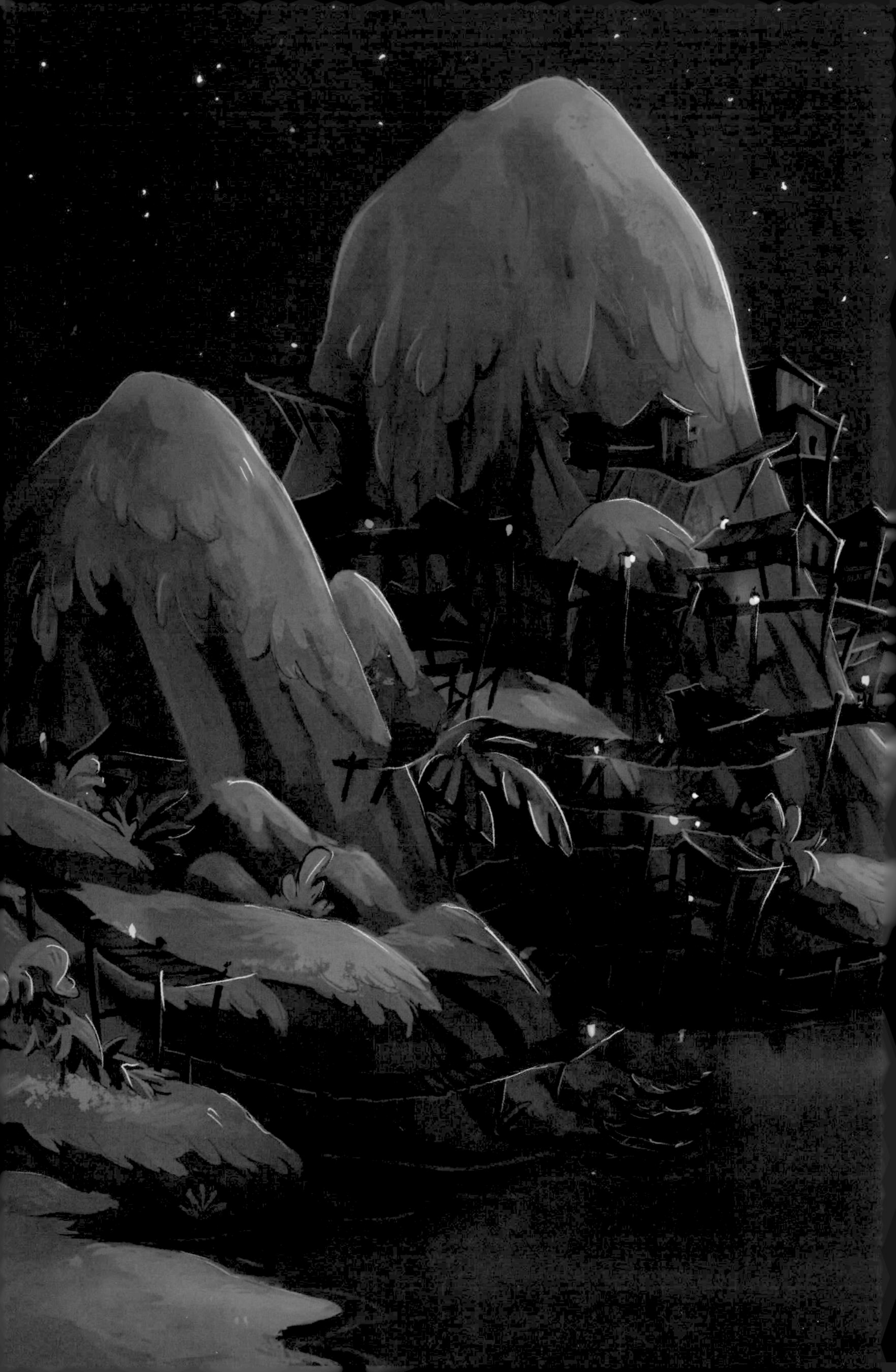

THE MASK DANCE

BY CHRYSTIN GARLAND

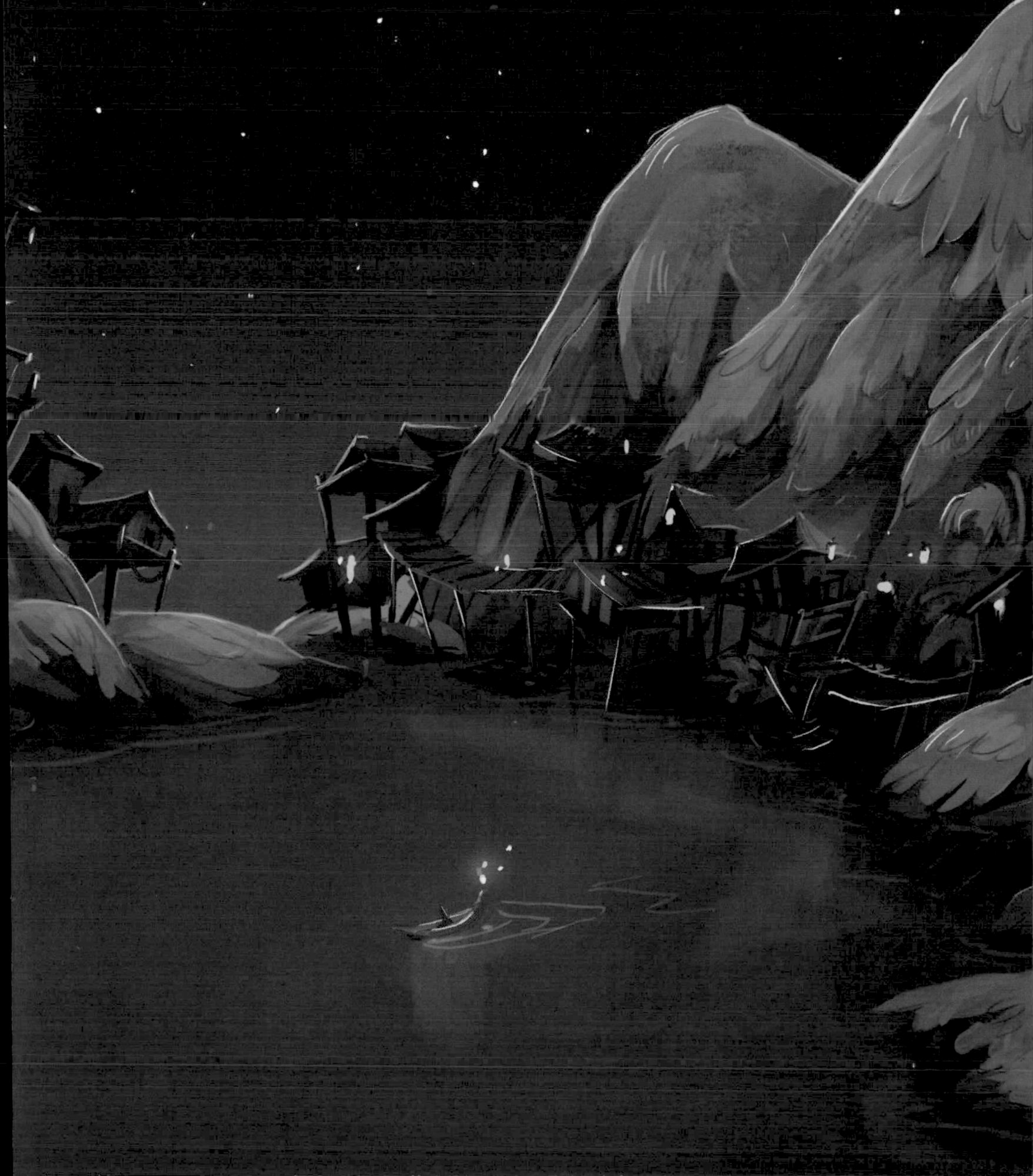

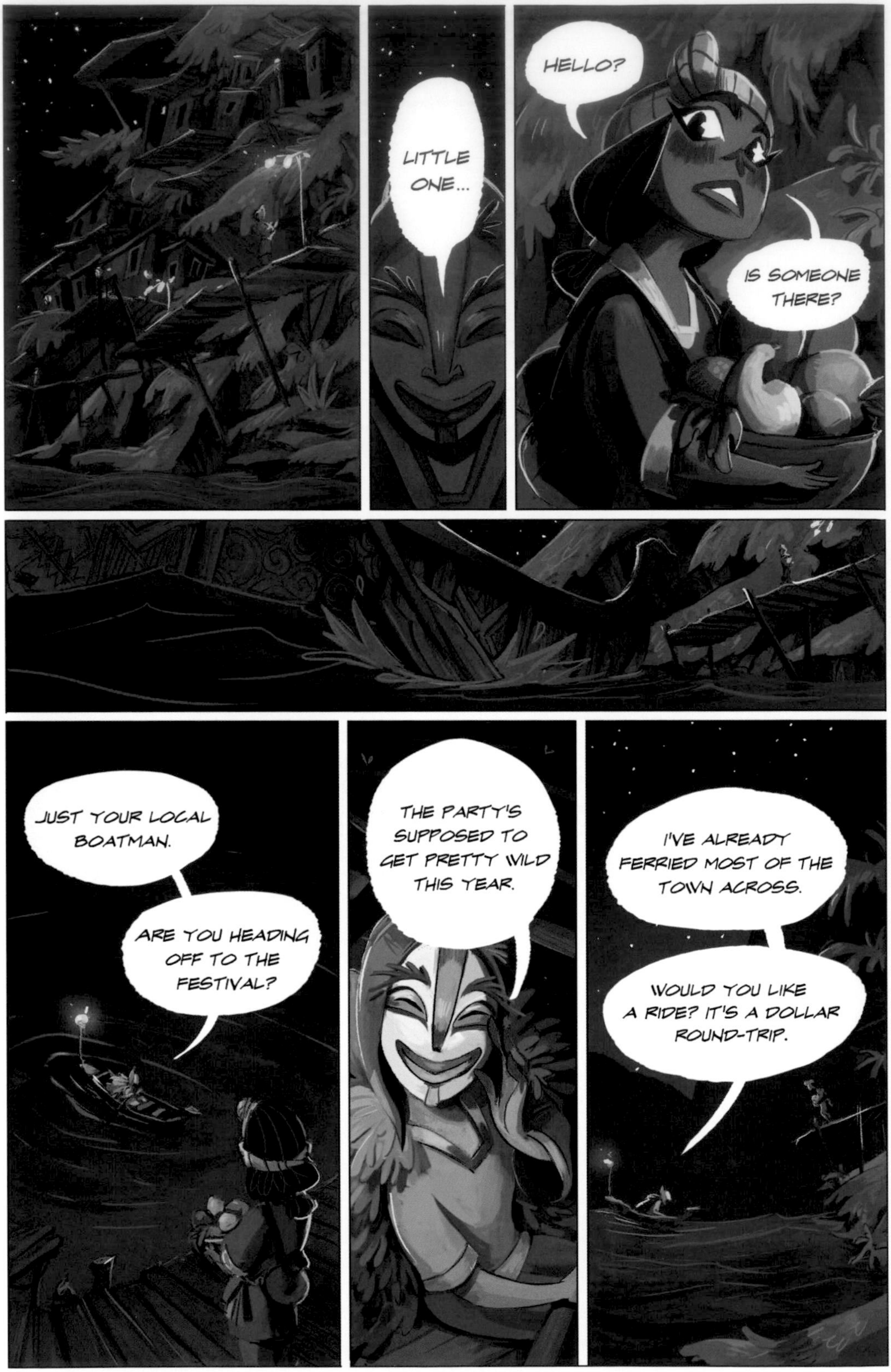
LITTLE ONE...
HELLO?
IS SOMEONE THERE?
JUST YOUR LOCAL BOATMAN.
ARE YOU HEADING OFF TO THE FESTIVAL?
THE PARTY'S SUPPOSED TO GET PRETTY WILD THIS YEAR.
I'VE ALREADY FERRIED MOST OF THE TOWN ACROSS.
WOULD YOU LIKE A RIDE? IT'S A DOLLAR ROUND-TRIP.

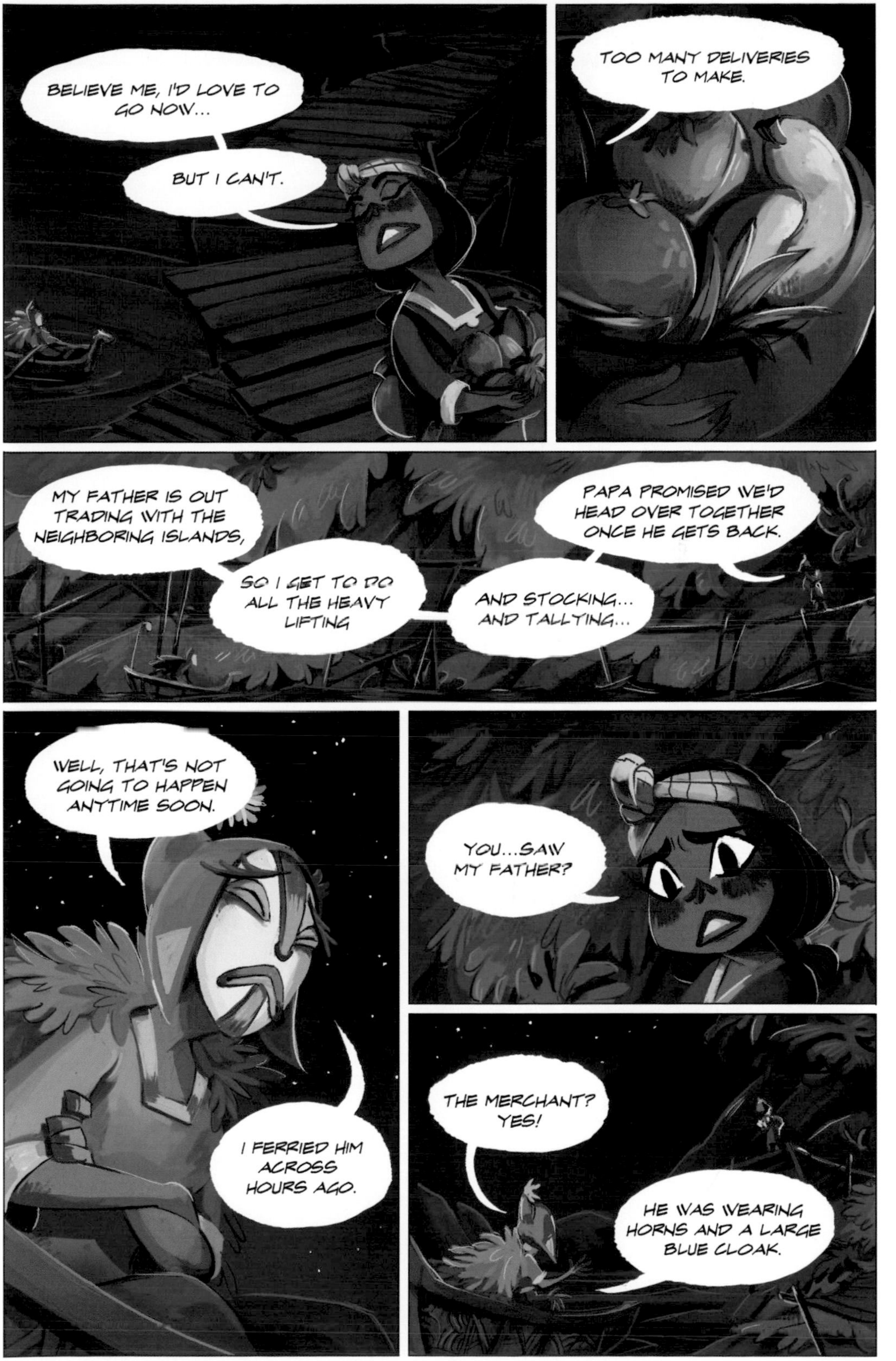
BELIEVE ME, I'D LOVE TO GO NOW...
BUT I CAN'T.
TOO MANY DELIVERIES TO MAKE.
MY FATHER IS OUT TRADING WITH THE NEIGHBORING ISLANDS,
SO I GET TO DO ALL THE HEAVY LIFTING
AND STOCKING... AND TALLYING...
PAPA PROMISED WE'D HEAD OVER TOGETHER ONCE HE GETS BACK.
WELL, THAT'S NOT GOING TO HAPPEN ANYTIME SOON.
I FERRIED HIM ACROSS HOURS AGO.
YOU...SAW MY FATHER?
THE MERCHANT? YES!
HE WAS WEARING HORNS AND A LARGE BLUE CLOAK.

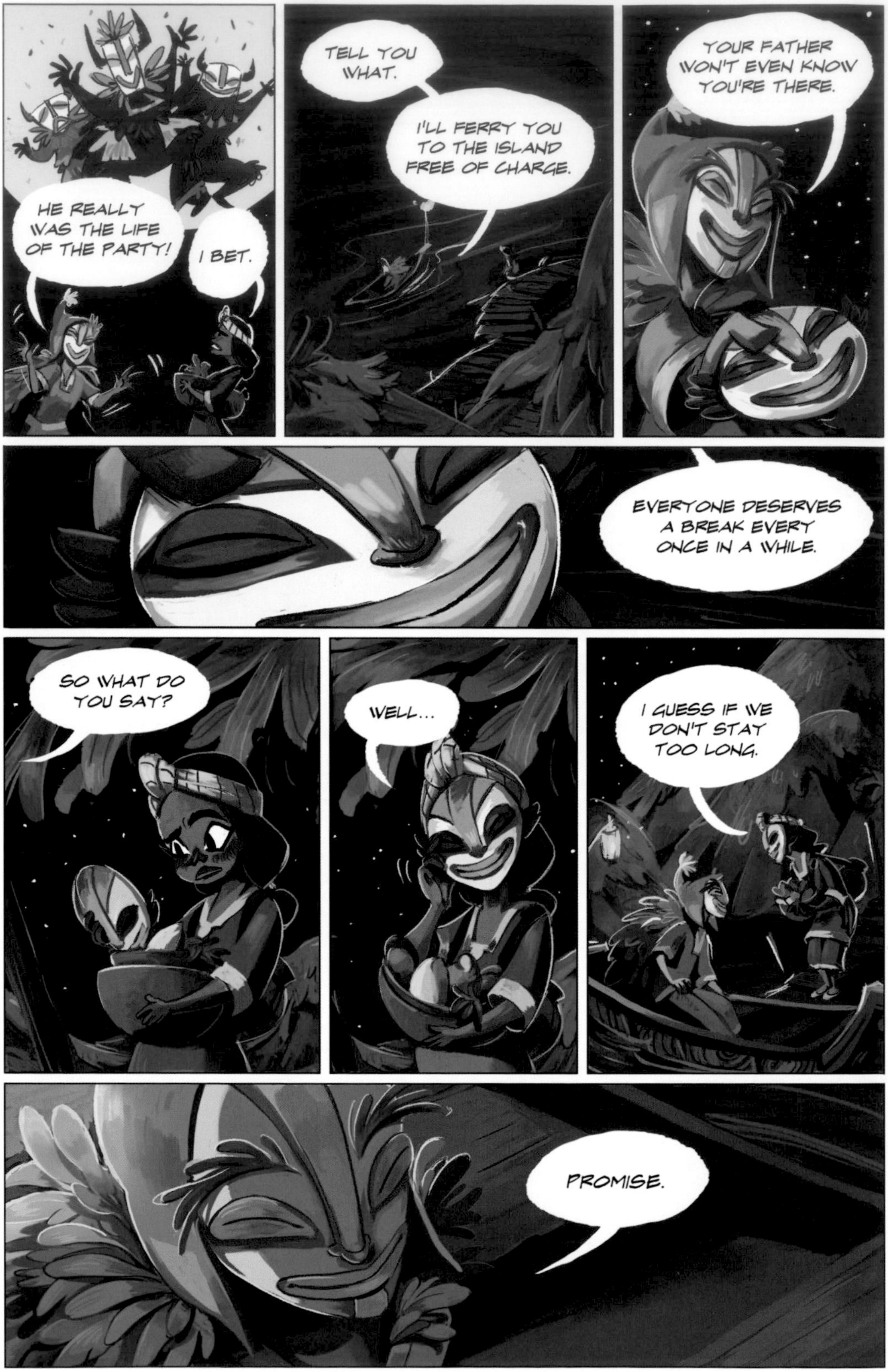
HE REALLY WAS THE LIFE OF THE PARTY!
I BET.
TELL YOU WHAT.
I'LL FERRY YOU TO THE ISLAND FREE OF CHARGE.
YOUR FATHER WON'T EVEN KNOW YOU'RE THERE.
EVERYONE DESERVES A BREAK EVERY ONCE IN A WHILE.
SO WHAT DO YOU SAY?
WELL...
I GUESS IF WE DON'T STAY TOO LONG.
PROMISE.

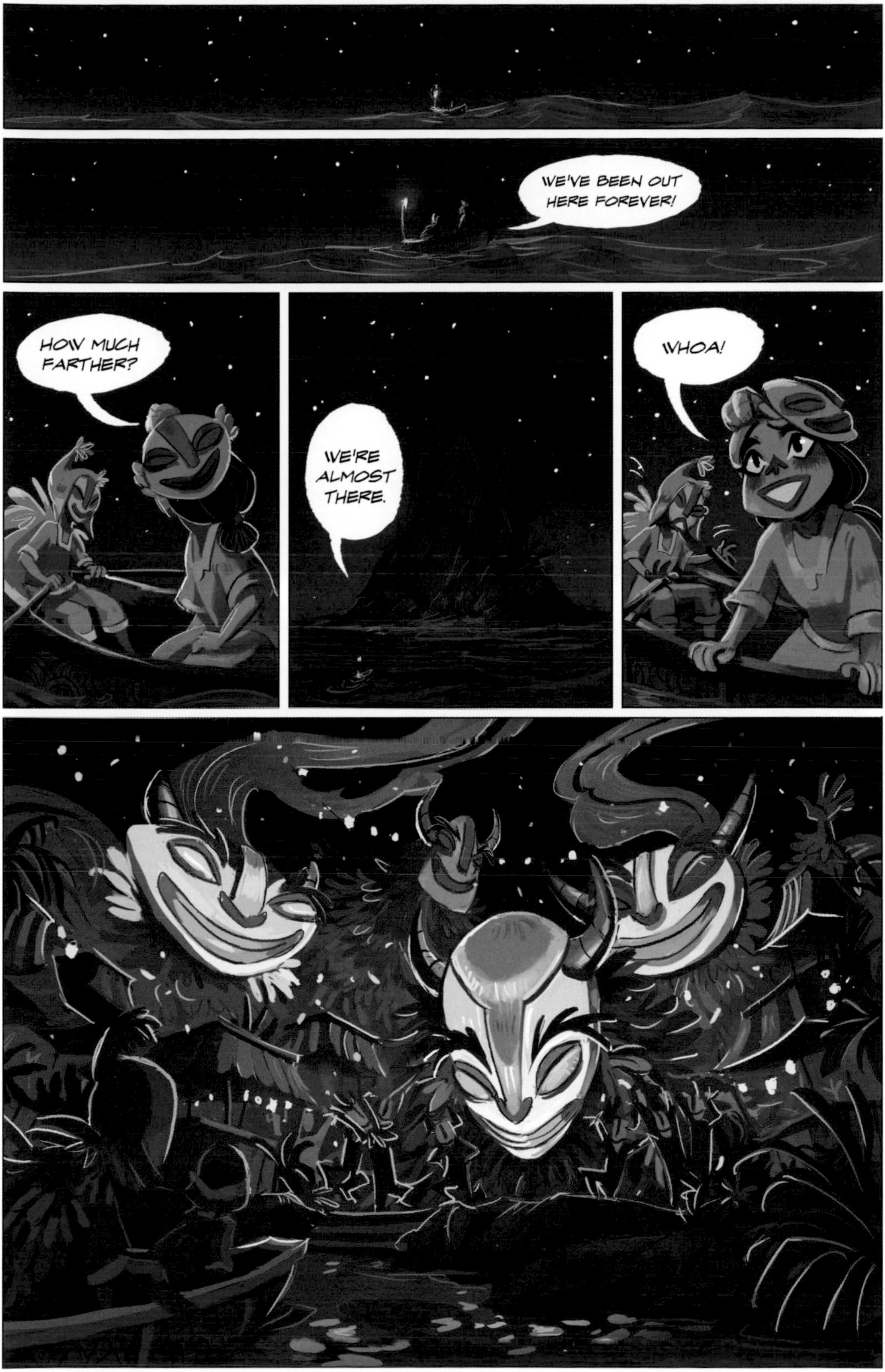
WE'VE BEEN OUT HERE FOREVER!
HOW MUCH FARTHER?
WE'RE ALMOST THERE.
WHOA!

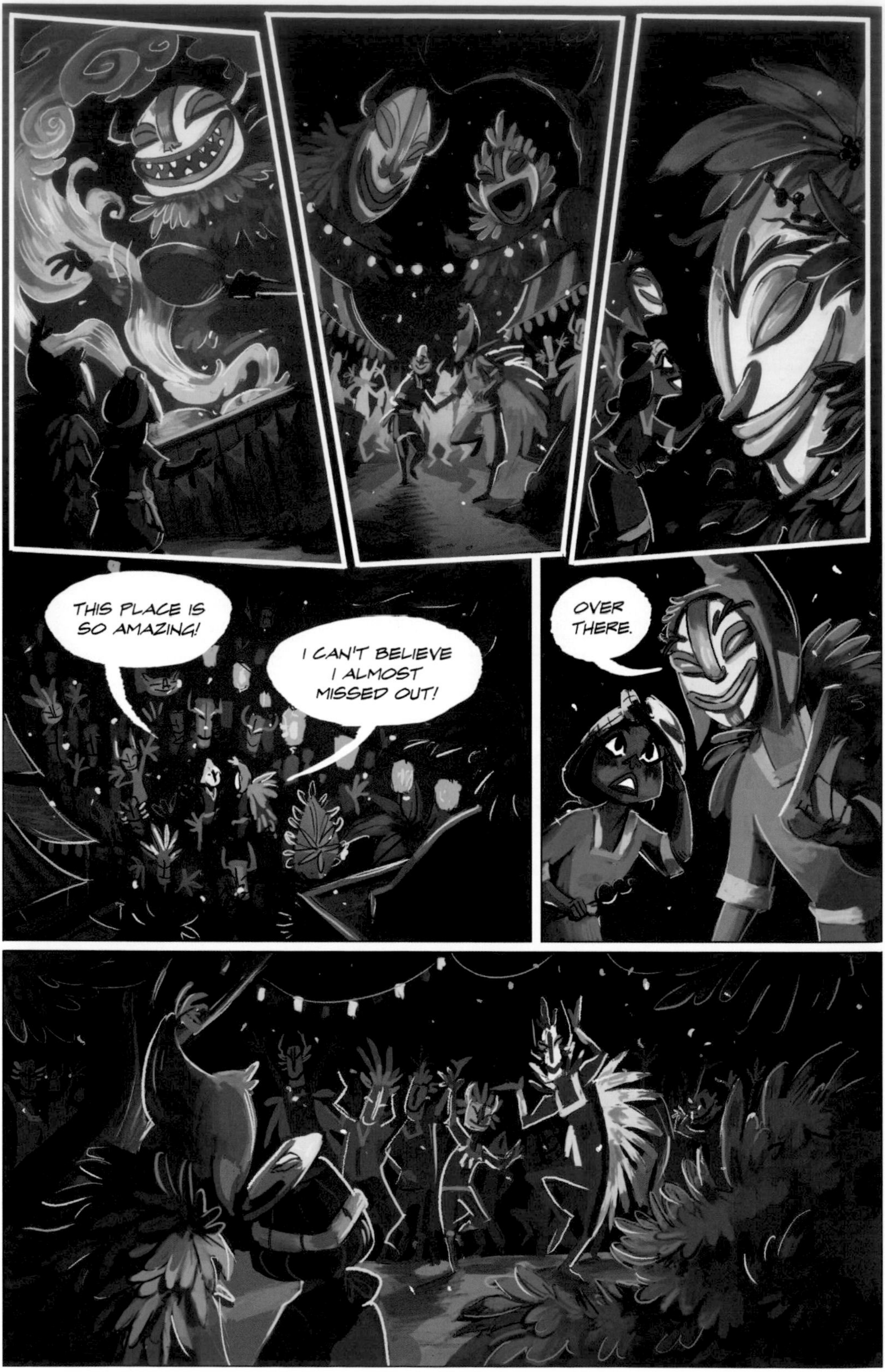
THIS PLACE IS SO AMAZING!
I CAN'T BELIEVE I ALMOST MISSED OUT!
OVER THERE.

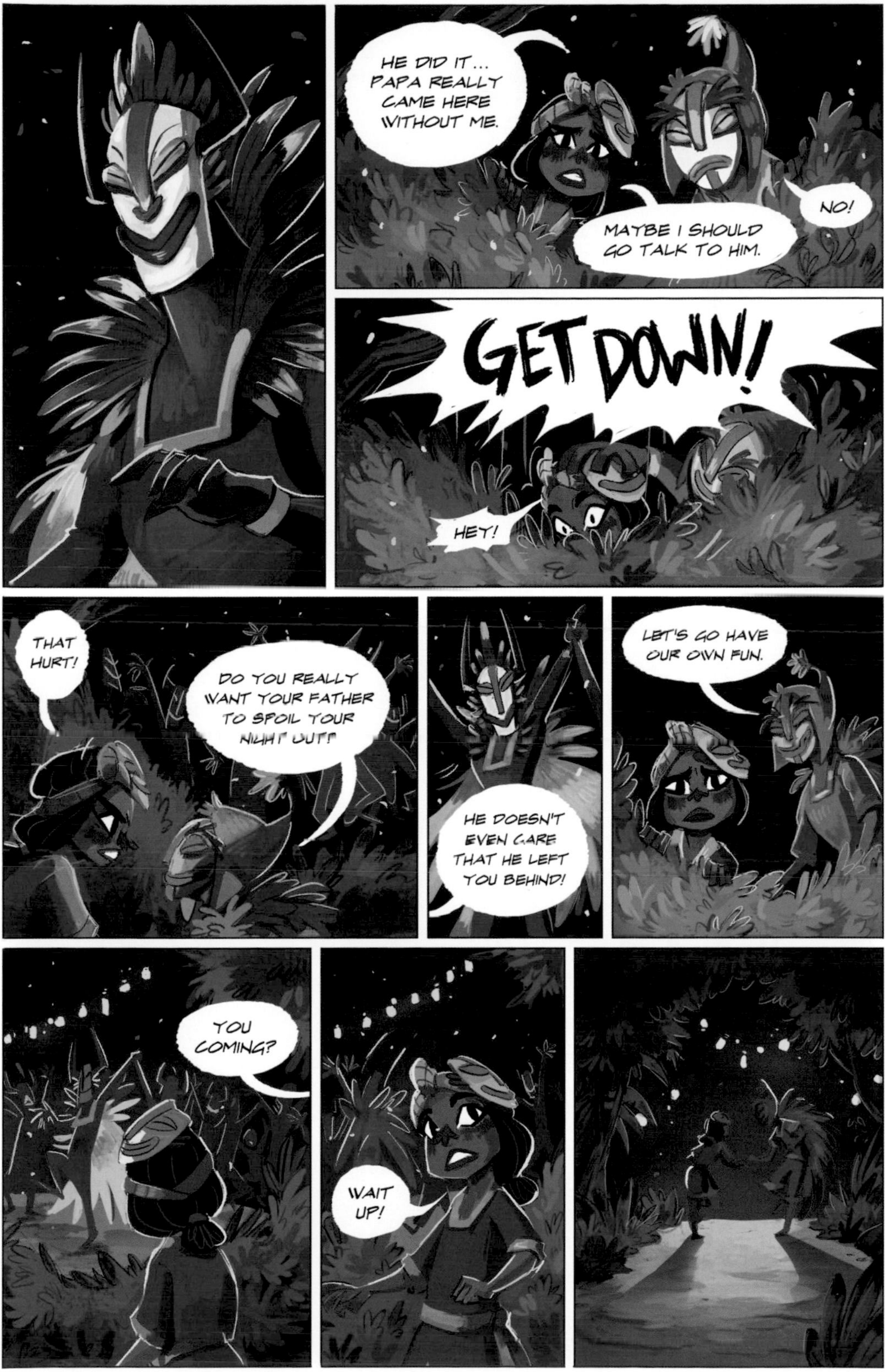
HE DID IT... PAPA REALLY CAME HERE WITHOUT ME.
MAYBE I SHOULD GO TALK TO HIM.
NO!
GET DOWN!
HEY!
THAT HURT!
DO YOU REALLY WANT YOUR FATHER TO SPOIL YOUR NIGHT OUT?
HE DOESN'T EVEN CARE THAT HE LEFT YOU BEHIND!
LET'S GO HAVE OUR OWN FUN.
YOU COMING?
WAIT UP!

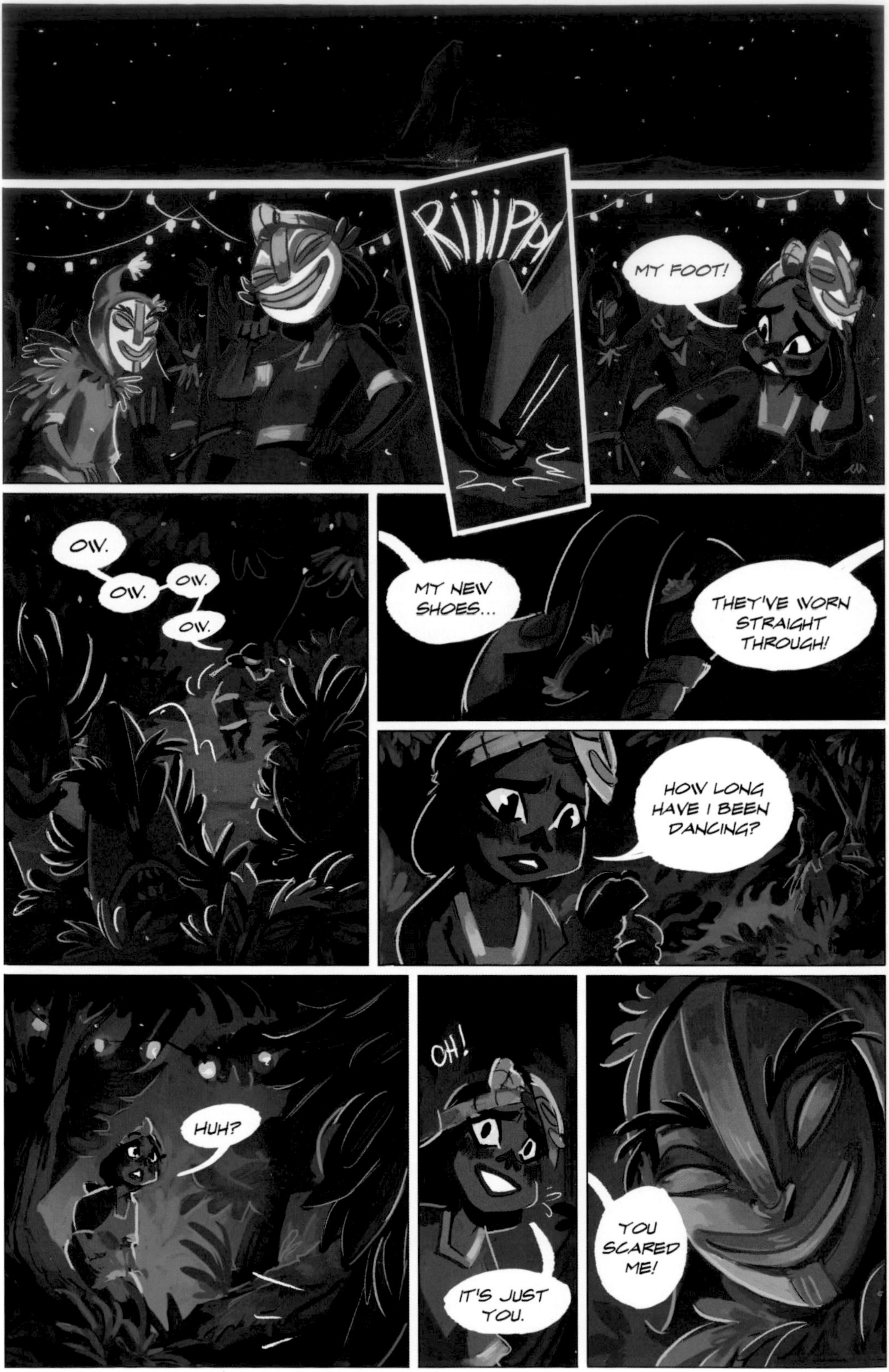
RIIIPP!
MY FOOT!
OW.
OW.
OW.
OW.
MY NEW SHOES...
THEY'VE WORN STRAIGHT THROUGH!
HOW LONG HAVE I BEEN DANCING?
HUH?
OH!
IT'S JUST YOU.
YOU SCARED ME!

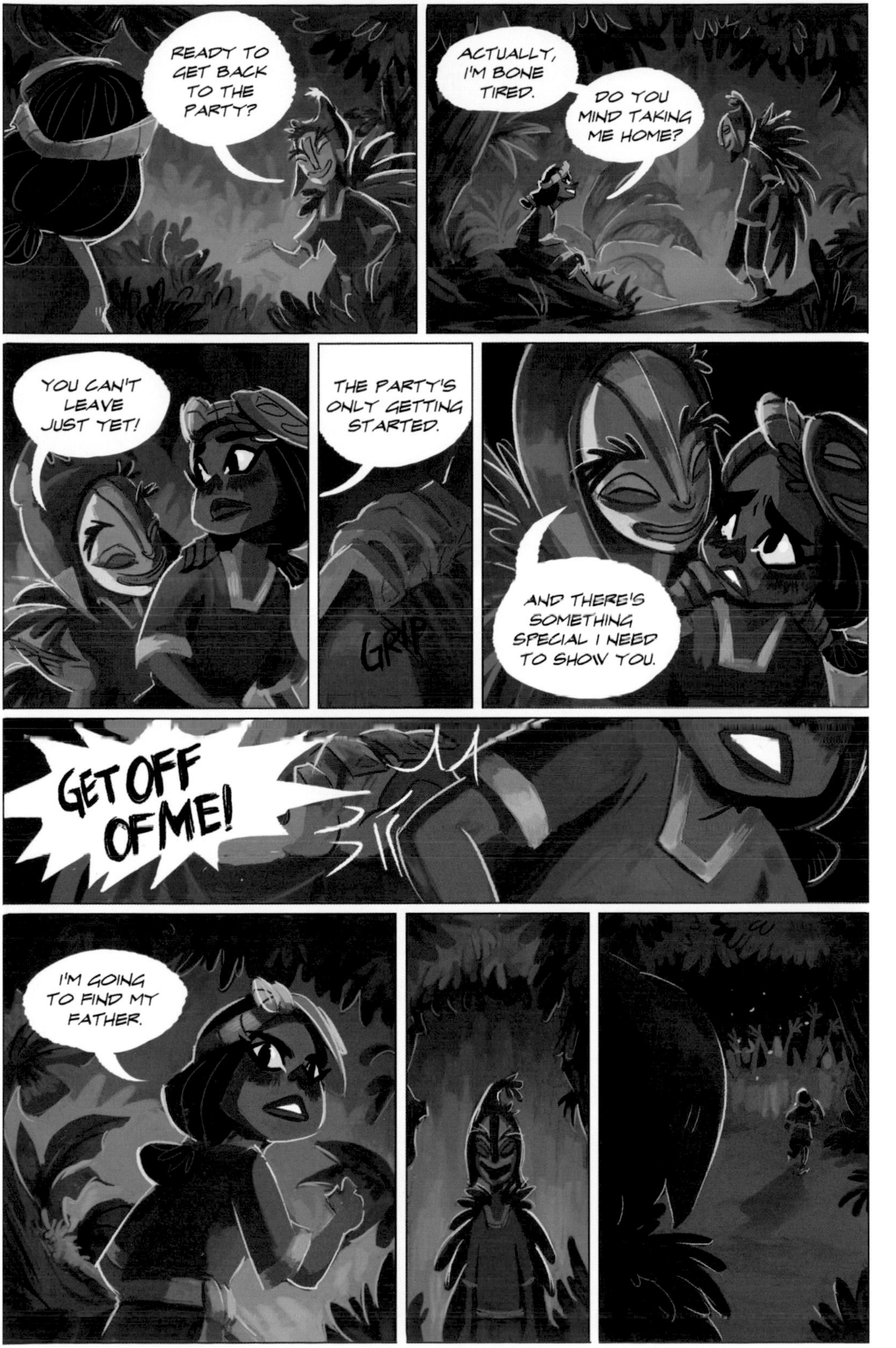
READY TO GET BACK TO THE PARTY?
ACTUALLY, I'M BONE TIRED.
DO YOU MIND TAKING ME HOME?
YOU CAN'T LEAVE JUST YET!
THE PARTY'S ONLY GETTING STARTED.
GRIP
AND THERE'S SOMETHING SPECIAL I NEED TO SHOW YOU.
GET OFF OF ME!
I'M GOING TO FIND MY FATHER.

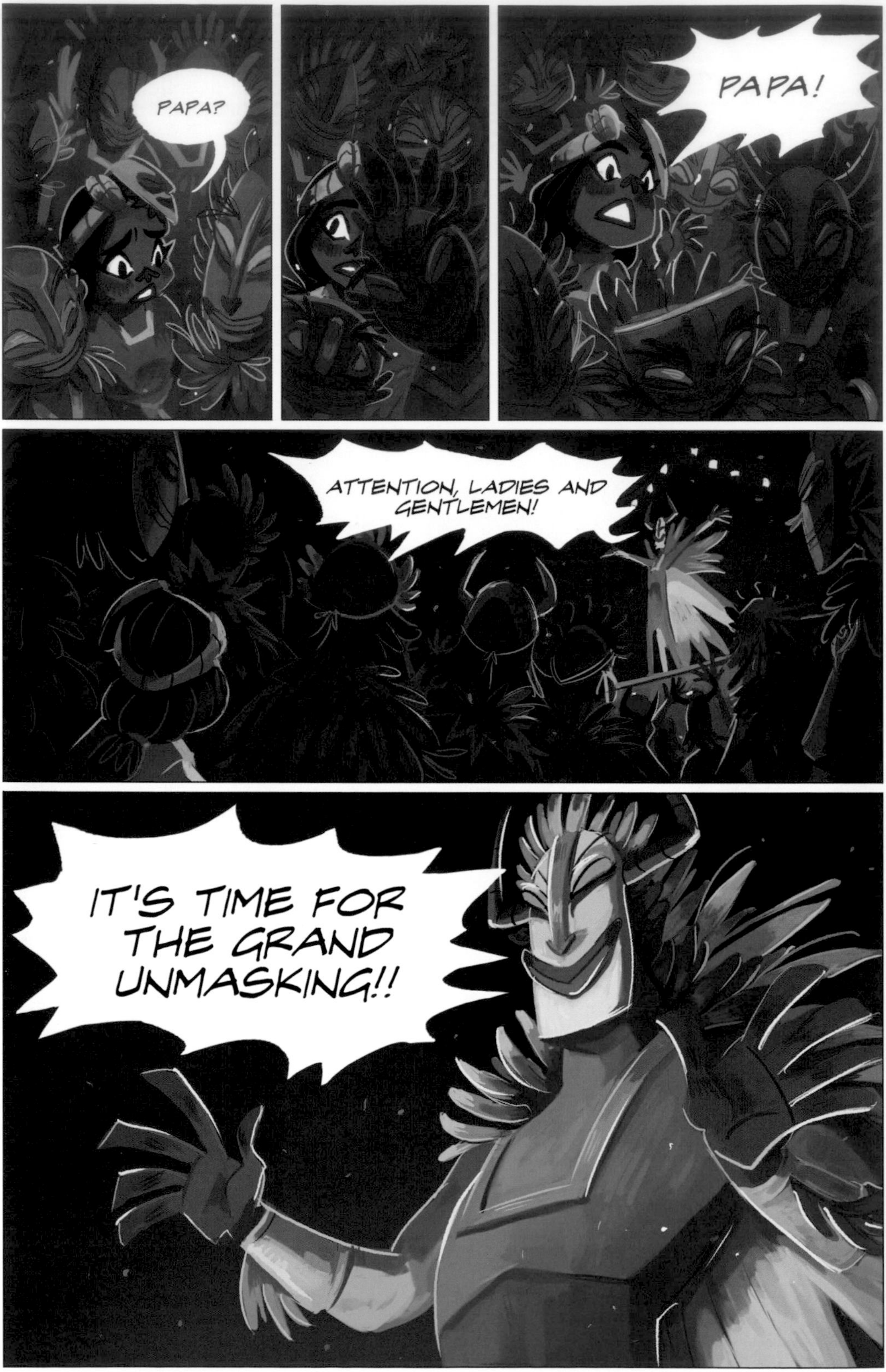
PAPA?
PAPA!
ATTENTION, LADIES AND GENTLEMEN!
IT'S TIME FOR THE GRAND UNMASKING!!

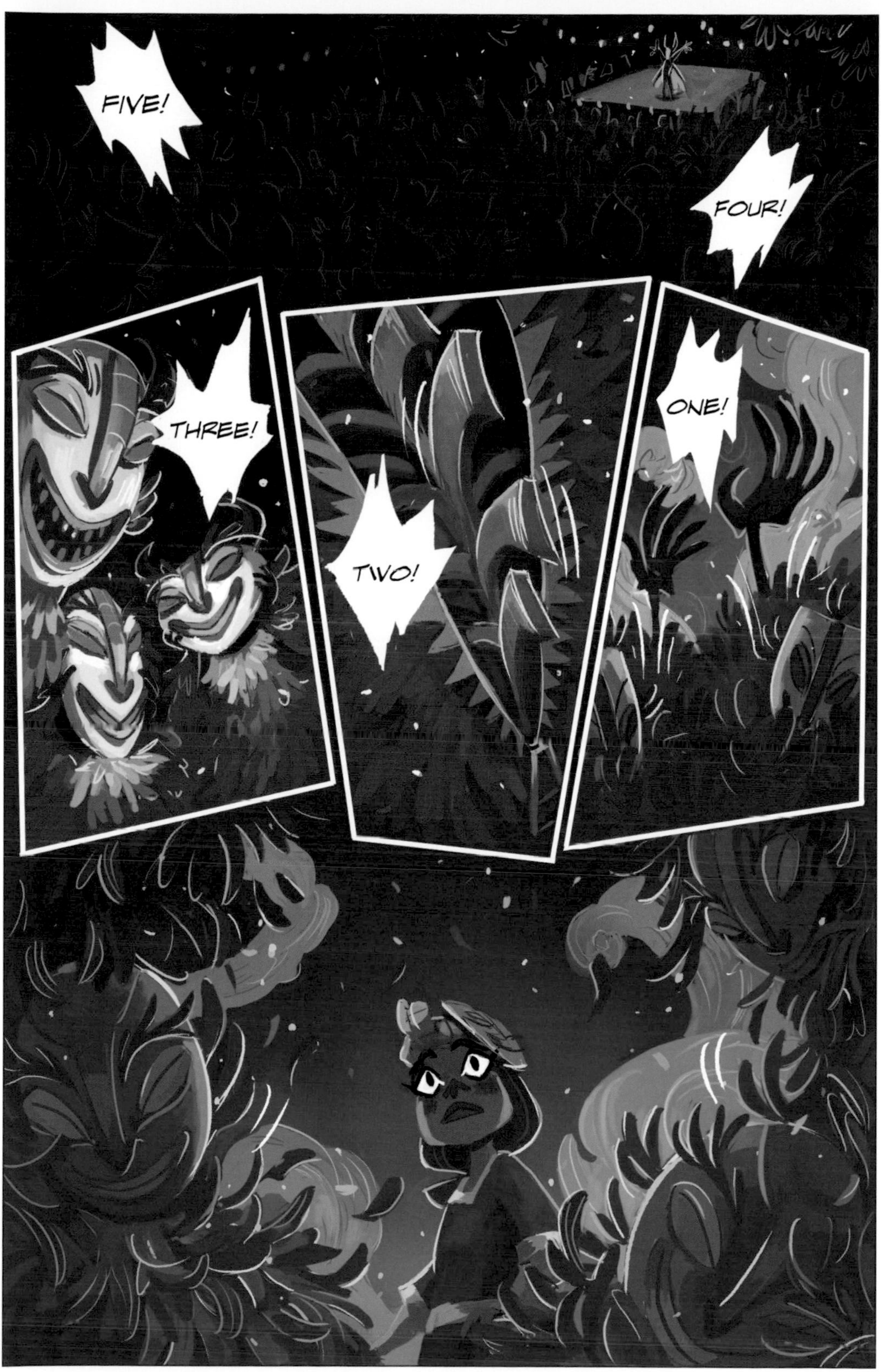
FIVE!
FOUR!
THREE!
TWO!
ONE!

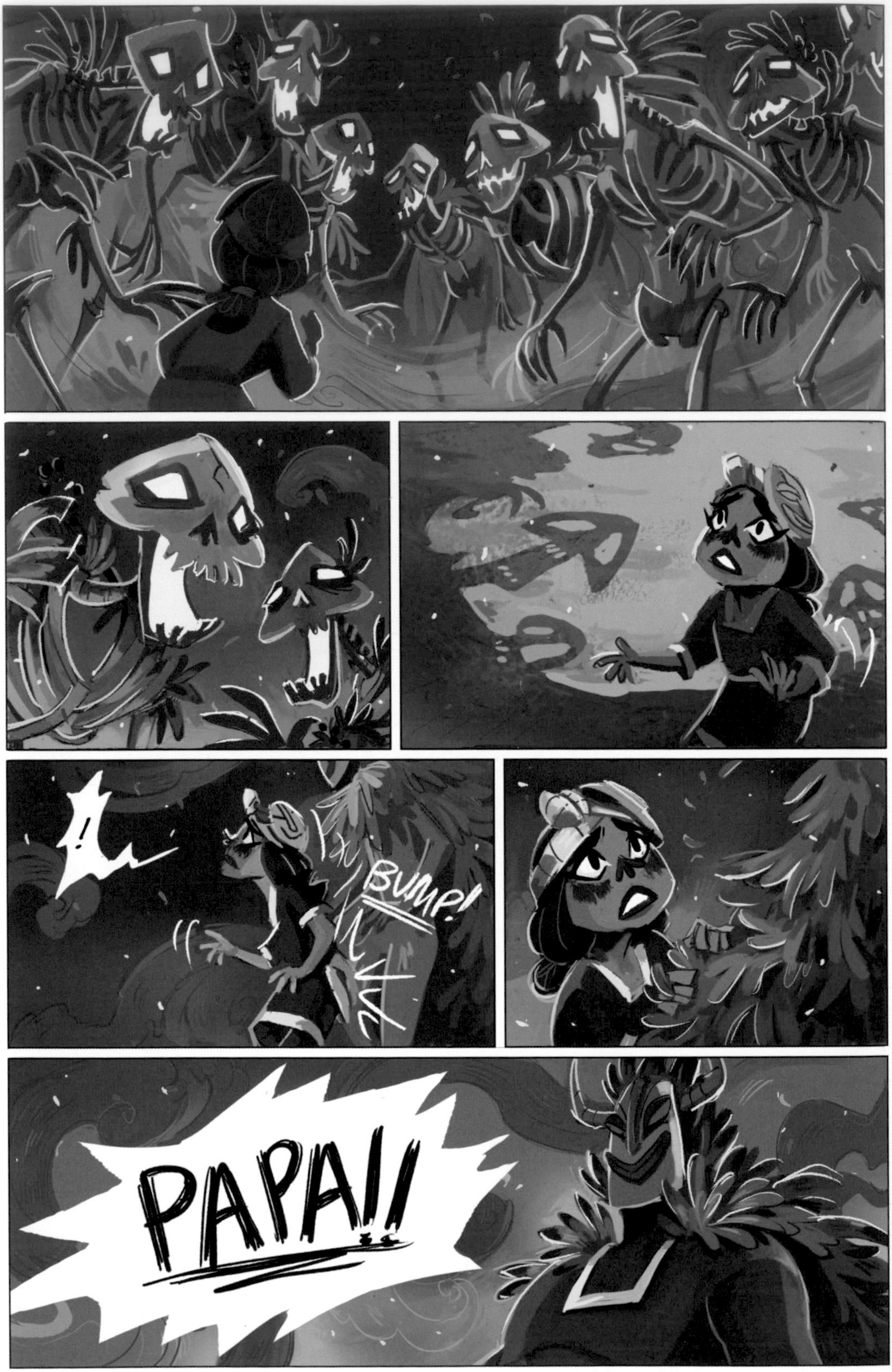
!
BUMP!
PAPA!!

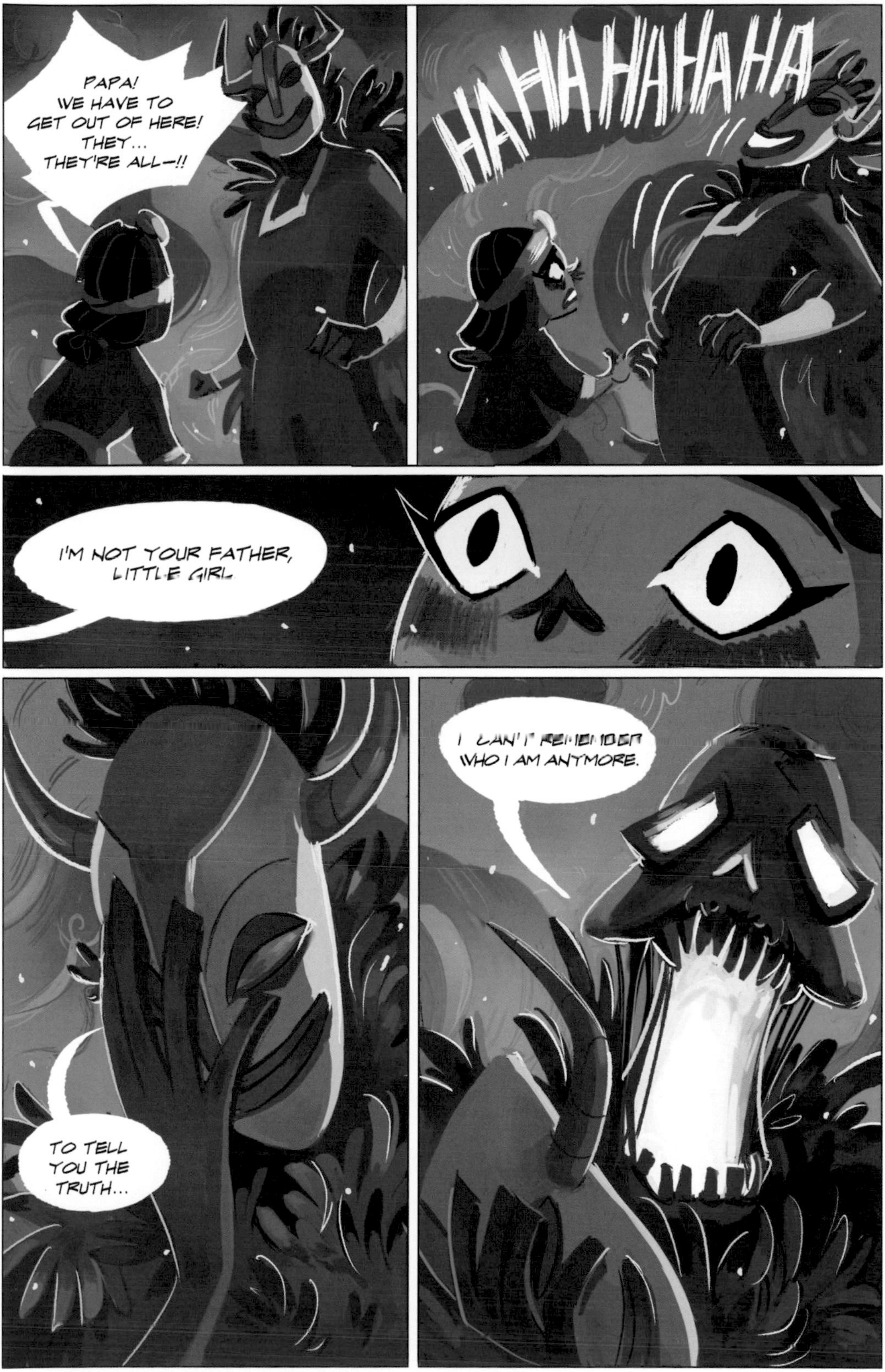
PAPA!
WE HAVE TO
GET OUT OF HERE!
THEY...
THEY'RE ALL—!!
HAHAHAHAHAHA
I'M NOT YOUR FATHER,
LITTLE GIRL.
TO TELL
YOU THE
TRUTH...
I CAN'T REMEMBER
WHO I AM ANYMORE.

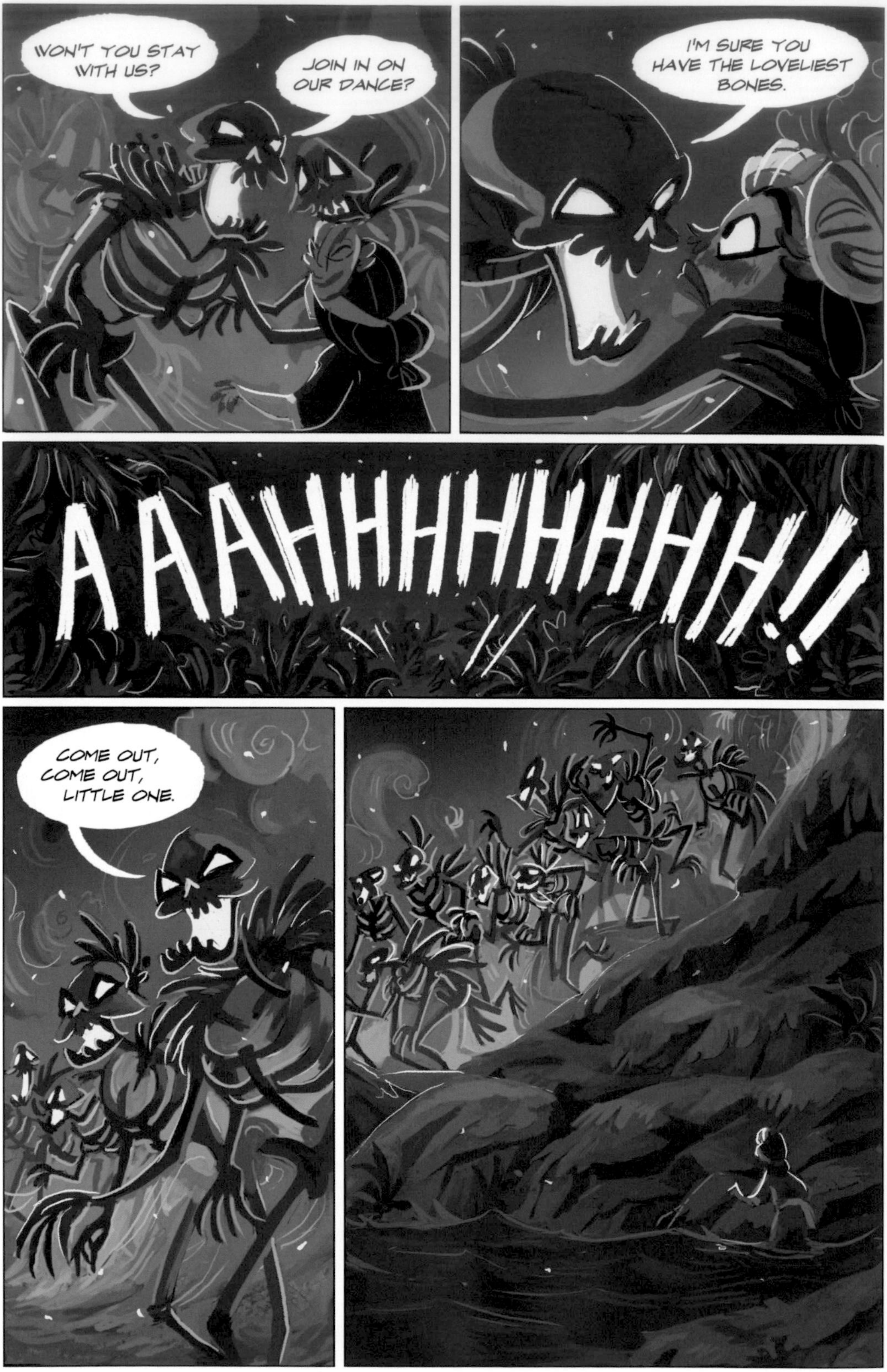
WON'T YOU STAY WITH US?
JOIN IN ON OUR DANCE?
I'M SURE YOU HAVE THE LOVELIEST BONES.
AAAHHHHHHHHHH!!
COME OUT, COME OUT, LITTLE ONE.

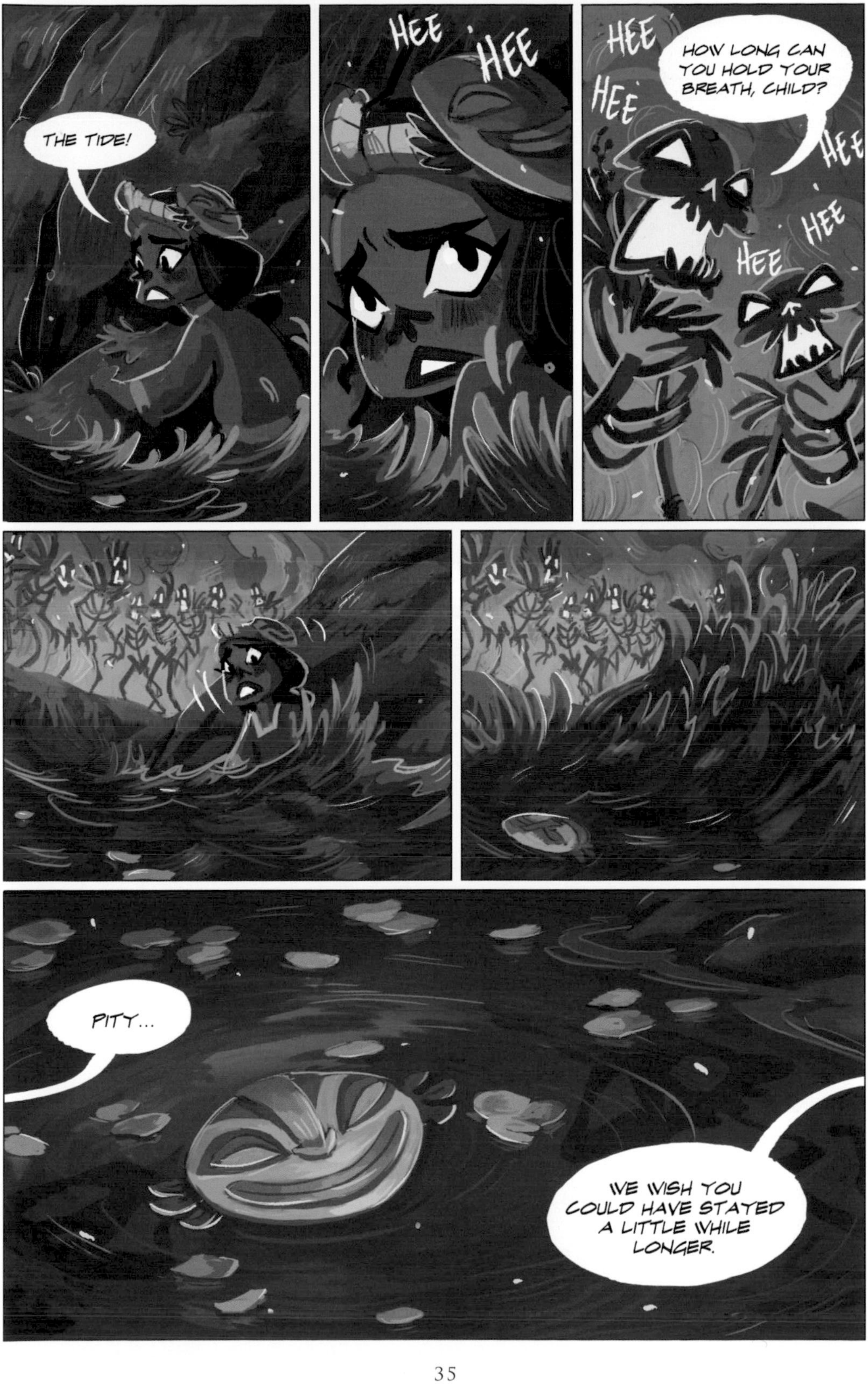
THE TIDE!
HEE
HEE
HEE
HEE
HOW LONG CAN YOU HOLD YOUR BREATH, CHILD?
HEE
HEE
HEE
PITY...
WE WISH YOU COULD HAVE STAYED A LITTLE WHILE LONGER.

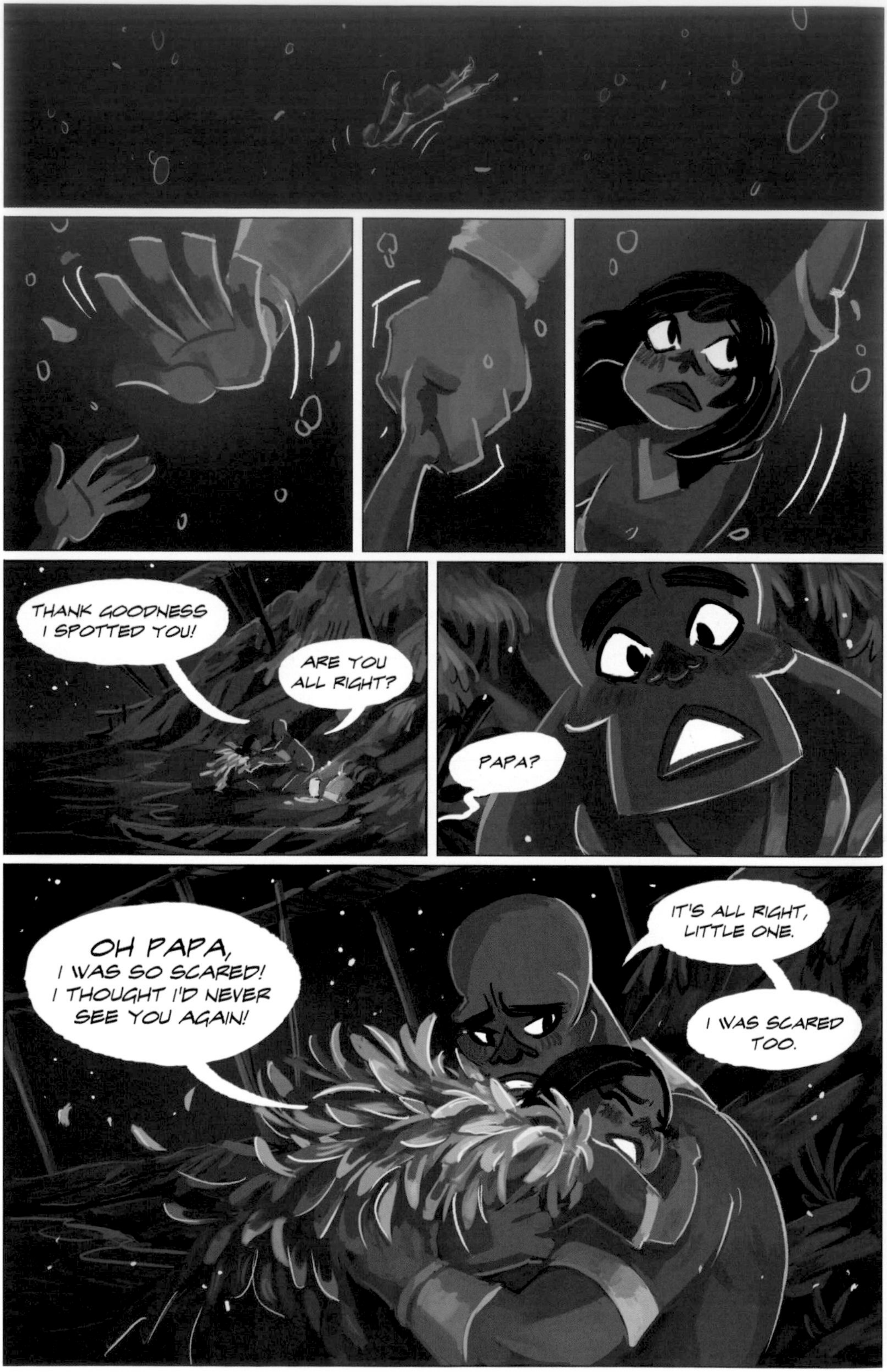
THANK GOODNESS I SPOTTED YOU!
ARE YOU ALL RIGHT?
PAPA?
OH PAPA, I WAS SO SCARED! I THOUGHT I'D NEVER SEE YOU AGAIN!
IT'S ALL RIGHT, LITTLE ONE.
I WAS SCARED TOO.

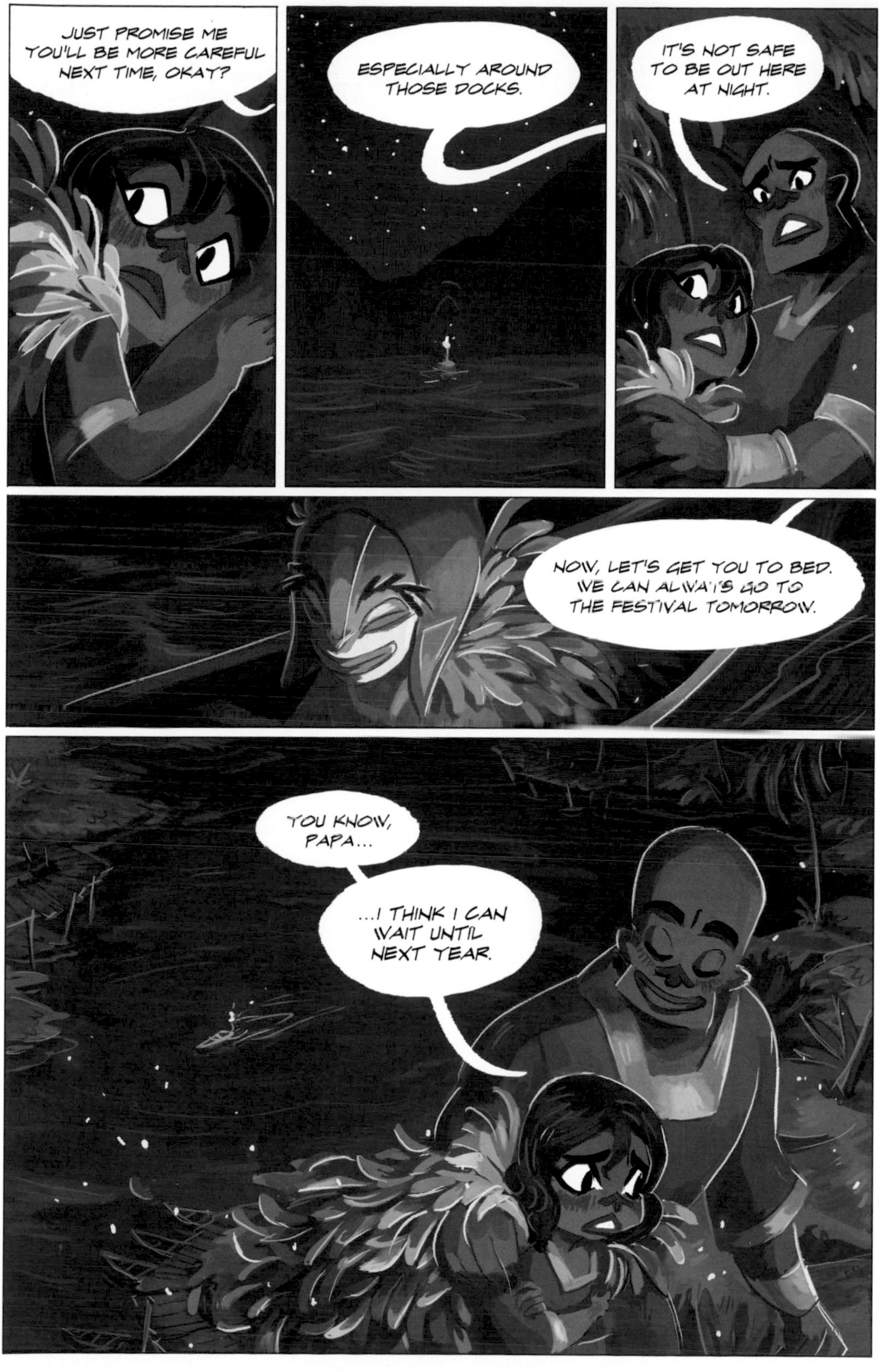
JUST PROMISE ME YOU'LL BE MORE CAREFUL NEXT TIME, OKAY?
ESPECIALLY AROUND THOSE DOCKS.
IT'S NOT SAFE TO BE OUT HERE AT NIGHT.
NOW, LET'S GET YOU TO BED. WE CAN ALWAYS GO TO THE FESTIVAL TOMORROW.
YOU KNOW, PAPA...
...I THINK I CAN WAIT UNTIL NEXT YEAR.

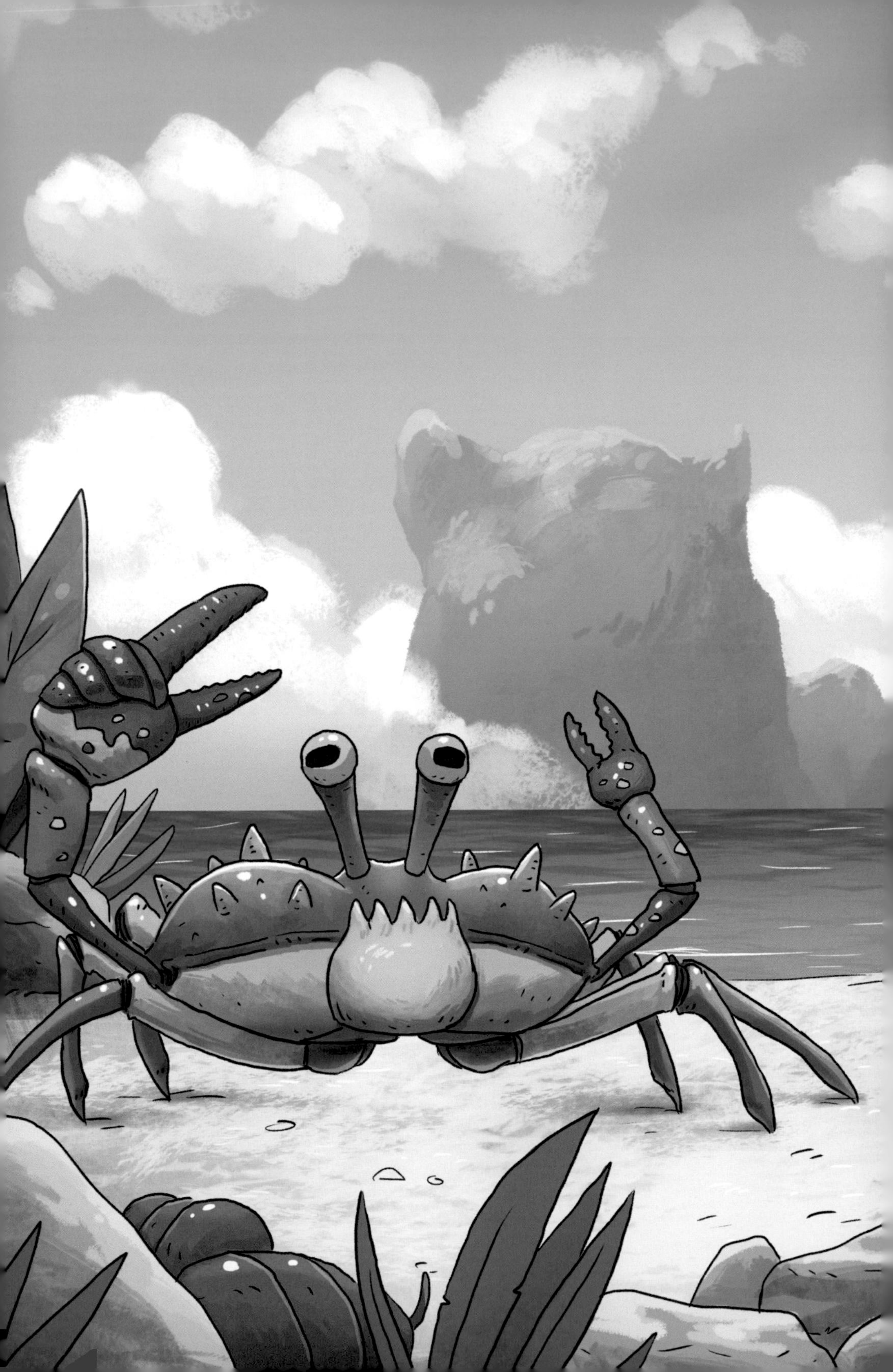

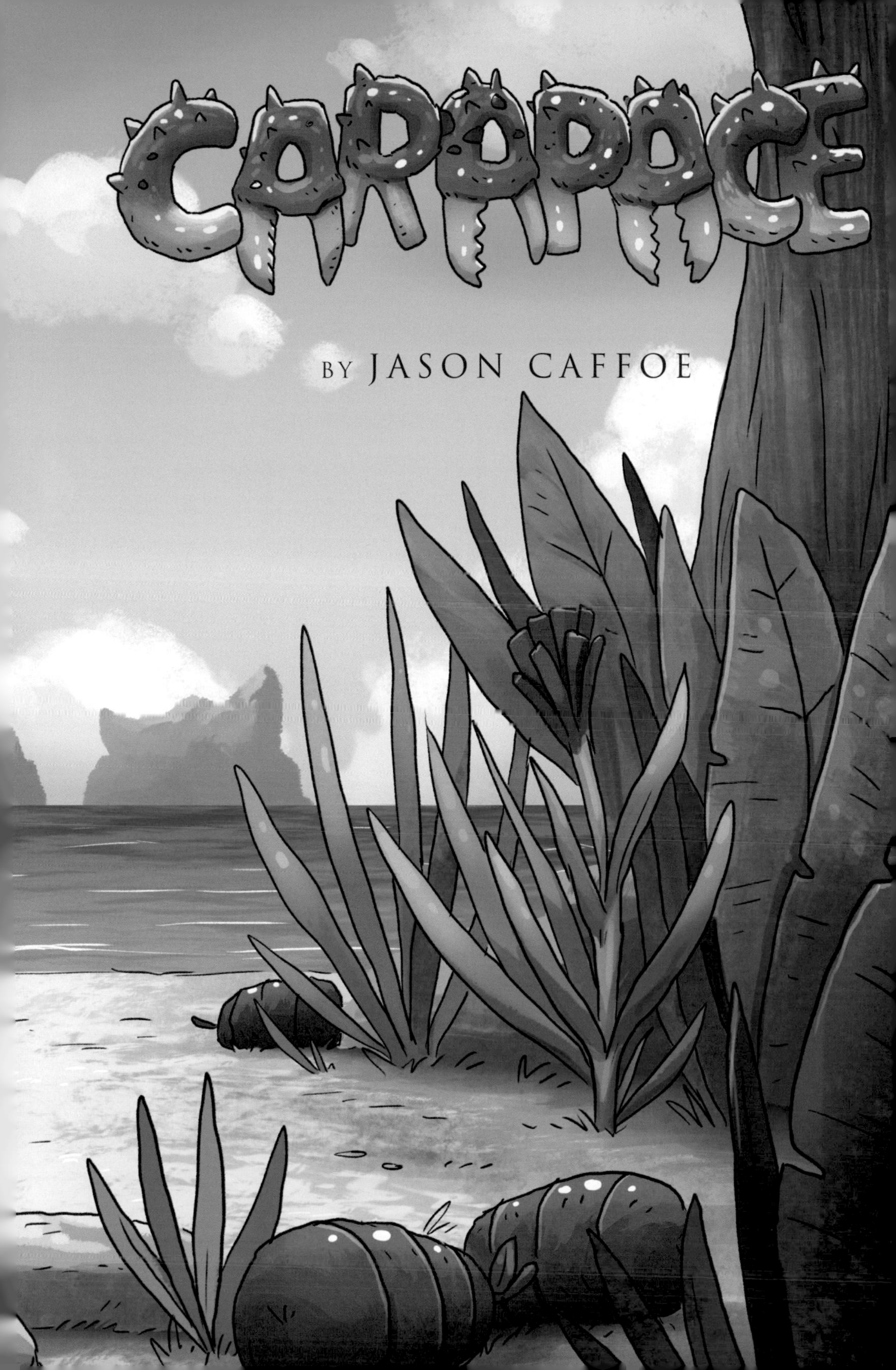
CARAPACE
BY JASON CAFFOE

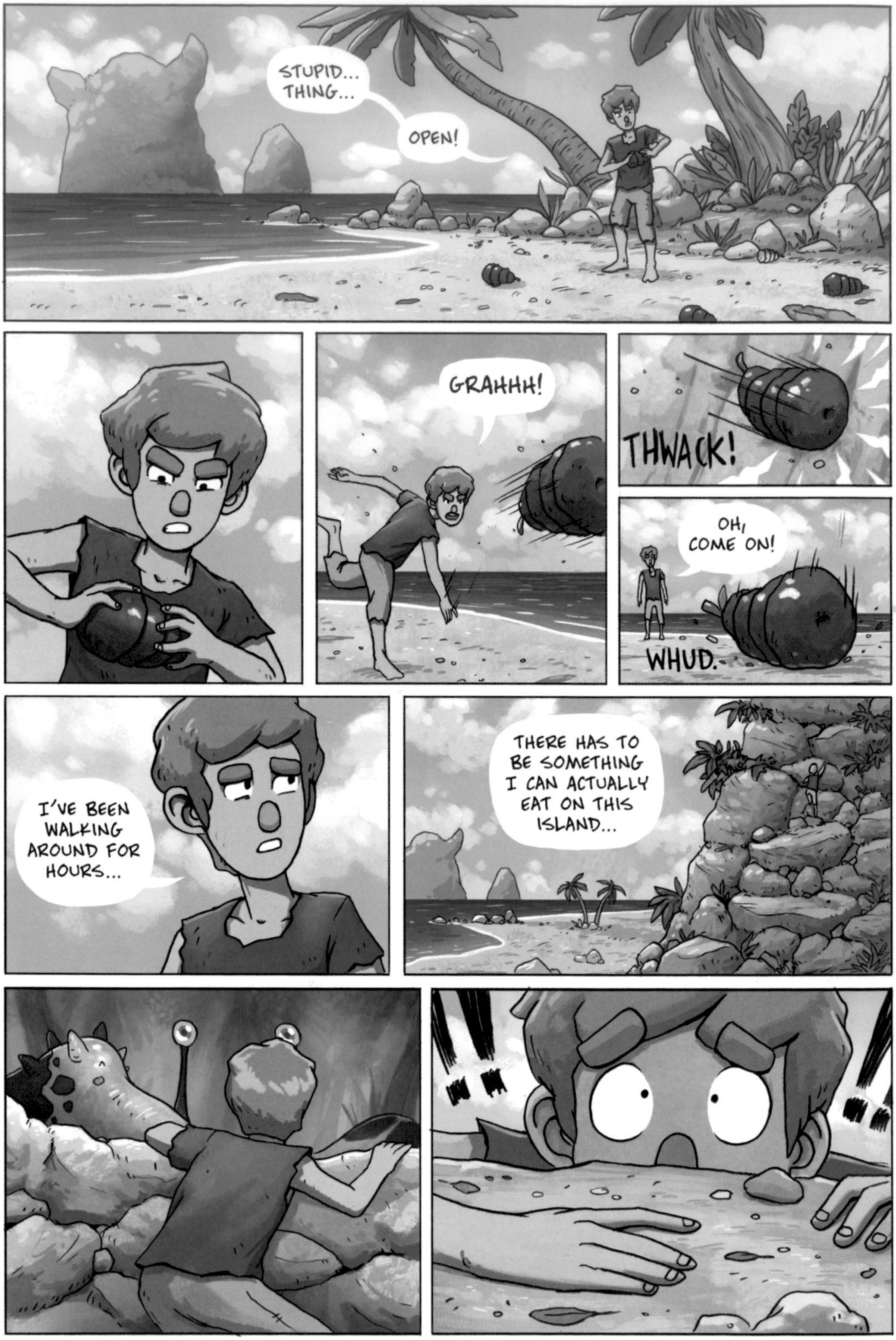
STUPID... THING...
OPEN!
GRAHHH!
THWACK!
OH, COME ON!
WHUD.
I'VE BEEN WALKING AROUND FOR HOURS...
THERE HAS TO BE SOMETHING I CAN ACTUALLY EAT ON THIS ISLAND...

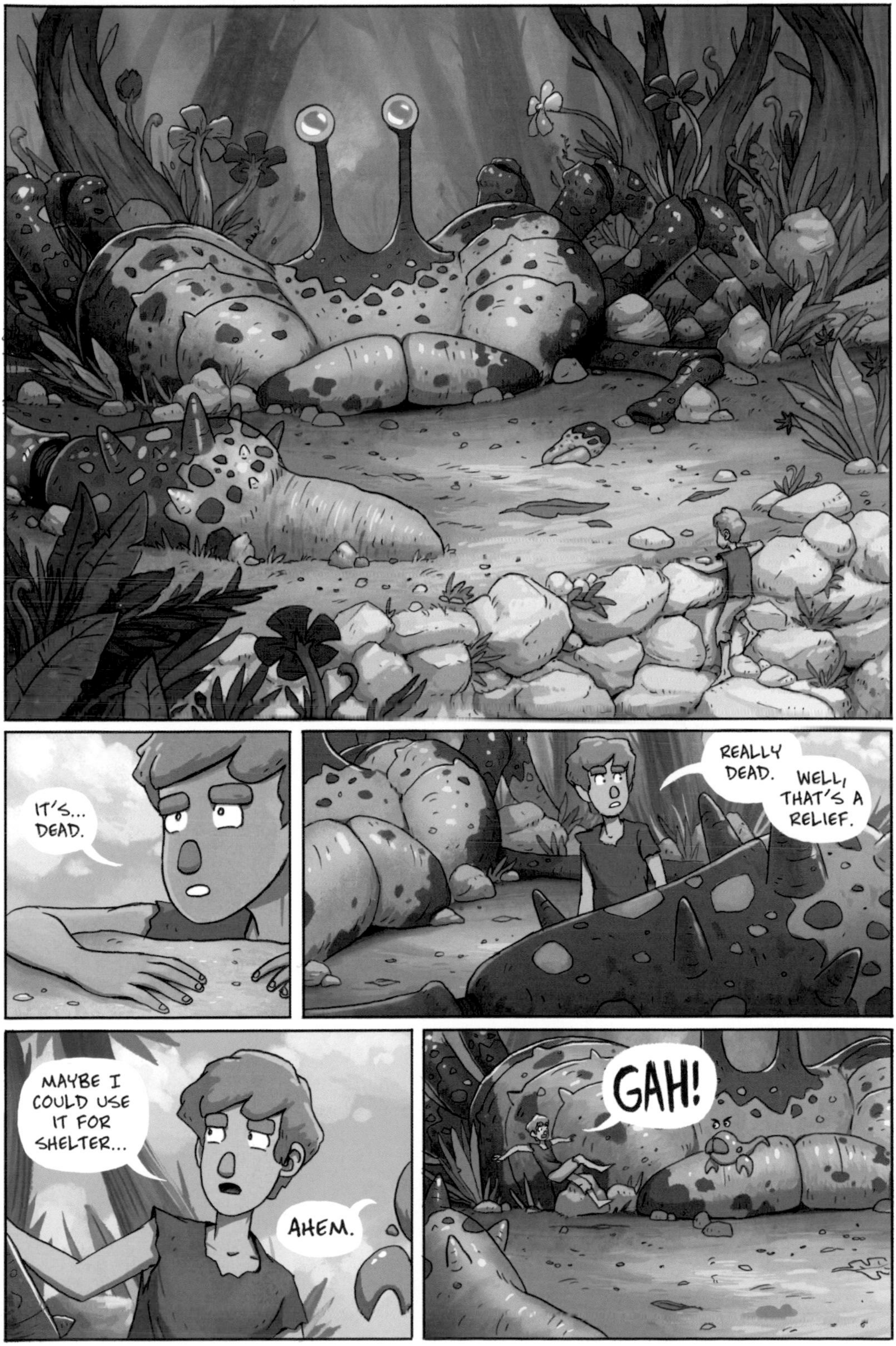
IT'S... DEAD.
REALLY DEAD.
WELL, THAT'S A RELIEF.
MAYBE I COULD USE IT FOR SHELTER...
AHEM.
GAH!

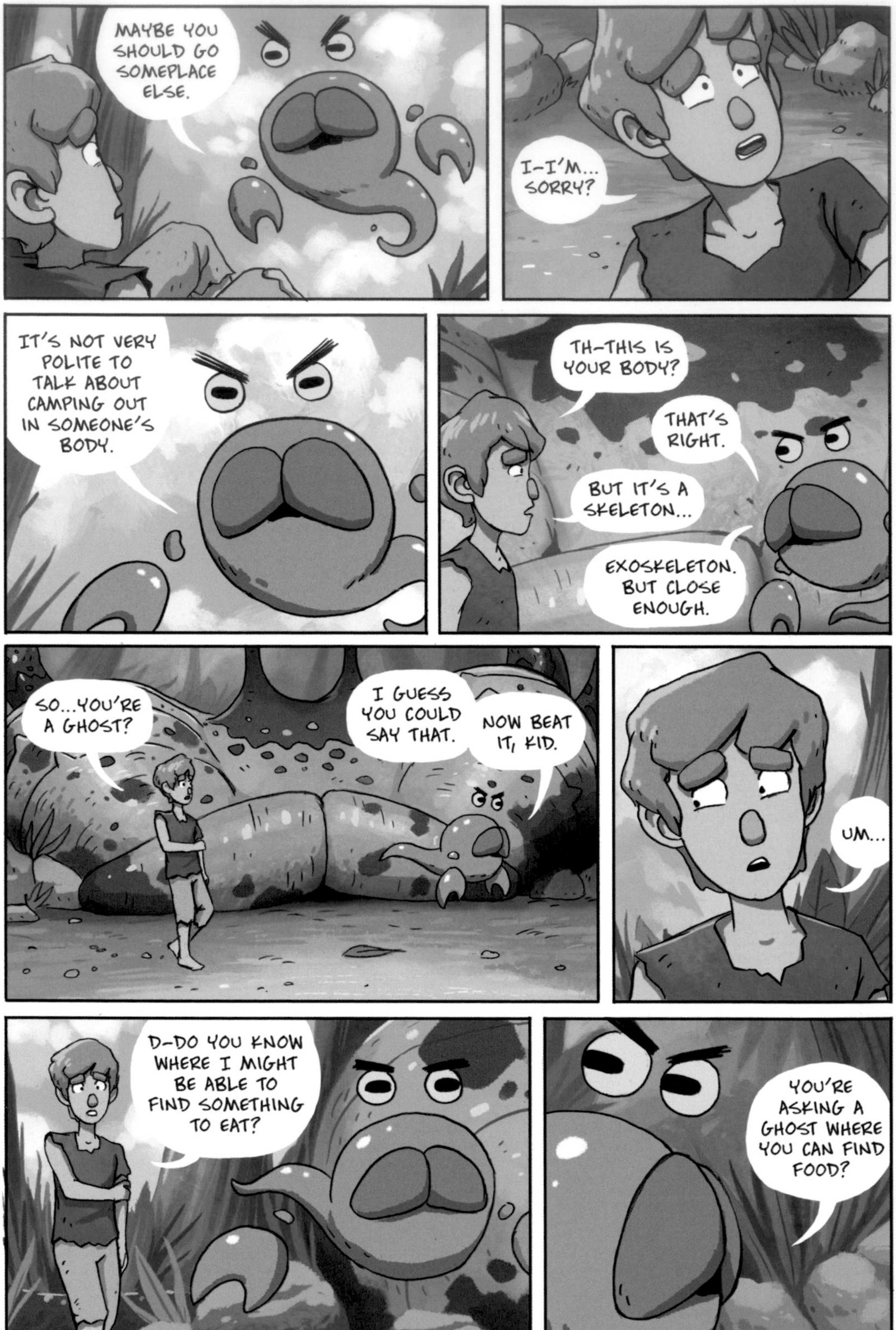
MAYBE YOU SHOULD GO SOMEPLACE ELSE.
I-I'M... SORRY?
IT'S NOT VERY POLITE TO TALK ABOUT CAMPING OUT IN SOMEONE'S BODY.
TH-THIS IS YOUR BODY?
THAT'S RIGHT.
BUT IT'S A SKELETON...
EXOSKELETON. BUT CLOSE ENOUGH.
SO...YOU'RE A GHOST?
I GUESS YOU COULD SAY THAT.
NOW BEAT IT, KID.
UM...
D-DO YOU KNOW WHERE I MIGHT BE ABLE TO FIND SOMETHING TO EAT?
YOU'RE ASKING A GHOST WHERE YOU CAN FIND FOOD?

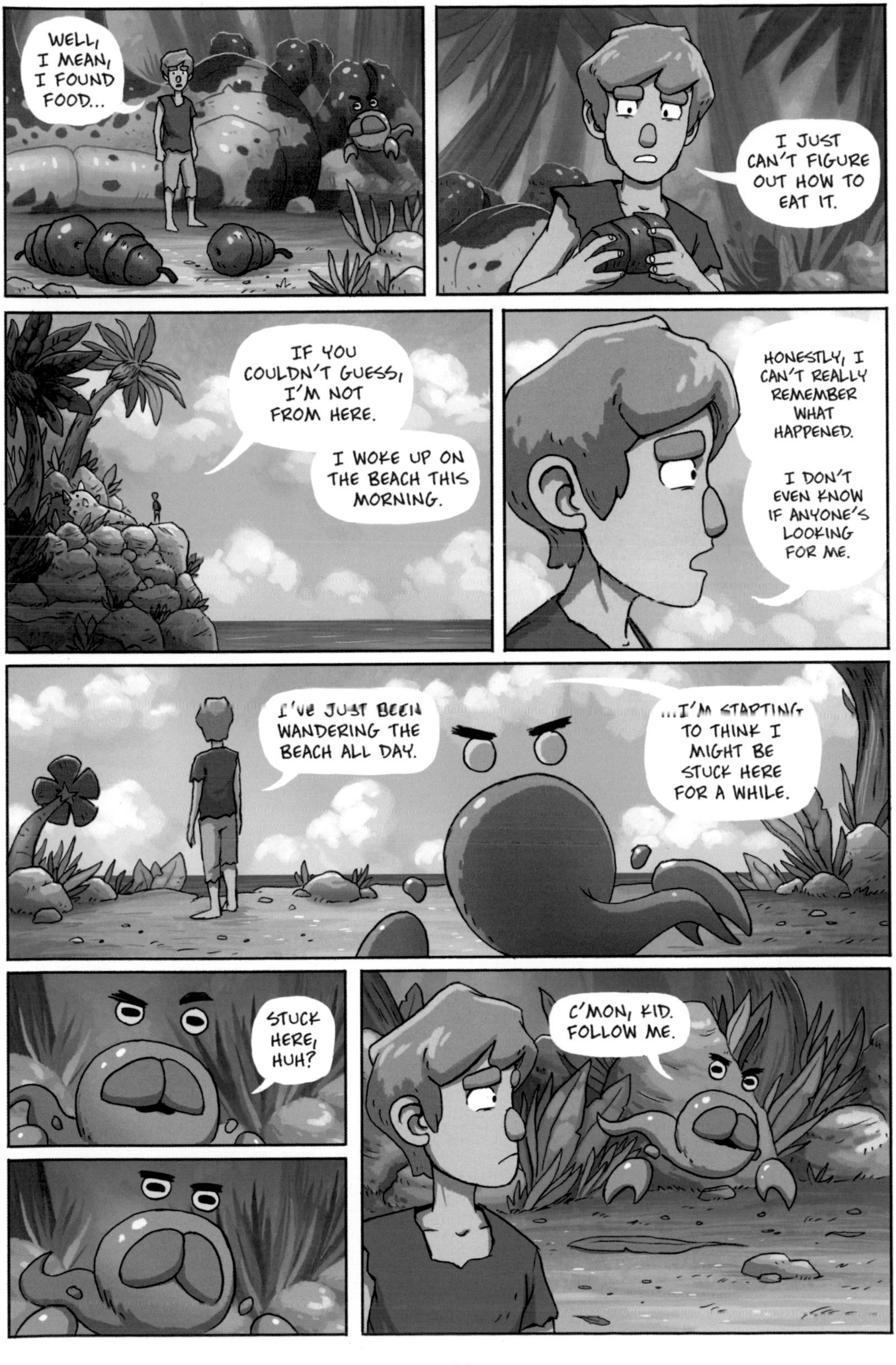
WELL, I MEAN, I FOUND FOOD...
I JUST CAN'T FIGURE OUT HOW TO EAT IT.
IF YOU COULDN'T GUESS, I'M NOT FROM HERE.
I WOKE UP ON THE BEACH THIS MORNING.
HONESTLY, I CAN'T REALLY REMEMBER WHAT HAPPENED.
I DON'T EVEN KNOW IF ANYONE'S LOOKING FOR ME.
I'VE JUST BEEN WANDERING THE BEACH ALL DAY.
...I'M STARTING TO THINK I MIGHT BE STUCK HERE FOR A WHILE.
STUCK HERE, HUH?
C'MON, KID. FOLLOW ME.

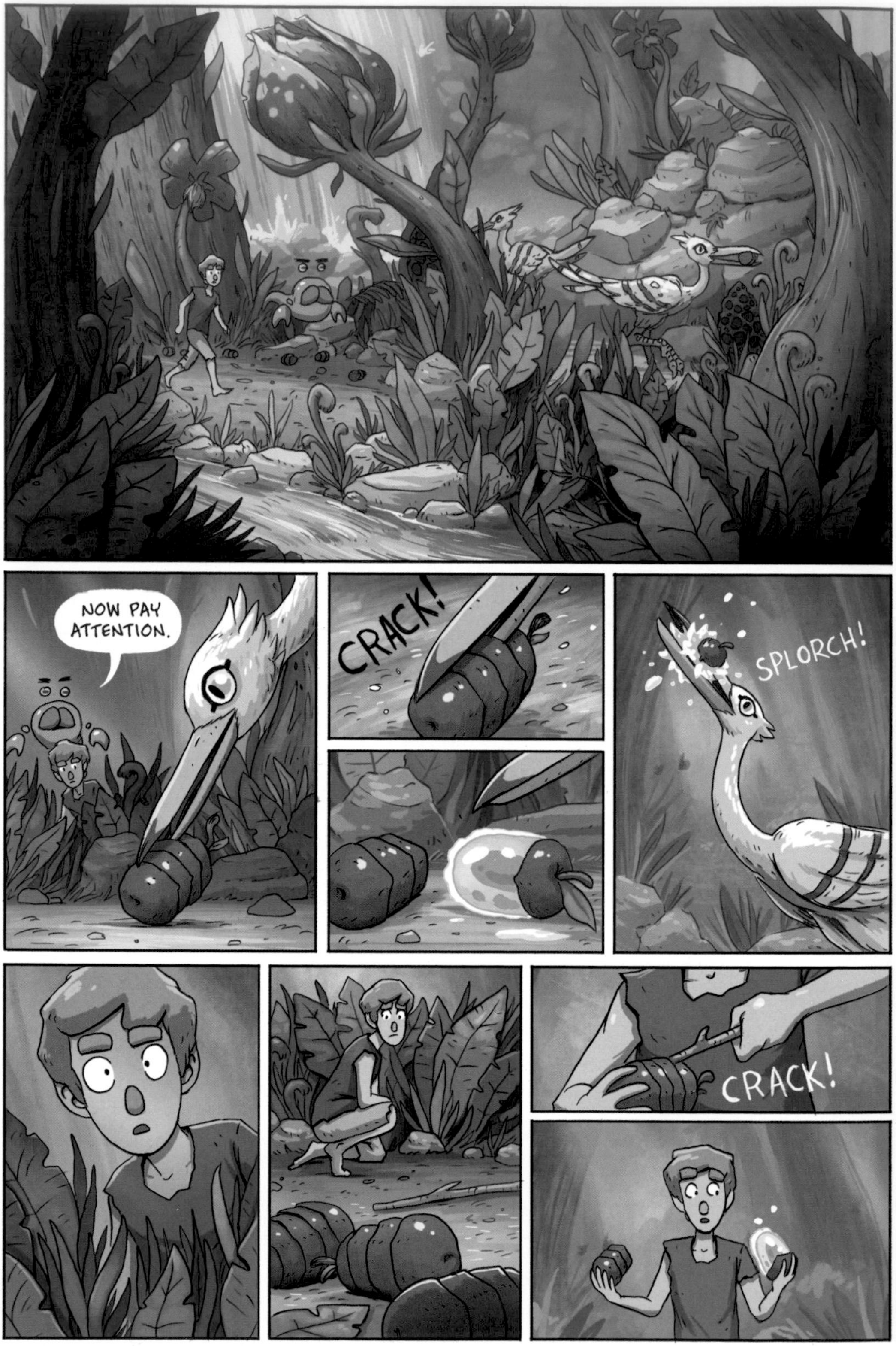
NOW PAY ATTENTION.
CRACK!
SPLORCH!
CRACK!

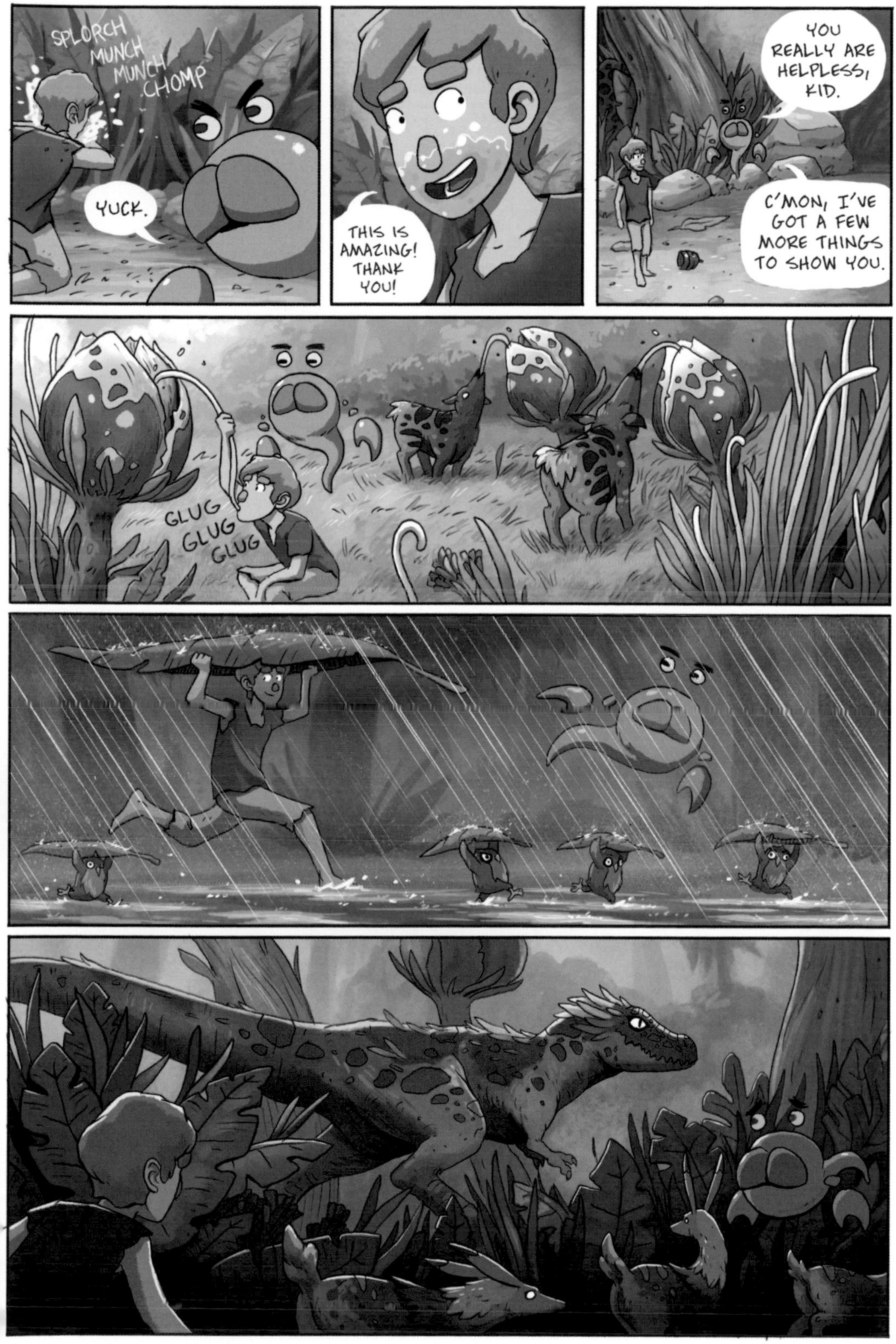
SPLORCH
MUNCH
MUNCH
CHOMP
YUCK.
THIS IS AMAZING! THANK YOU!
YOU REALLY ARE HELPLESS, KID.
C'MON, I'VE GOT A FEW MORE THINGS TO SHOW YOU.
GLUG
GLUG
GLUG

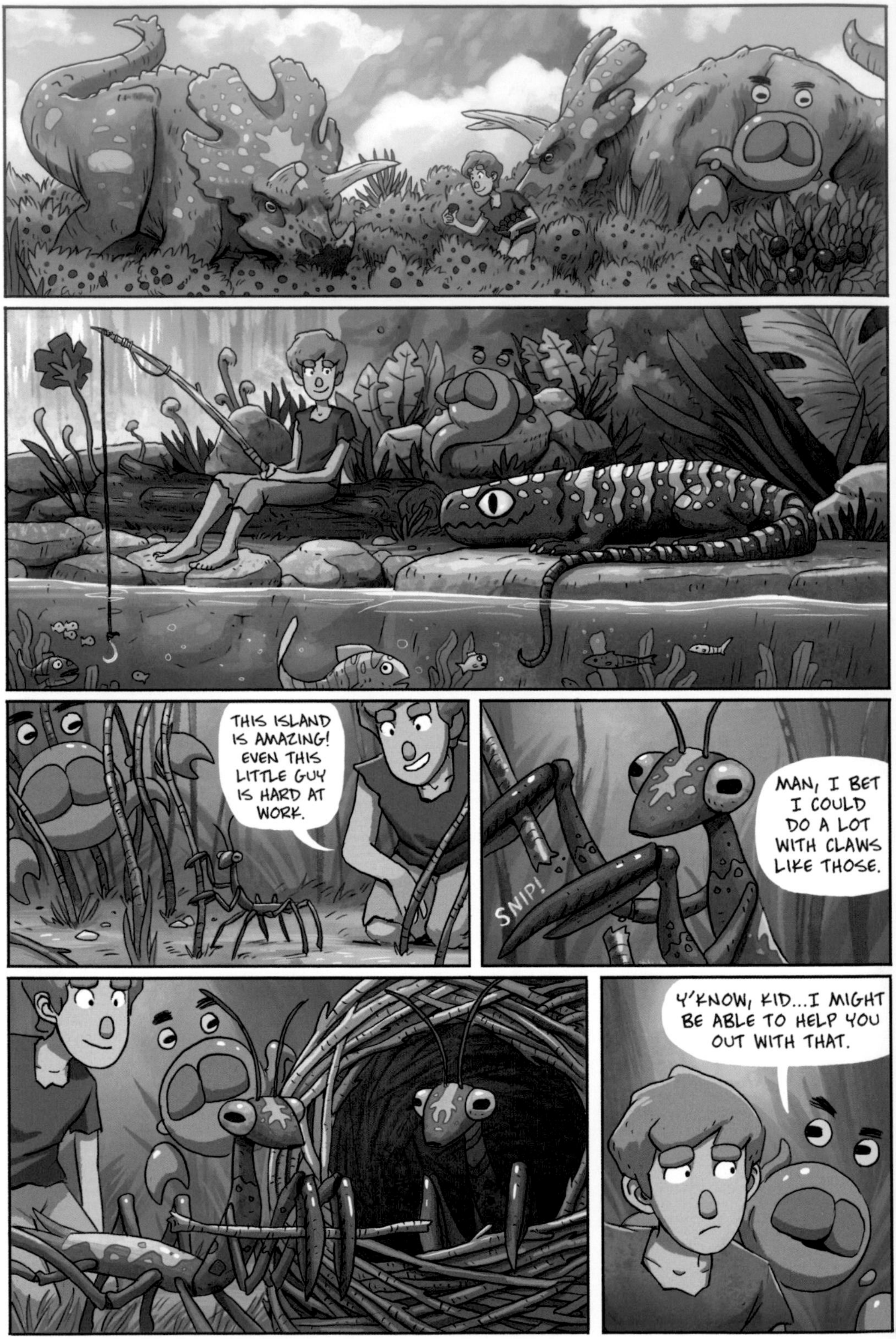
THIS ISLAND IS AMAZING! EVEN THIS LITTLE GUY IS HARD AT WORK.
SNIP!
MAN, I BET I COULD DO A LOT WITH CLAWS LIKE THOSE.
Y'KNOW, KID...I MIGHT BE ABLE TO HELP YOU OUT WITH THAT.

48

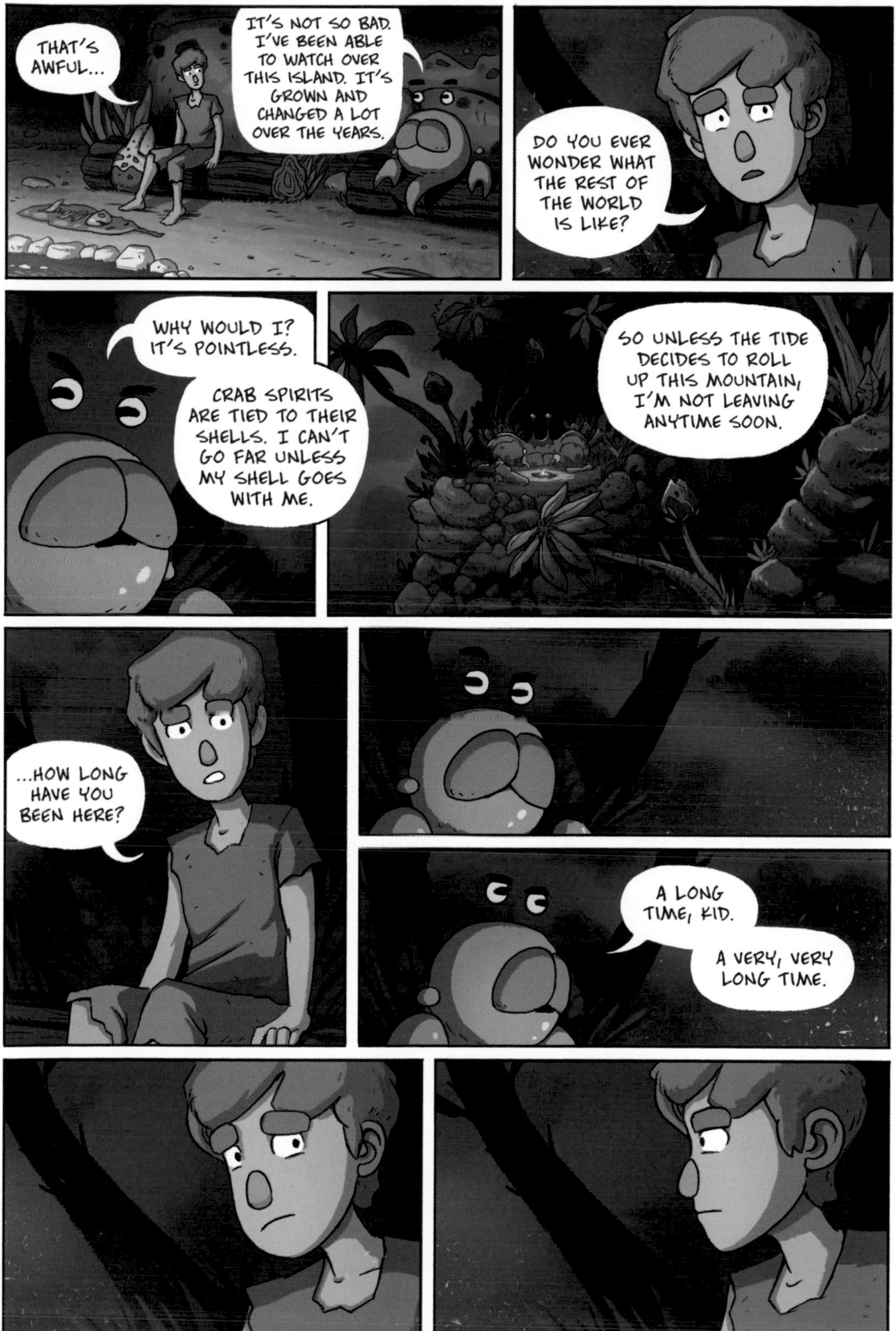
THAT'S AWFUL...
IT'S NOT SO BAD. I'VE BEEN ABLE TO WATCH OVER THIS ISLAND. IT'S GROWN AND CHANGED A LOT OVER THE YEARS.
DO YOU EVER WONDER WHAT THE REST OF THE WORLD IS LIKE?
WHY WOULD I? IT'S POINTLESS.
CRAB SPIRITS ARE TIED TO THEIR SHELLS. I CAN'T GO FAR UNLESS MY SHELL GOES WITH ME.
SO UNLESS THE TIDE DECIDES TO ROLL UP THIS MOUNTAIN, I'M NOT LEAVING ANYTIME SOON.
...HOW LONG HAVE YOU BEEN HERE?
A LONG TIME, KID.
A VERY, VERY LONG TIME.

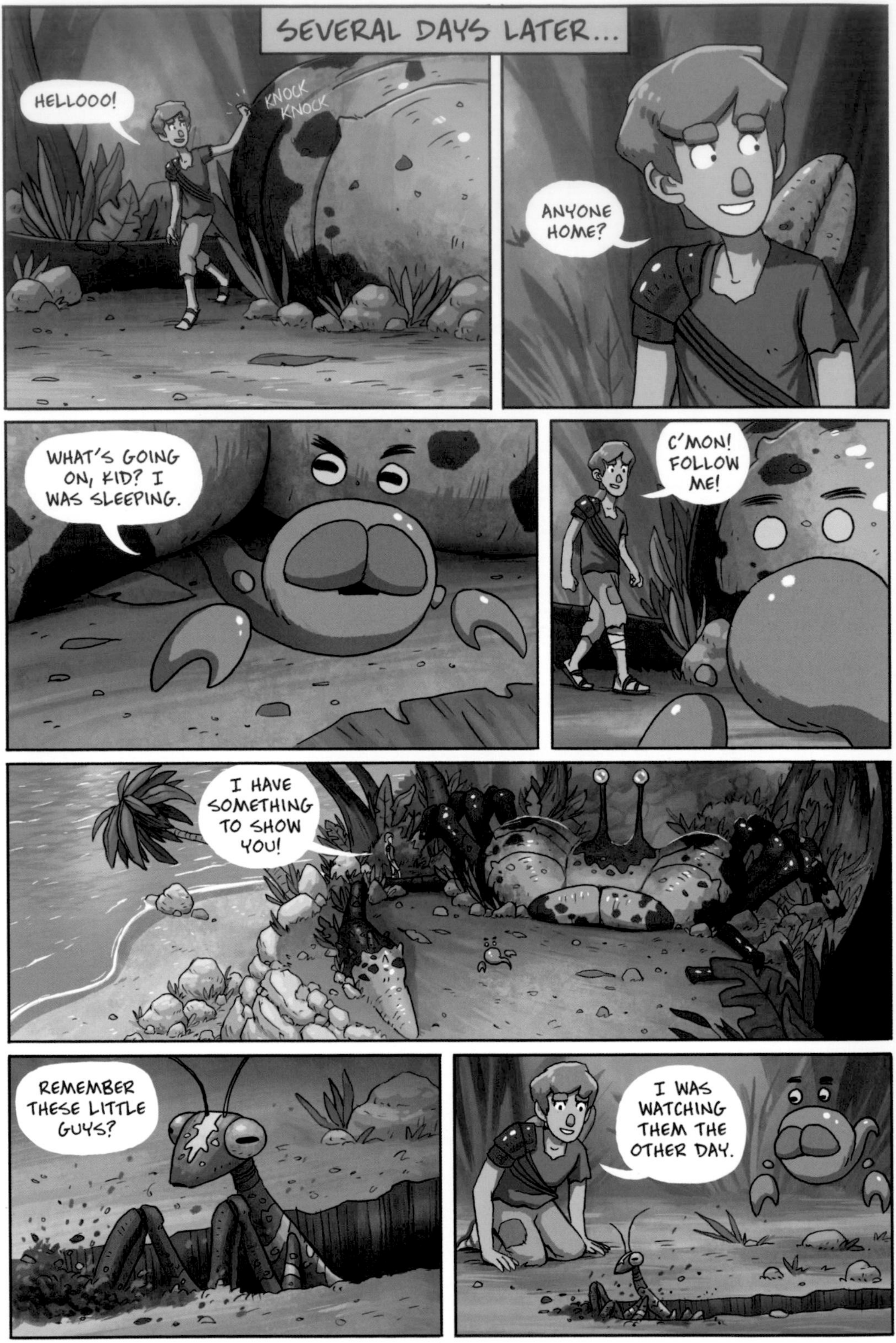
SEVERAL DAYS LATER...
HELLOOO!
KNOCK KNOCK
ANYONE HOME?
WHAT'S GOING ON, KID? I WAS SLEEPING.
C'MON! FOLLOW ME!
I HAVE SOMETHING TO SHOW YOU!
REMEMBER THESE LITTLE GUYS?
I WAS WATCHING THEM THE OTHER DAY.

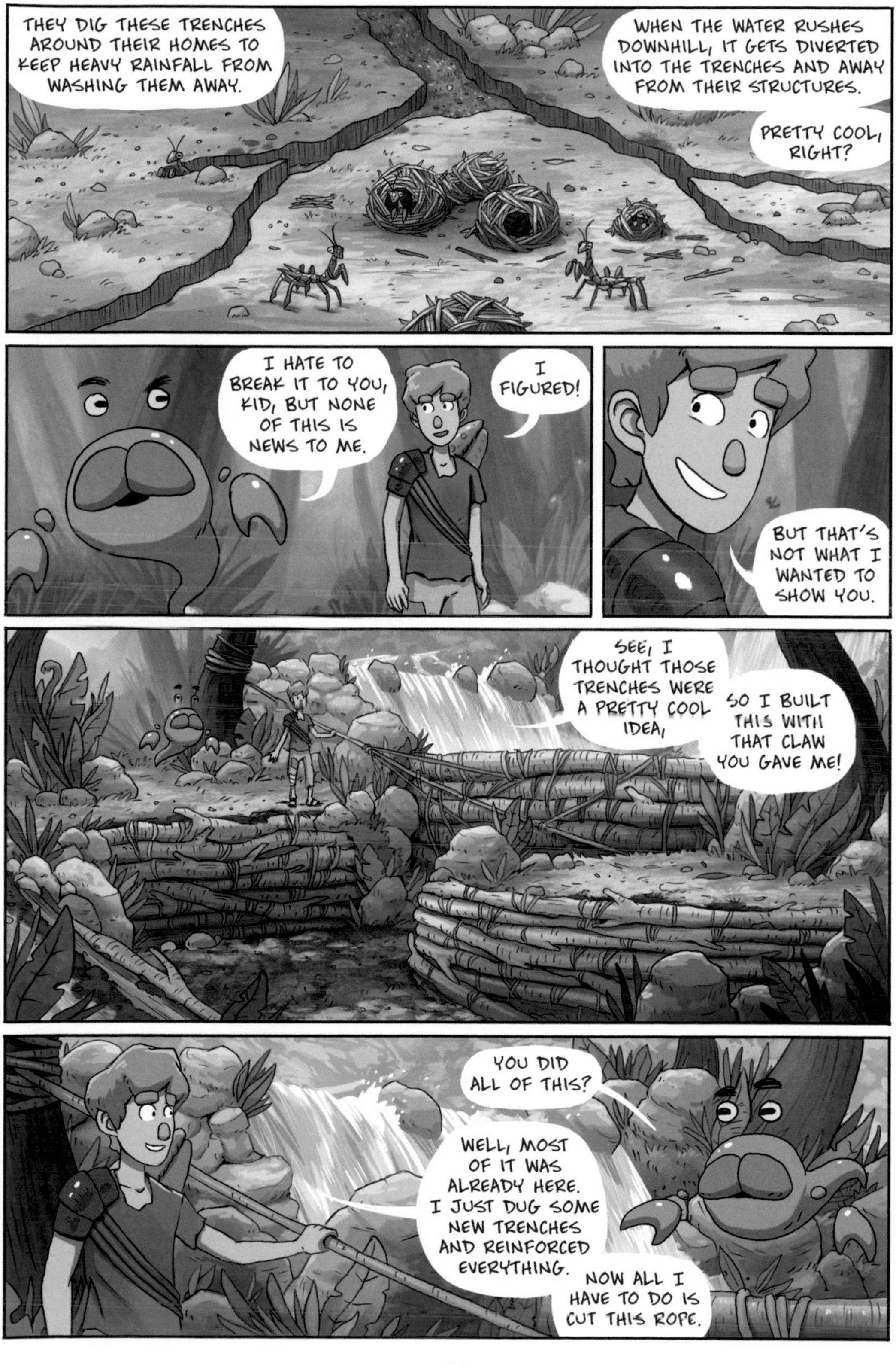
THEY DIG THESE TRENCHES AROUND THEIR HOMES TO KEEP HEAVY RAINFALL FROM WASHING THEM AWAY.
WHEN THE WATER RUSHES DOWNHILL, IT GETS DIVERTED INTO THE TRENCHES AND AWAY FROM THEIR STRUCTURES.
PRETTY COOL, RIGHT?
I HATE TO BREAK IT TO YOU, KID, BUT NONE OF THIS IS NEWS TO ME.
I FIGURED!
BUT THAT'S NOT WHAT I WANTED TO SHOW YOU.
SEE, I THOUGHT THOSE TRENCHES WERE A PRETTY COOL IDEA,
SO I BUILT THIS WITH THAT CLAW YOU GAVE ME!
YOU DID ALL OF THIS?
WELL, MOST OF IT WAS ALREADY HERE. I JUST DUG SOME NEW TRENCHES AND REINFORCED EVERYTHING.
NOW ALL I HAVE TO DO IS CUT THIS ROPE.

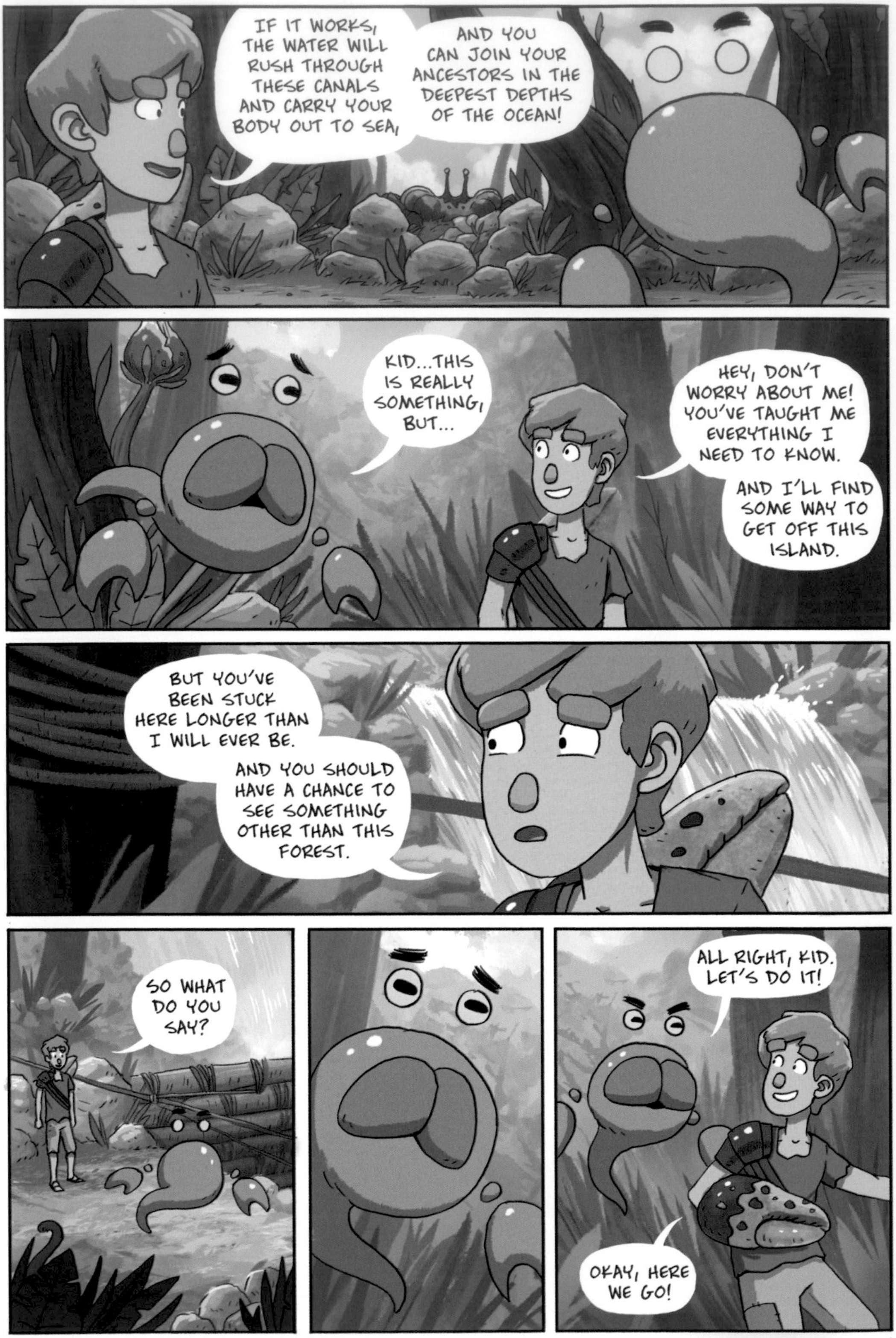
IF IT WORKS, THE WATER WILL RUSH THROUGH THESE CANALS AND CARRY YOUR BODY OUT TO SEA,
AND YOU CAN JOIN YOUR ANCESTORS IN THE DEEPEST DEPTHS OF THE OCEAN!
KID...THIS IS REALLY SOMETHING, BUT...
HEY, DON'T WORRY ABOUT ME! YOU'VE TAUGHT ME EVERYTHING I NEED TO KNOW.
AND I'LL FIND SOME WAY TO GET OFF THIS ISLAND.
BUT YOU'VE BEEN STUCK HERE LONGER THAN I WILL EVER BE.
AND YOU SHOULD HAVE A CHANCE TO SEE SOMETHING OTHER THAN THIS FOREST.
SO WHAT DO YOU SAY?
ALL RIGHT, KID. LET'S DO IT!
OKAY, HERE WE GO!

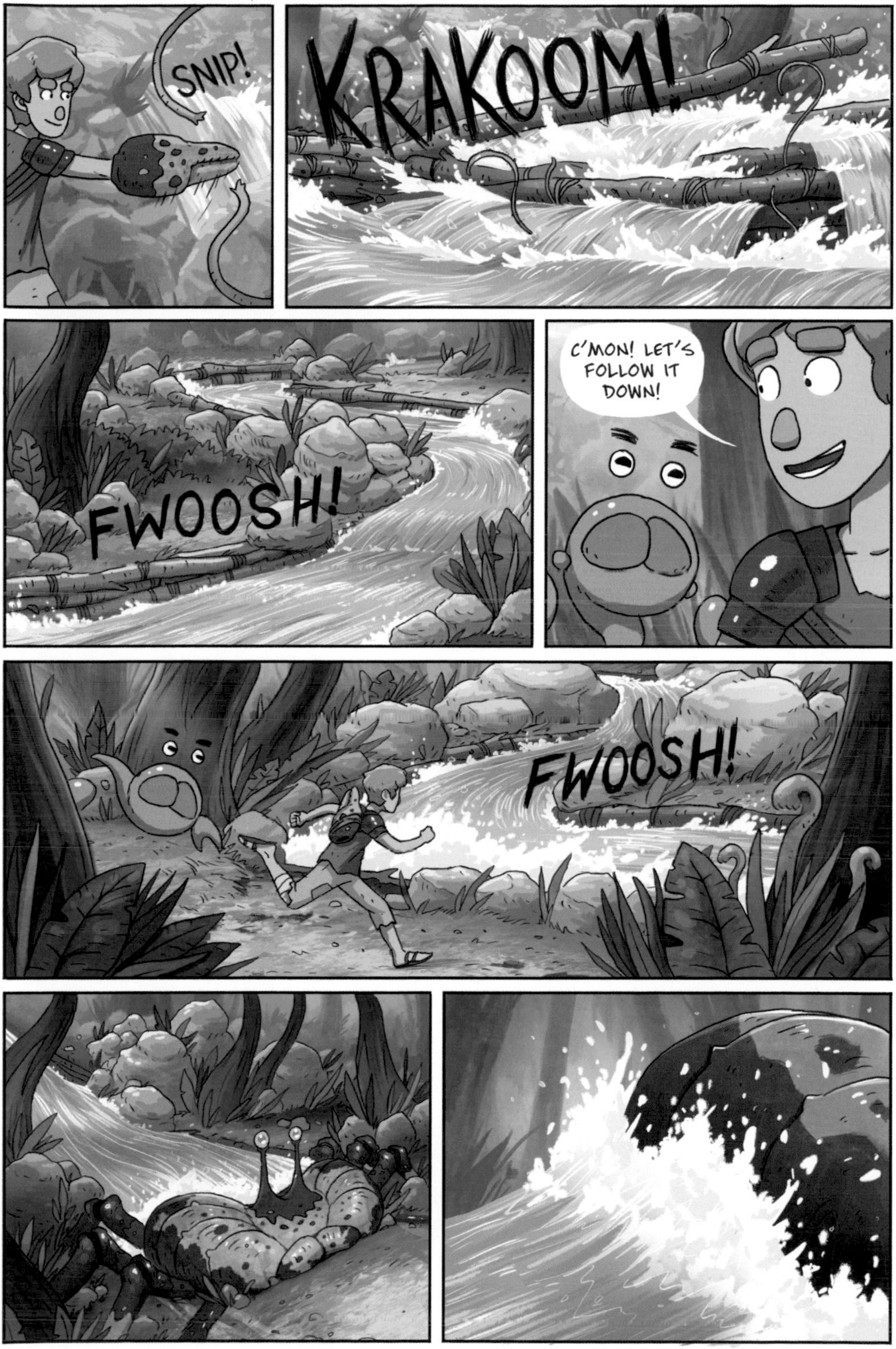
SNIP!
KRAKOOM!
FWOOSH!
C'MON! LET'S FOLLOW IT DOWN!
FWOOSH!

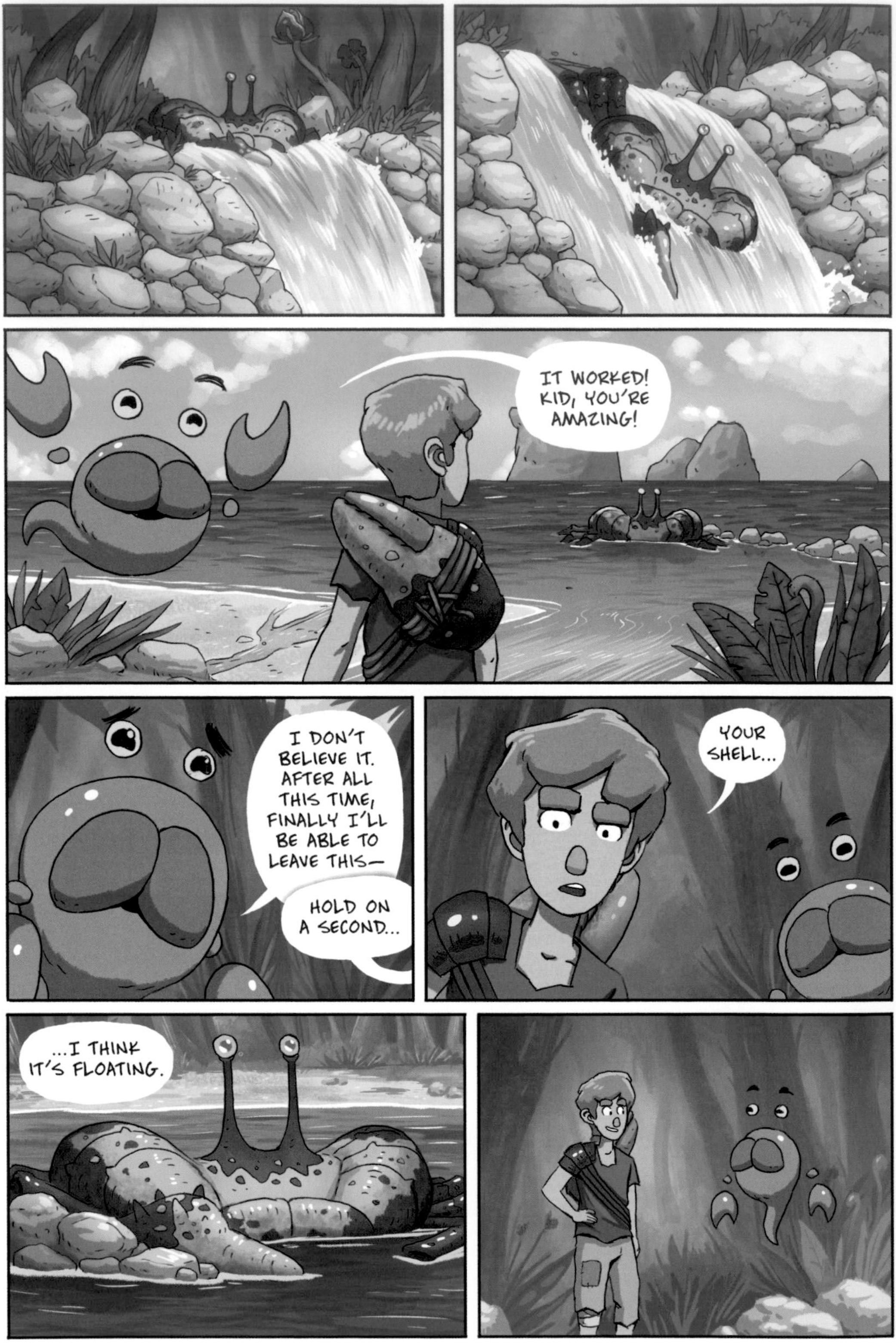
IT WORKED! KID, YOU'RE AMAZING!
I DON'T BELIEVE IT. AFTER ALL THIS TIME, FINALLY I'LL BE ABLE TO LEAVE THIS—
HOLD ON A SECOND...
YOUR SHELL...
...I THINK IT'S FLOATING.

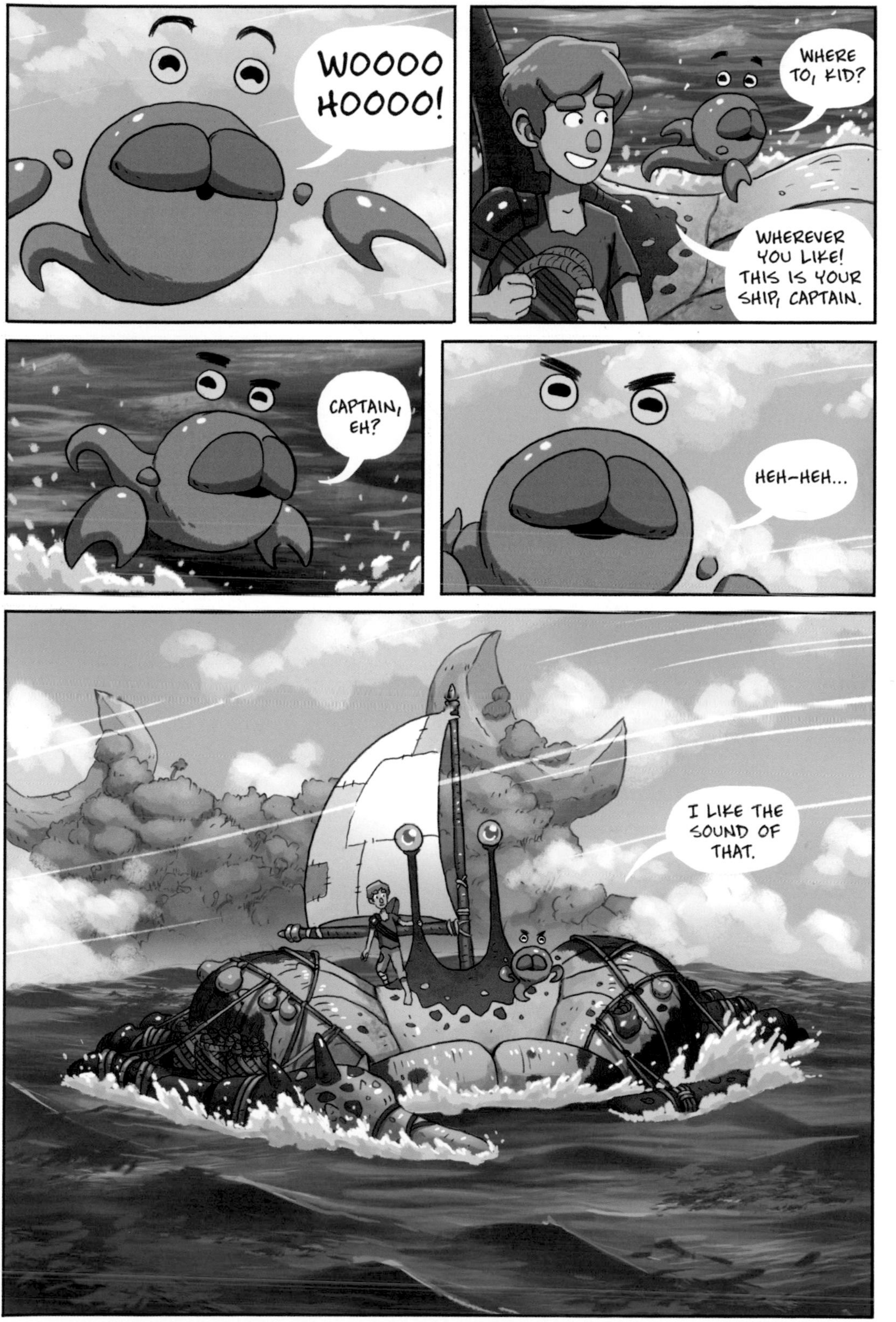
WOOOO HOOOO!
WHERE TO, KID?
WHEREVER YOU LIKE! THIS IS YOUR SHIP, CAPTAIN.
CAPTAIN, EH?
HEH-HEH...
I LIKE THE SOUND OF THAT.

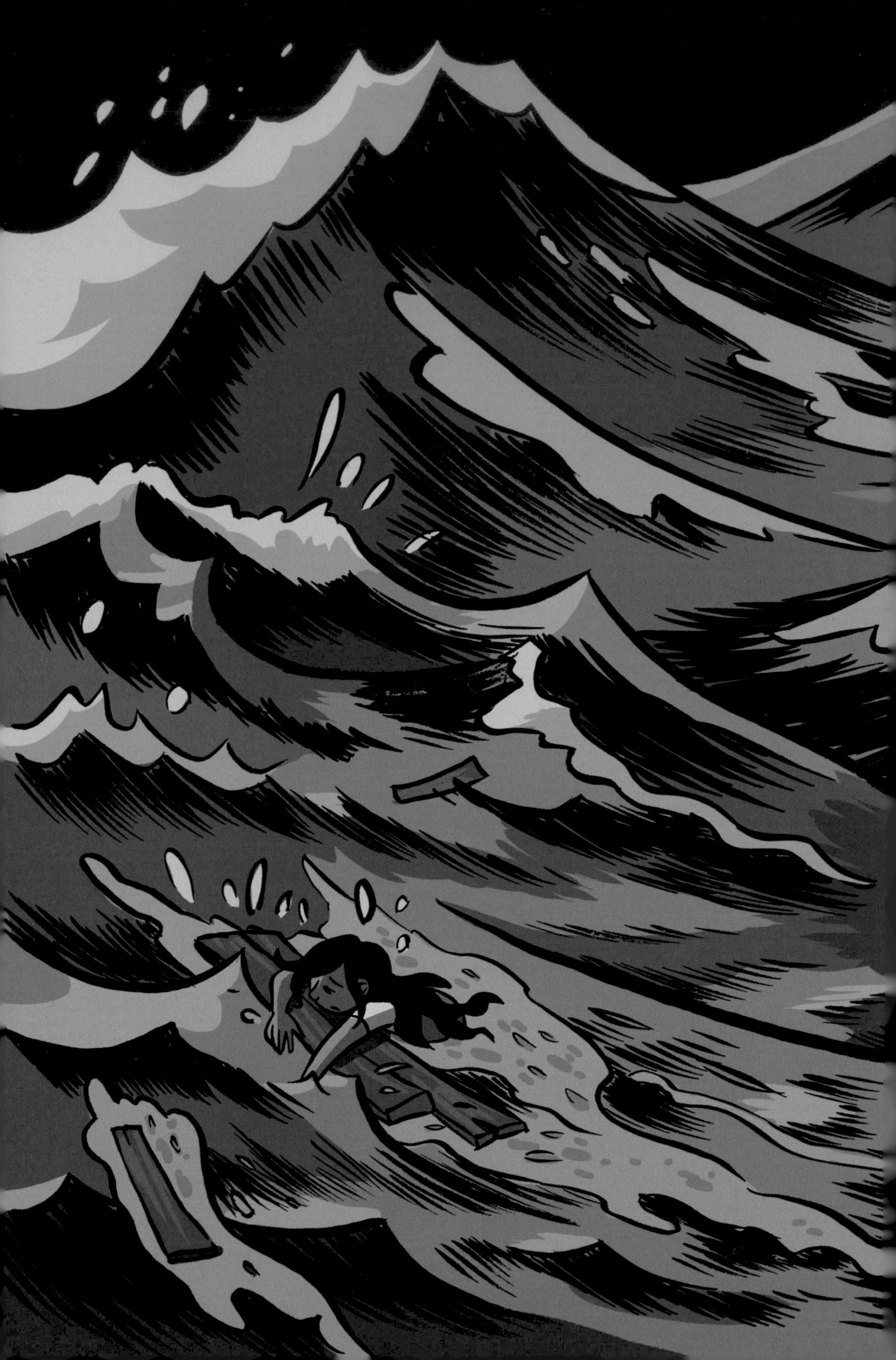

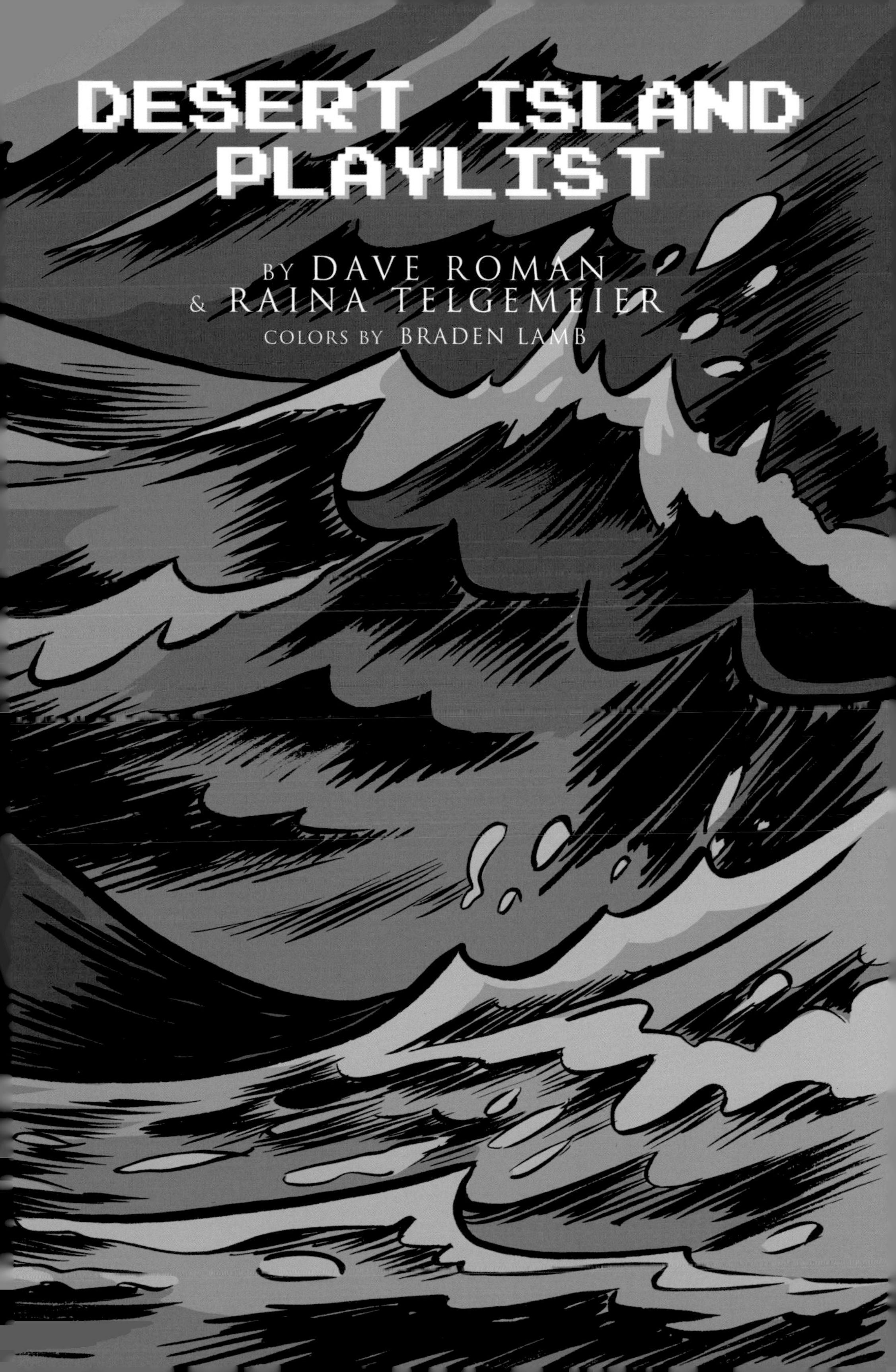
DESERT ISLAND PLAYLIST
BY DAVE ROMAN
& RAINA TELGEMEIER
COLORS BY BRADEN LAMB

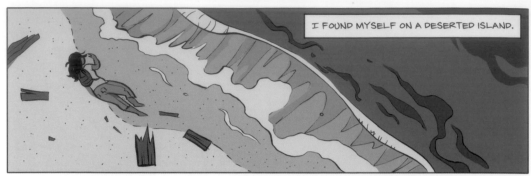

I FOUND MYSELF ON A DESERTED ISLAND.

WITH ONLY A BACKPACK...

Brush
Brush

A FEW KEEPSAKES...

ZZZZZZIP

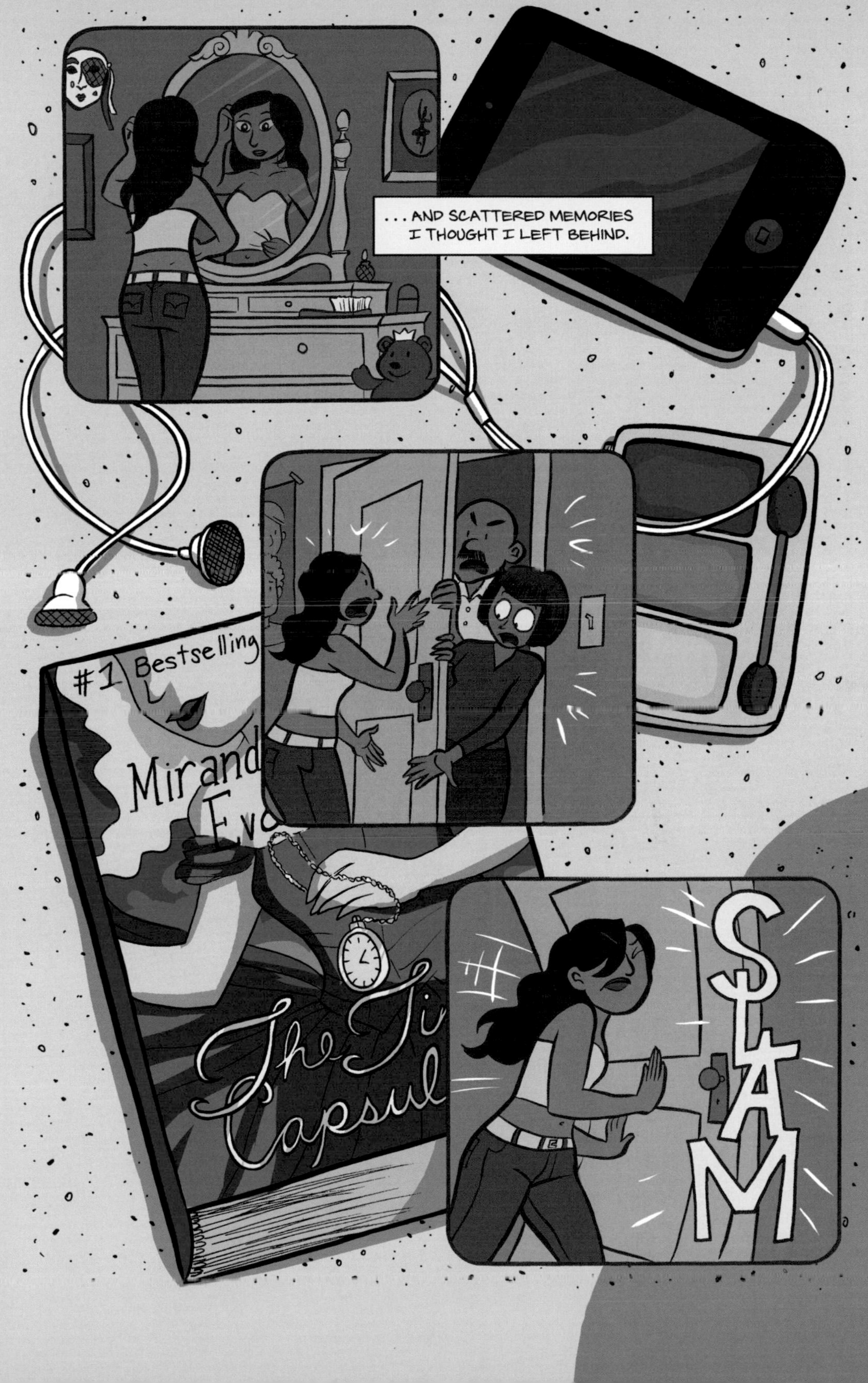
. . . AND SCATTERED MEMORIES I THOUGHT I LEFT BEHIND.
#1 Bestselling
Mirand
Eva
The Ti
Capsul
SLAM

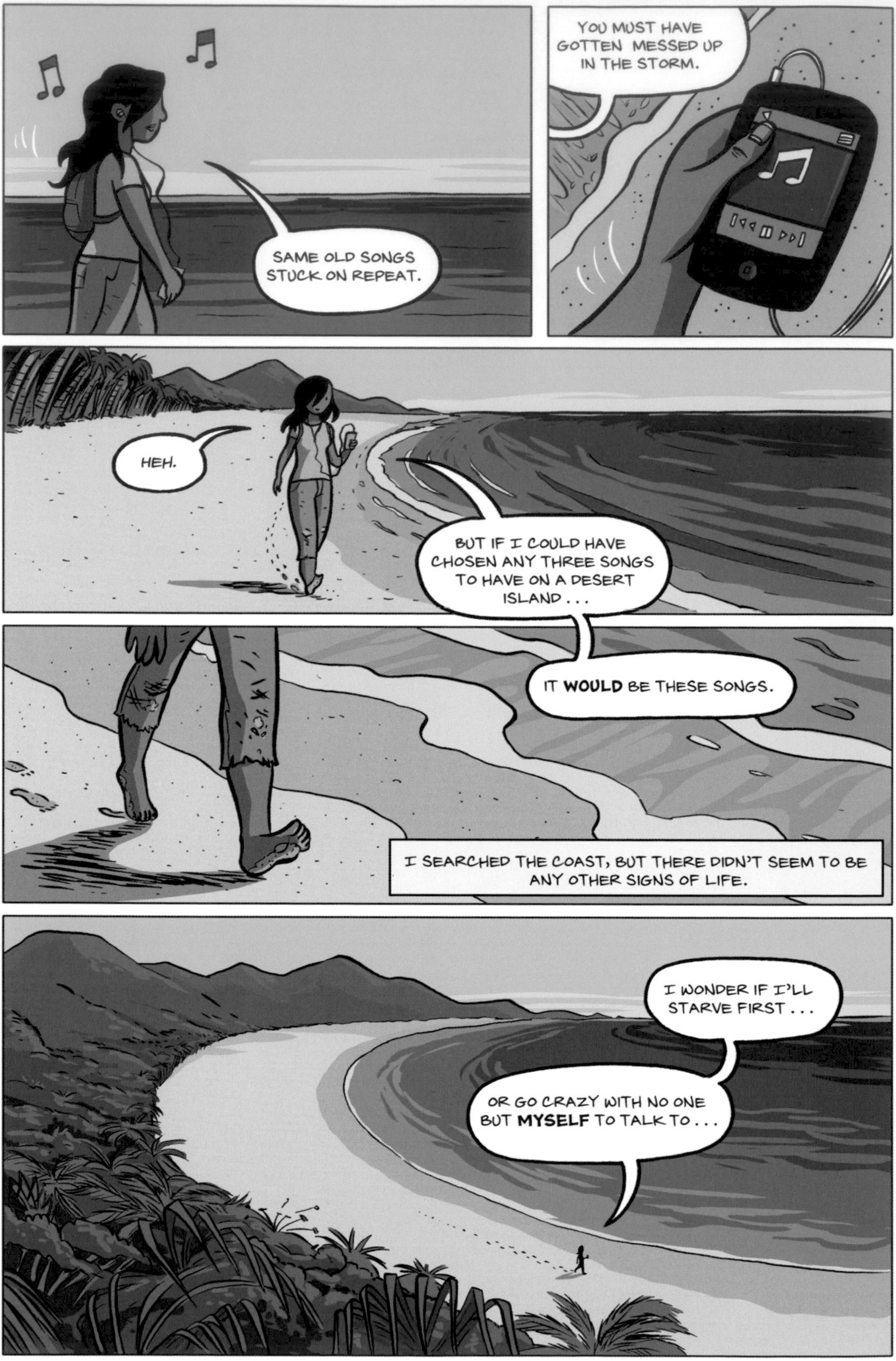
SAME OLD SONGS STUCK ON REPEAT.
YOU MUST HAVE GOTTEN MESSED UP IN THE STORM.
HEH.
BUT IF I COULD HAVE CHOSEN ANY THREE SONGS TO HAVE ON A DESERT ISLAND . . .
IT **WOULD** BE THESE SONGS.
I SEARCHED THE COAST, BUT THERE DIDN'T SEEM TO BE ANY OTHER SIGNS OF LIFE.
I WONDER IF I'LL STARVE FIRST . . .
OR GO CRAZY WITH NO ONE BUT **MYSELF** TO TALK TO . . .

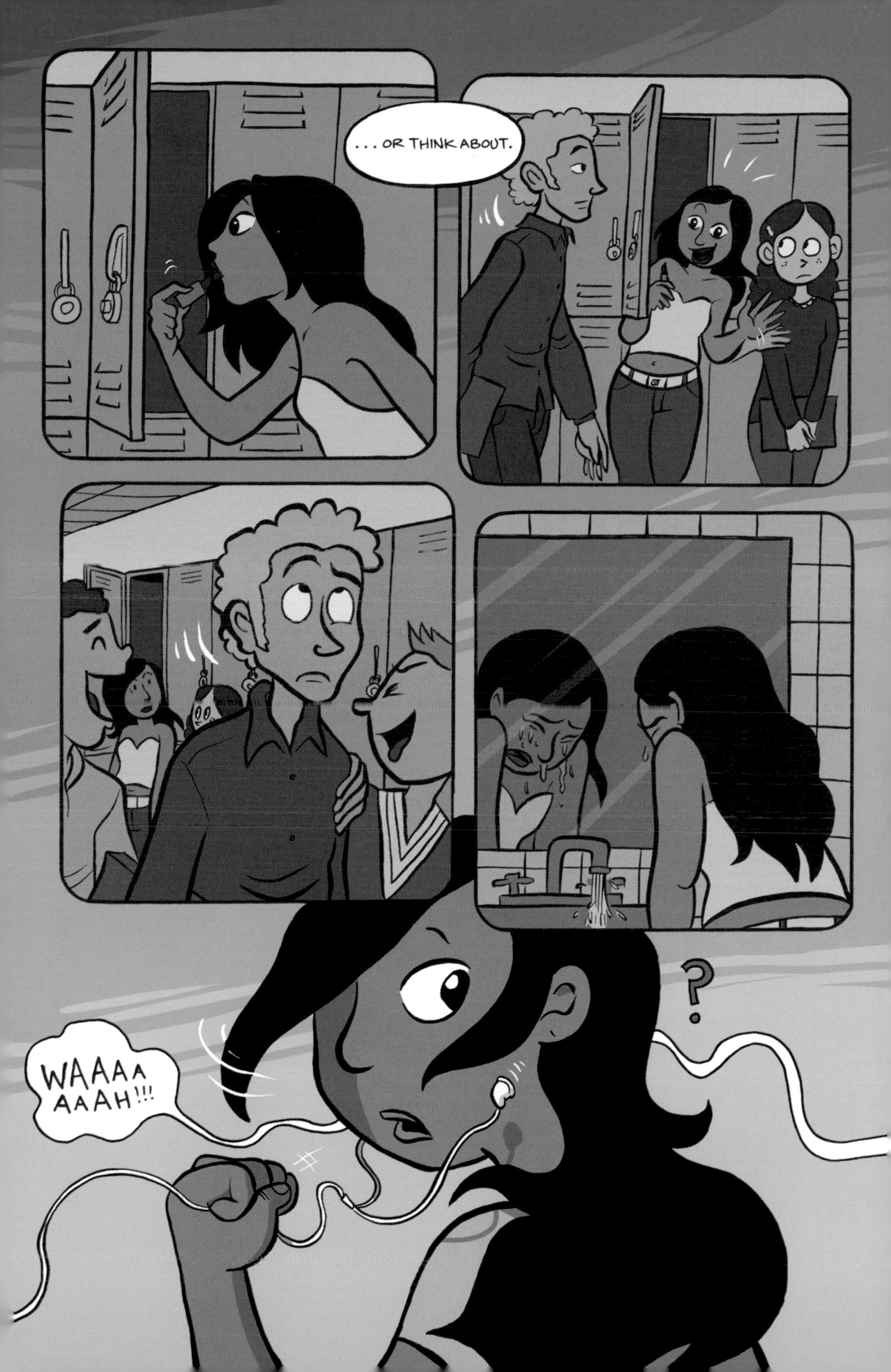
. . . OR THINK ABOUT.
?
WAAAA AAAH!!!

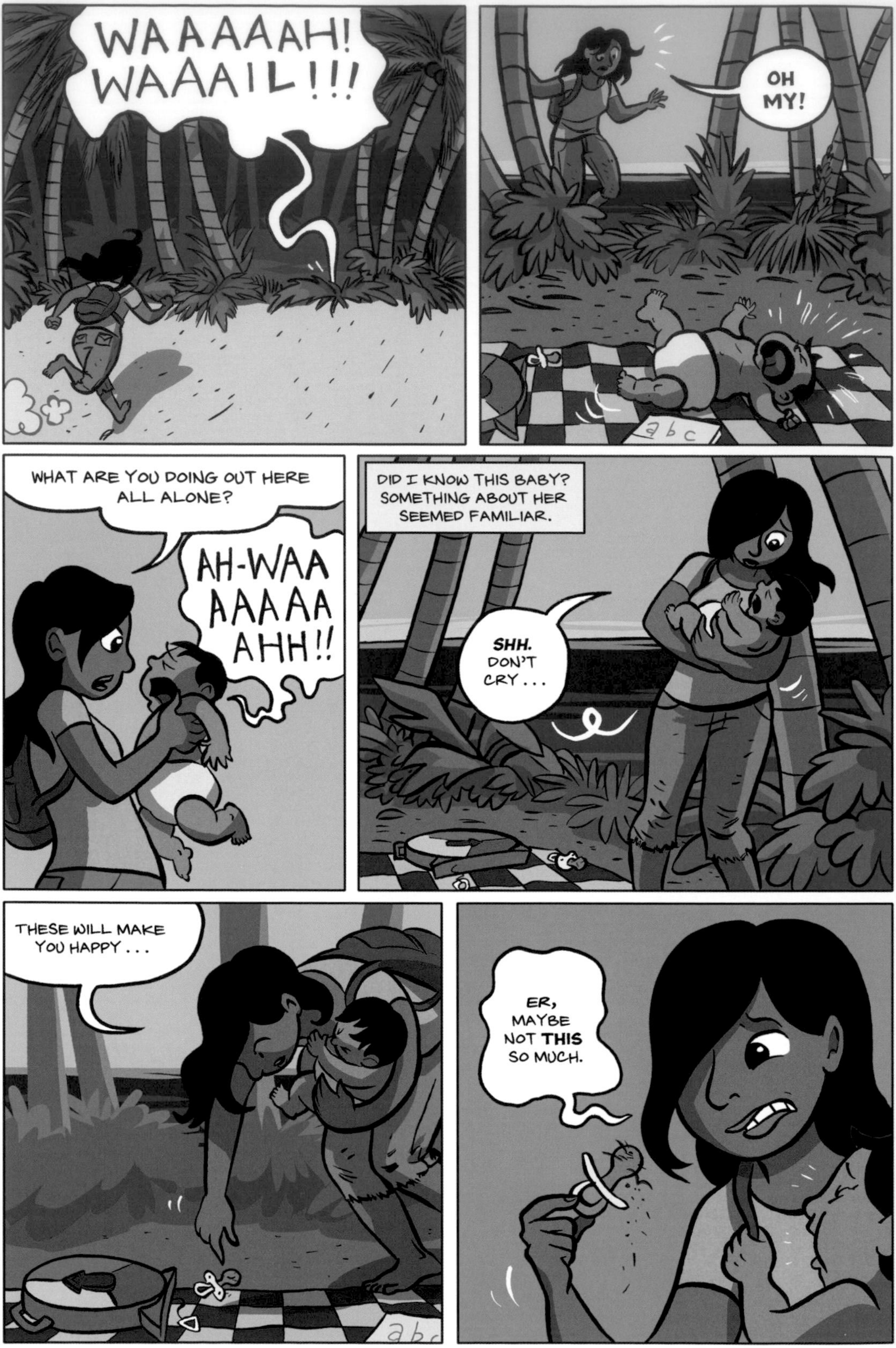

WAAAAAH! WAAAIL!!!
OH MY!
WHAT ARE YOU DOING OUT HERE ALL ALONE?
AH-WAA AAAAA AHH!!
DID I KNOW THIS BABY? SOMETHING ABOUT HER SEEMED FAMILIAR.
SHH. DON'T CRY . . .
THESE WILL MAKE YOU HAPPY . . .
ER, MAYBE NOT THIS SO MUCH.

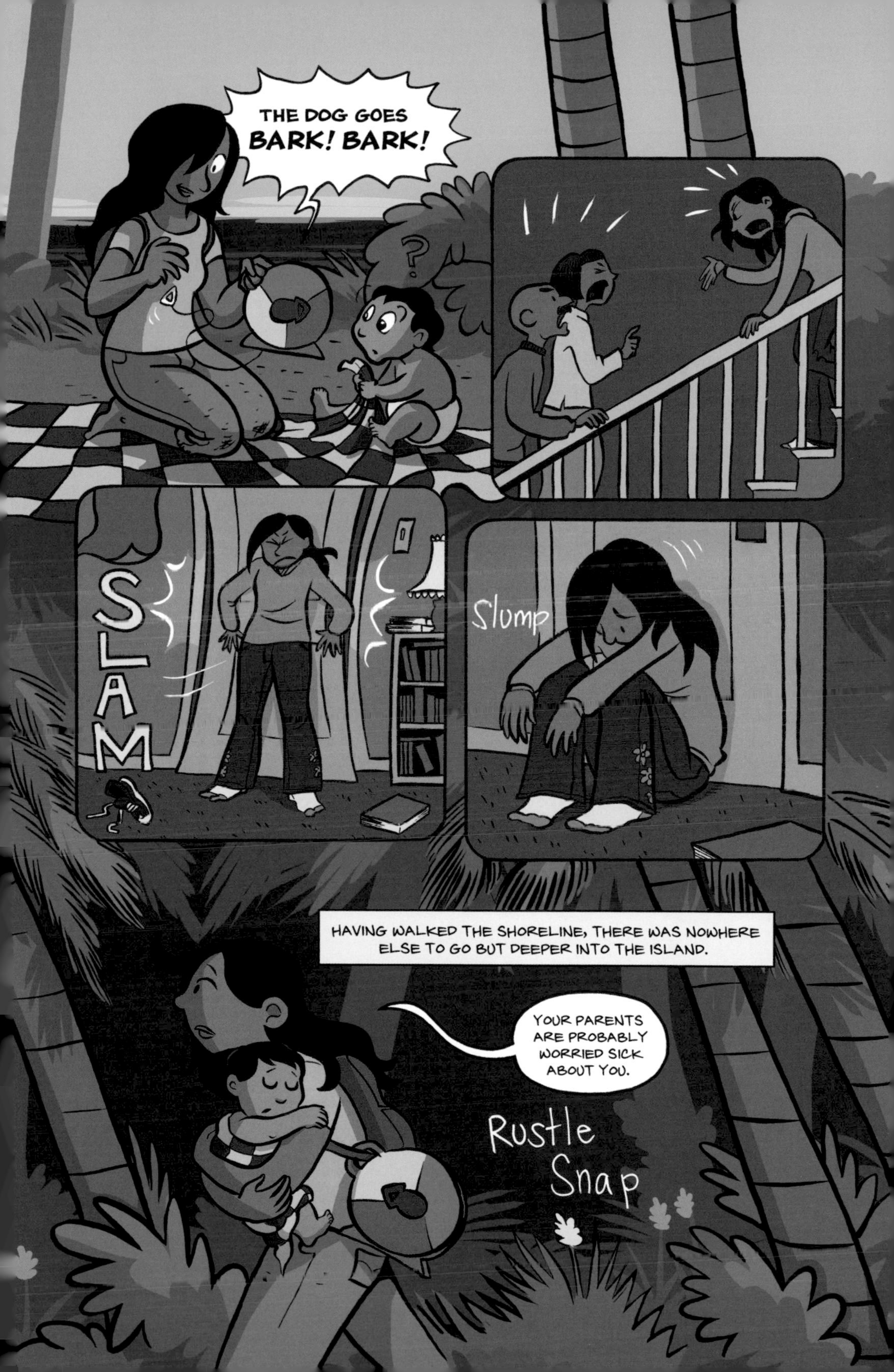
THE DOG GOES BARK! BARK!
?
SLAM
Slump
HAVING WALKED THE SHORELINE, THERE WAS NOWHERE ELSE TO GO BUT DEEPER INTO THE ISLAND.
YOUR PARENTS ARE PROBABLY WORRIED SICK ABOUT YOU.
Rustle
Snap

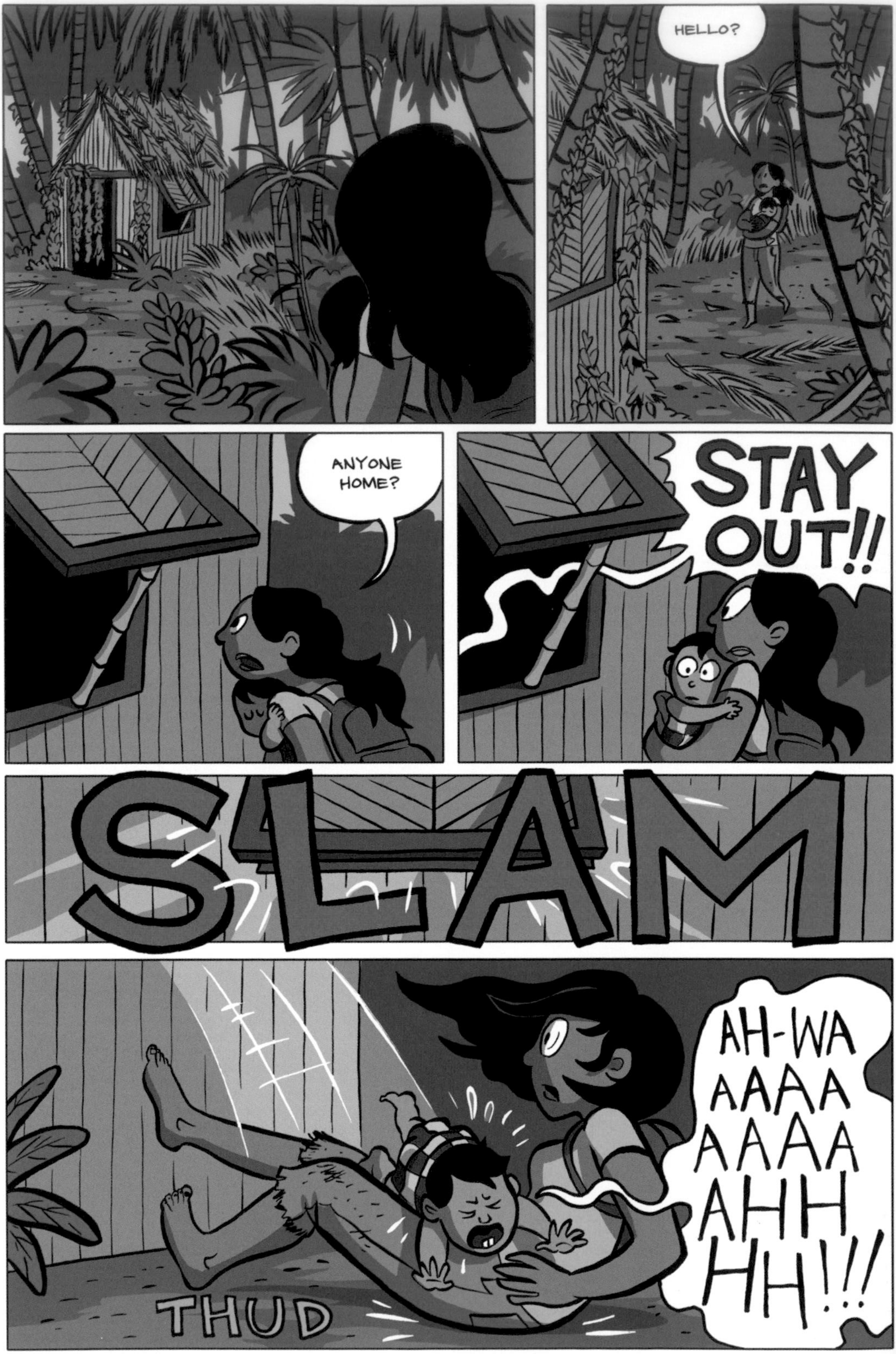
HELLO?
ANYONE HOME?
STAY OUT!!
SLAM
AH-WA AAAA AAAA AHH HH!!!
THUD

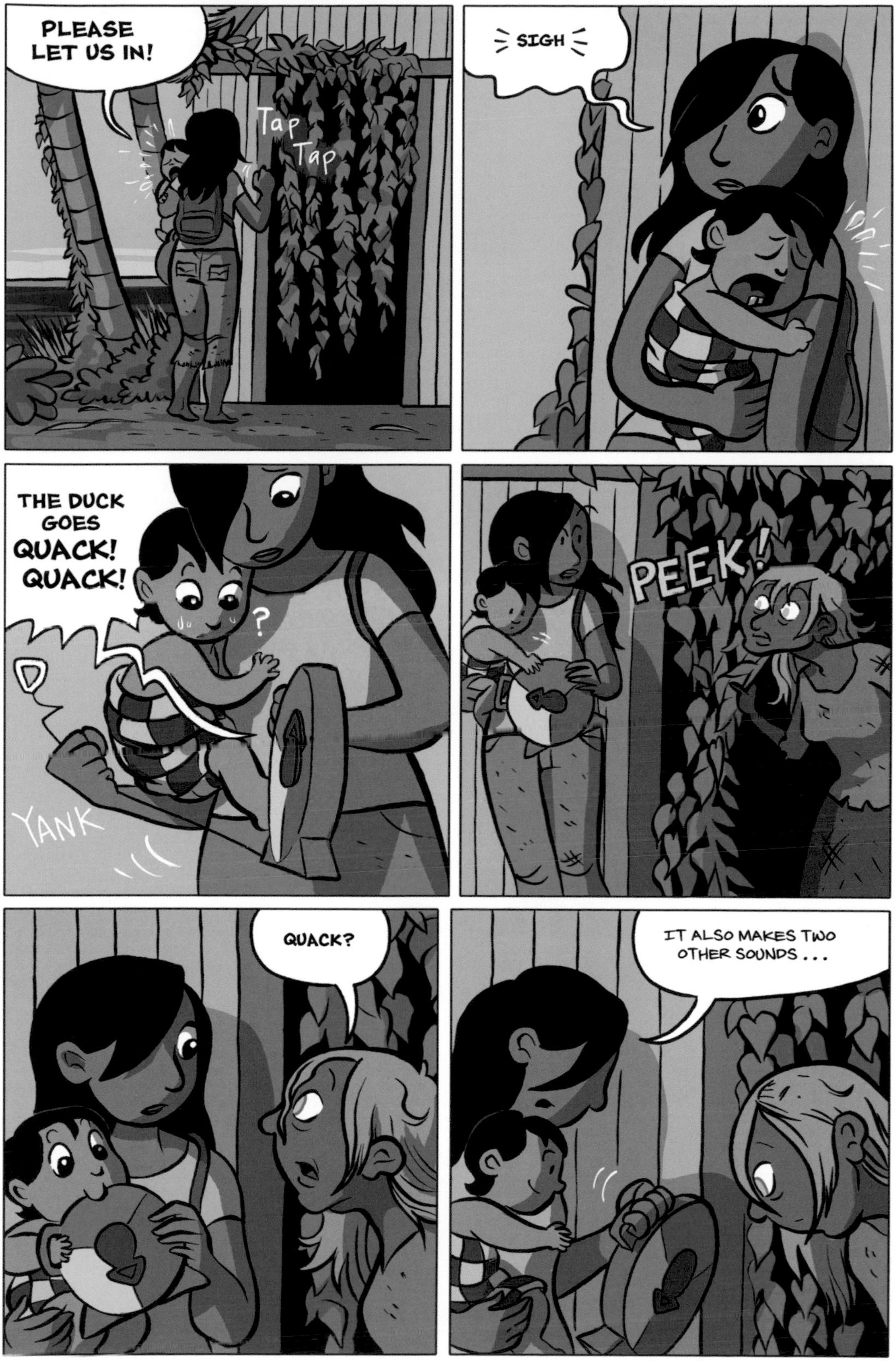
PLEASE LET US IN!
Tap Tap
SIGH
THE DUCK GOES QUACK! QUACK!
YANK
PEEK!
QUACK?
IT ALSO MAKES TWO OTHER SOUNDS . . .

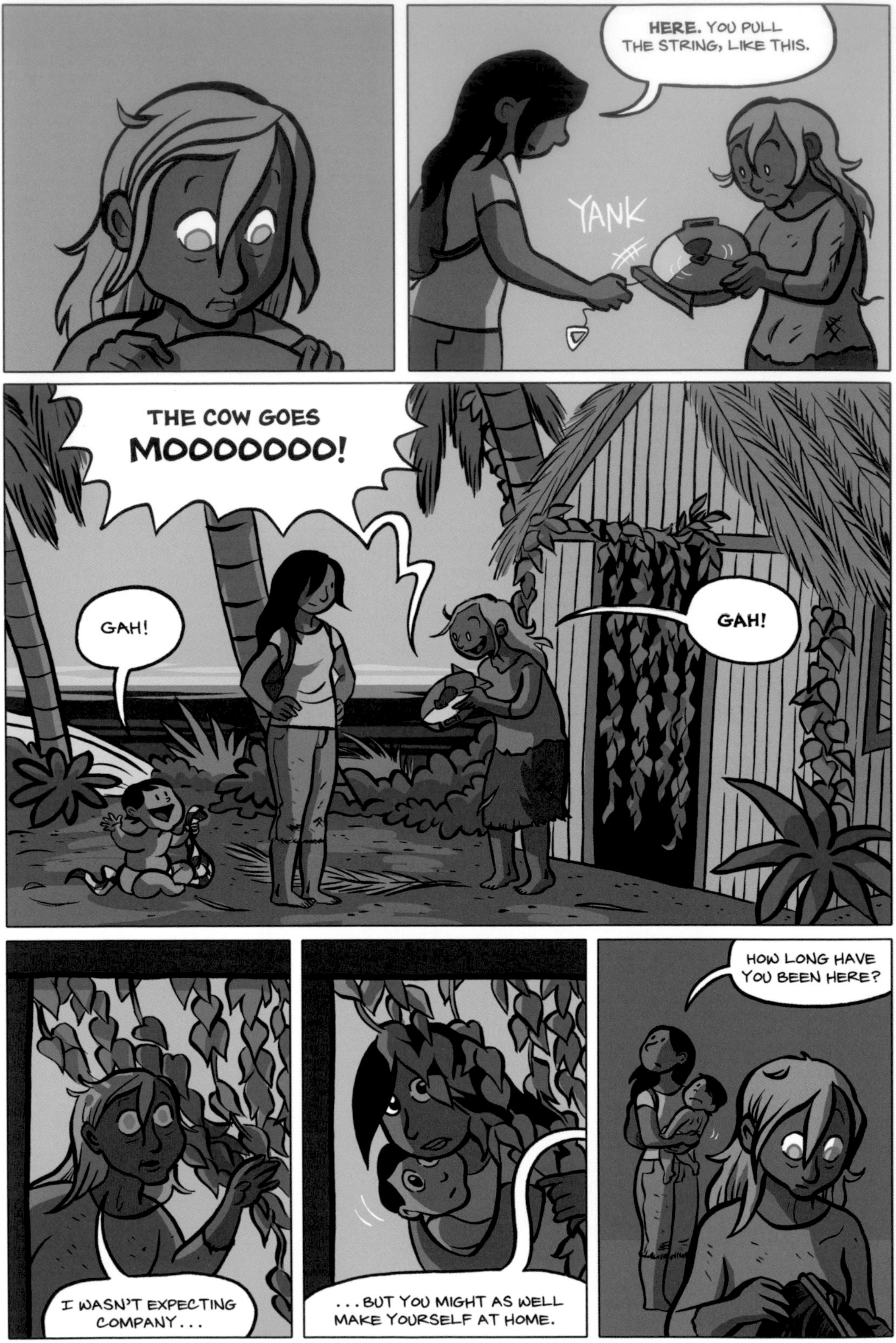

HERE. YOU PULL THE STRING, LIKE THIS.
YANK
THE COW GOES MOOOOOOO!
GAH!
GAH!
I WASN'T EXPECTING COMPANY...
...BUT YOU MIGHT AS WELL MAKE YOURSELF AT HOME.
HOW LONG HAVE YOU BEEN HERE?

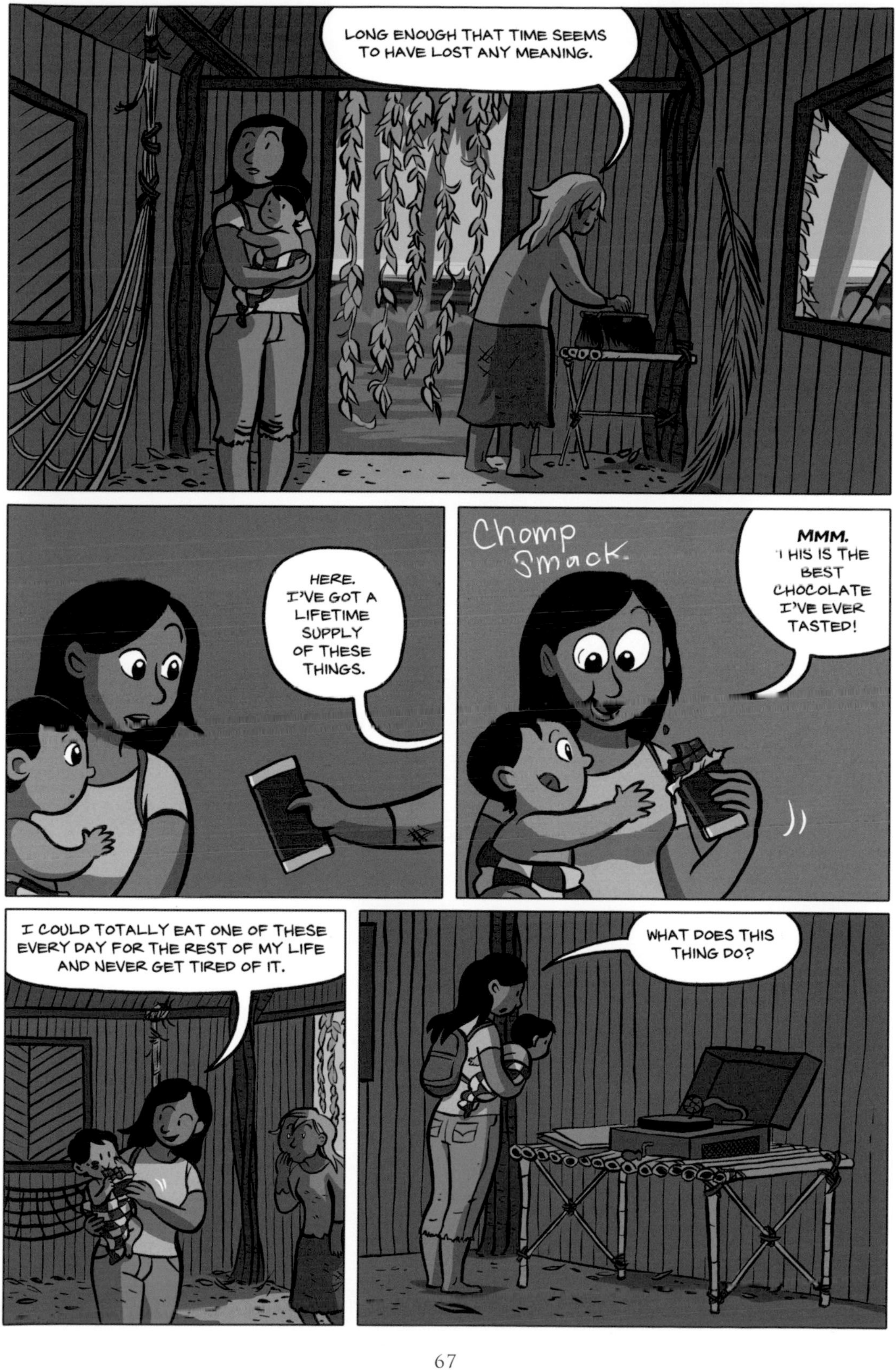
LONG ENOUGH THAT TIME SEEMS TO HAVE LOST ANY MEANING.
HERE. I'VE GOT A LIFETIME SUPPLY OF THESE THINGS.
Chomp Smack
MMM. THIS IS THE BEST CHOCOLATE I'VE EVER TASTED!
I COULD TOTALLY EAT ONE OF THESE EVERY DAY FOR THE REST OF MY LIFE AND NEVER GET TIRED OF IT.
WHAT DOES THIS THING DO?

IT'S A RECORD PLAYER. **YOU KNOW**, FOR MUSIC.

I BROUGHT IT HERE WITH ME. **I THINK** . . .

THEY'RE ANTIQUES.

WORTH A LOT OF MONEY?

TO **ME** THEY ARE.

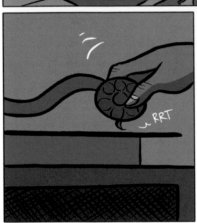

~RRT

HEY! I HAVE THIS SAME SONG ON MY MP3 PLAYER!

Crank crank

I DON'T RECOGNIZE THESE OTHER TWO. ARE THEY ANY GOOD?

YOU COULD SAY THEY'RE SORTA LIKE MY SOUL FOOD.

AS TIME PASSES, THERE ARE A LOT OF THINGS I LOSE SIGHT OF.

BUT WHEN I LISTEN TO THESE SONGS, I CATCH A GLIMPSE OF HAPPIER TIMES.

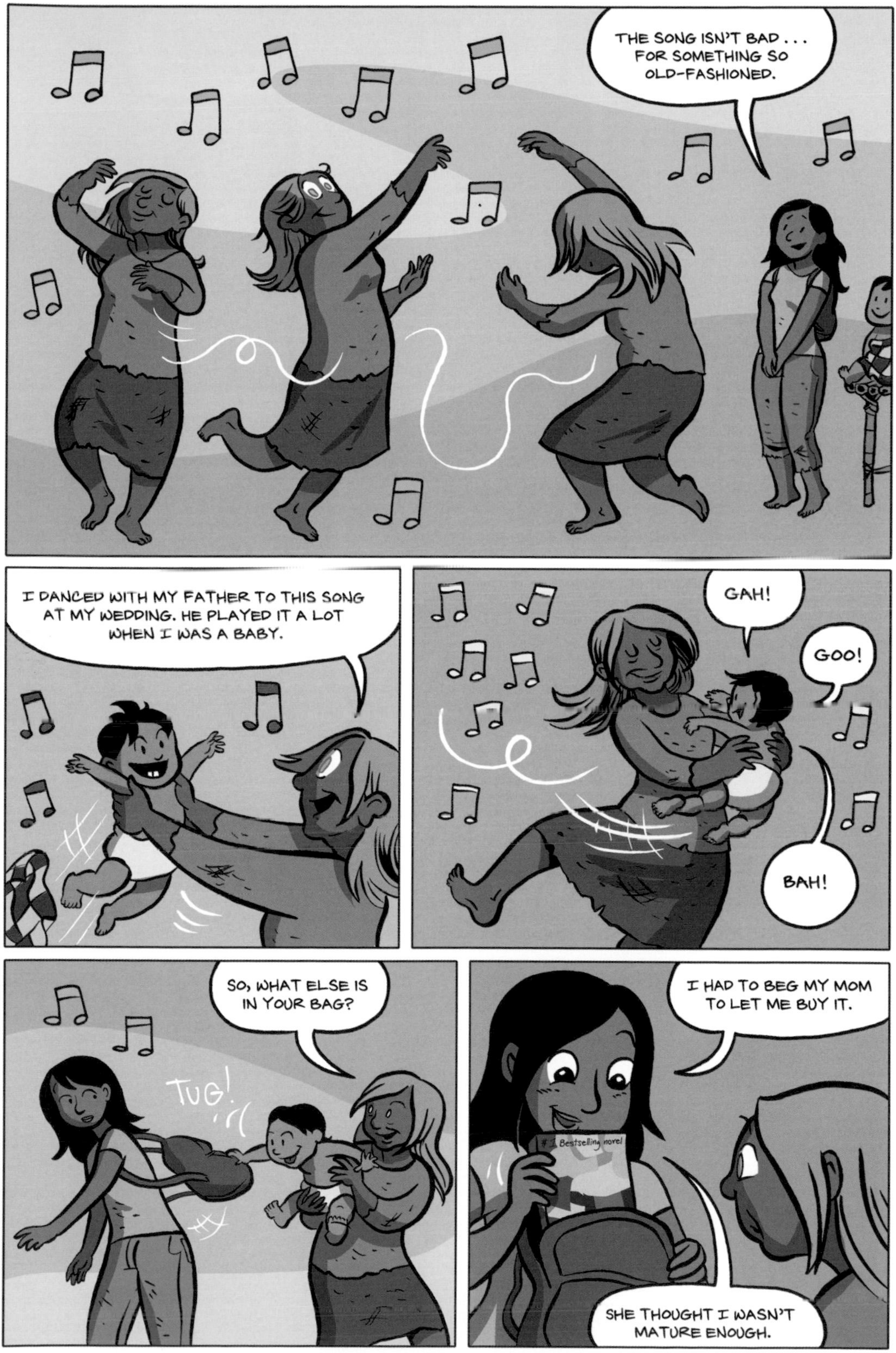
THE SONG ISN'T BAD . . . FOR SOMETHING SO OLD-FASHIONED.
I DANCED WITH MY FATHER TO THIS SONG AT MY WEDDING. HE PLAYED IT A LOT WHEN I WAS A BABY.
GAH!
GOO!
BAH!
SO, WHAT ELSE IS IN YOUR BAG?
TUG!
I HAD TO BEG MY MOM TO LET ME BUY IT.
#1 Bestselling novel
SHE THOUGHT I WASN'T MATURE ENOUGH.

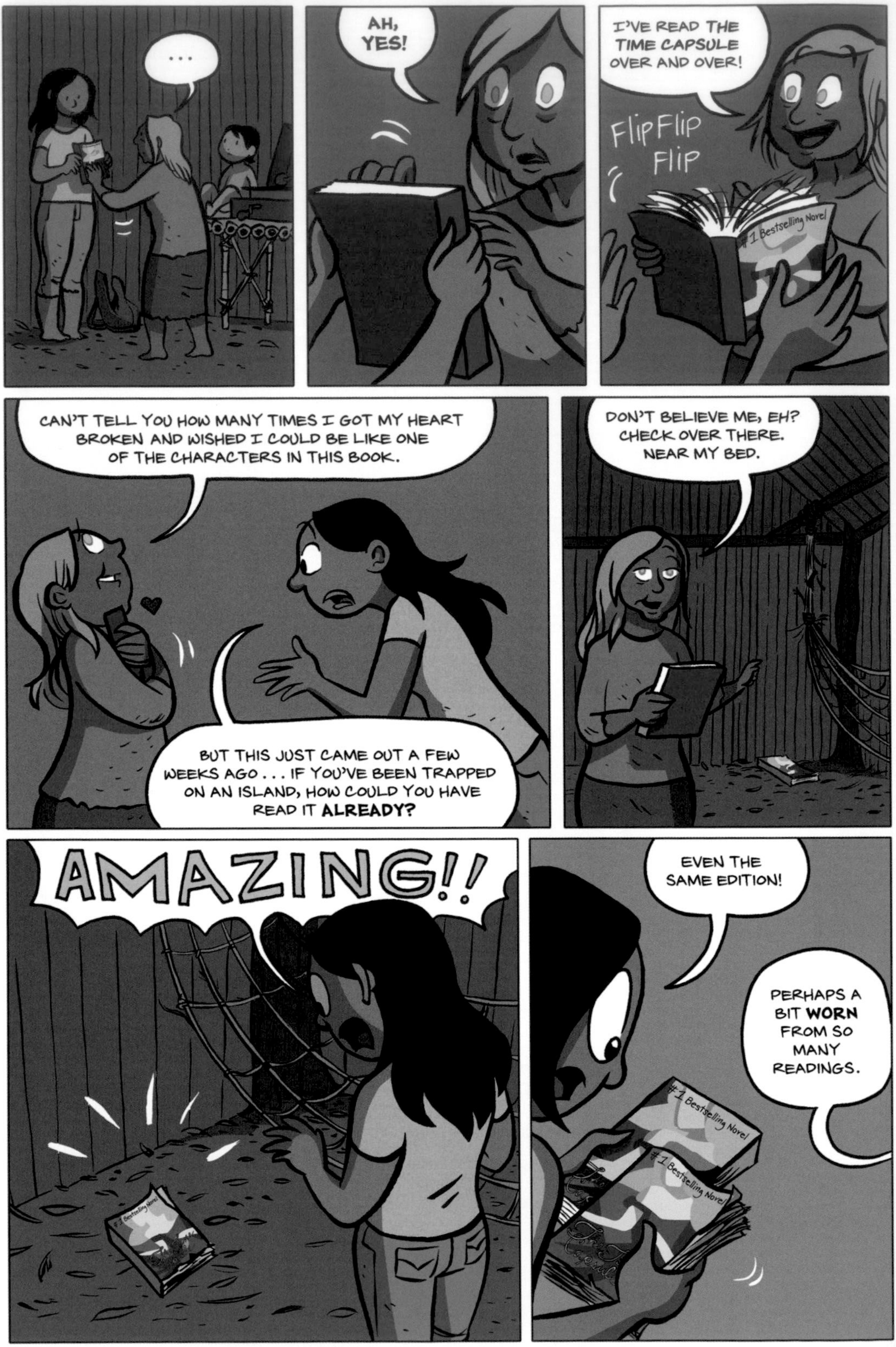
. . .
AH, YES!
I'VE READ THE TIME CAPSULE OVER AND OVER!
FlipFlip Flip
#1 Bestselling Novel
CAN'T TELL YOU HOW MANY TIMES I GOT MY HEART BROKEN AND WISHED I COULD BE LIKE ONE OF THE CHARACTERS IN THIS BOOK.
BUT THIS JUST CAME OUT A FEW WEEKS AGO . . . IF YOU'VE BEEN TRAPPED ON AN ISLAND, HOW COULD YOU HAVE READ IT **ALREADY?**
DON'T BELIEVE ME, EH? CHECK OVER THERE. NEAR MY BED.
AMAZING!!
EVEN THE SAME EDITION!
PERHAPS A BIT **WORN** FROM SO MANY READINGS.
#1 Bestselling Novel
#1 Bestselling Novel

I ALWAYS LOVED THE PART WHERE THE WOMAN REALIZES THAT THE MONSTERS SHE **THOUGHT** WERE HER ENEMY . . .
#1 Bestselling Novel
. . . WERE PROTECTING HER THE WHOLE TIME.
SNIP
Bzzz
Bzz
Bzzz
SNIP

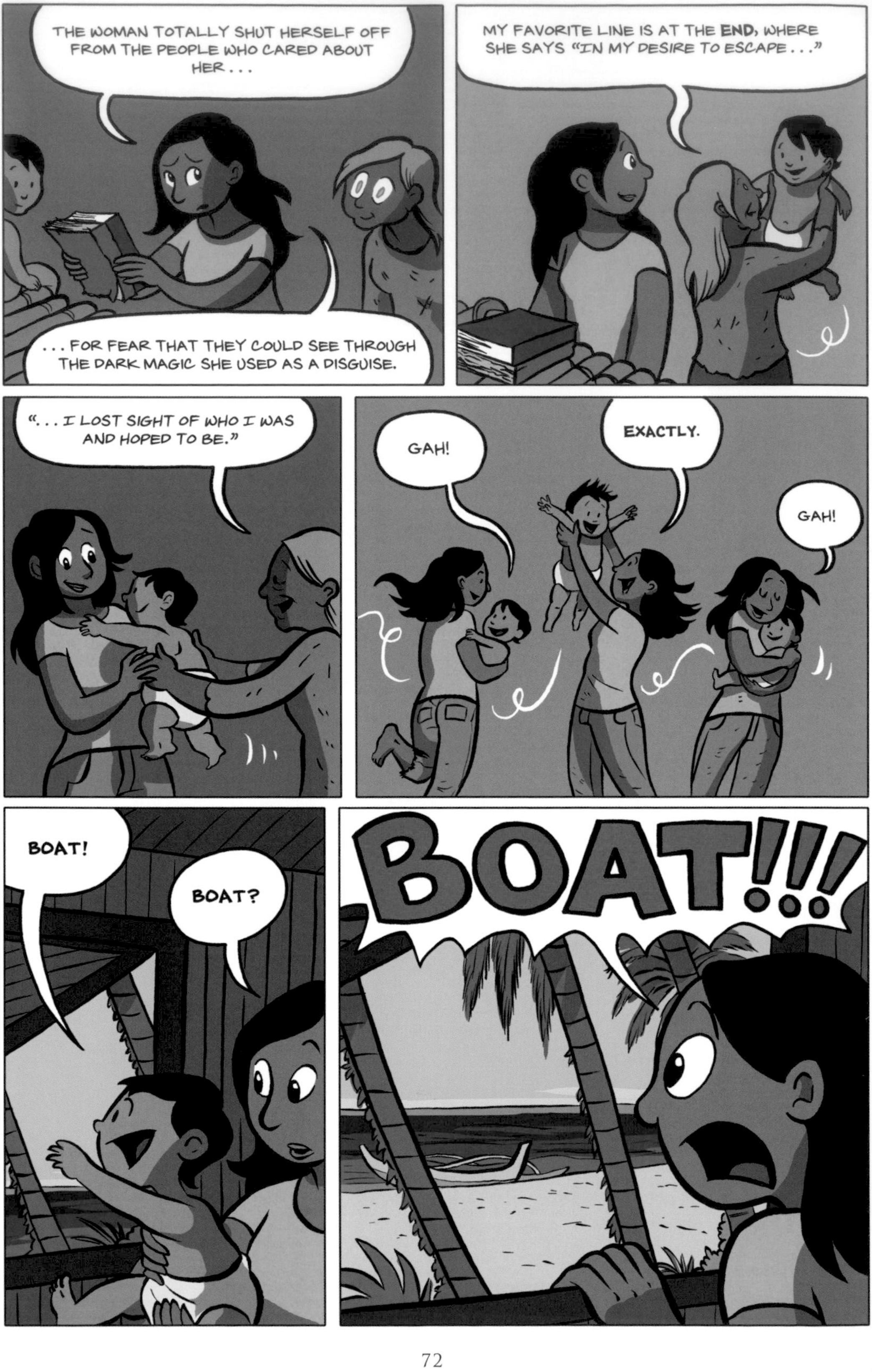
THE WOMAN TOTALLY SHUT HERSELF OFF FROM THE PEOPLE WHO CARED ABOUT HER . . .
. . . FOR FEAR THAT THEY COULD SEE THROUGH THE DARK MAGIC SHE USED AS A DISGUISE.
MY FAVORITE LINE IS AT THE **END**, WHERE SHE SAYS "IN MY DESIRE TO ESCAPE . . ."
". . . I LOST SIGHT OF WHO I WAS AND HOPED TO BE."
GAH!
EXACTLY.
GAH!
BOAT!
BOAT?
BOAT!!!

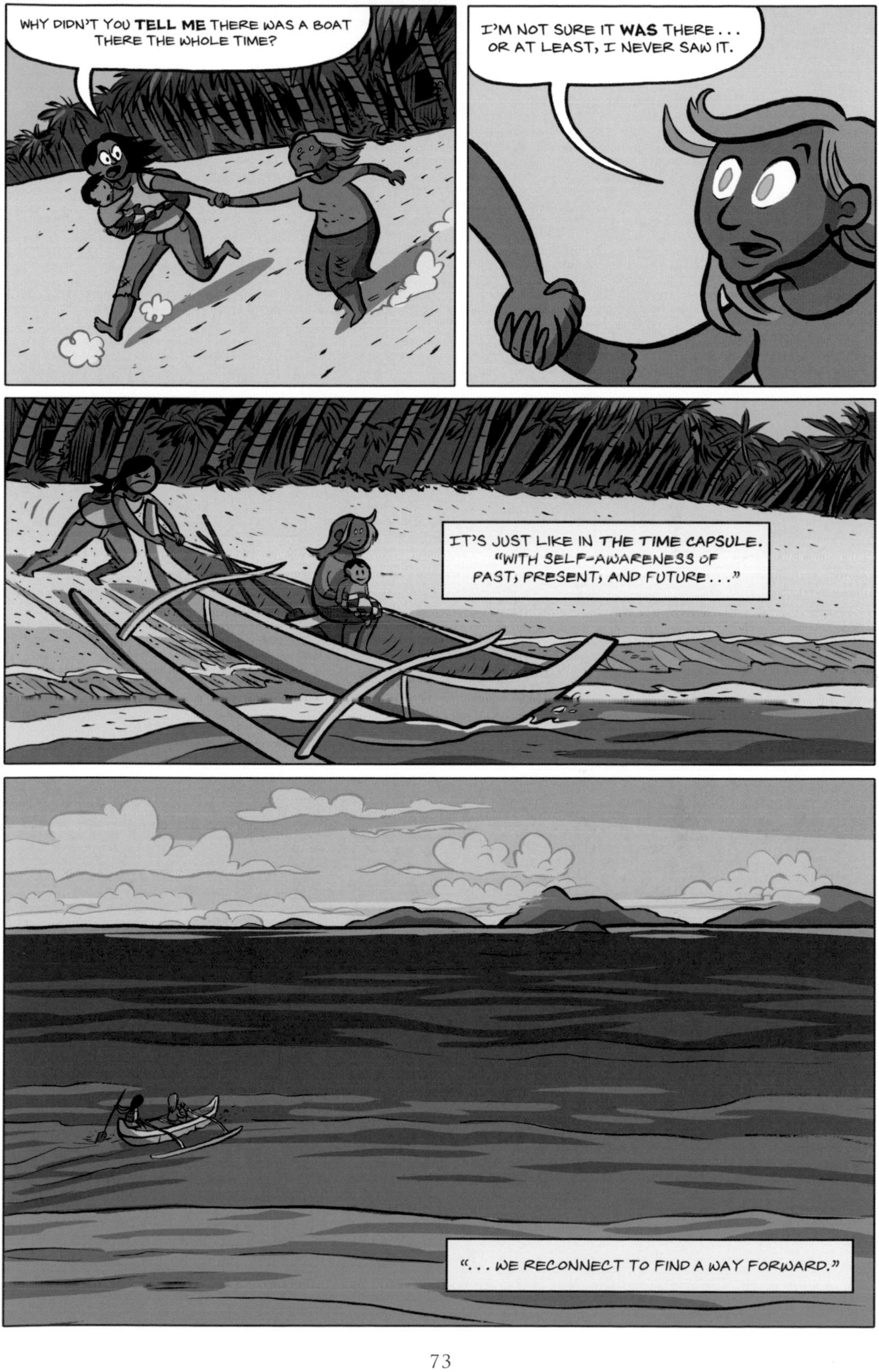
WHY DIDN'T YOU TELL ME THERE WAS A BOAT THERE THE WHOLE TIME?
I'M NOT SURE IT WAS THERE . . . OR AT LEAST, I NEVER SAW IT.
IT'S JUST LIKE IN THE TIME CAPSULE. "WITH SELF-AWARENESS OF PAST, PRESENT, AND FUTURE . . ."
". . . WE RECONNECT TO FIND A WAY FORWARD."

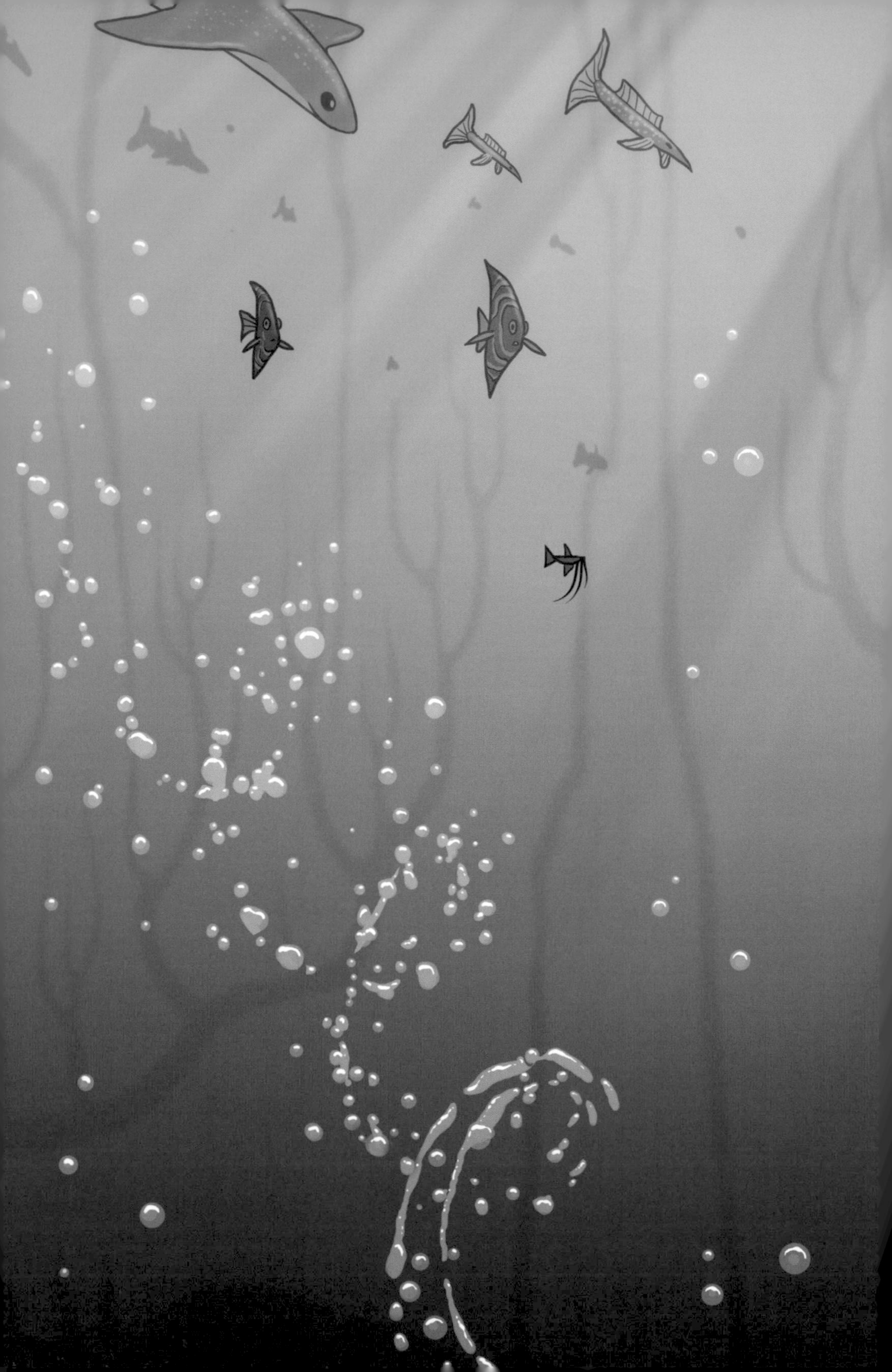

CLOAH

BY MICHEL GAGNÉ

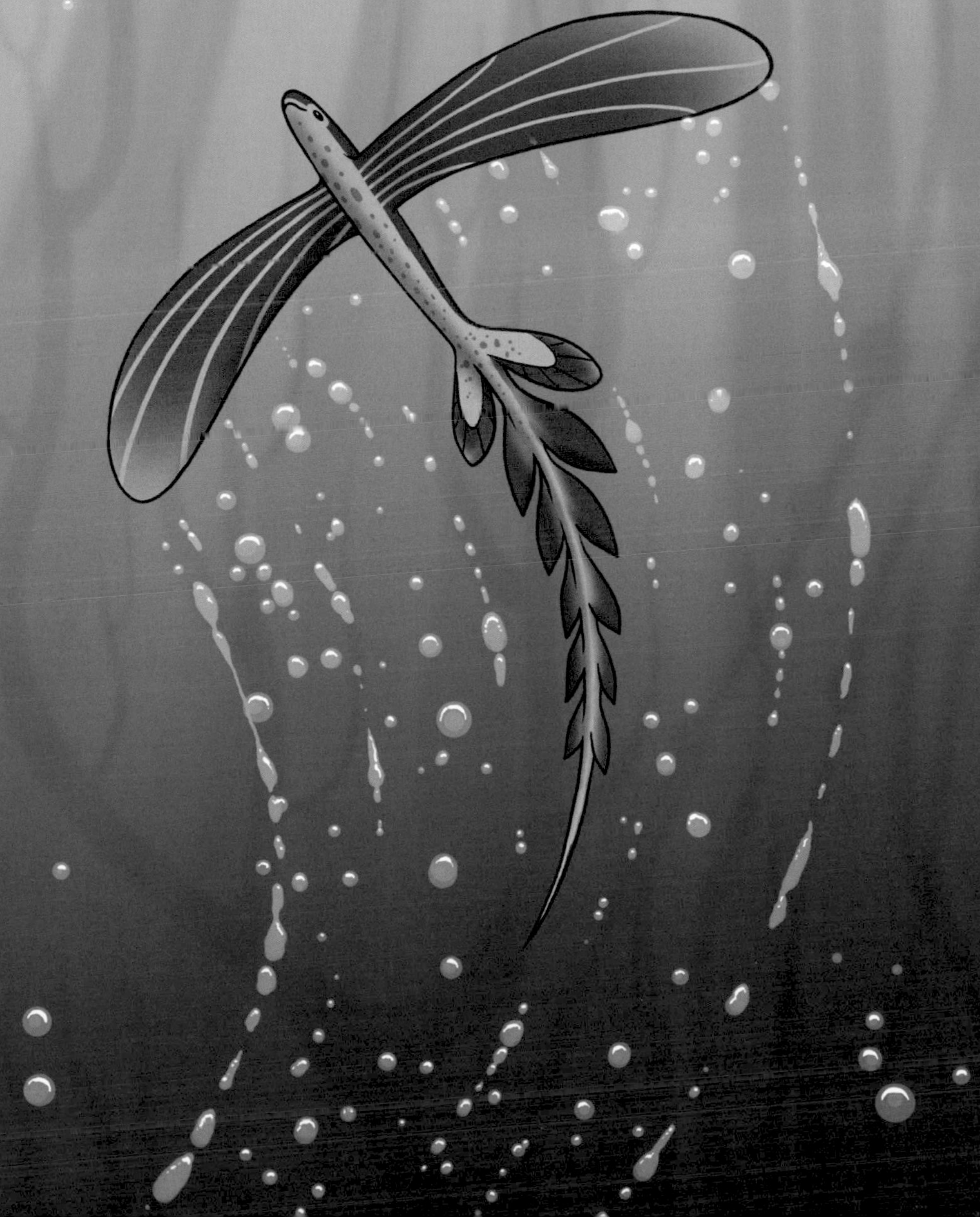

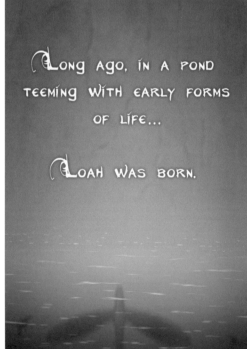
Long ago, in a pond teeming with early forms of life...

Loah was born.

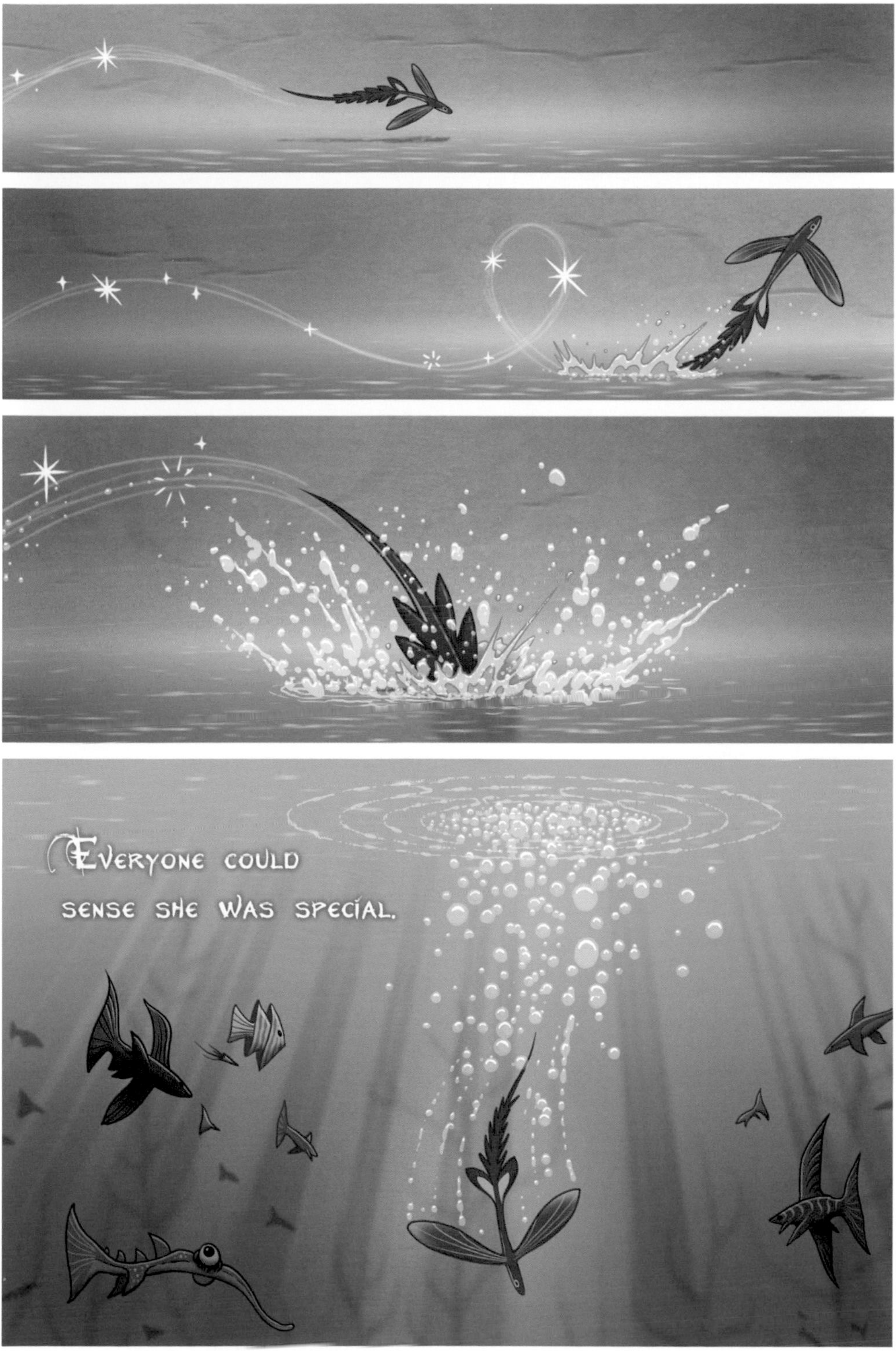
Everyone could
sense she was special.

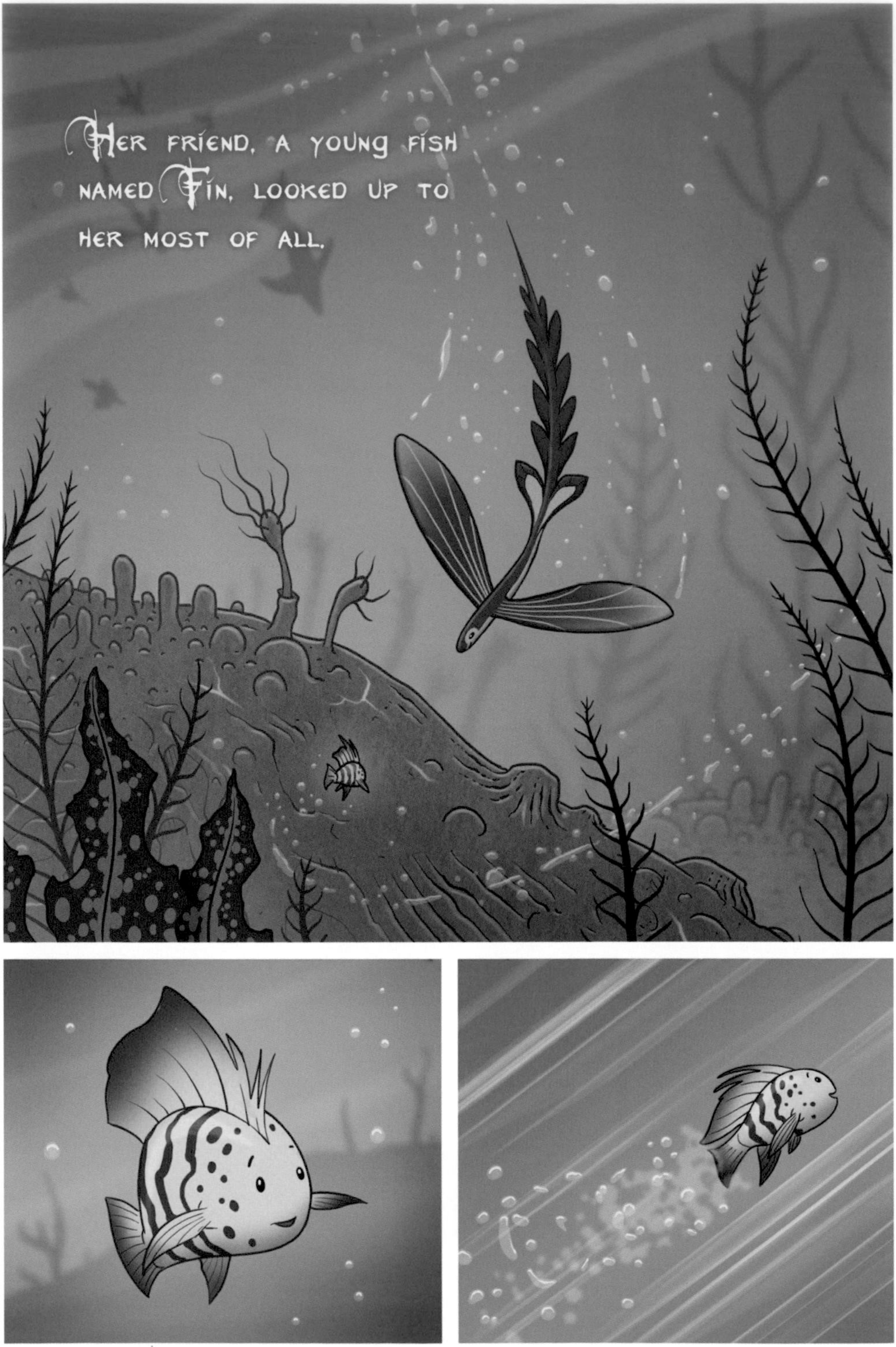
Her friend, a young fish named Fin, looked up to her most of all.

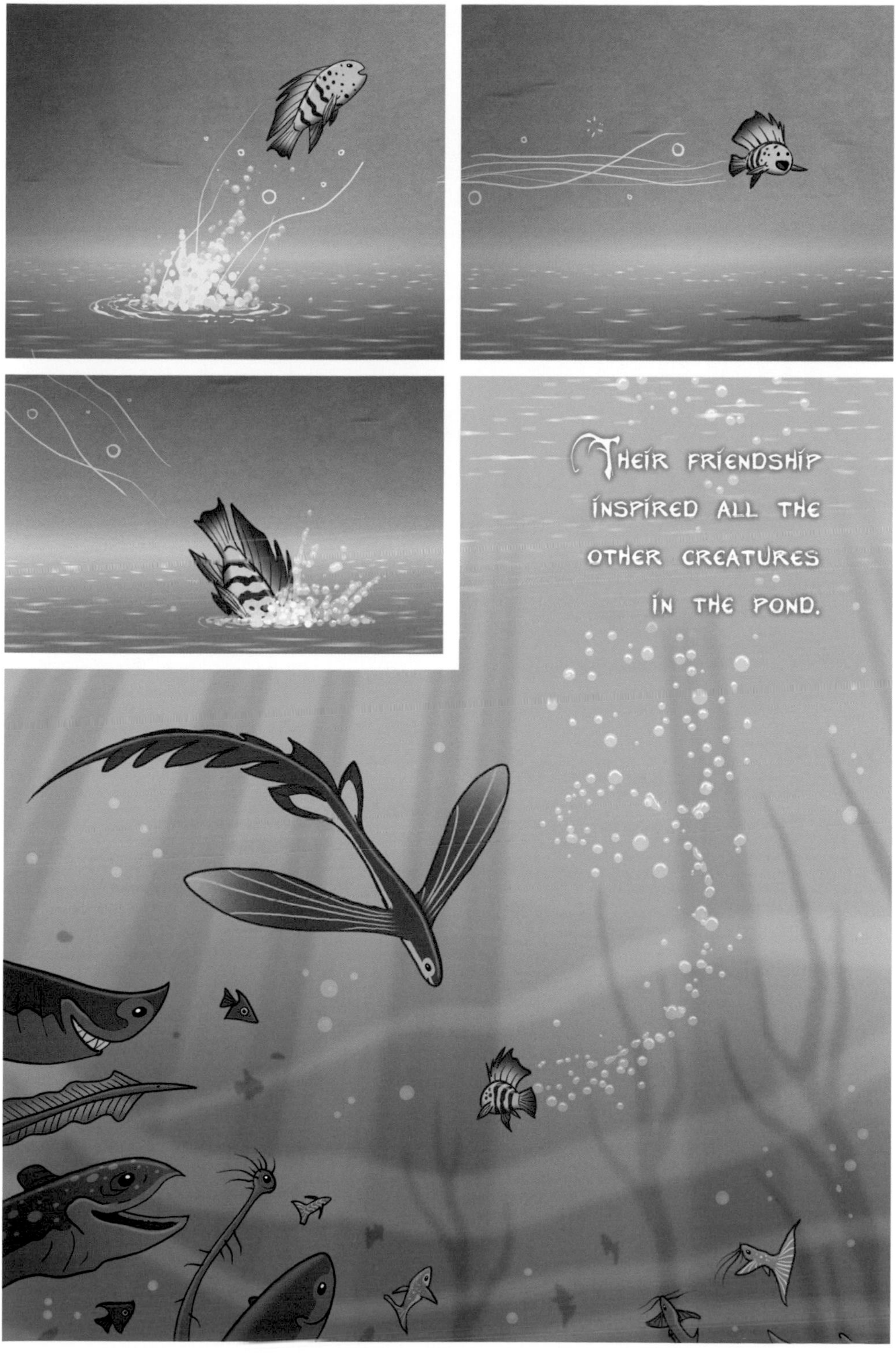
Their friendship inspired all the other creatures in the pond.

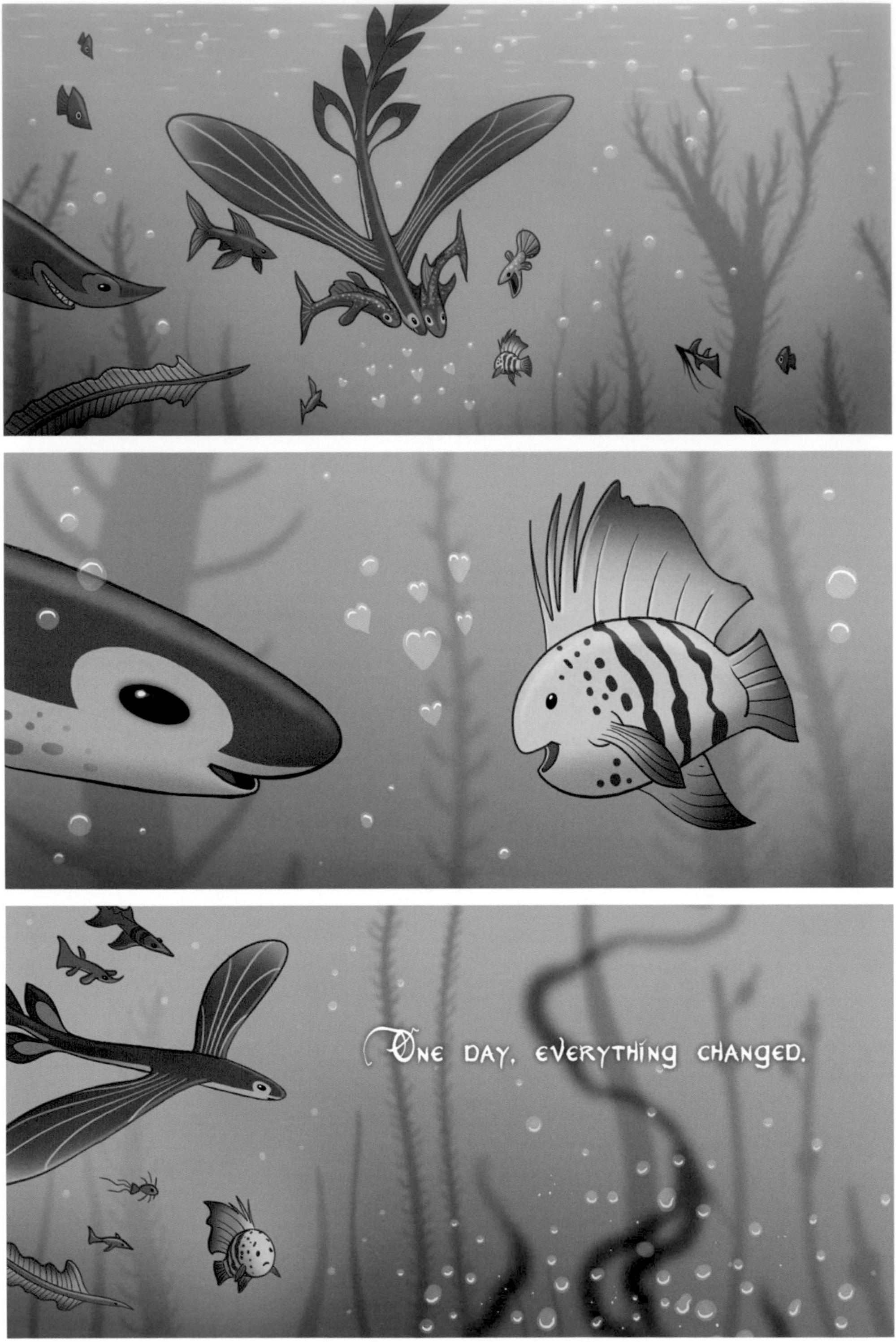
One day, everything changed.

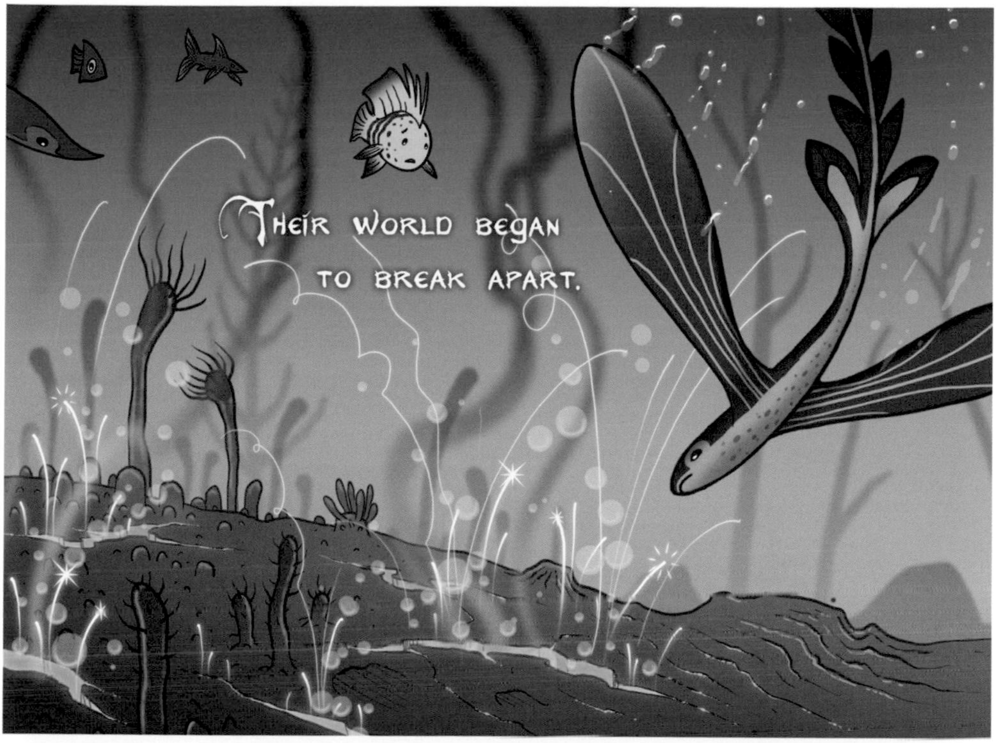
Their world began
to break apart.

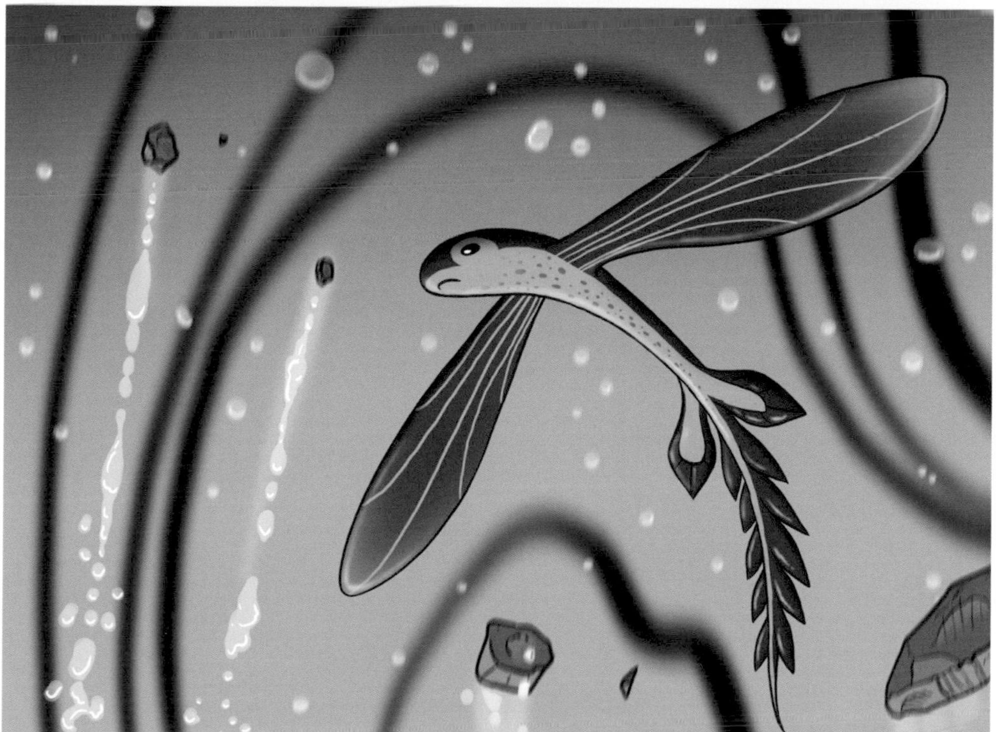

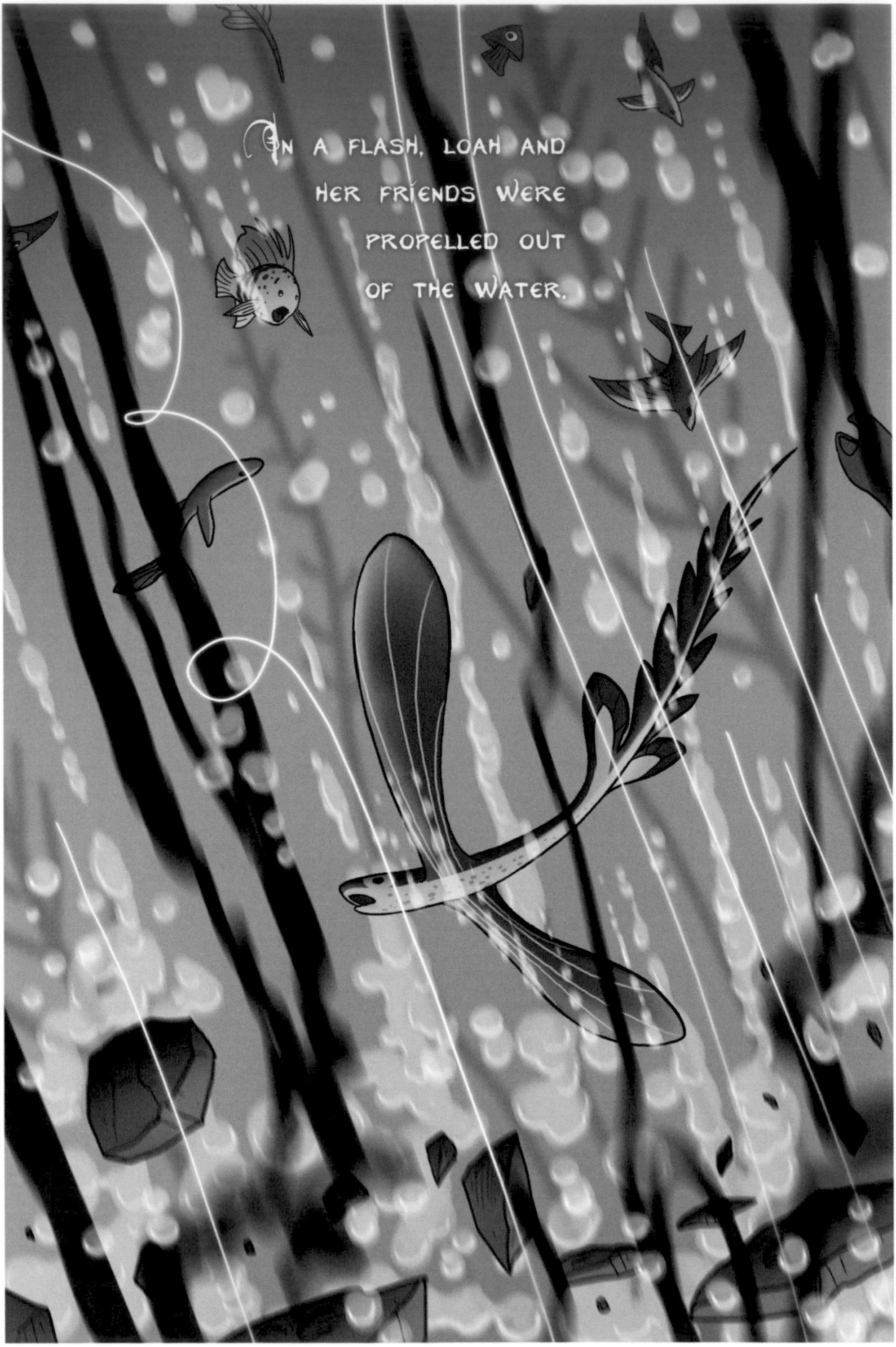
In a flash, Loah and
her friends were
propelled out
of the water.

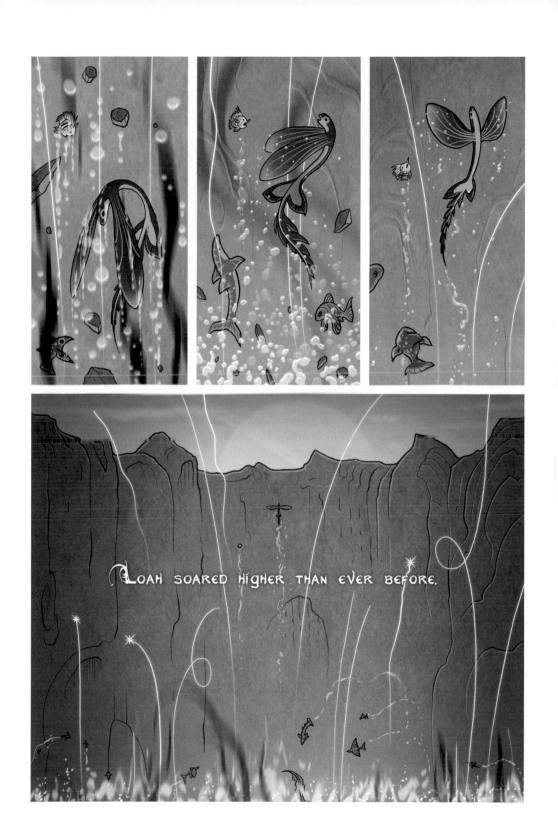

LOAH SOARED HIGHER THAN EVER BEFORE.

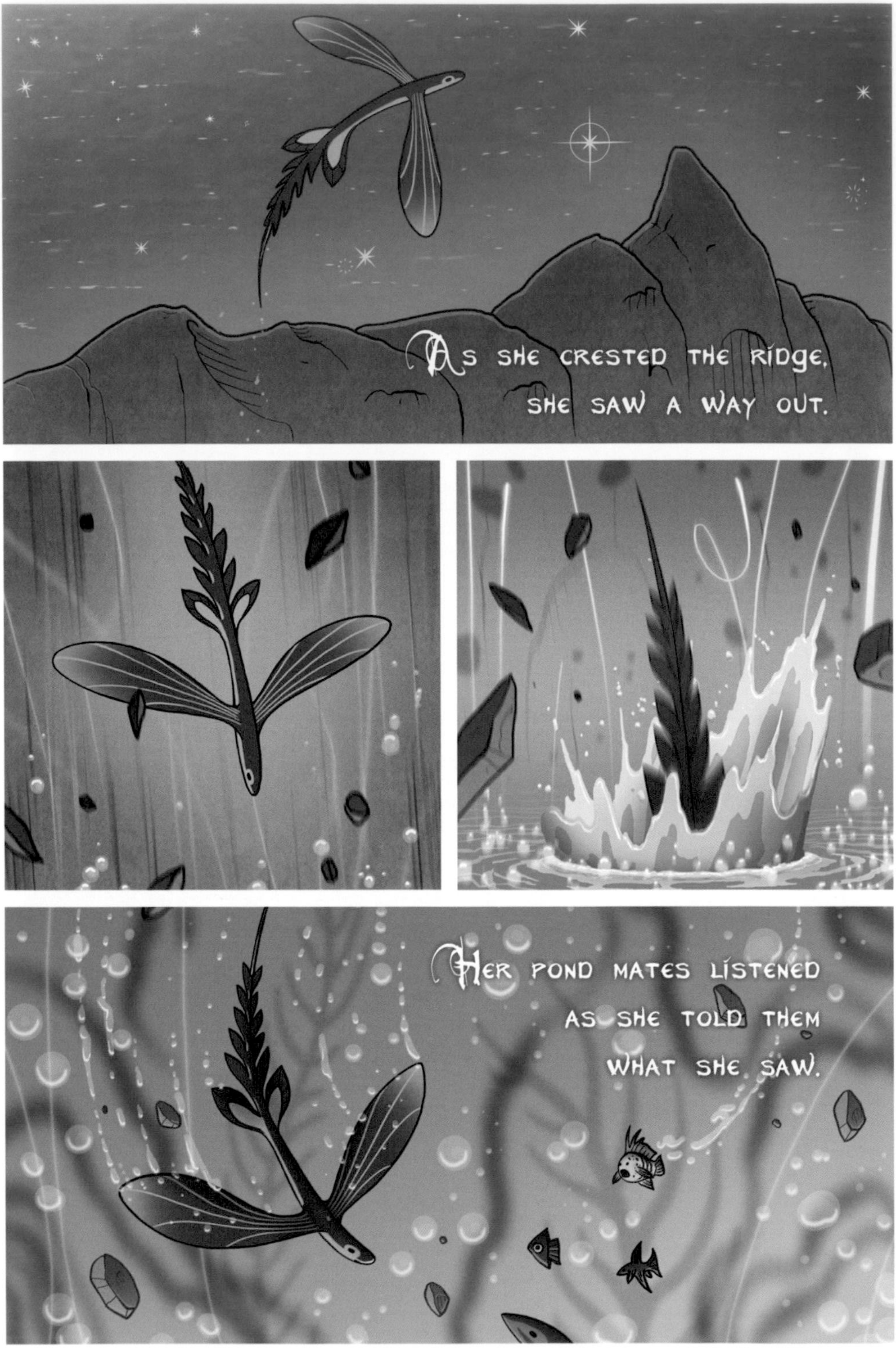
As she crested the ridge,
she saw a way out.
Her pond mates listened
as she told them
what she saw.

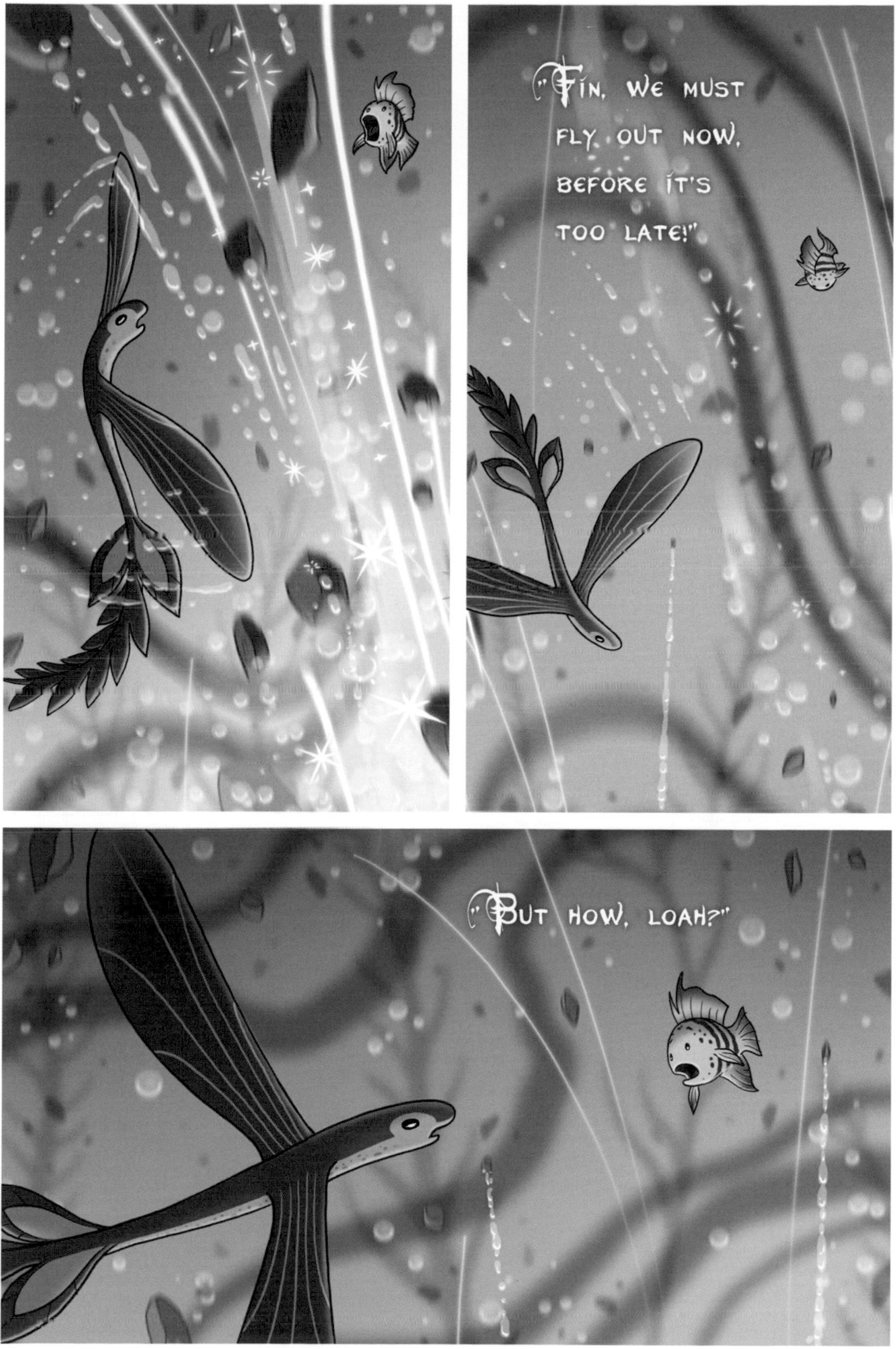
"FIN, WE MUST FLY OUT NOW, BEFORE IT'S TOO LATE!"
"BUT HOW, LOAH?"

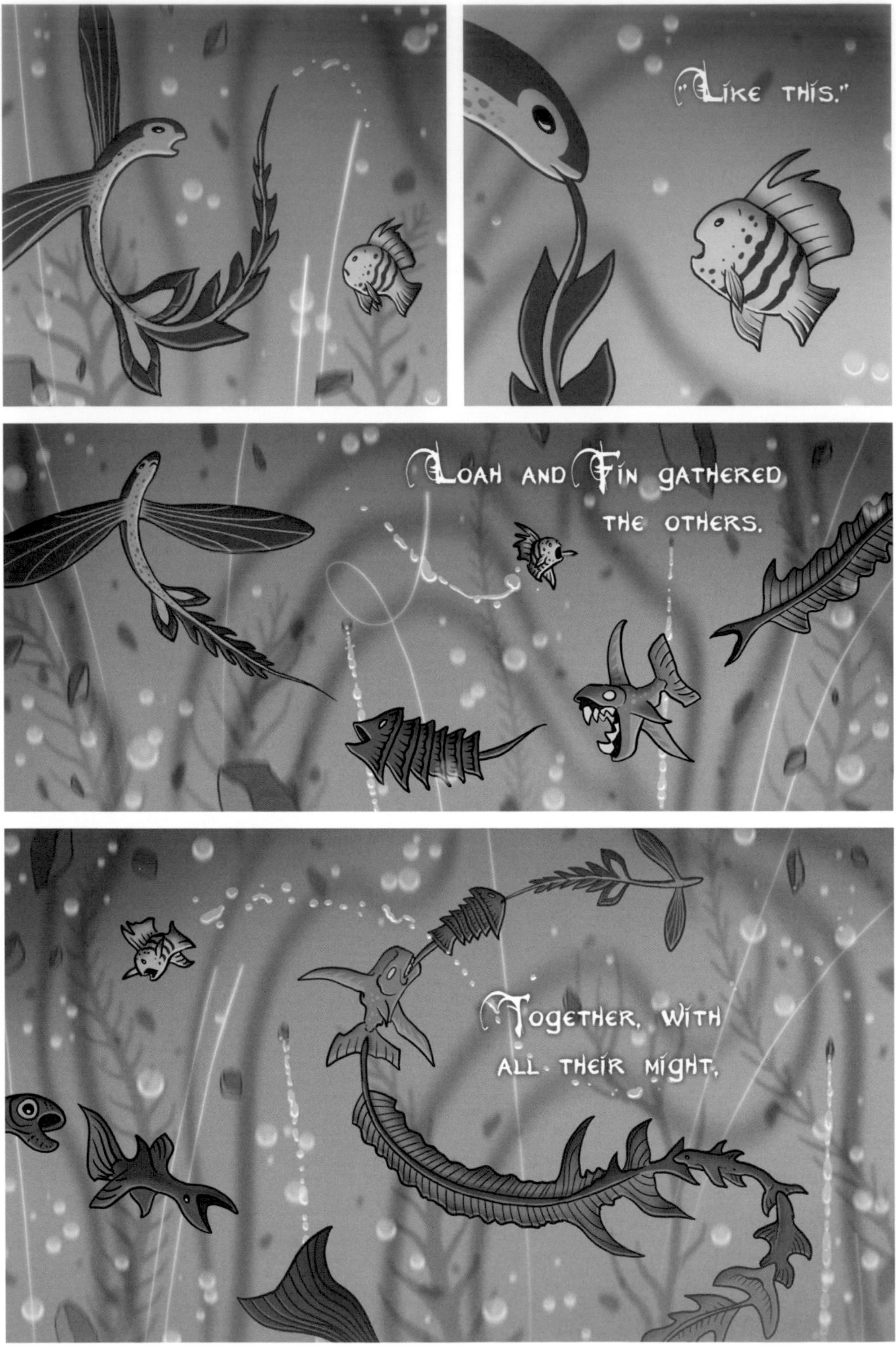
"Like this."
Loah and Fin gathered the others.
Together, with all their might,

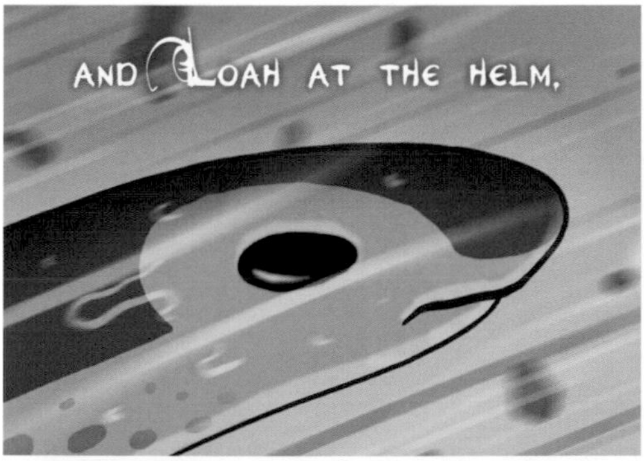
AND NOAH AT THE HELM,

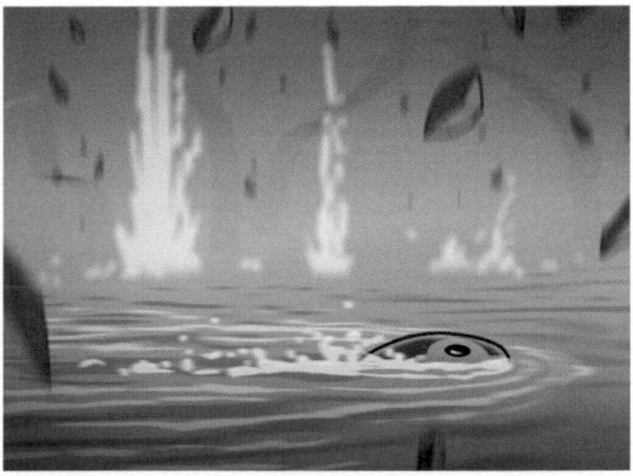

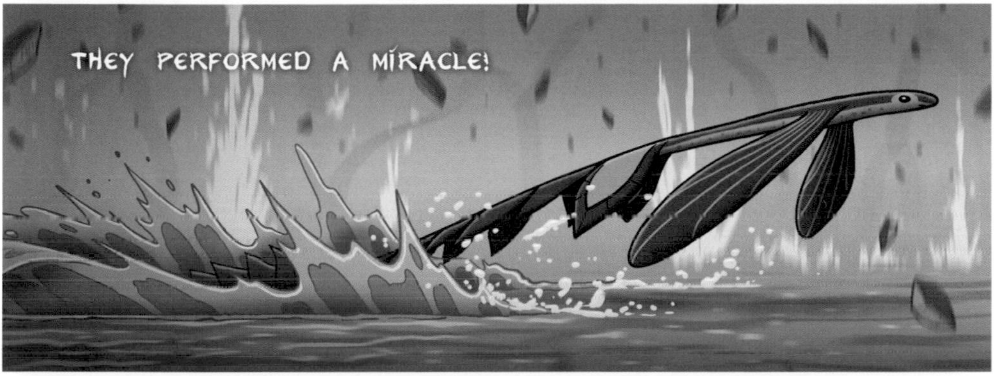
THEY PERFORMED A MIRACLE!

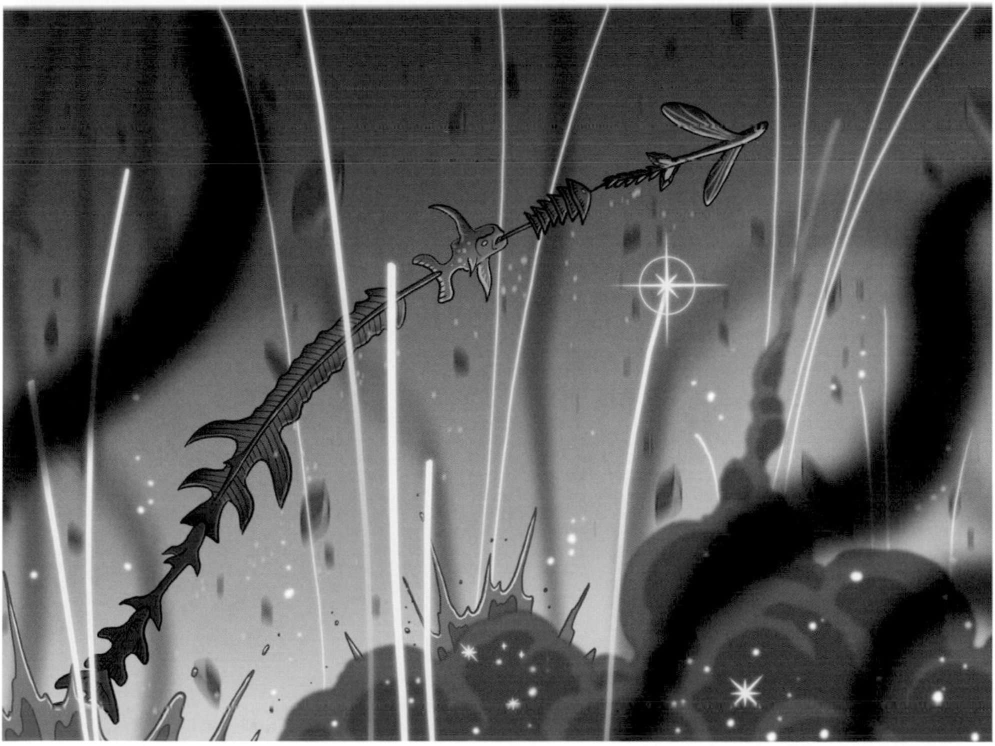

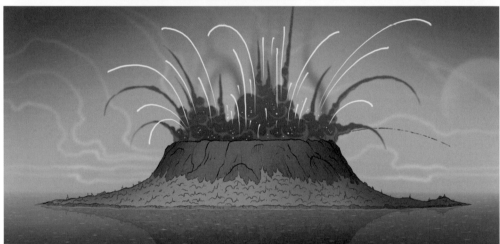

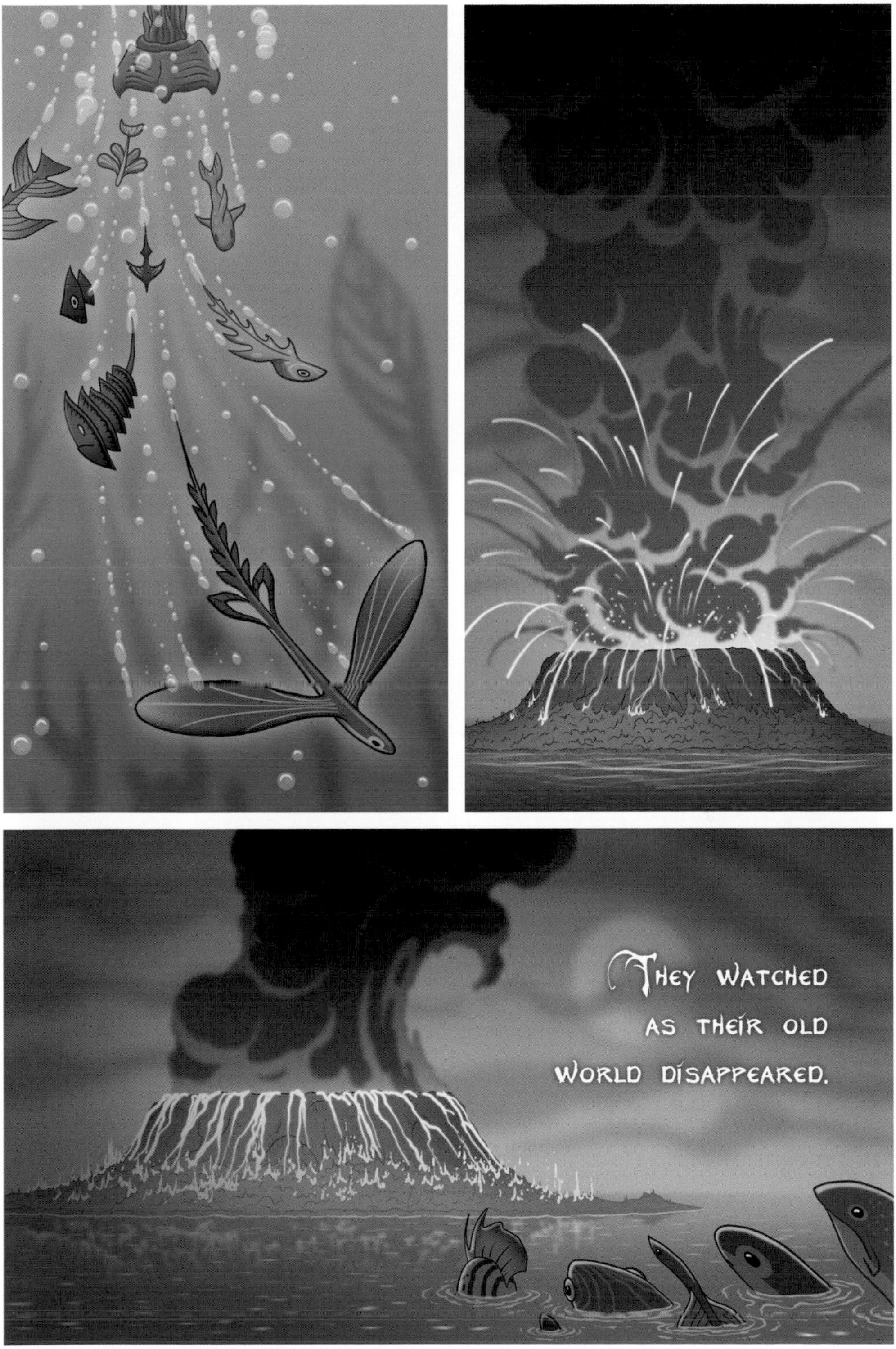
THEY WATCHED AS THEIR OLD WORLD DISAPPEARED.

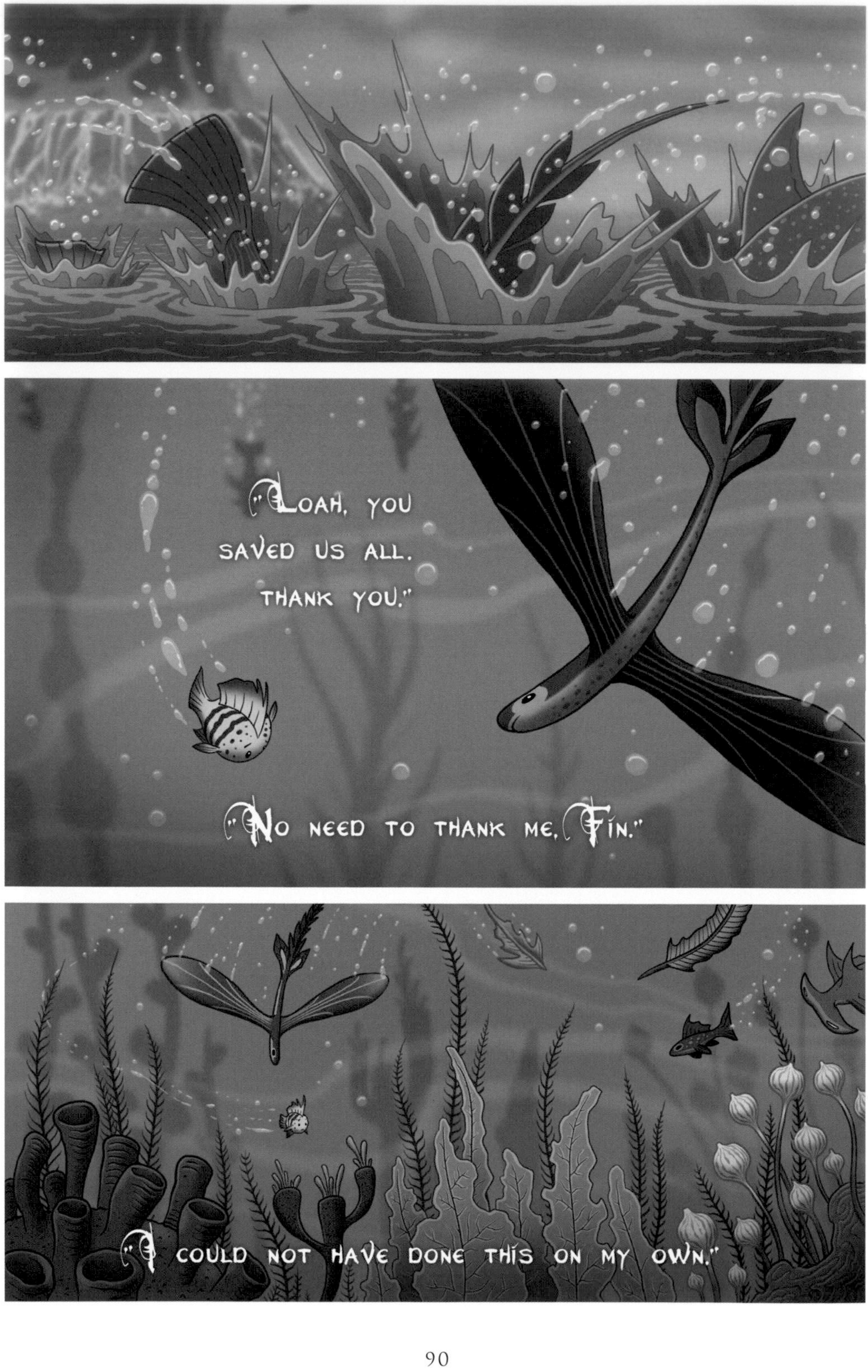
"Loah, you saved us all. thank you."
"No need to thank me, Fin."
"I could not have done this on my own."

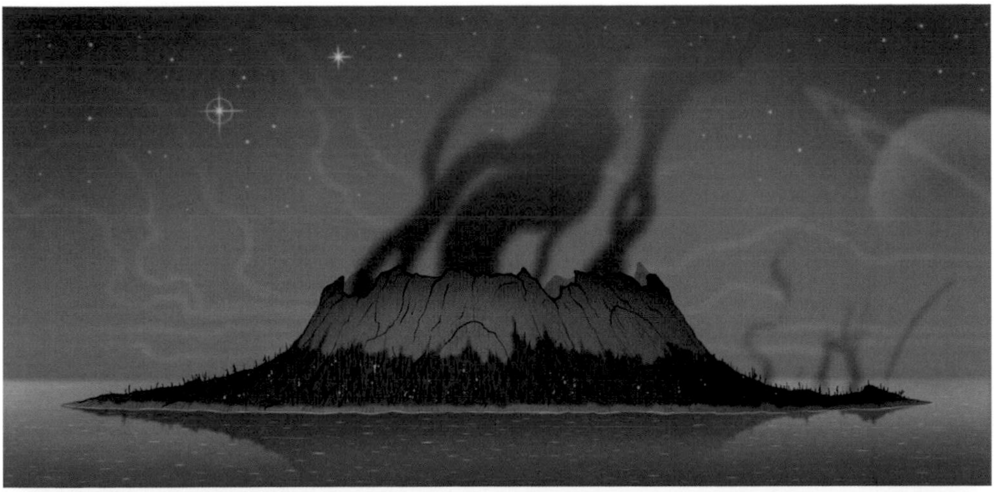

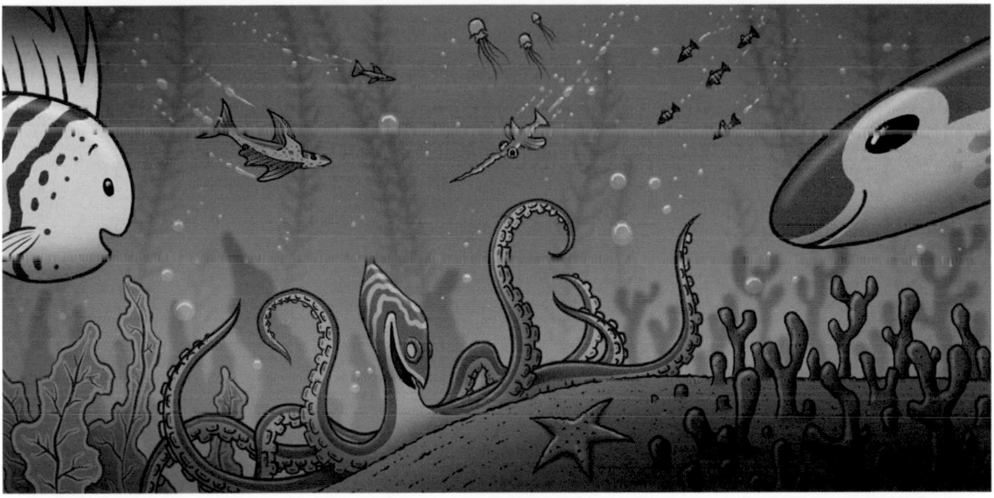

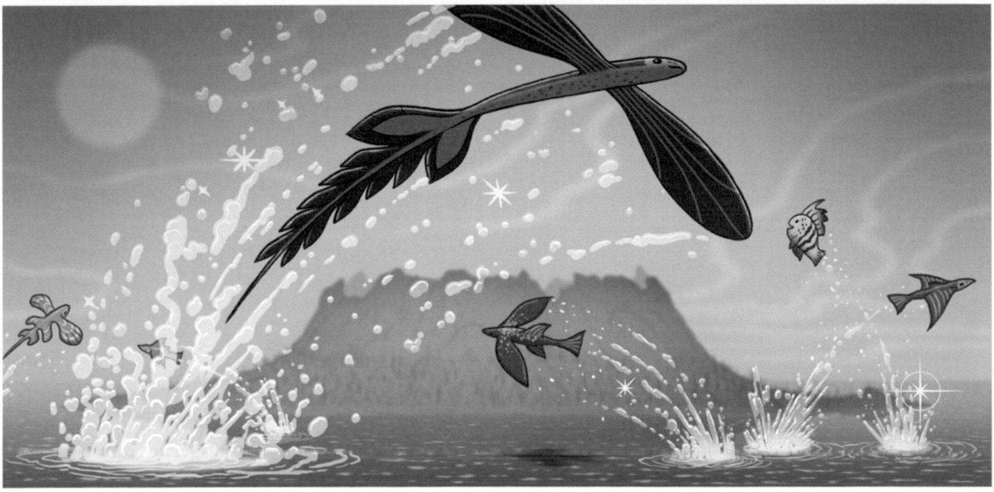

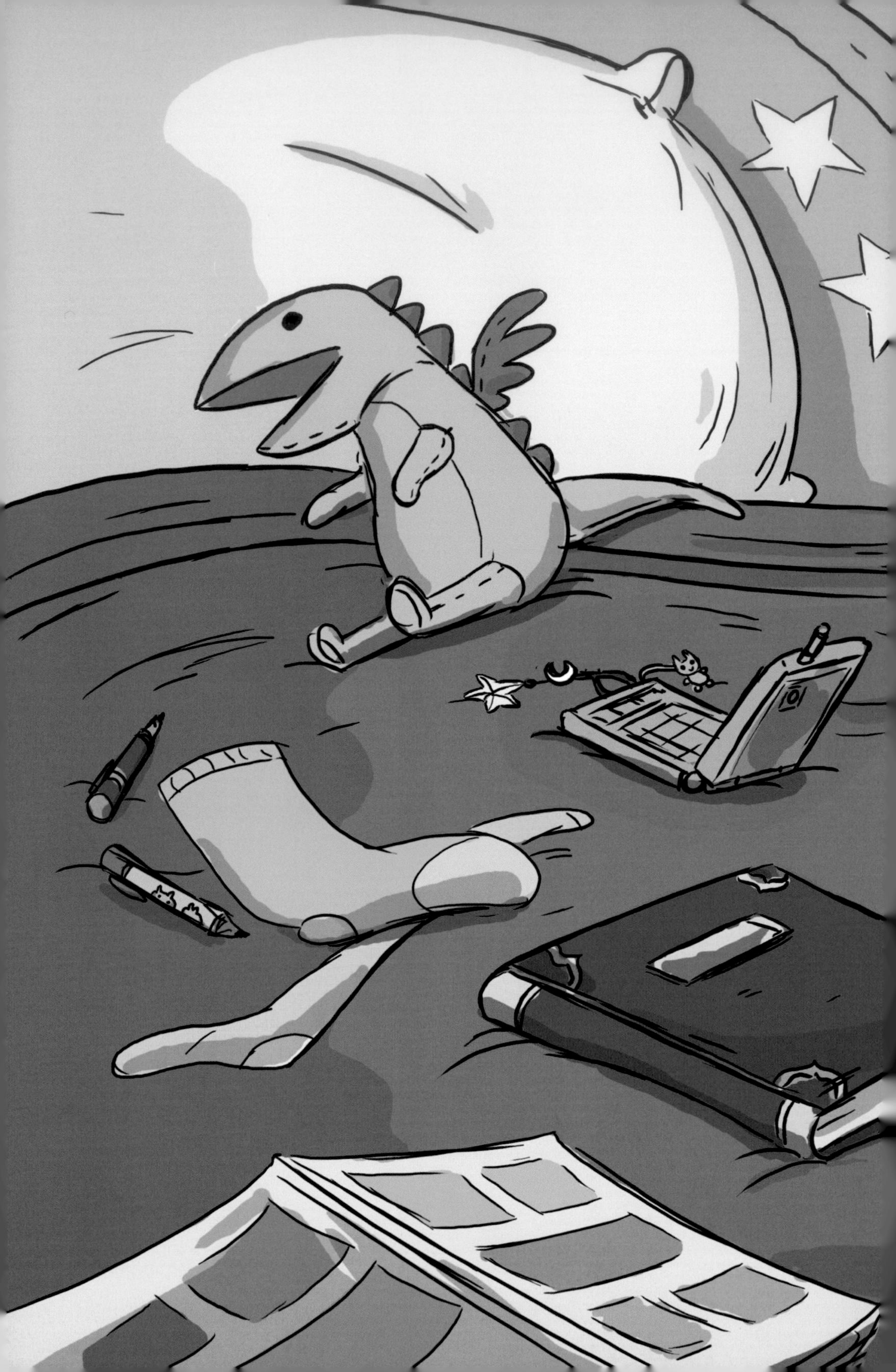

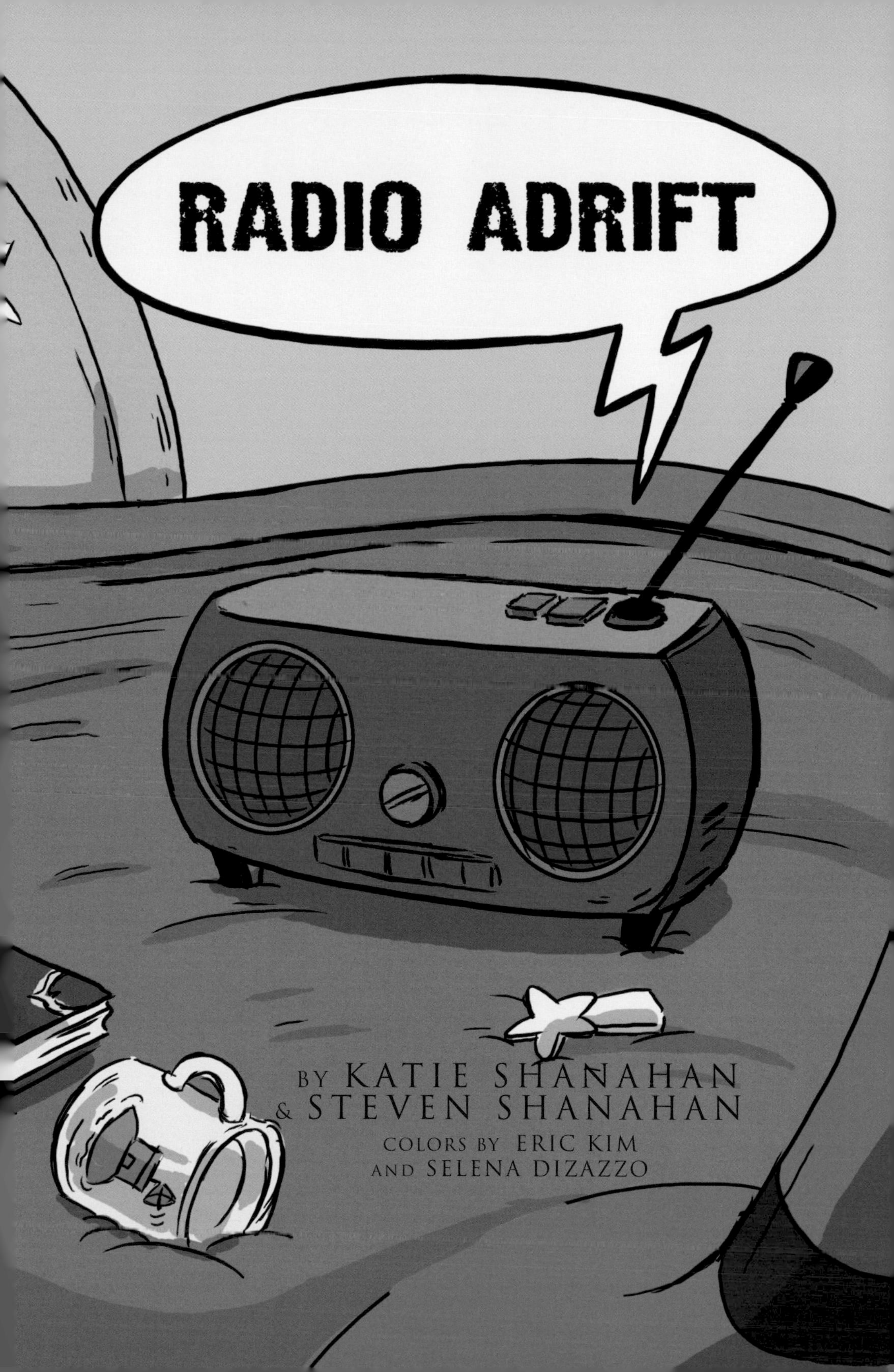
RADIO ADRIFT
BY KATIE SHANAHAN
& STEVEN SHANAHAN
COLORS BY ERIC KIM
AND SELENA DIZAZZO

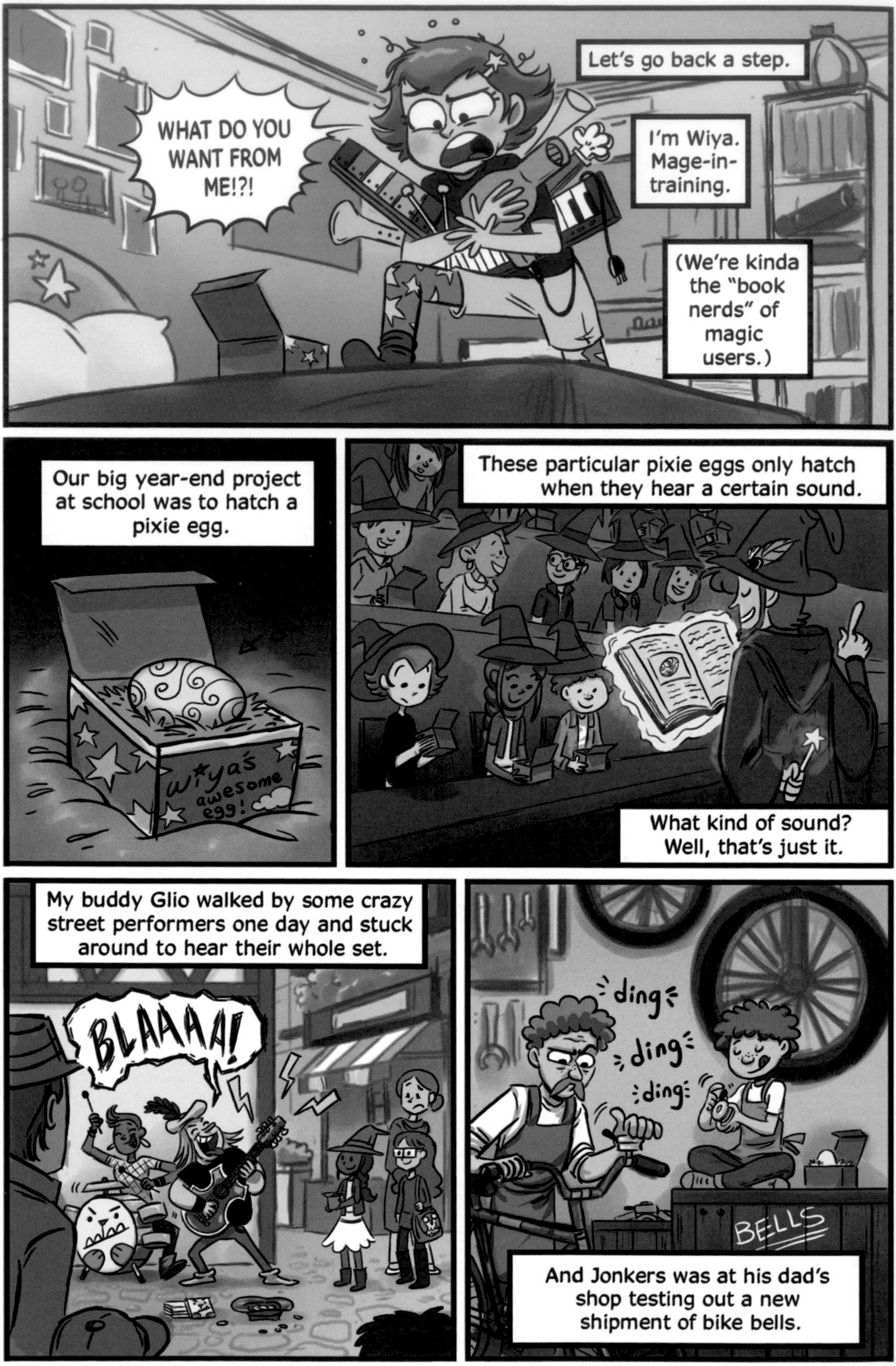
WHAT DO YOU WANT FROM ME!?!
Let's go back a step.
I'm Wiya. Mage-in-training.
(We're kinda the "book nerds" of magic users.)
Our big year-end project at school was to hatch a pixie egg.
Wiya's awesome egg!
These particular pixie eggs only hatch when they hear a certain sound.
What kind of sound? Well, that's just it.
My buddy Glio walked by some crazy street performers one day and stuck around to hear their whole set.
BLAAAA!
ding
ding
ding
BELLS
And Jonkers was at his dad's shop testing out a new shipment of bike bells.

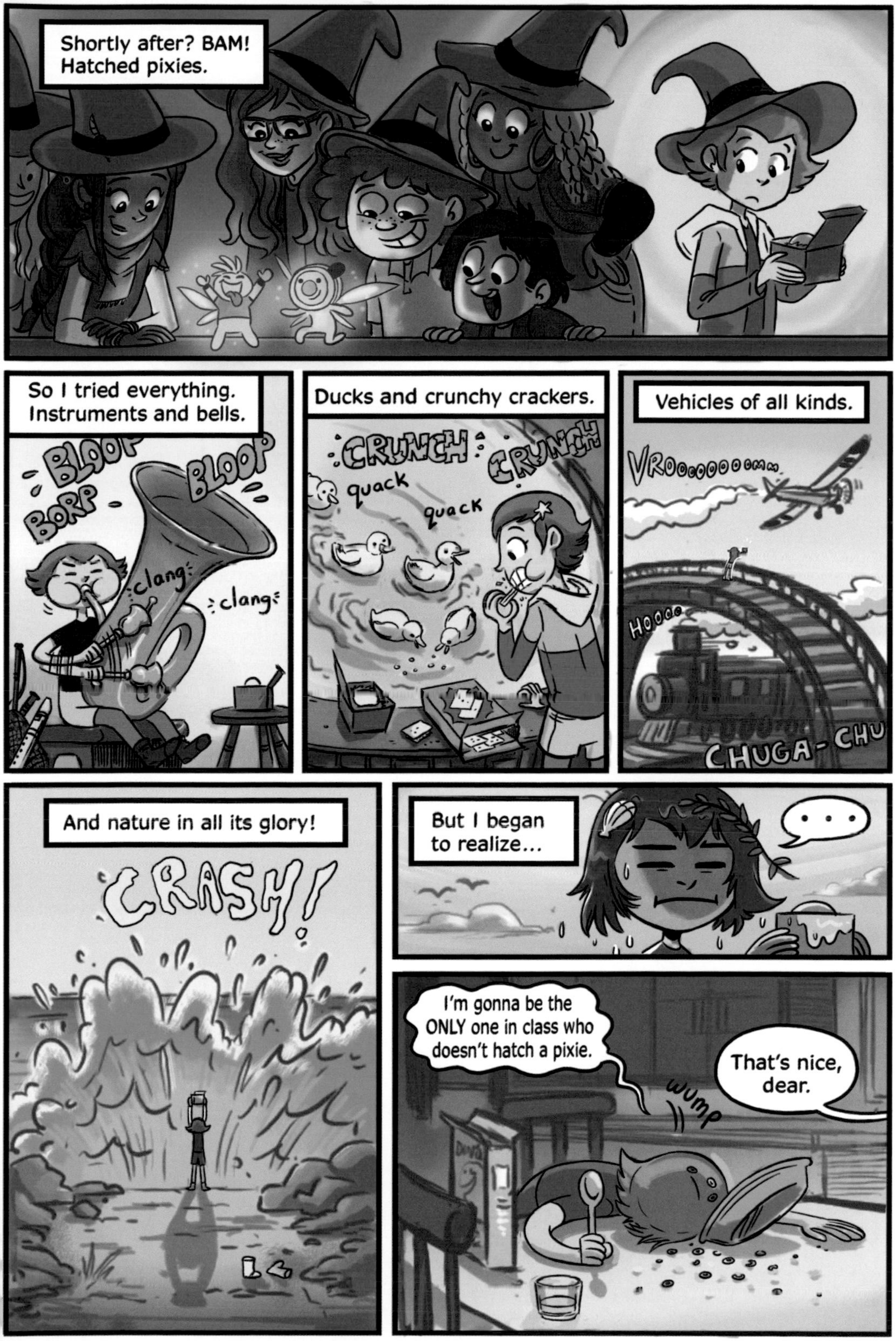
Shortly after? BAM! Hatched pixies.
So I tried everything. Instruments and bells.
BLOOP
BORP
BLOOP
clang
clang
Ducks and crunchy crackers.
CRUNCH
CRUNCH
quack
quack
Vehicles of all kinds.
VROOOOOOOOOMM
HOOOO
CHUGA-CHU
And nature in all its glory!
CRASH!
But I began to realize...
...
I'm gonna be the ONLY one in class who doesn't hatch a pixie.
WUMP
That's nice, dear.

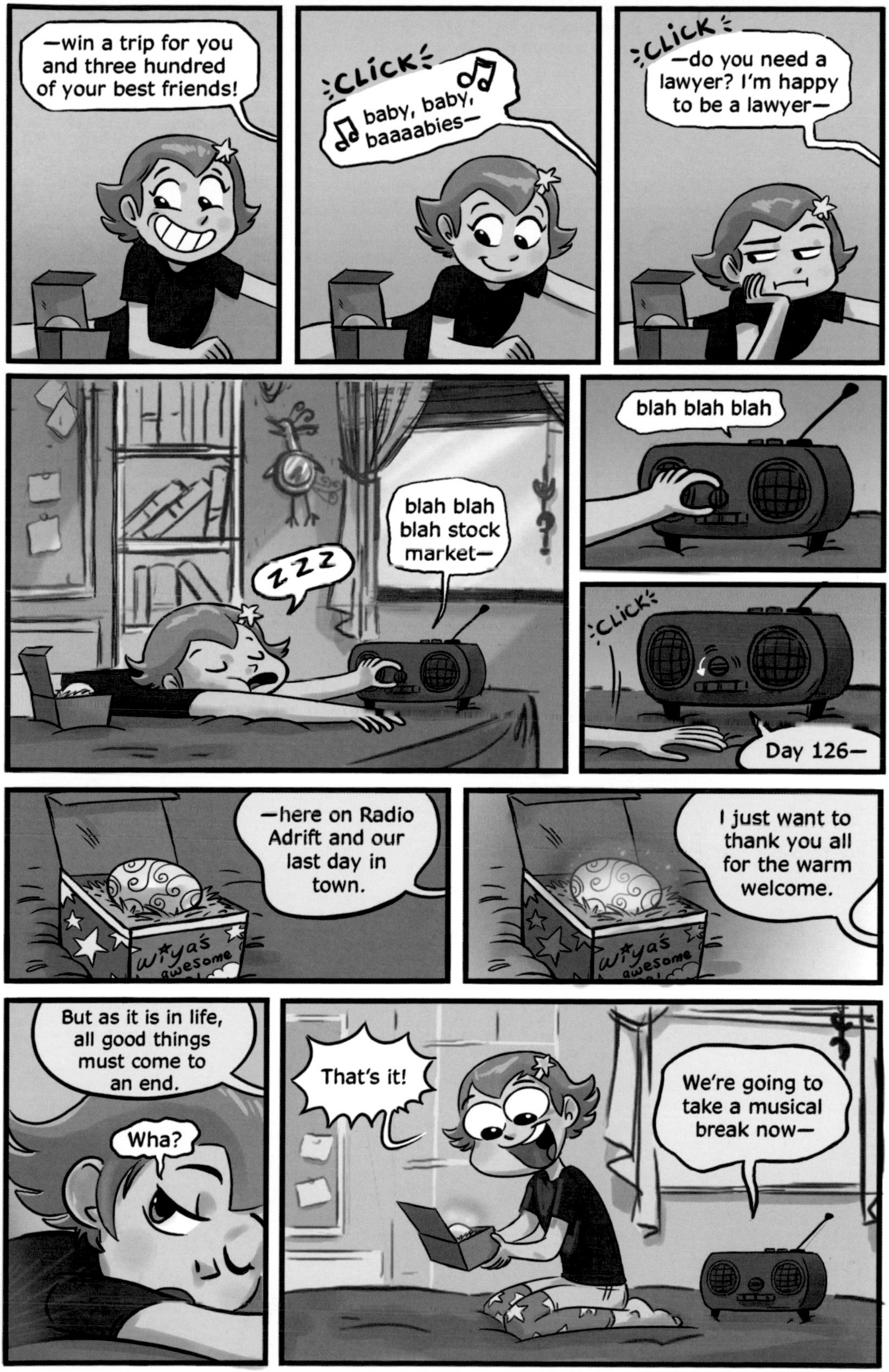
—win a trip for you and three hundred of your best friends!
CLICK
baby, baby, baaaabies—
CLICK
—do you need a lawyer? I'm happy to be a lawyer—
z z z
blah blah blah stock market—
blah blah blah
CLICK
Day 126—
—here on Radio Adrift and our last day in town.
Wiya's awesome
I just want to thank you all for the warm welcome.
Wiya's awesome
But as it is in life, all good things must come to an end.
Wha?
That's it!
We're going to take a musical break now—

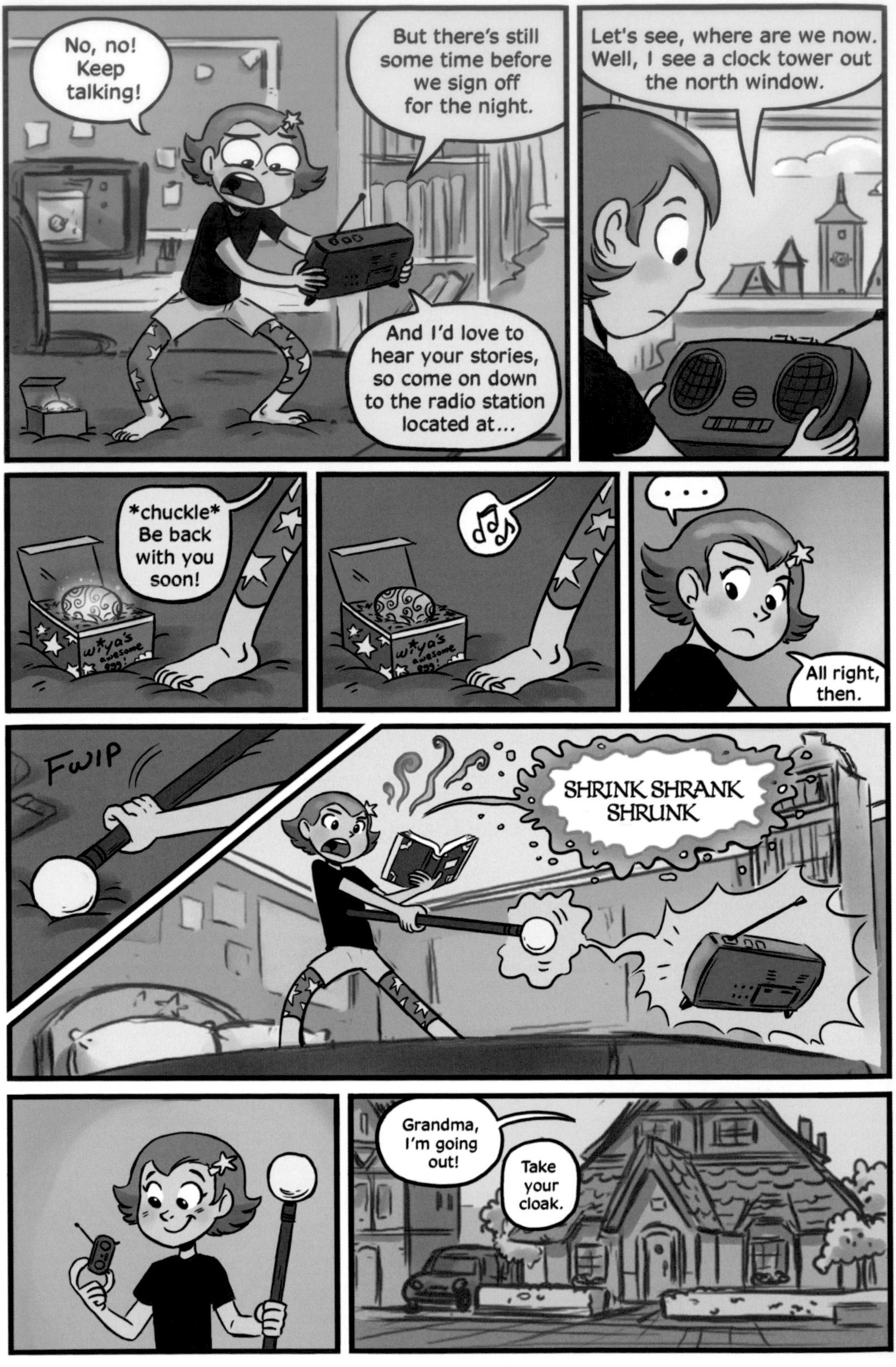
No, no! Keep talking!
But there's still some time before we sign off for the night.
And I'd love to hear your stories, so come on down to the radio station located at...
Let's see, where are we now. Well, I see a clock tower out the north window.
chuckle Be back with you soon!
wiya's awesome egg!
wiya's awesome egg!
. . .
All right, then.
FWIP
SHRINK SHRANK SHRUNK
Grandma, I'm going out!
Take your cloak.

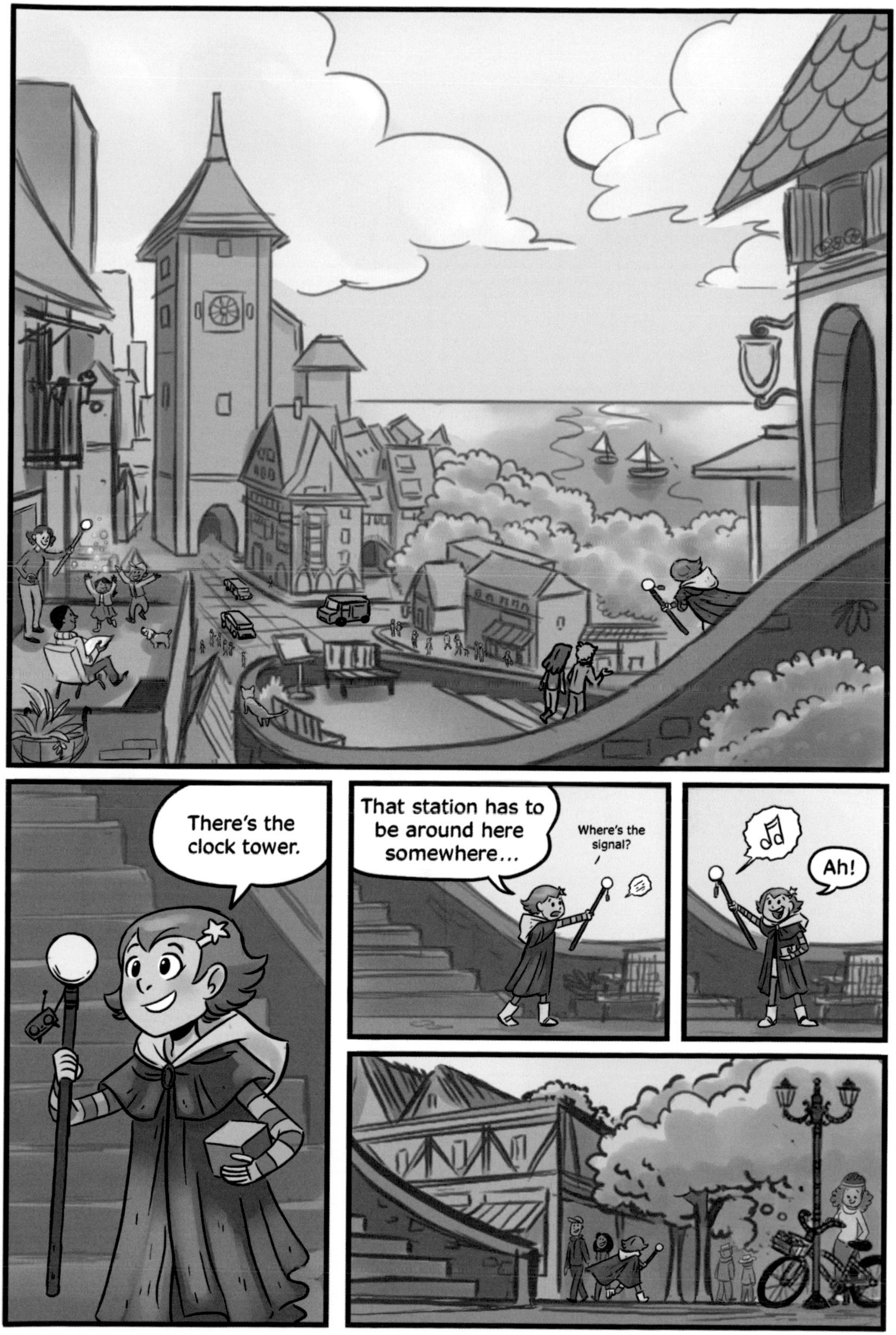
There's the clock tower.
That station has to be around here somewhere...
Where's the signal?
Ah!

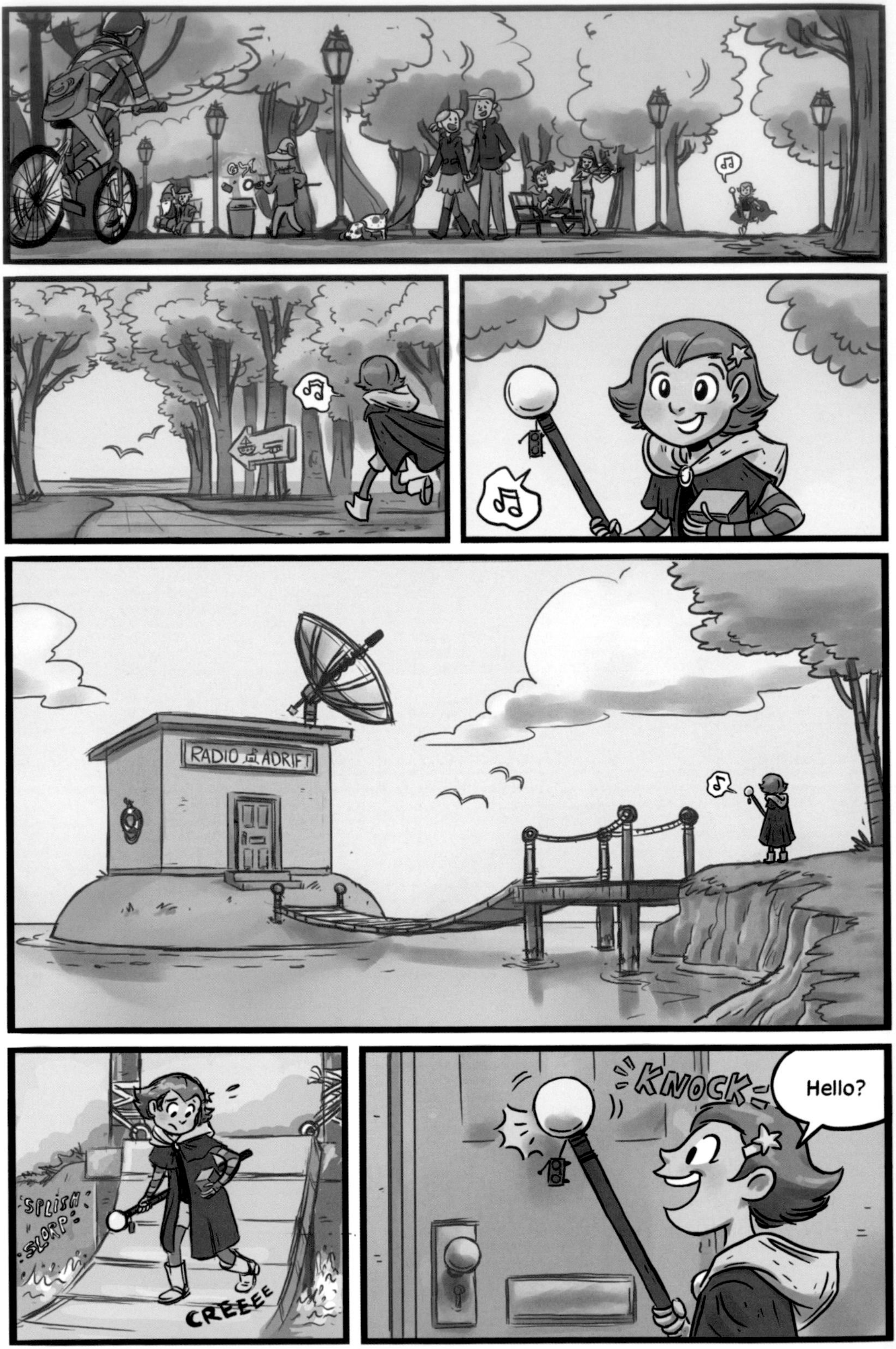
RADIO ADRIFT
SPLISH
SLORP
CREEEE
KNOCK
Hello?

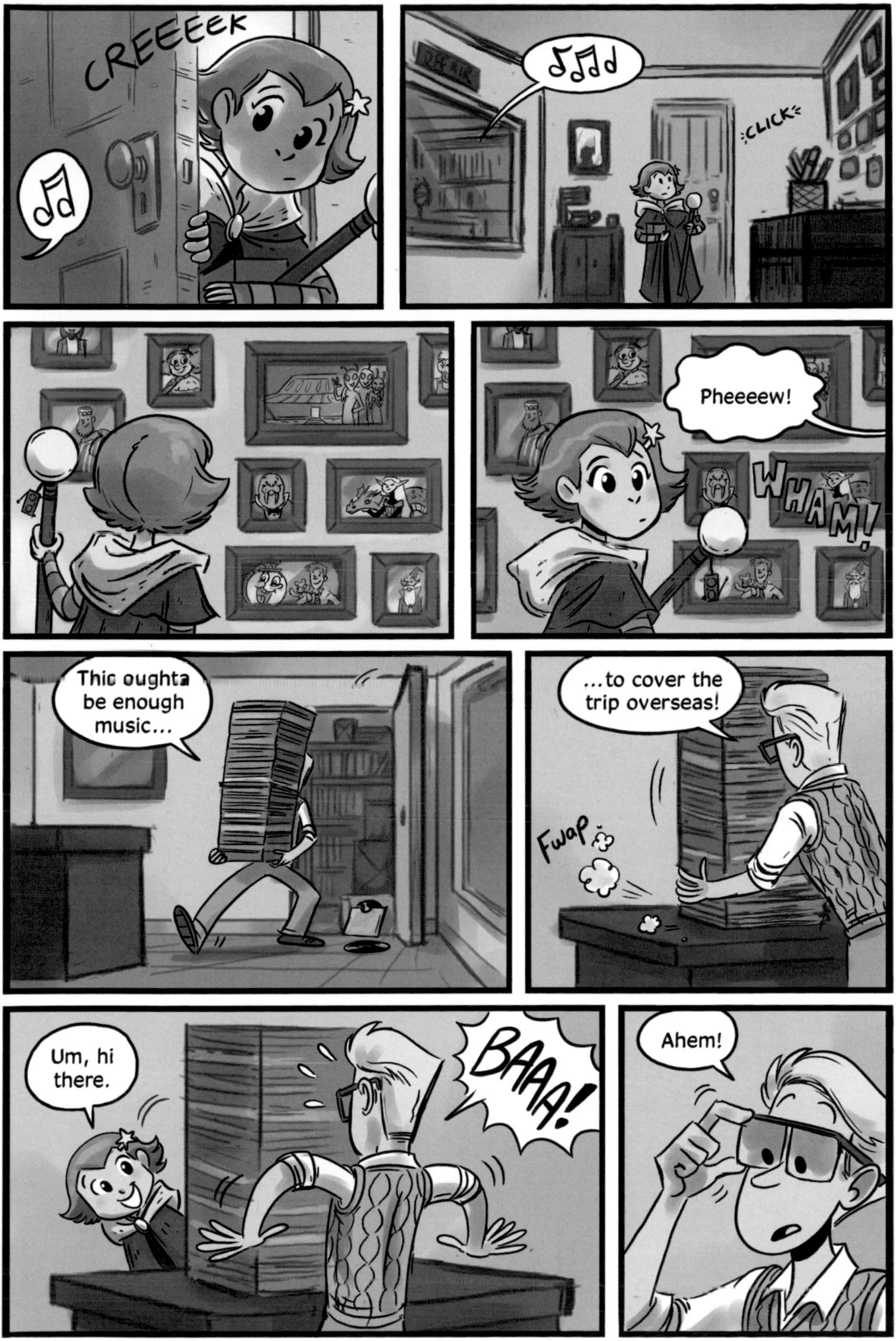
CREEEEK
CLICK
Pheeeew!
WHAM!
This oughta be enough music...
...to cover the trip overseas!
Fwap
Um, hi there.
BAAA!
Ahem!

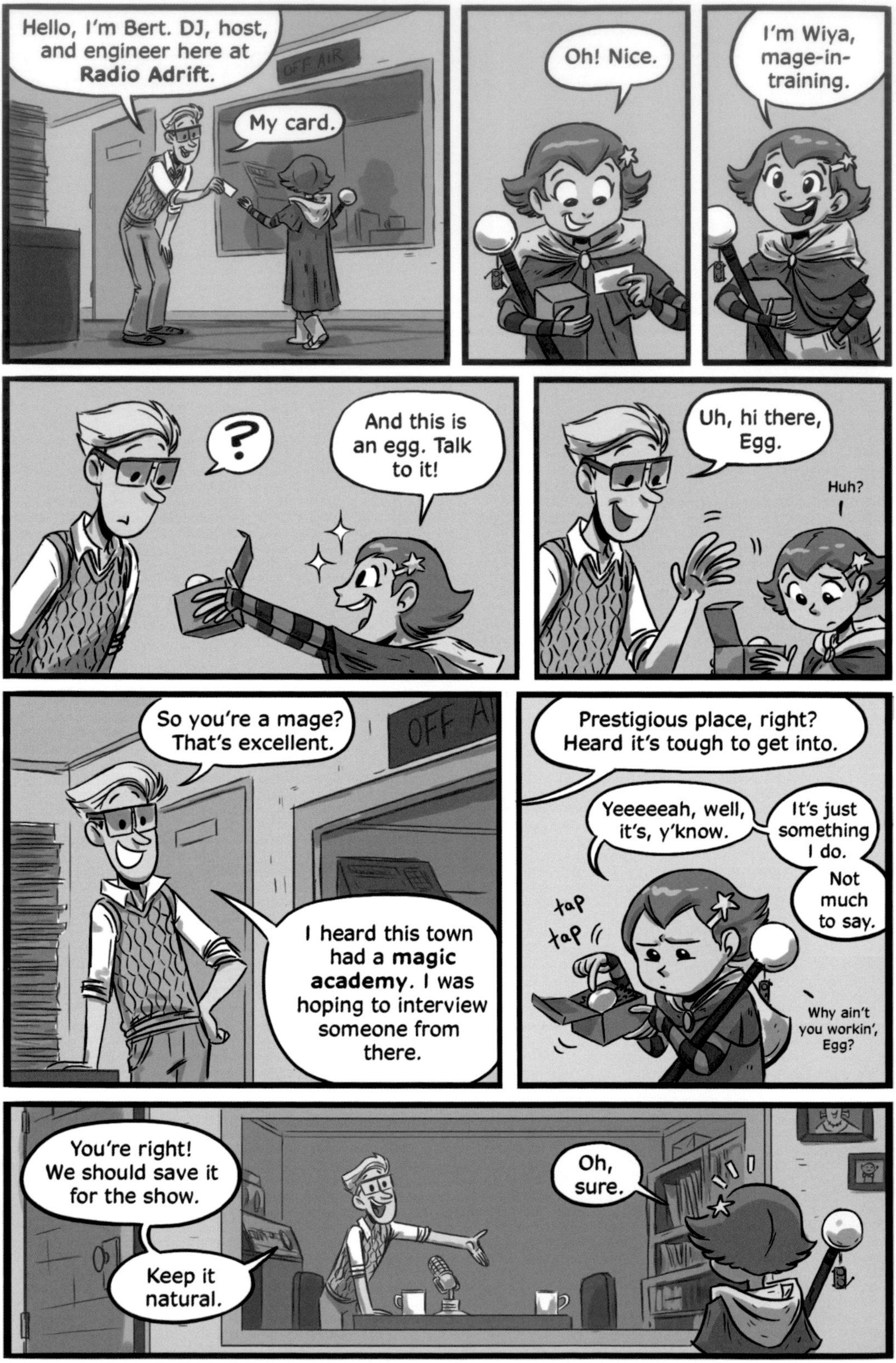

Hello, I'm Bert. DJ, host, and engineer here at **Radio Adrift**.
OFF AIR
My card.
Oh! Nice.
I'm Wiya, mage-in-training.
?
And this is an egg. Talk to it!
Uh, hi there, Egg.
Huh?
So you're a mage? That's excellent.
OFF A
I heard this town had a **magic academy**. I was hoping to interview someone from there.
Prestigious place, right? Heard it's tough to get into.
Yeeeeeah, well, it's, y'know.
It's just something I do.
Not much to say.
tap
tap
Why ain't you workin', Egg?
You're right! We should save it for the show.
Keep it natural.
Oh, sure.

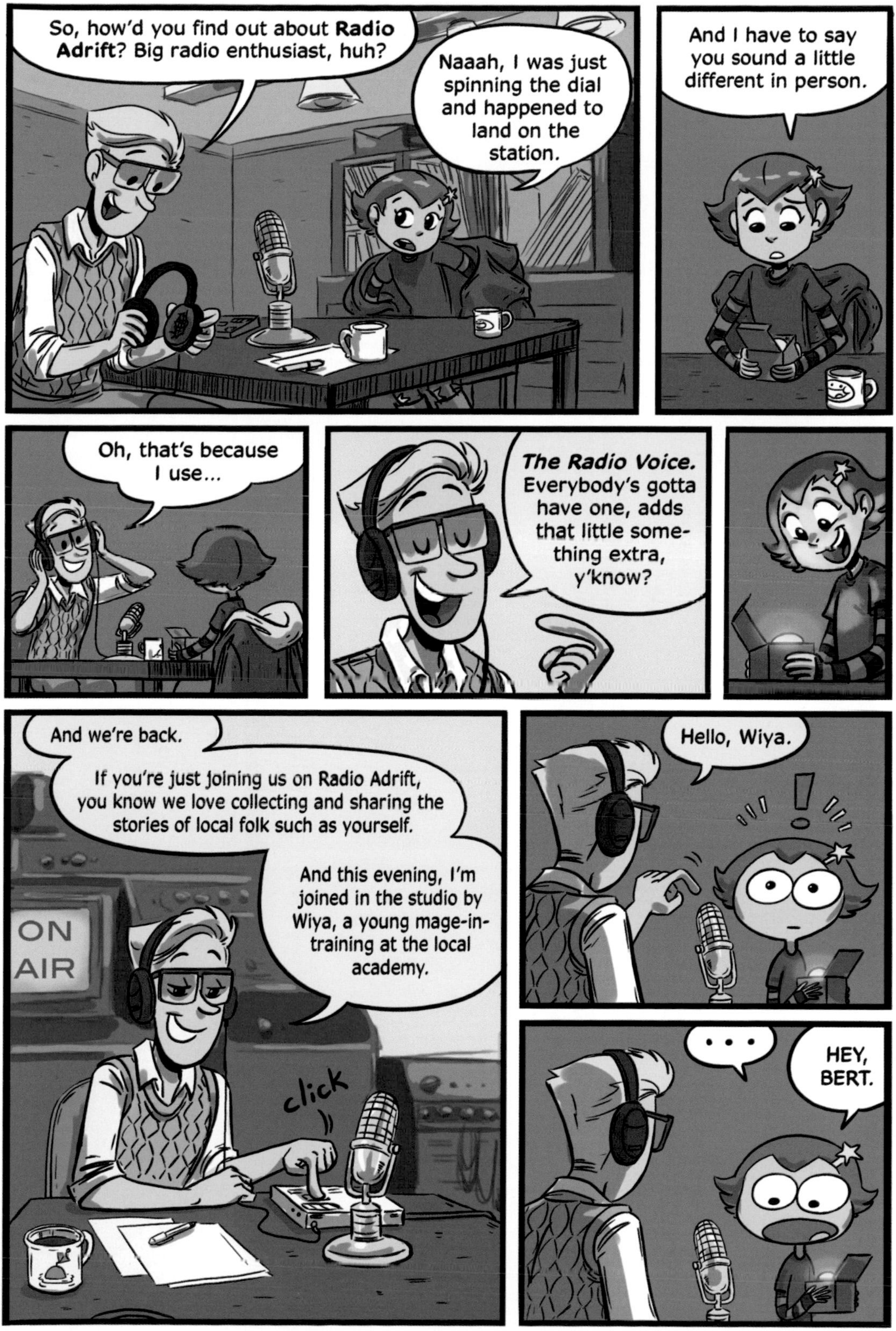

So, how'd you find out about **Radio Adrift**? Big radio enthusiast, huh?
Naaah, I was just spinning the dial and happened to land on the station.
And I have to say you sound a little different in person.
Oh, that's because I use...
The Radio Voice. Everybody's gotta have one, adds that little something extra, y'know?
And we're back.
If you're just joining us on Radio Adrift, you know we love collecting and sharing the stories of local folk such as yourself.
And this evening, I'm joined in the studio by Wiya, a young mage-in-training at the local academy.
ON AIR
click
Hello, Wiya.
!
. . .
HEY, BERT.

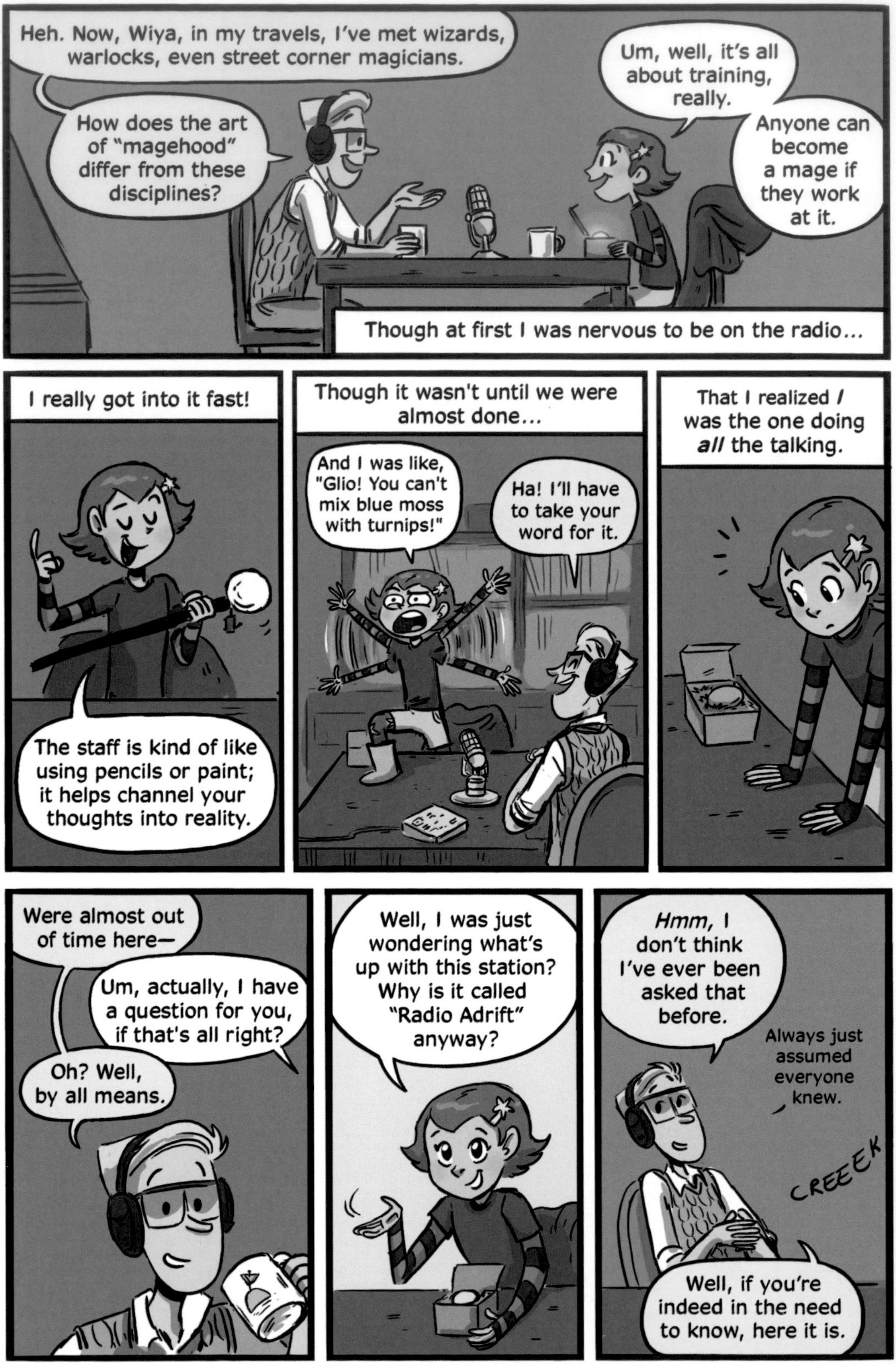
Heh. Now, Wiya, in my travels, I've met wizards, warlocks, even street corner magicians.
How does the art of "magehood" differ from these disciplines?
Um, well, it's all about training, really.
Anyone can become a mage if they work at it.
Though at first I was nervous to be on the radio...
I really got into it fast!
The staff is kind of like using pencils or paint; it helps channel your thoughts into reality.
Though it wasn't until we were almost done...
And I was like, "Glio! You can't mix blue moss with turnips!"
Ha! I'll have to take your word for it.
That I realized *I* was the one doing *all* the talking.
Were almost out of time here—
Um, actually, I have a question for you, if that's all right?
Oh? Well, by all means.
Well, I was just wondering what's up with this station? Why is it called "Radio Adrift" anyway?
Hmm, I don't think I've ever been asked that before.
Always just assumed everyone knew.
CREEEK
Well, if you're indeed in the need to know, here it is.

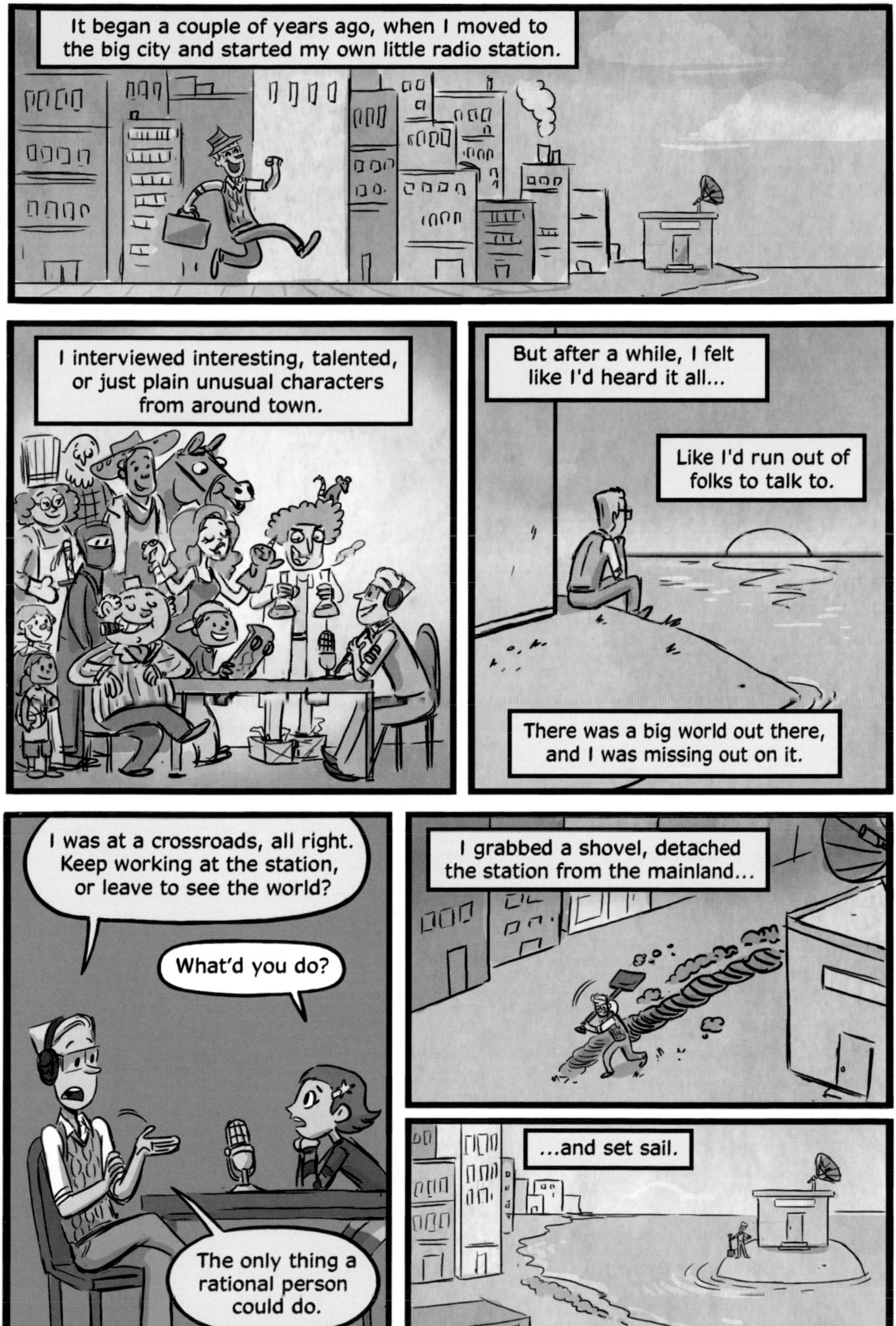
It began a couple of years ago, when I moved to the big city and started my own little radio station.
I interviewed interesting, talented, or just plain unusual characters from around town.
But after a while, I felt like I'd heard it all...
Like I'd run out of folks to talk to.
There was a big world out there, and I was missing out on it.
I was at a crossroads, all right. Keep working at the station, or leave to see the world?
What'd you do?
The only thing a rational person could do.
I grabbed a shovel, detached the station from the mainland...
...and set sail.

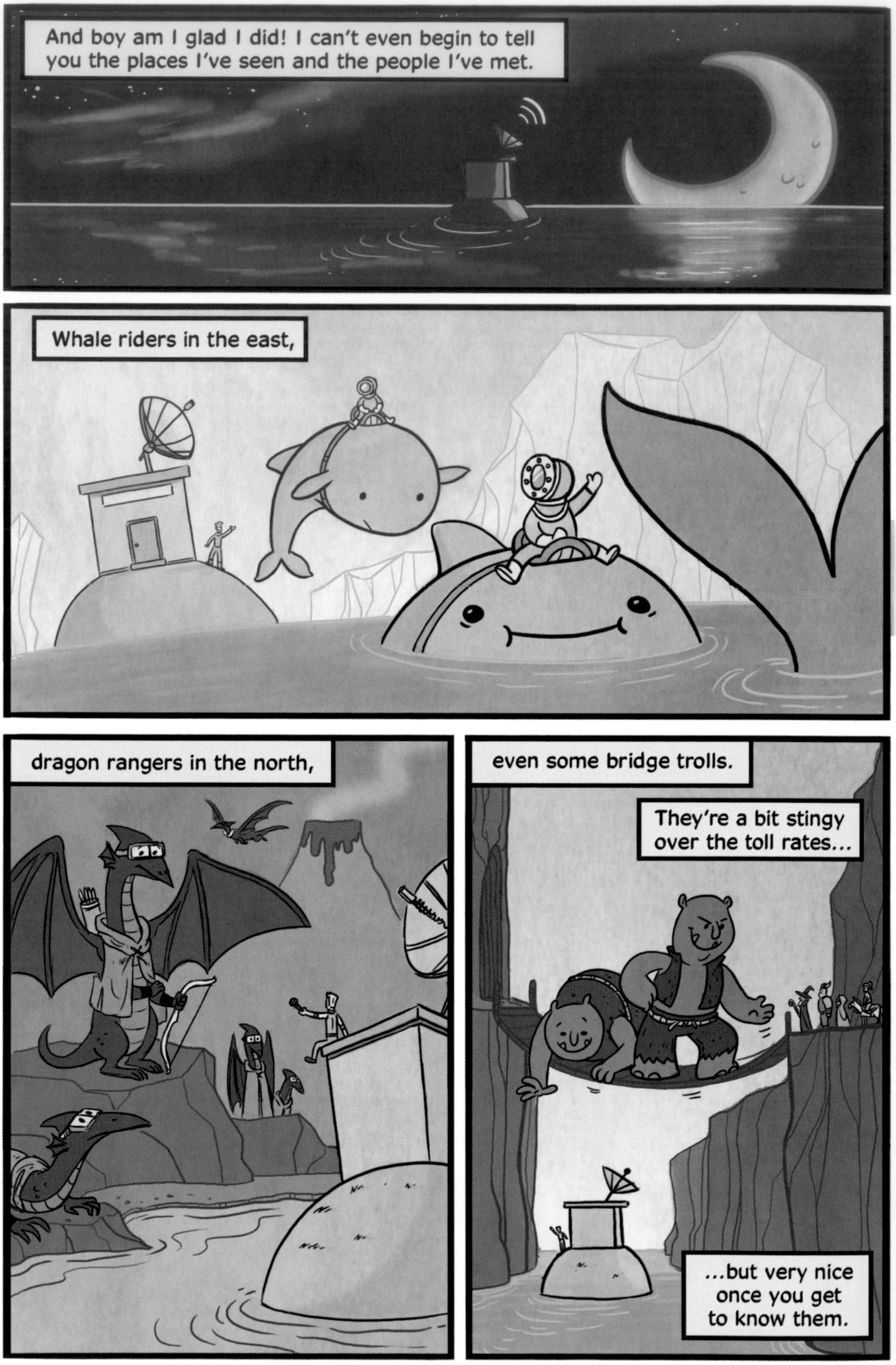
And boy am I glad I did! I can't even begin to tell you the places I've seen and the people I've met.
Whale riders in the east,
dragon rangers in the north,
even some bridge trolls.
They're a bit stingy over the toll rates...
...but very nice once you get to know them.

From the looks of these photos, seems like you got everybody to chat with you.

Oh, it was tricky at times.

When I offered the microphone to some guests, they tried to eat it. *chuckle*

Now, is it just me...

...or is that egg about to—

Huh?

Oh m'gosh!

Wi'ya's awesome egg!

vreeee

Wi'ya's awesome egg!

SHA-BOOM!

TA-DAH!

For you listeners at home, this is by far the strangest thing to happen here on Radio Adrift.

eeee!

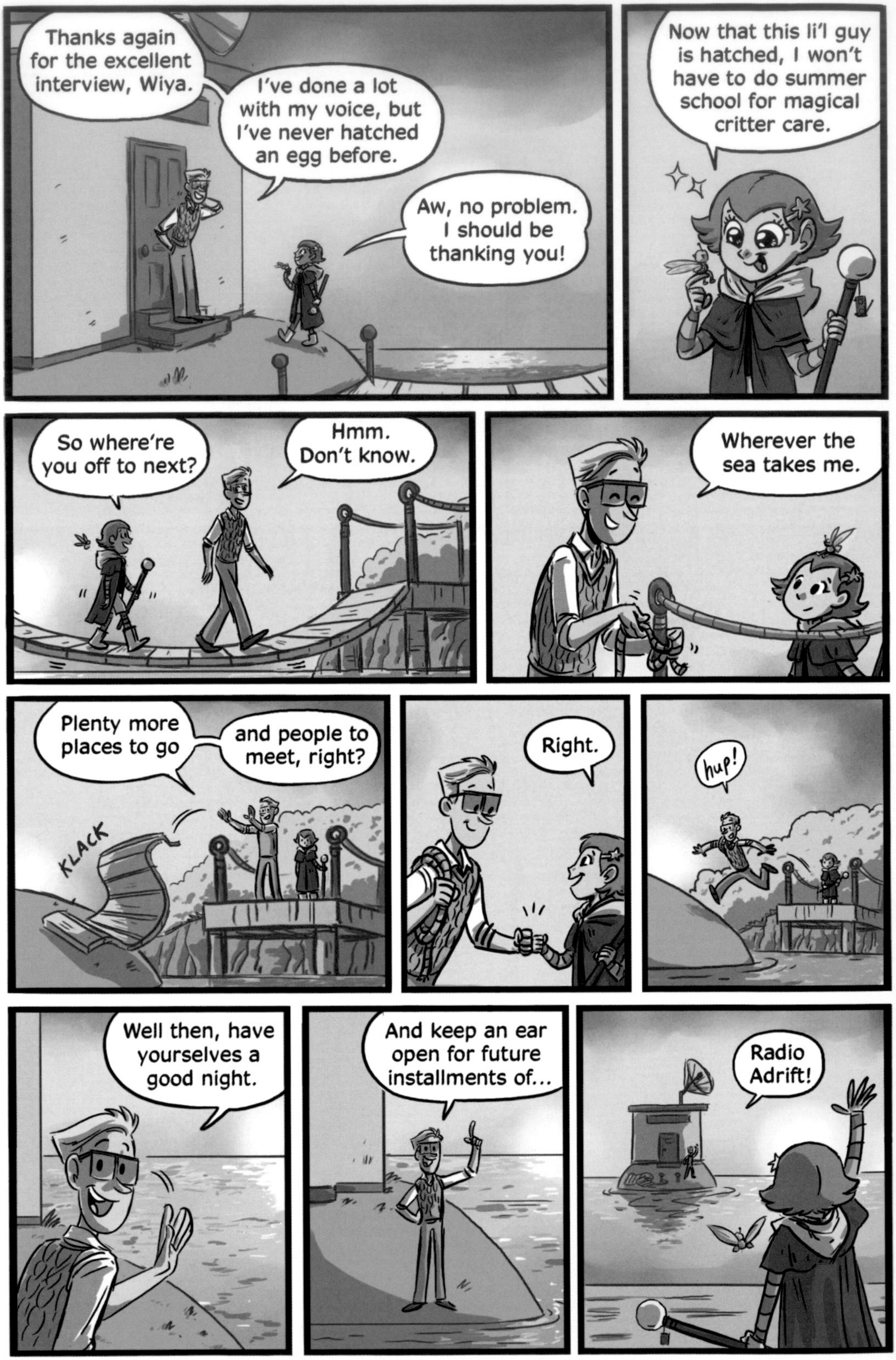
Thanks again for the excellent interview, Wiya.
I've done a lot with my voice, but I've never hatched an egg before.
Aw, no problem. I should be thanking you!
Now that this li'l guy is hatched, I won't have to do summer school for magical critter care.
So where're you off to next?
Hmm. Don't know.
Wherever the sea takes me.
Plenty more places to go
and people to meet, right?
KLACK
Right.
hup!
Well then, have yourselves a good night.
And keep an ear open for future installments of...
Radio Adrift!

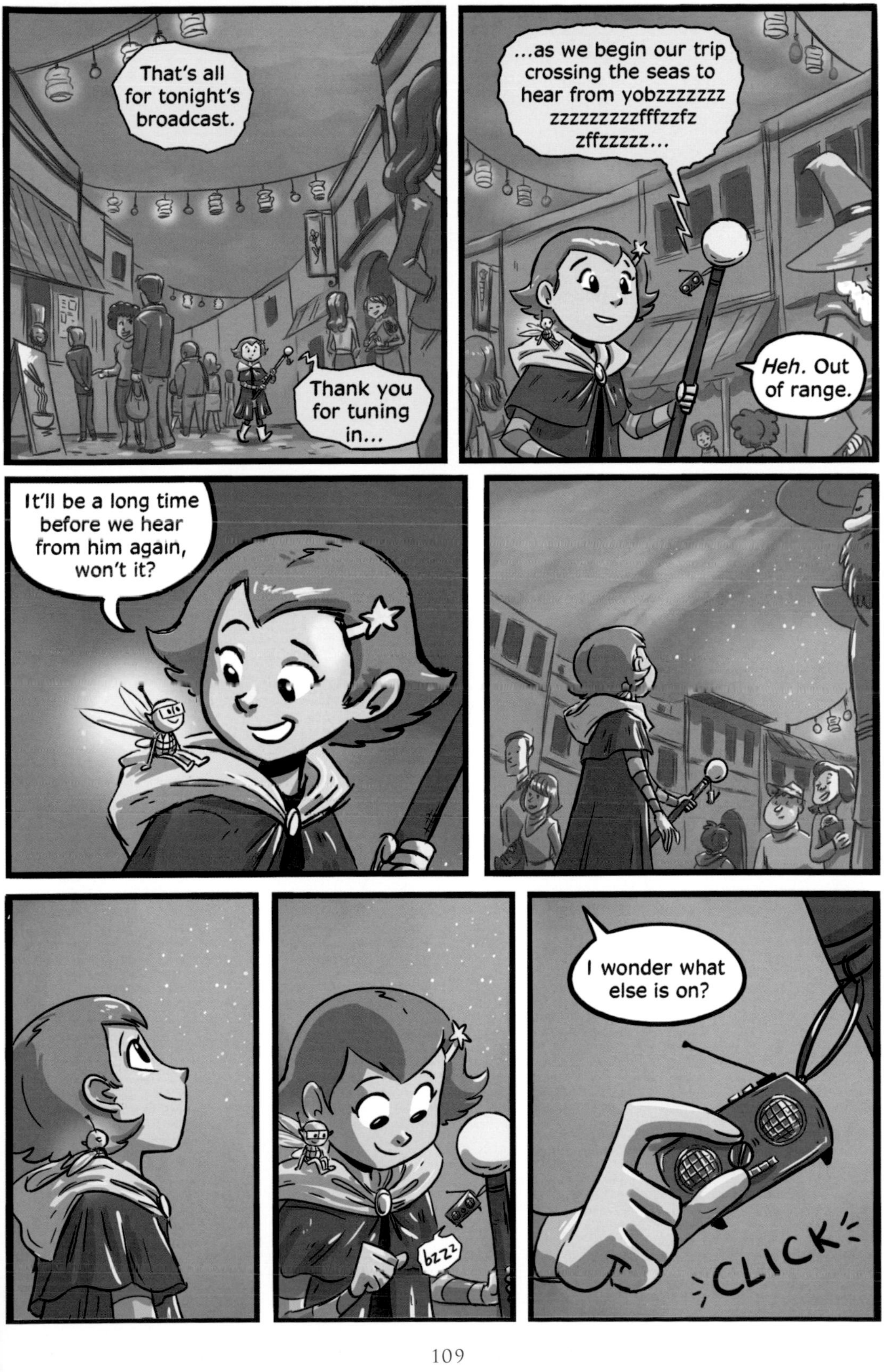
That's all for tonight's broadcast.
Thank you for tuning in...
...as we begin our trip crossing the seas to hear from yobzzzzzzz zzzzzzzzzfffzzfz zffzzzzz...
Heh. Out of range.
It'll be a long time before we hear from him again, won't it?
bzzz
I wonder what else is on?
CLICK

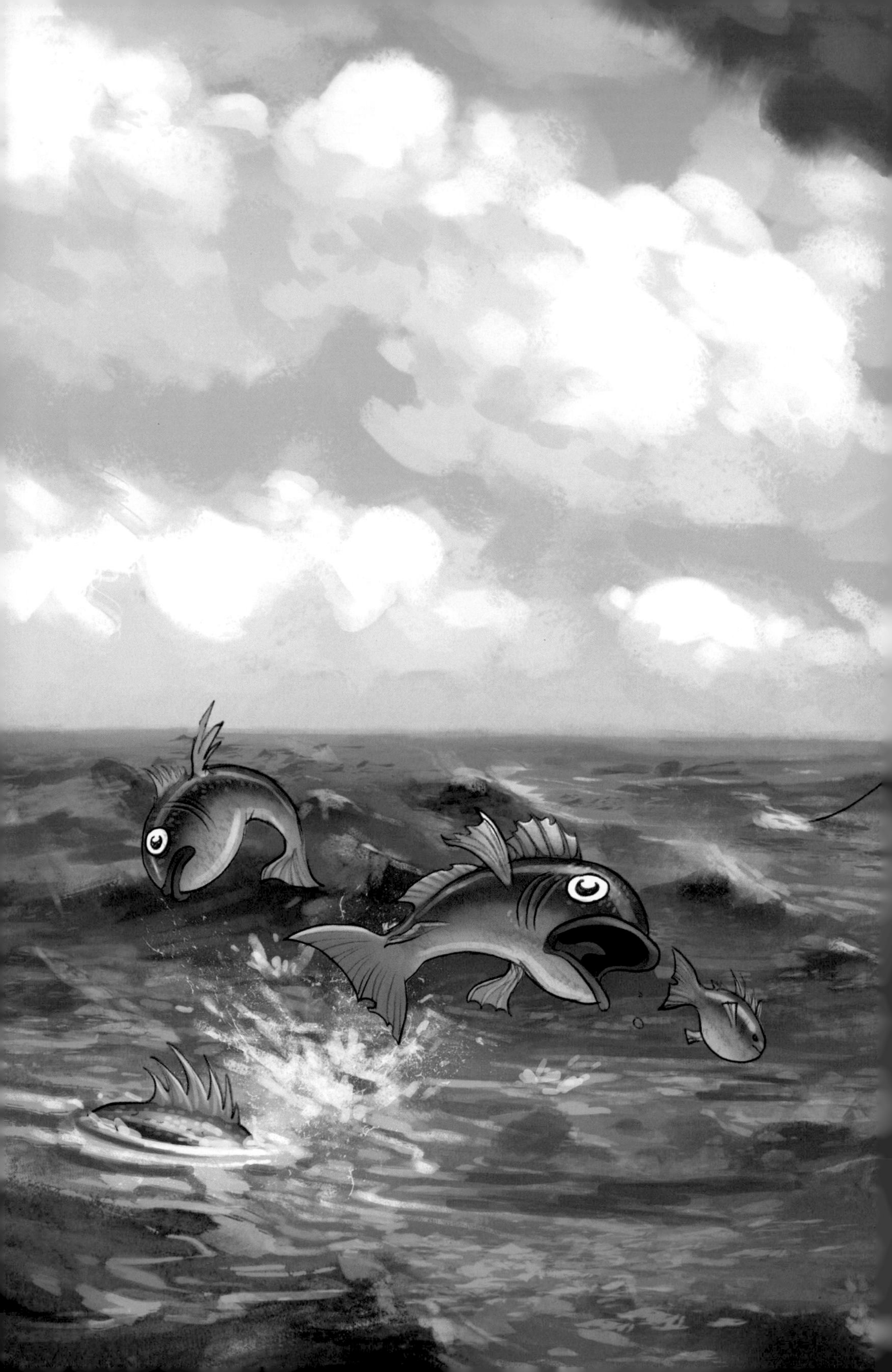

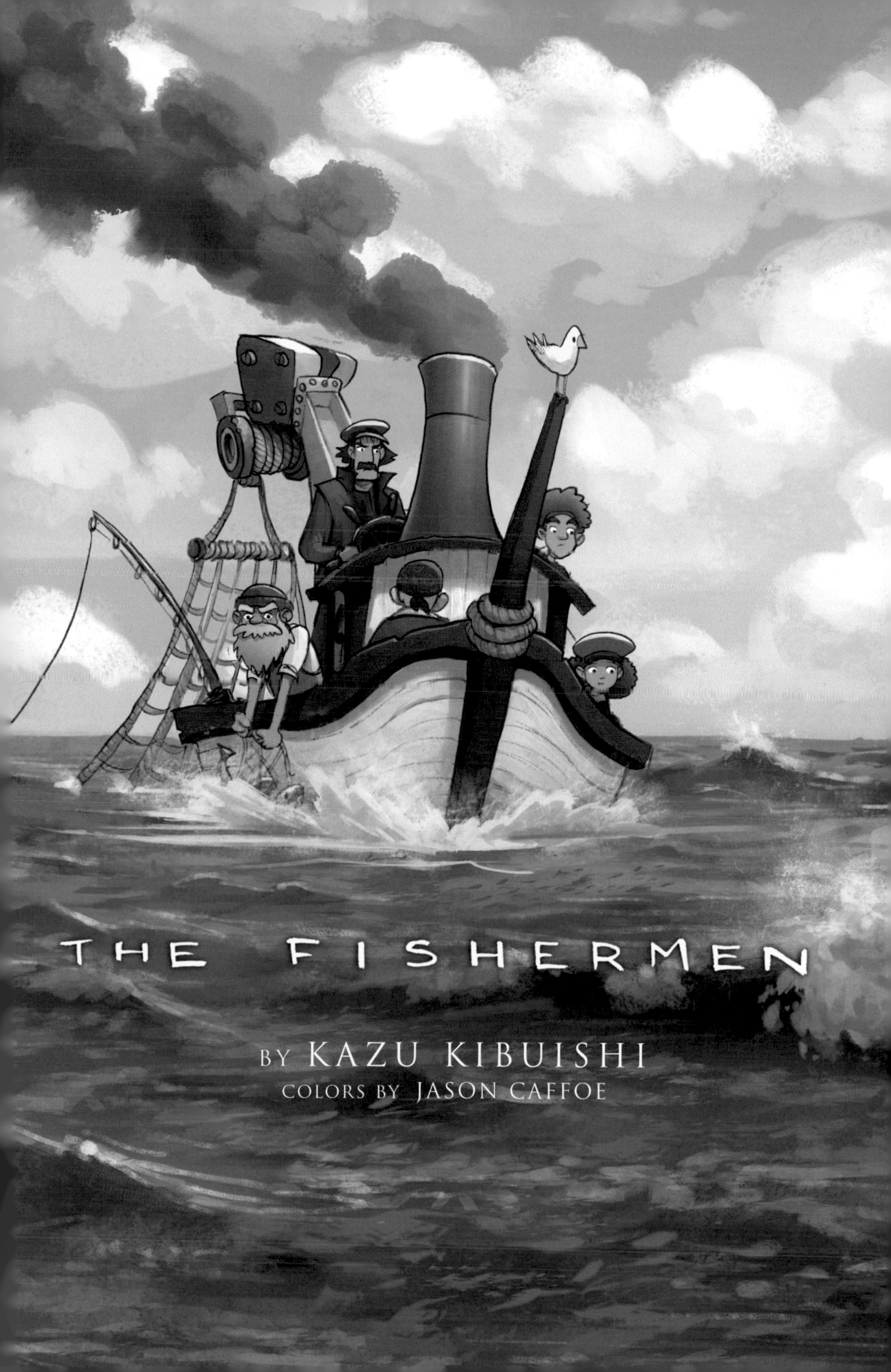

THE FISHERMEN

BY KAZU KIBUISHI

COLORS BY JASON CAFFOE

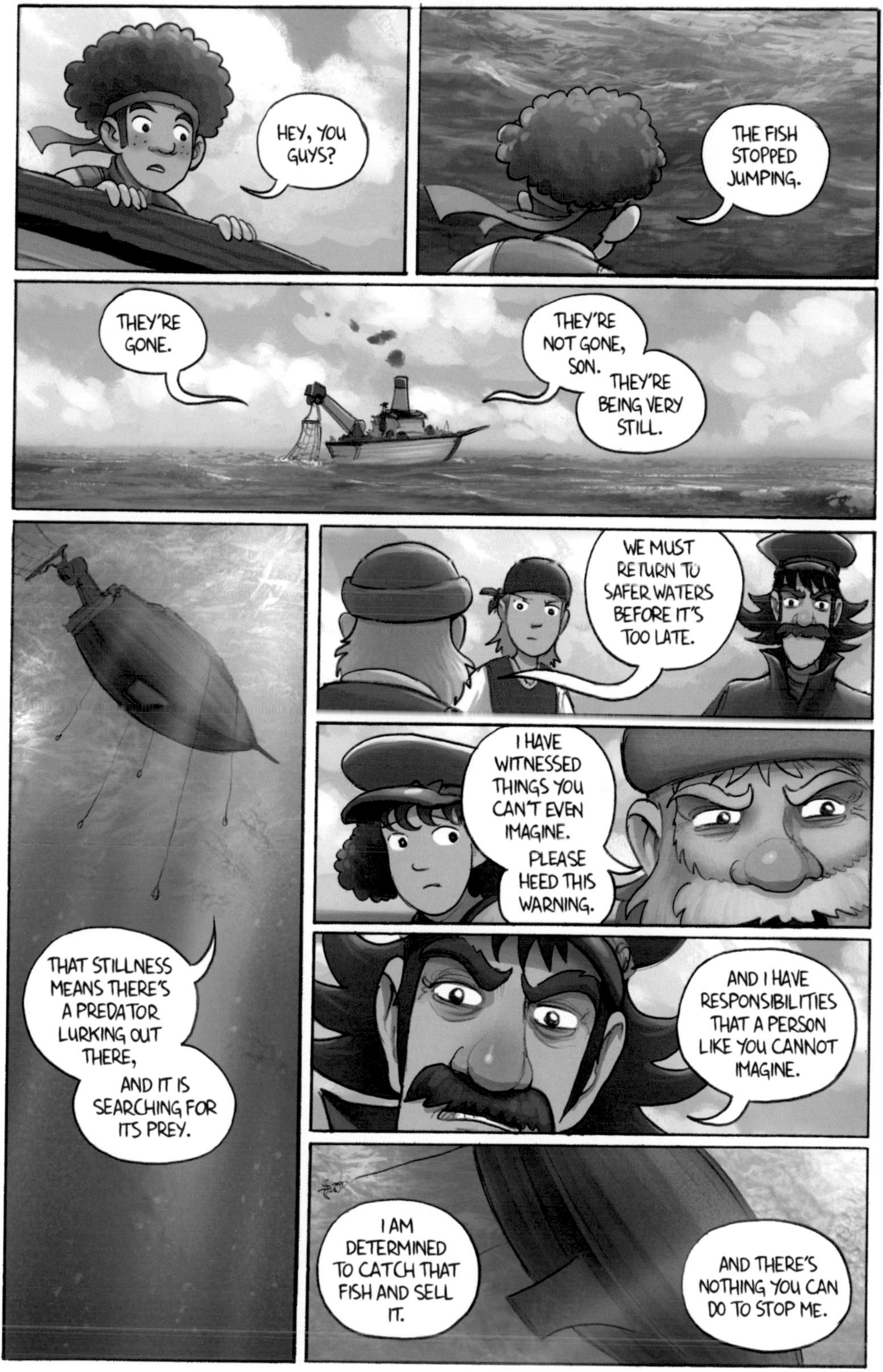
HEY, YOU GUYS?
THE FISH STOPPED JUMPING.
THEY'RE GONE.
THEY'RE NOT GONE, SON.
THEY'RE BEING VERY STILL.
THAT STILLNESS MEANS THERE'S A PREDATOR LURKING OUT THERE,
AND IT IS SEARCHING FOR ITS PREY.
WE MUST RETURN TO SAFER WATERS BEFORE IT'S TOO LATE.
I HAVE WITNESSED THINGS YOU CAN'T EVEN IMAGINE.
PLEASE HEED THIS WARNING.
AND I HAVE RESPONSIBILITIES THAT A PERSON LIKE YOU CANNOT IMAGINE.
I AM DETERMINED TO CATCH THAT FISH AND SELL IT.
AND THERE'S NOTHING YOU CAN DO TO STOP ME.

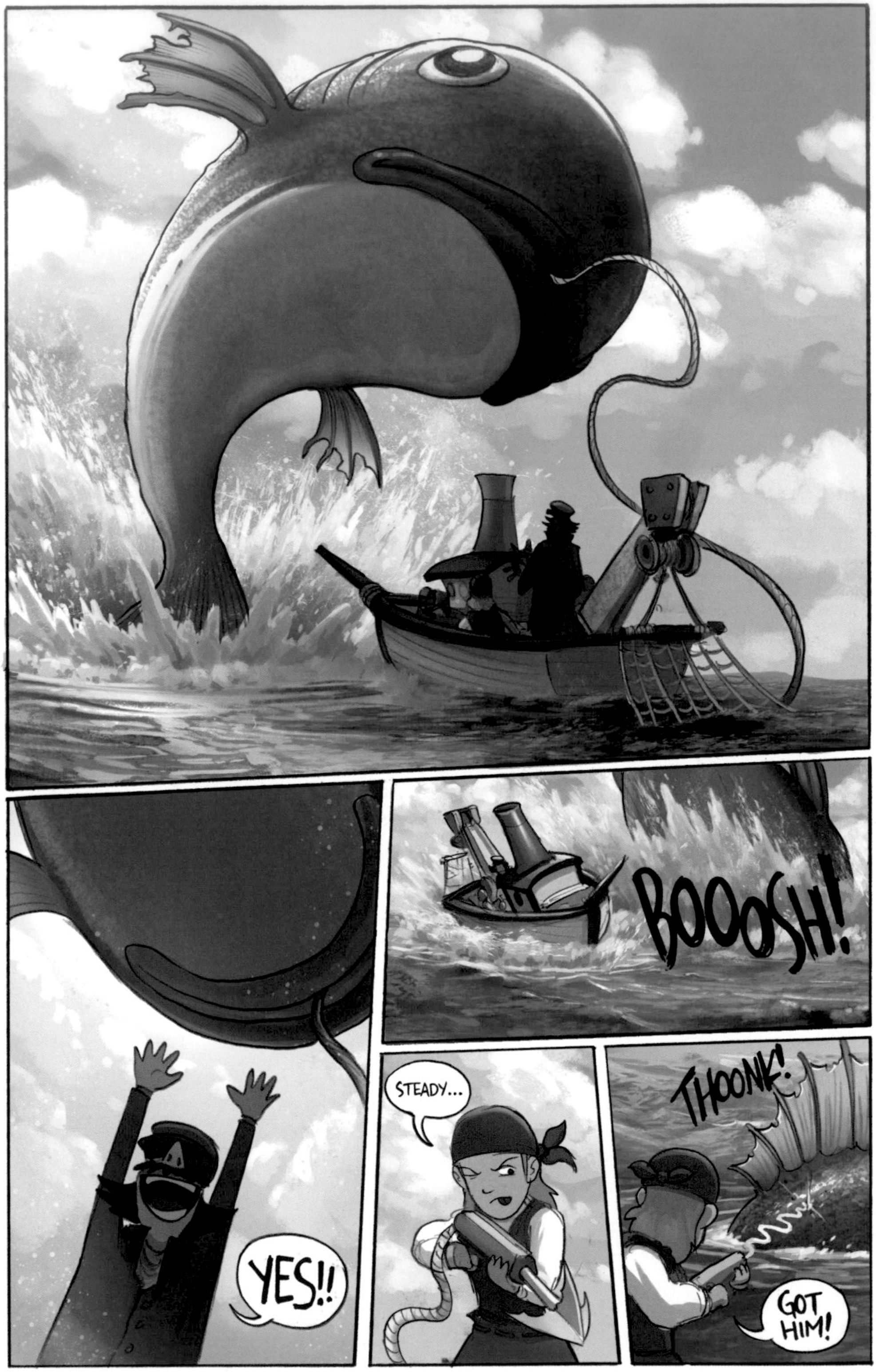
BOOOSH!
YES!!
STEADY...
THOONK!
GOT HIM!

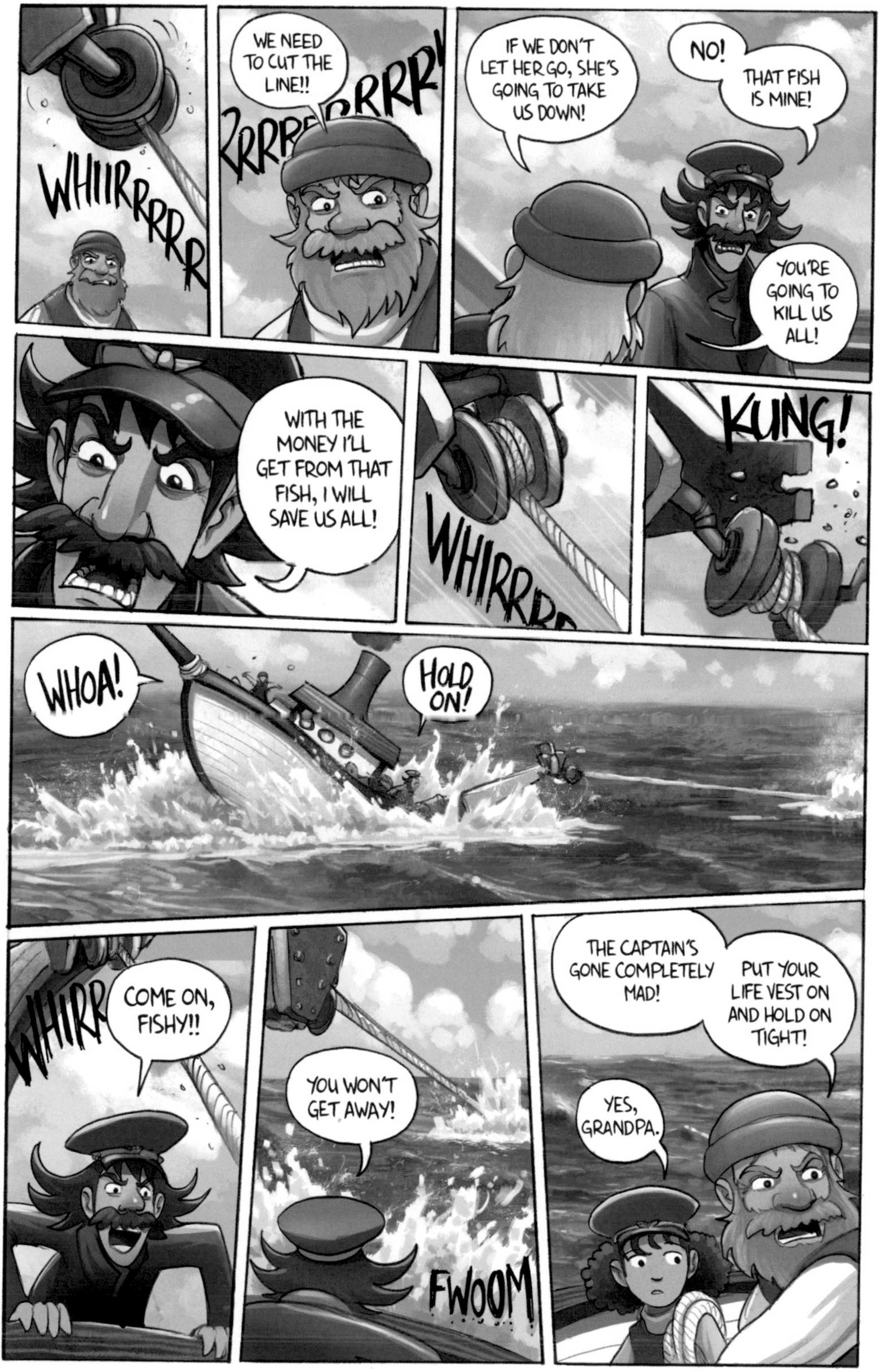

WHIIRRRRR
WE NEED TO CUT THE LINE!!
RRRRRRRRR!
IF WE DON'T LET HER GO, SHE'S GOING TO TAKE US DOWN!
NO!
THAT FISH IS MINE!
YOU'RE GOING TO KILL US ALL!
WITH THE MONEY I'LL GET FROM THAT FISH, I WILL SAVE US ALL!
WHIRRRR
KUNG!
WHOA!
HOLD ON!
WHIRR
COME ON, FISHY!!
YOU WON'T GET AWAY!
FWOOM
THE CAPTAIN'S GONE COMPLETELY MAD!
PUT YOUR LIFE VEST ON AND HOLD ON TIGHT!
YES, GRANDPA.

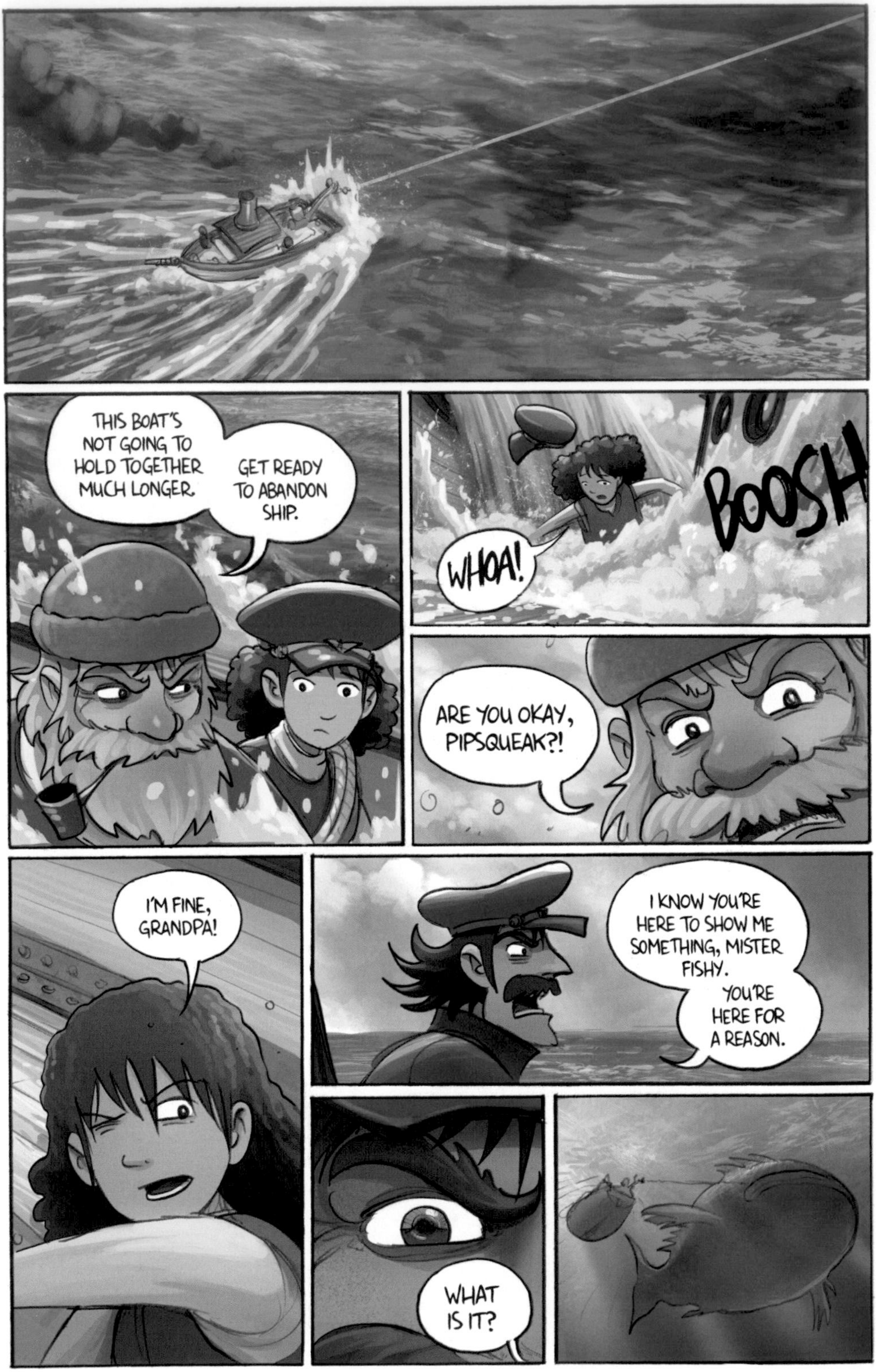
THIS BOAT'S NOT GOING TO HOLD TOGETHER MUCH LONGER.
GET READY TO ABANDON SHIP.
WHOA!
BOOSH
ARE YOU OKAY, PIPSQUEAK?!
I'M FINE, GRANDPA!
I KNOW YOU'RE HERE TO SHOW ME SOMETHING, MISTER FISHY.
YOU'RE HERE FOR A REASON.
WHAT IS IT?

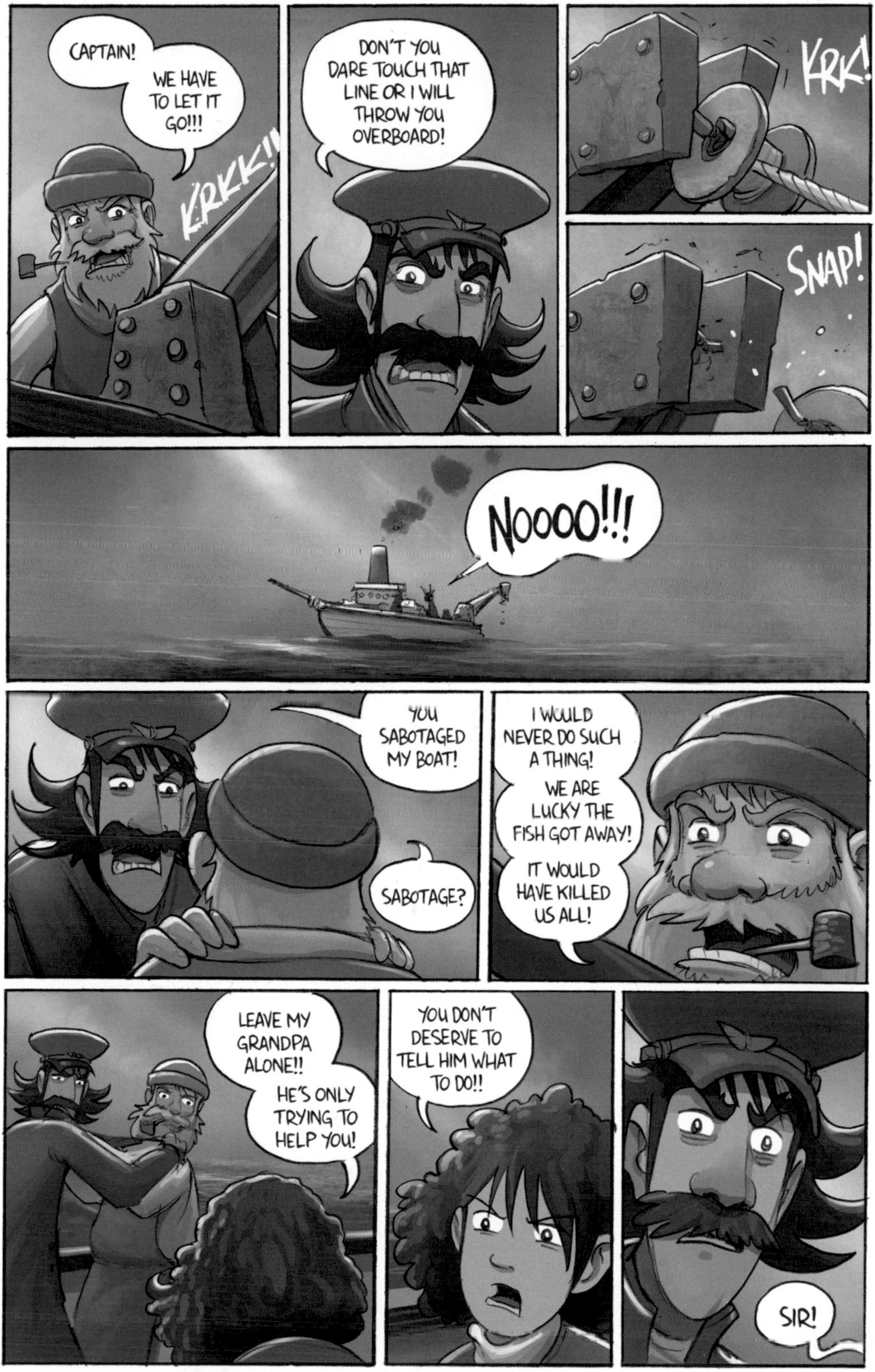
CAPTAIN!
WE HAVE TO LET IT GO!!!
KRKK!!
DON'T YOU DARE TOUCH THAT LINE OR I WILL THROW YOU OVERBOARD!
KRK!
SNAP!
NOOOO!!!
YOU SABOTAGED MY BOAT!
SABOTAGE?
I WOULD NEVER DO SUCH A THING!
WE ARE LUCKY THE FISH GOT AWAY!
IT WOULD HAVE KILLED US ALL!
LEAVE MY GRANDPA ALONE!!
HE'S ONLY TRYING TO HELP YOU!
YOU DON'T DESERVE TO TELL HIM WHAT TO DO!!
SIR!

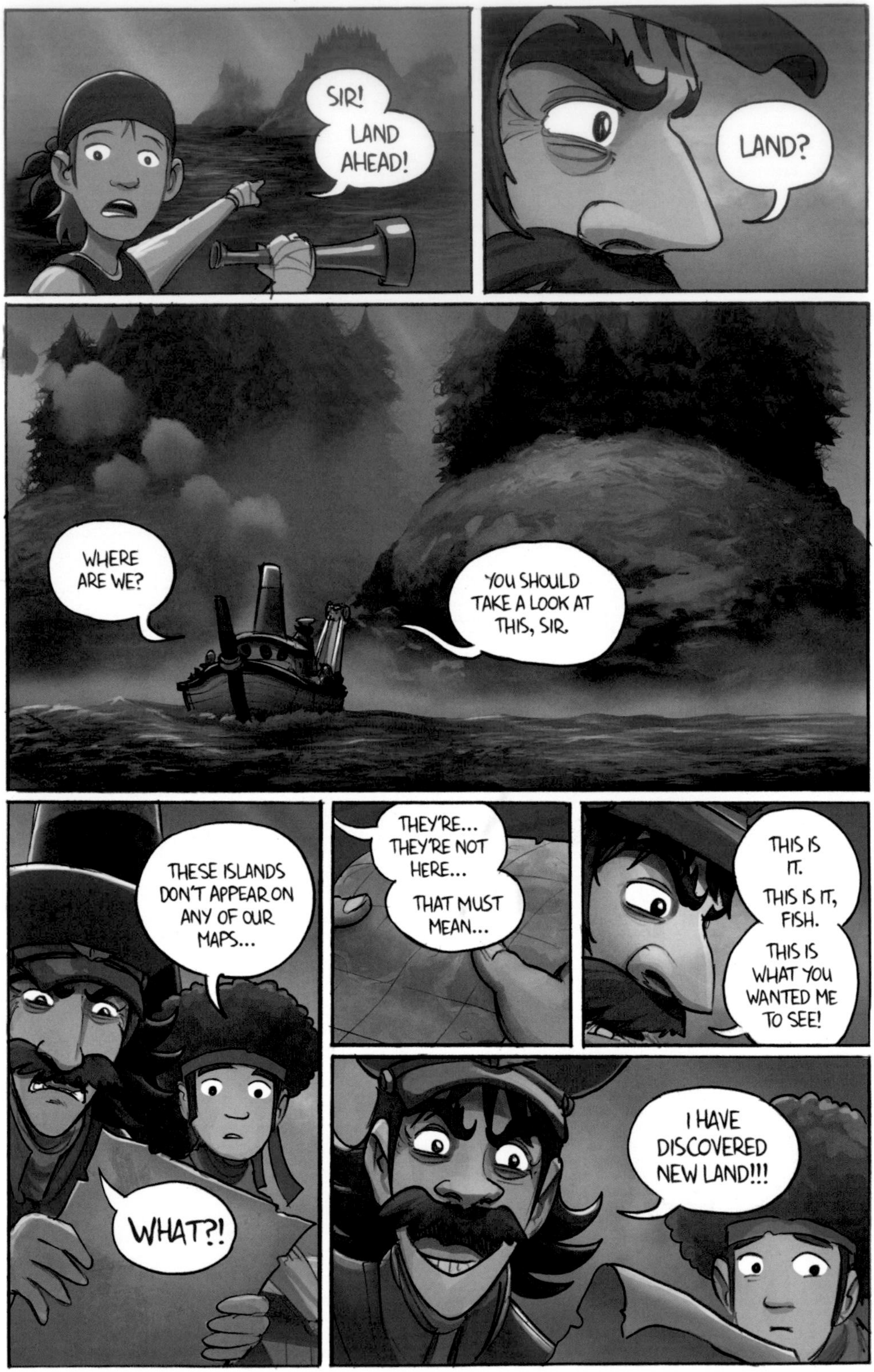
SIR!
LAND AHEAD!
LAND?
WHERE ARE WE?
YOU SHOULD TAKE A LOOK AT THIS, SIR.
THESE ISLANDS DON'T APPEAR ON ANY OF OUR MAPS...
WHAT?!
THEY'RE... THEY'RE NOT HERE...
THAT MUST MEAN...
THIS IS IT.
THIS IS IT, FISH.
THIS IS WHAT YOU WANTED ME TO SEE!
I HAVE DISCOVERED NEW LAND!!!

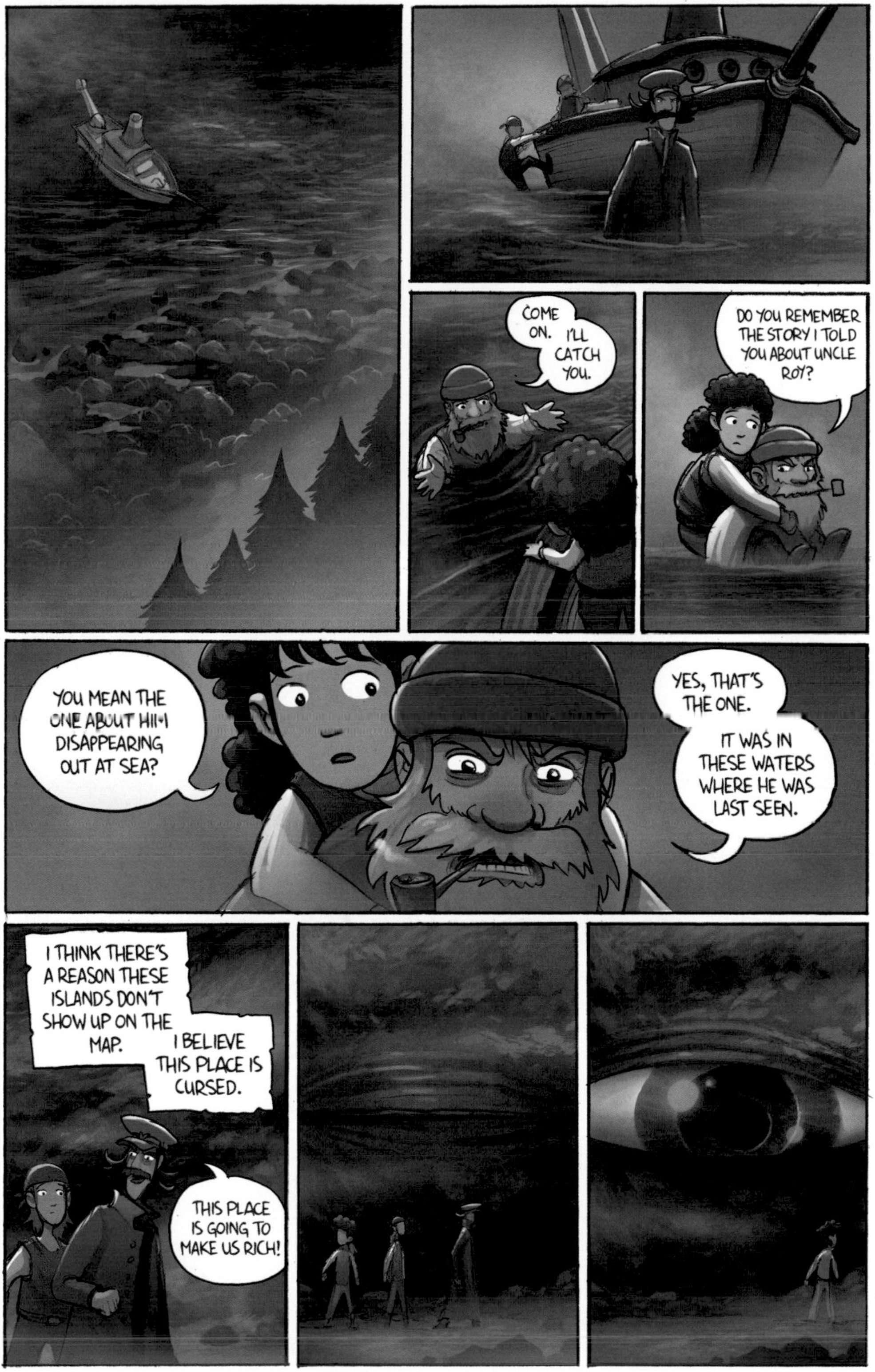

COME ON. I'LL CATCH YOU.
DO YOU REMEMBER THE STORY I TOLD YOU ABOUT UNCLE ROY?
YOU MEAN THE ONE ABOUT HIM DISAPPEARING OUT AT SEA?
YES, THAT'S THE ONE.
IT WAS IN THESE WATERS WHERE HE WAS LAST SEEN.
I THINK THERE'S A REASON THESE ISLANDS DON'T SHOW UP ON THE MAP.
I BELIEVE THIS PLACE IS CURSED.
THIS PLACE IS GOING TO MAKE US RICH!

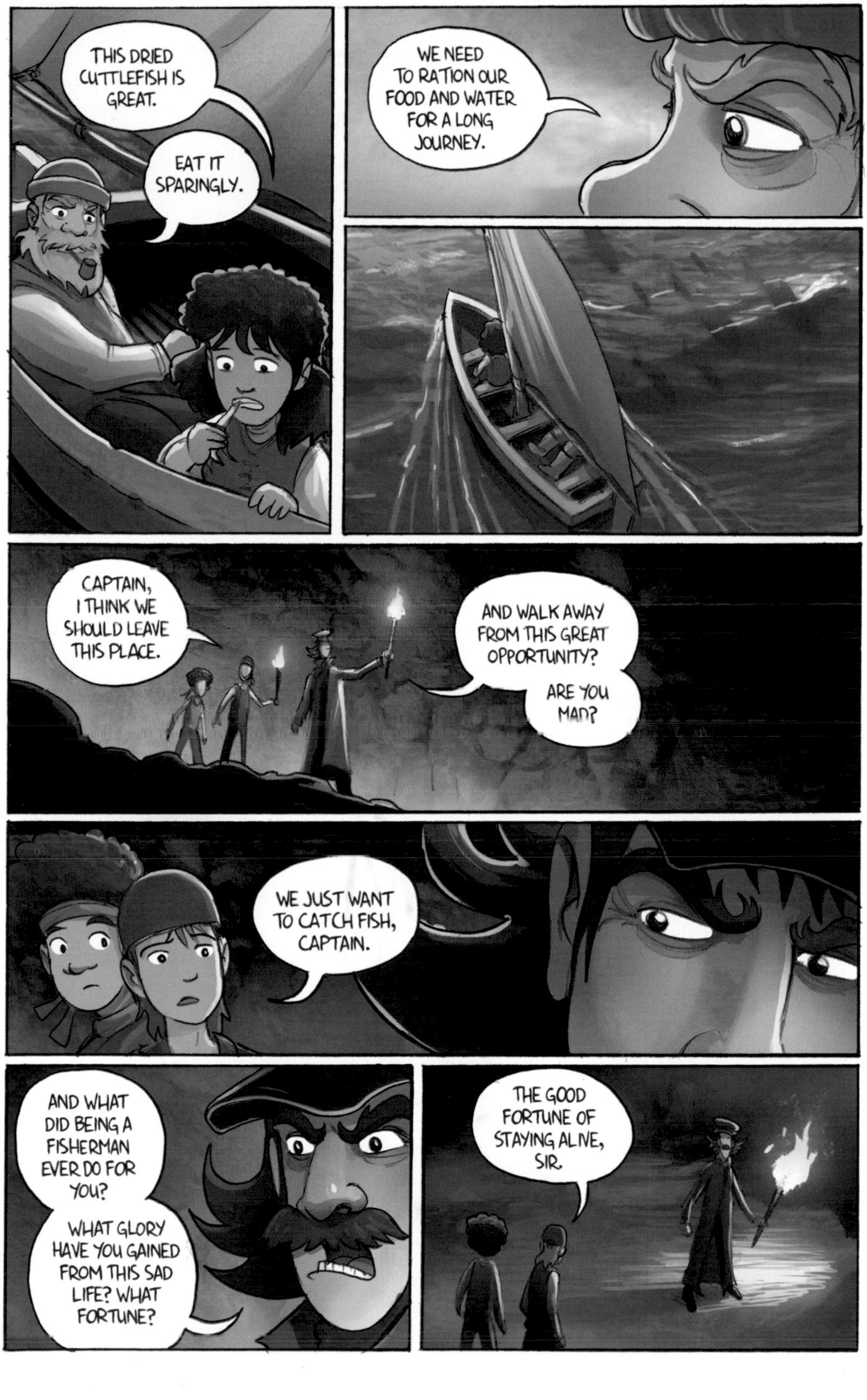
THIS DRIED CUTTLEFISH IS GREAT.
EAT IT SPARINGLY.
WE NEED TO RATION OUR FOOD AND WATER FOR A LONG JOURNEY.
CAPTAIN, I THINK WE SHOULD LEAVE THIS PLACE.
AND WALK AWAY FROM THIS GREAT OPPORTUNITY?
ARE YOU MAD?
WE JUST WANT TO CATCH FISH, CAPTAIN.
AND WHAT DID BEING A FISHERMAN EVER DO FOR YOU?
WHAT GLORY HAVE YOU GAINED FROM THIS SAD LIFE? WHAT FORTUNE?
THE GOOD FORTUNE OF STAYING ALIVE, SIR.

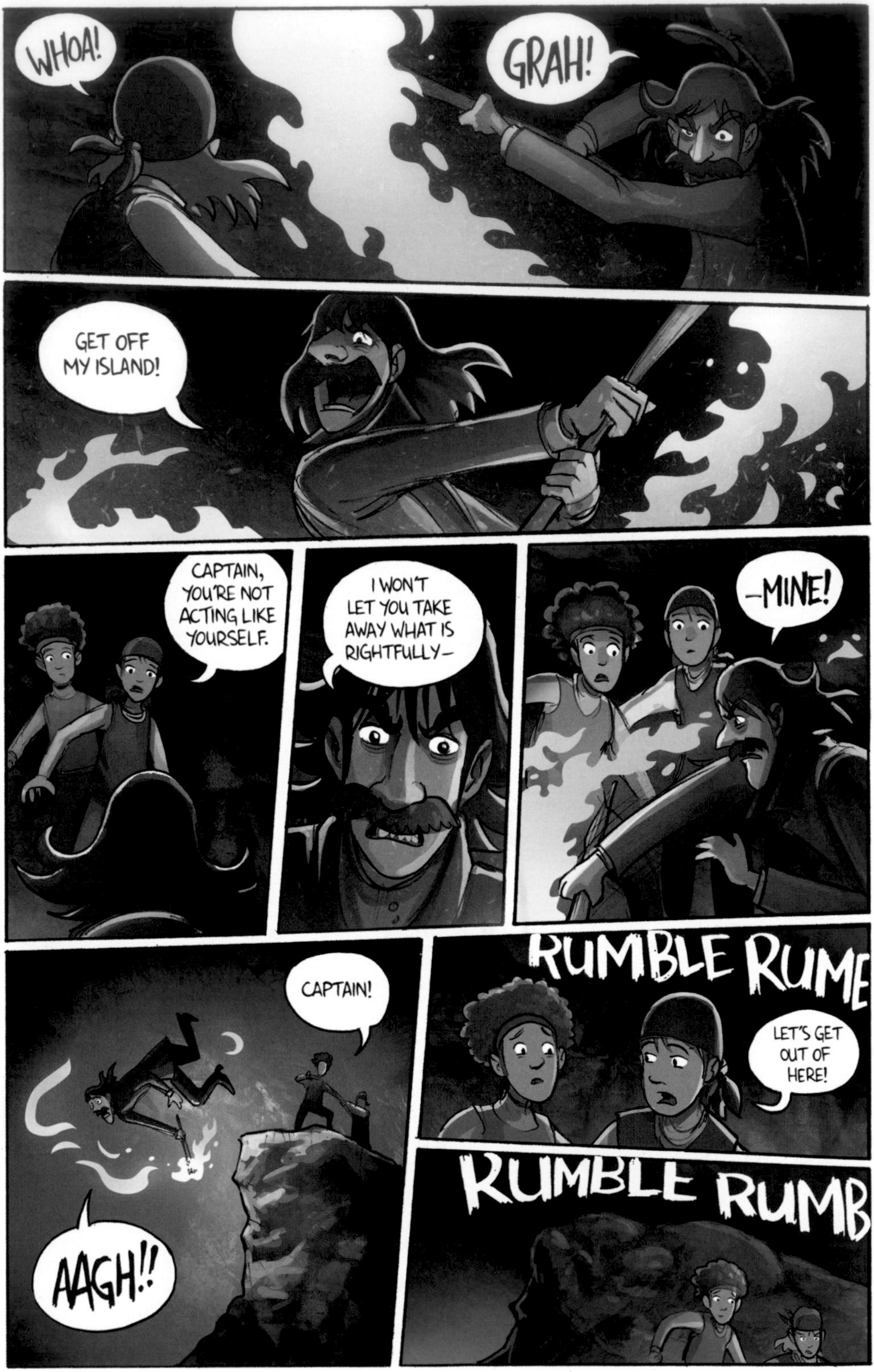
WHOA!
GRAH!
GET OFF MY ISLAND!
CAPTAIN, YOU'RE NOT ACTING LIKE YOURSELF.
I WON'T LET YOU TAKE AWAY WHAT IS RIGHTFULLY—
—MINE!
CAPTAIN!
AAGH!!
RUMBLE RUME
LET'S GET OUT OF HERE!
RUMBLE RUMB

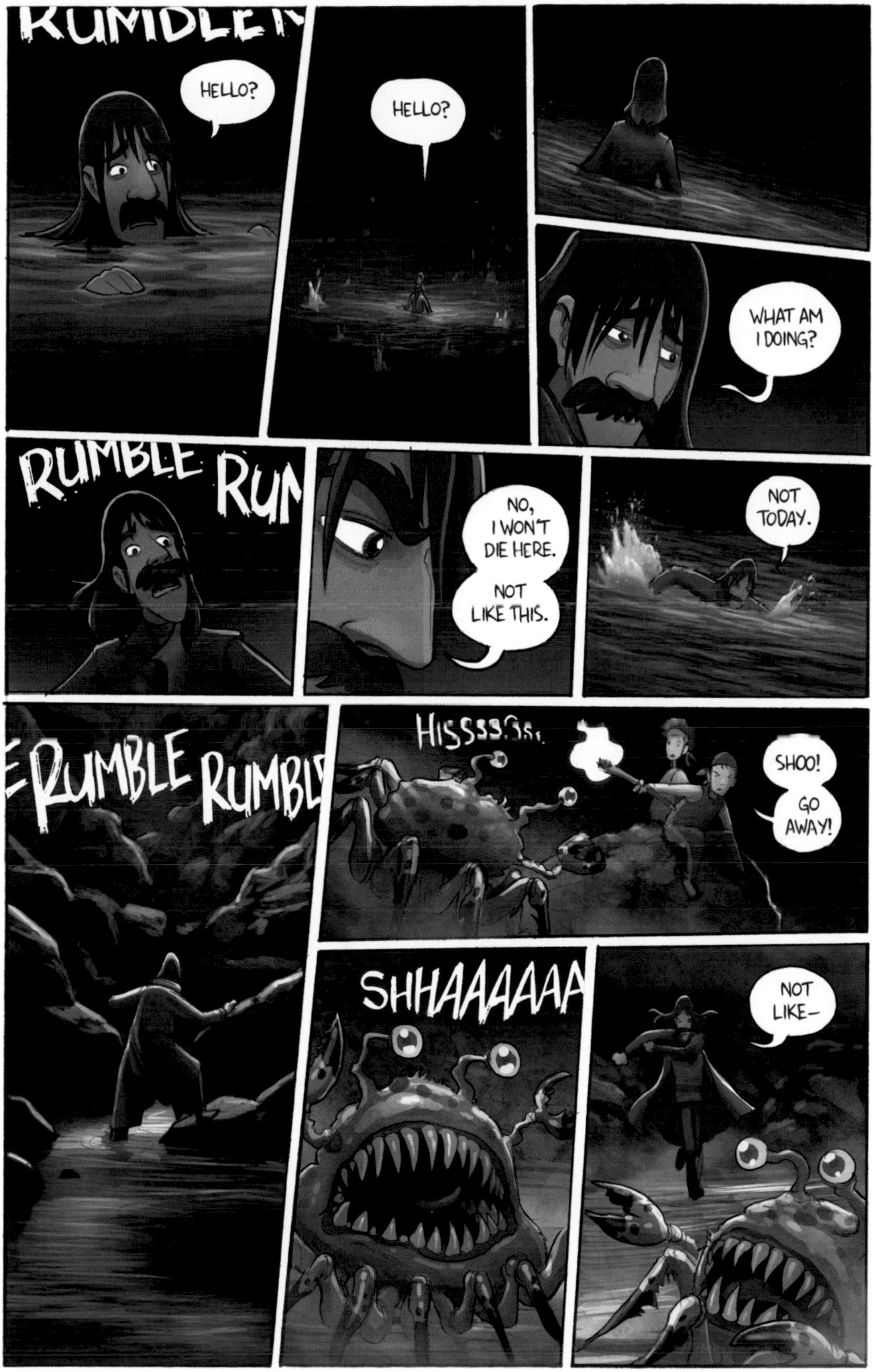
RUMBLE
HELLO?
HELLO?
WHAT AM I DOING?
RUMBLE RUM
NO, I WON'T DIE HERE.
NOT LIKE THIS.
NOT TODAY.
RUMBLE RUMBL
HISSSSSSS
SHOO!
GO AWAY!
SHHAAAAAA
NOT LIKE—

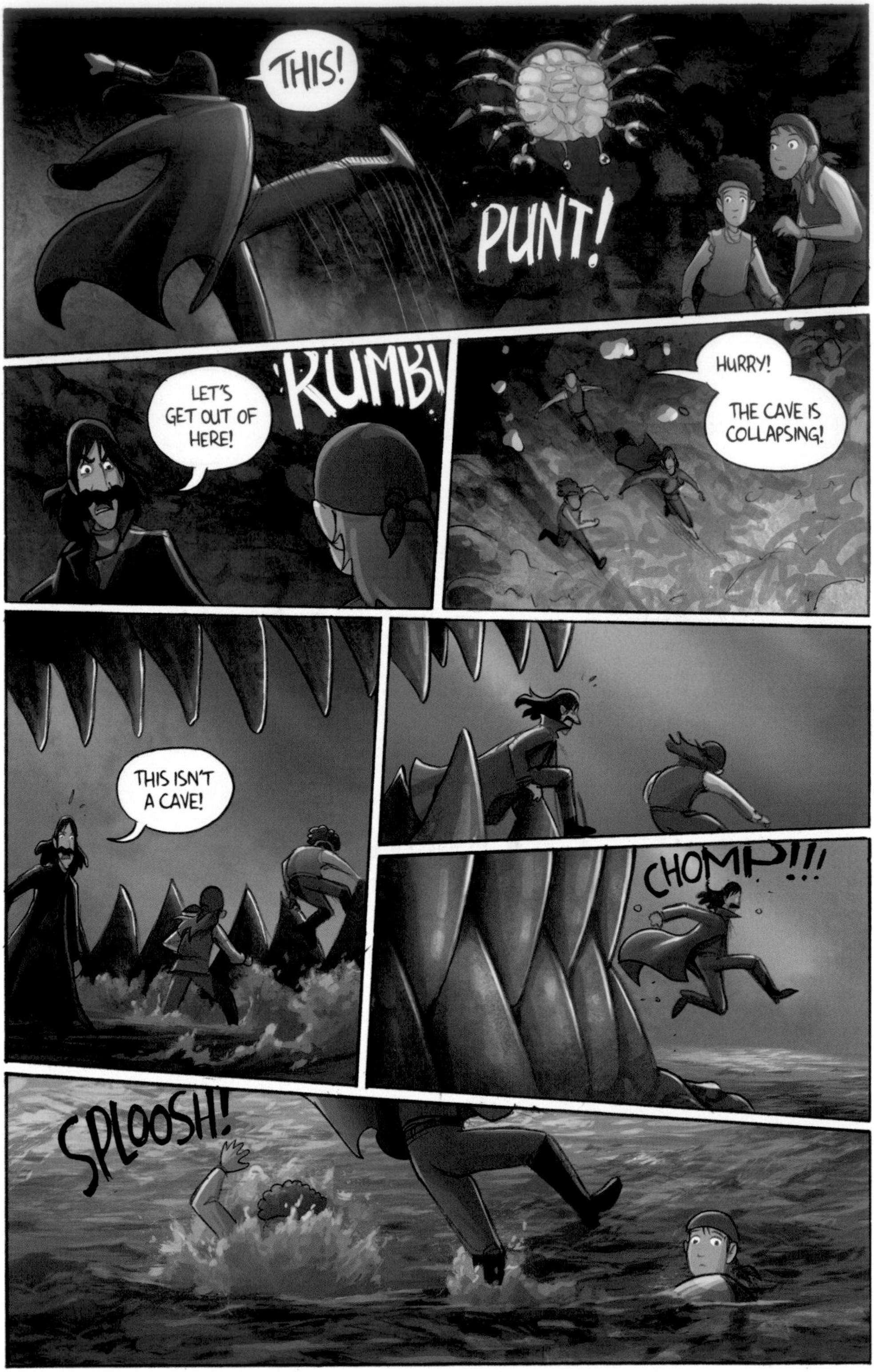
THIS!
PUNT!
LET'S GET OUT OF HERE!
'KRUMB!
HURRY!
THE CAVE IS COLLAPSING!
THIS ISN'T A CAVE!
CHOMP!!!
SPLOOSH!

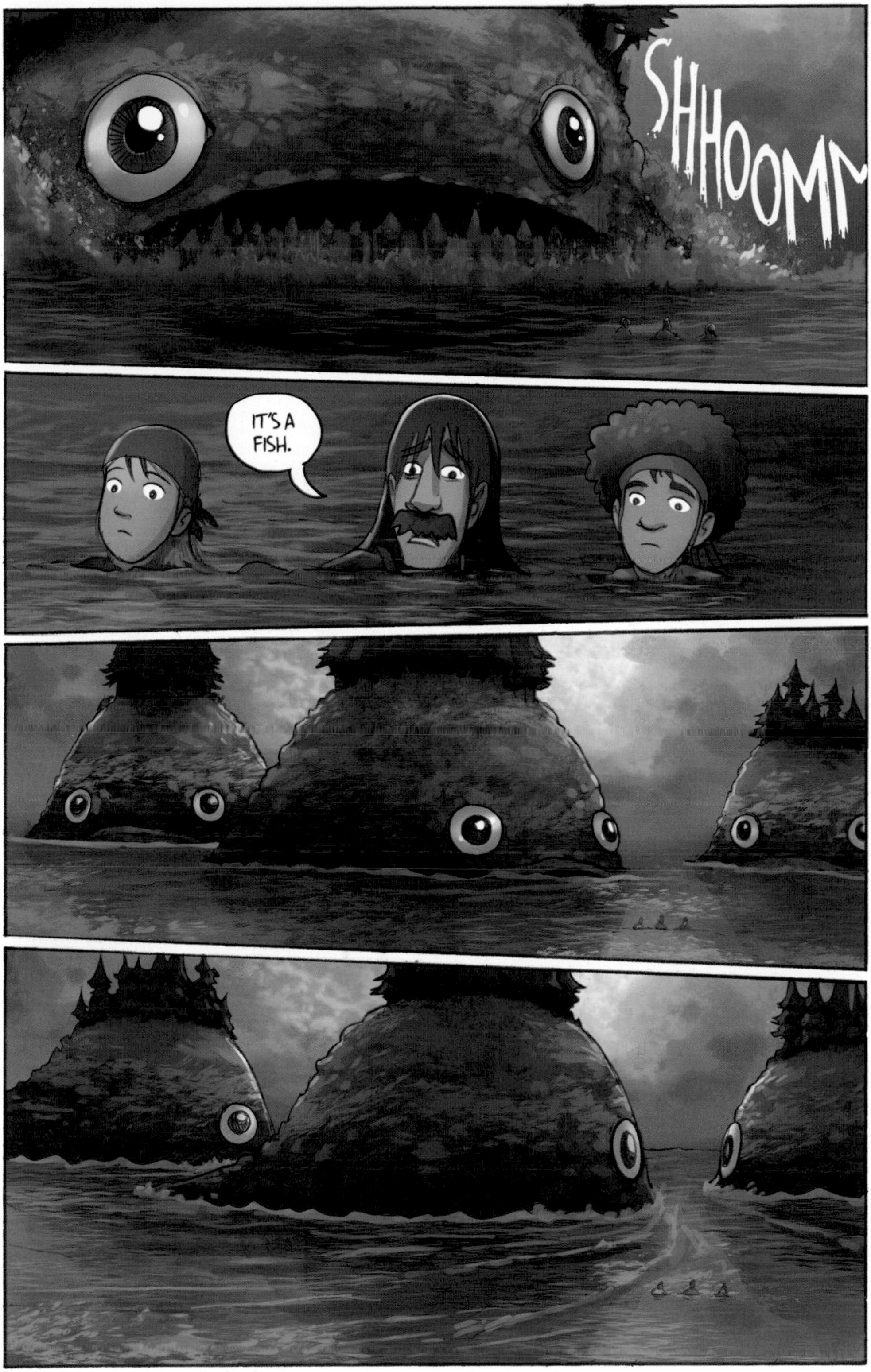
SHHOOMM
IT'S A FISH.

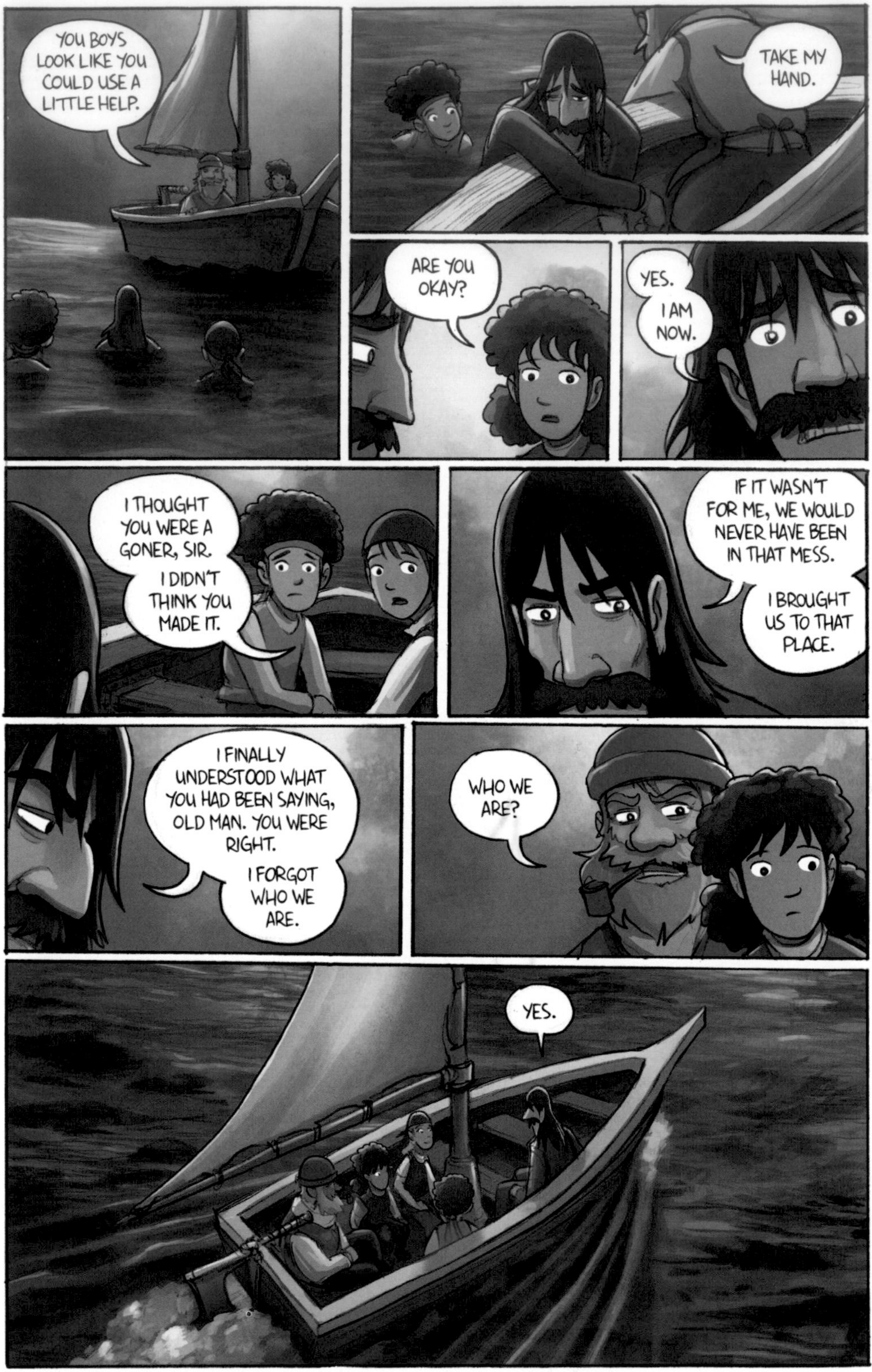
YOU BOYS LOOK LIKE YOU COULD USE A LITTLE HELP.
TAKE MY HAND.
ARE YOU OKAY?
YES.
I AM NOW.
I THOUGHT YOU WERE A GONER, SIR.
I DIDN'T THINK YOU MADE IT.
IF IT WASN'T FOR ME, WE WOULD NEVER HAVE BEEN IN THAT MESS.
I BROUGHT US TO THAT PLACE.
I FINALLY UNDERSTOOD WHAT YOU HAD BEEN SAYING, OLD MAN. YOU WERE RIGHT.
I FORGOT WHO WE ARE.
WHO WE ARE?
YES.

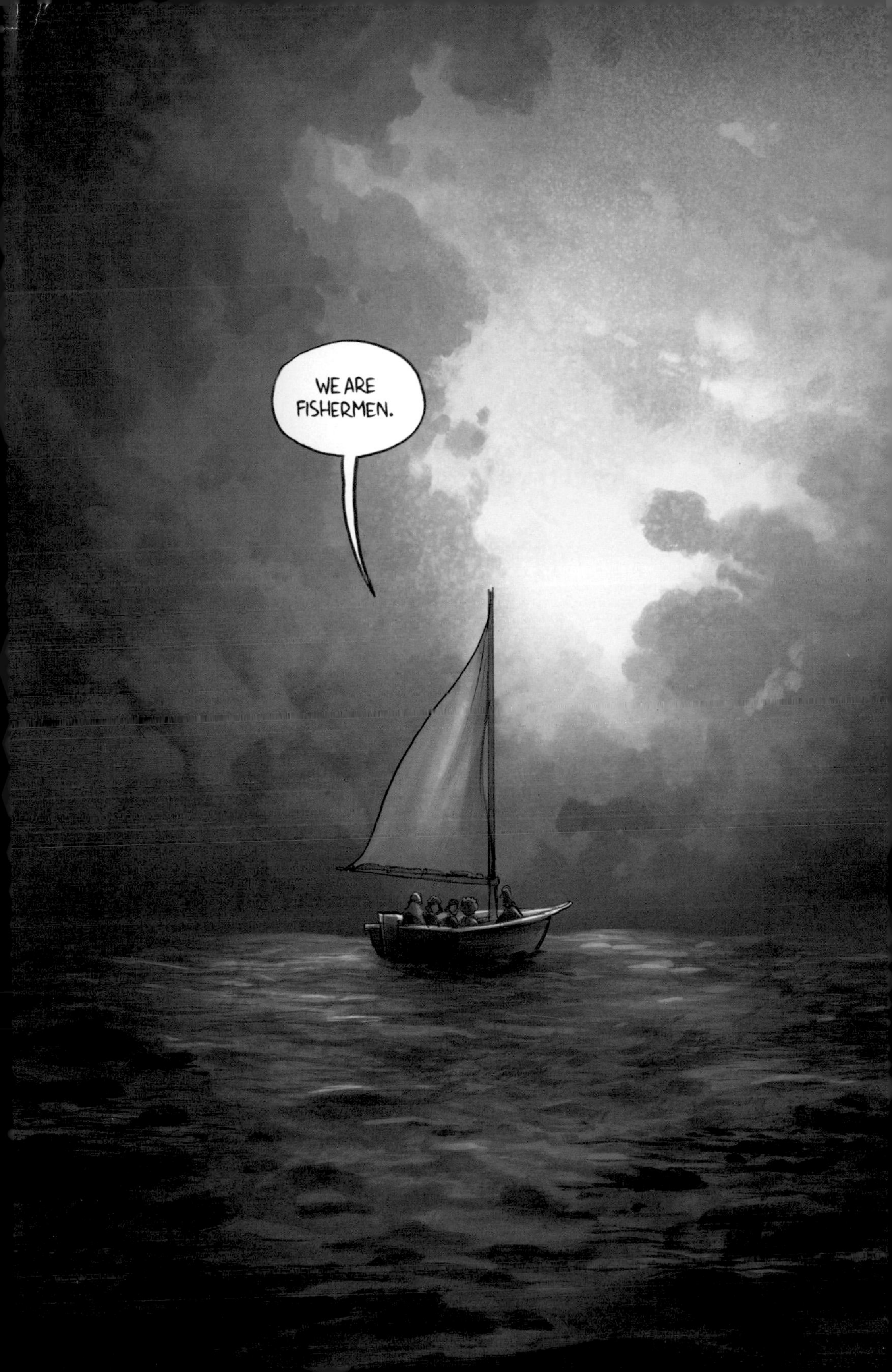
WE ARE FISHERMEN.

ABOUT THE CREATORS

JASON CAFFOE is a contributor to *Explorer: The Mystery Boxes* and the *Flight* anthologies and is the lead production assistant for the *Amulet* series. Visit him at jasoncaffoe.com.

MICHEL GAGNÉ works in film animation and is the BAFTA/Annie Award–winning creator of the graphic novels *The Saga of Rex* and *ZED: A Cosmic Tale*, as well as the award-winning video game Insanely Twisted Shadow Planet. Learn more at gagneint.com.

CHRYSTIN GARLAND graduated from the Savannah College of Art and Design and now works as a storyboard artist and animator. You can see her work at ladygarland.com.

KAZU KIBUISHI is the creator of the *New York Times*–bestselling graphic novel series *Amulet*. He was also the editor and art director of eight volumes of *Flight*, the groundbreaking Eisner-nominated graphic anthology. His comics collection *Copper* was a Junior Library Guild selection; an earlier work, *Daisy Kutter*, was named a YALSA Best Book for Young Adults. Kibuishi recently created cover art for the new paperback editions of J.K. Rowling's *Harry Potter* series. For more on Kazu, check out boltcity.com.

JAKE PARKER illustrated Michael Chabon's picture book *The Astonishing Secret of Awesome Man* and is the creator of the *Missile Mouse* graphic novel series. Visit him at mrjakeparker.com.

DAVE ROMAN is the creator of the *Astronaut Academy* and *Teen Boat!* graphic novels, both of which were Junior Library Guild selections. He has contributed stories to *Explorer: The Mystery Boxes* and *Nursery Rhyme Comics* and is the coauthor of two *New York Times* bestsellers, *The Last Airbender: Zuko's Story* and *X-Men: Misfits*. See more of Dave's work at yaytime.com.

KATIE SHANAHAN is a storyboard artist for animated children's TV shows. She and her brother Steven have contributed to *Flight* and created the popular comic *Silly Kingdom*, which was nominated for two Joe Shuster Awards. Check out more at ktshy.blogspot.ca.

STEVEN SHANAHAN is a writer, editor, and graphic animator who also collaborates on comics with his sister Katie. More about their digital comic can be found at sillykingdom-comic.blogspot.com.

RAINA TELGEMEIER is the Eisner Award–winning, *New York Times*–bestselling creator of *Smile* and *Drama*. Her graphic novels have been selected for the *New York Times* Editors' Choice and the *Boston Globe–Horn Book* Honor Award, and have been named a *Kirkus* Best Teen Book, a YALSA Great Graphic Novel for Teens, an ALA Top 10 Graphic Novel for Youth, and an ALA Notable Children's Book. See more of Raina's work at goraina.com.

* * *

SELENA DIZAZZO is a storyboard artist and graduate of Sheridan College who worked on the colors for "Radio Adrift."

ERIC KIM helped color "Radio Adrift." He is a comics artist whose work has been published by Oni Press.

BRADEN LAMB colored "Desert Island Playlist." He is an artist and animator whose credits include the *Adventure Time* comics series.